EVERYTHING I LEFT UNSAID

EVERYTHING I LEFT UNSAID

A Novel

M. O'Keefe

Bantam Books • New York

A Bantam Books Trade Paperback Original

Copyright © 2015 by Molly Fader
Excerpt from *The Truth About Him* by M. O'Keefe copyright © 2015 by Molly Fader

Published in the United States by Bantam Books, an imprint of Random House, a division of Penguin Random House LLC, New York.

BANTAM BOOKS and the HOUSE colophon are registered trademarks of Penguin Random House LLC.

This book contains an excerpt from the forthcoming book *The Truth About Him* by M. O'Keefe. This excerpt has been set for this edition only and may not reflect the final content of the forthcoming edition.

LIBRARY OF CONGRESS CATALOGING-IN-PUBLICATION DATA
O'Keefe, Molly.
Everything I left unsaid : a novel / M. O'Keefe.
pages cm
"A Bantam Books trade paperback original"—Verso title page.
ISBN 978-1-101-88448-5 (paperback)—ISBN 978-1-101-88449-2 (eBook)
1. Runaway wives—Fiction. 2. Abused wives—Fiction. I. Title.
PS3615.K44E38 2015
813'.6—dc23
2015007597

Printed in the United States of America on acid-free paper

randomhousebooks.com

9 8 7 6 5 4 3 2 1

Book design by Karin Batten

For Adam. For everything.

Acknowledgments

My life is rich with friends who inspire and help me. My gratitude is endless.

To Maureen McGowan, Ripley Vaughn, and Stephanie Doyle: you are the foundation of so many great things in my life. Thank you.

To Bonnie Staring, Shari Slade, and Carolyn Crane: thank you for your comments and support—your input made the books so much better. I'm really honored to have you in my corner.

To the Toronto Romance Writers, the Western New York Romance Writers, and the Ottawa Romance Writers: your workshops and the resulting lightbulb moments I had made these books possible.

Simone St. James, between the beers and the writer's retreats, we've got a good thing going.

Pam Hopkins, my agent—an amazing compass constantly pointing me in the right direction.

Shauna Summers, Gina Wachtel, Sarah Murphy, and the rest of the amazing team at Bantam: your hard work and faith in these books has been humbling and inspiring.

And to my readers: I am just so blessed. Thank you.

PART ONE

1

ANNIE

Escape smelled like a thick layer of Febreze over stale cigarette smoke.

I dropped my duffle bag on the patch of linoleum in front of the trailer's stove and closed the thin metal door behind me. It didn't latch the first time and I had to slam it.

The whole trailer shook.

I'll need better locks.

Not that locks had kept me safe before. Locks and sitting very still and being very small had not kept me safe at all.

Everyone minds their own here. They all keep to themselves. That's what Kevin, the park manager, had said when I put down my cash for the trailer. *It's safe and it's quiet and we don't truck with no nonsense.*

Safe, quiet, and no nonsense made this little scrap of swamp a perfect place to end my week of helter-skelter traveling. Doubling back, buying a ticket west only to go east. Buses. Trains.

Out in front of my trailer, there was a used car—a POS Toyota with bad brakes and a broken radio. I bought it in Virginia, from a high school football player with dreams the crappy car could not hold, and drove north before heading south again.

But I had to stop somewhere. I couldn't drive forever.

So, seven days, hundreds of miles to here. To this place that didn't even show up on a state map of North Carolina.

"Home sweet home," I sighed, putting my hands on my hips and surveying my new kingdom.

Kevin called it a trailer, but really it was an old RV that had rolled to a stop at the Flowered Manor Trailer Park and Camp Ground and refused to keep going. Someone had taken off the wheels and put the RV up on blocks and maybe that same someone had carefully, lovingly planted the morning glory vines to hide those cement blocks.

The flowers were a nice touch, admirable really in their delusional quality, but didn't much hide the fact that it was an RV.

A crappy one. In a crappy trailer park so off the beaten path it was practically impossible to find.

Perfect. So, so perfect.

My deep breath shuddered through me and I allowed some of the fear I lived with to lift away, like crows startled from a winter field. Usually I gathered the fear back because fear kept me safe.

Fear was familiar.

But in this crazy little trailer, there was no need.

We don't truck with no nonsense.

Good, I thought, smiling for the first time in a long time. Bravado making me giddy. *Neither do I.*

I also didn't truck with the smell of this place.

It was two steps from the kitchen to the dining area and I leaned over the Formica table and beige banquette seating to pull back the curtains and yank open the windows. A fetid breeze blew through, slipping across my neck and down the collar of my white cotton shirt.

I closed my eyes because I was tired down to my bones and . . . it felt good. The breeze, on my skin . . . it just felt good. Different.

And these days I was in the business of *different*.

My entire life I'd had long hair against my neck or pulled back in a ponytail so heavy it made my head hurt. My hair was naturally red and curly and thick. So thick.

Suffocatingly thick.

Mom used to say it was the prettiest thing about me. Which is one of those kinds of compliments that isn't really a compliment at all, because it leaves so much room for awful to grow up around it. But it was the nicest thing she said about me, so I took it to heart, because she was my mom.

Chopping it off had been a weird relief. Not just from headaches and the heat, but this new butchered hair allowed me to feel the breeze like I never had before. The sun against the nape of my neck was a revelation.

When the wind blew, my short hair lifted and the feeling rippled down my back, like a domino fall of nerve endings.

I liked it. A lot.

The quiet was broken by the distant, muffled sound of a phone ringing.

It wasn't mine. I'd left my cell in the bottom of a trash can in the Tulsa bus station. The other trailers were close, but not so close that I'd be able to hear a cell phone ringing in a purse. And that's what it sounded like.

The counters of my small kitchen were empty. The driver and front-seat-passenger captain seats that had been turned to create a little sitting area were both bare.

There were no purses left forgotten by the previous tenant.

I glanced down at the fabric of the bench seats that made up the banquettes.

Am I really thinking about putting my hand in there? It

looked clean enough, for all its shabbiness, but still . . . disgusting things fell between seat cushions. It was a fact.

The phone rang again and with it the instinct to answer a ringing phone kicked in, and I shoved my hand down into the crease between the top and bottom cushions and then wedged it along sideways, running into nothing, not even cracker crumbs or the odd toy car, until I hit the plastic case of a phone. I pulled it out and glanced at its face.

Dylan.

Accept. Decline.

With a small brush of my thumb, I touched accept.

So small a thing. Really. In the crazy mix of drastic shit I'd been doing this week—answering that phone seemed like nothing.

Just goes to show, I guess.

"Hello?"

"Jesus, Megan, where the hell have you been?" a guy said, his voice not angry so much as exasperated. Relieved, almost.

"I'm sorry." I wedged my hand back into the cushions to see if anything else had slid in there. Money. Money would be nice. "This isn't Megan."

Aha! I pulled out three quarters and a nickel.

The guy sighed. The kind of sigh I was terribly used to. The put-out sigh. The angry sigh. The *this is your fault* sigh.

And I had this visceral reaction, screwed into the marrow of my bones over the last five years, to do everything in my power and some things incredibly outside of my power to appease the anger behind that sigh. To make it all okay.

But those days were officially over.

Sorry, Dylan. No one sighs like that at me. Not anymore. Not ever.

I pulled the phone away from my ear and lifted my thumb to turn it off, but his voice stopped me just before I disconnected the call.

"I'm sorry," he said. "I got no reason to treat you like that. Is Megan there?"

"No." Okay, I was pulled back in by an apology. Because apologies were nice and they were rare. And this guy sounded sincerely worried. Megan might be his wife. Or girlfriend. His daughter. "She moved out a few days ago. She must have left the phone behind."

His chuckle was deep and very masculine, and it made me think that I haven't heard many guys laughing in my life. And that was too bad. It was a nice sound.

"She must have," he agreed. "Have you moved into the trailer?"

My protective instincts were new and fragile but they were working, and they rose on shaky legs to stop the unthinking answer that came to my lips.

I don't know this man. I don't know him at all.

"Just cleaning it," I said. "I don't live here."

"I hope that's not as bad a job as it sounds."

"No. It's fine. Megan must have kept it real clean." I rolled my eyes at myself.

"What's your name?"

This is a man. Not a boy. Not a guy. But a man. His voice had a low quality, a rumble and a rasp, like maybe he hadn't done a lot of talking today. Or maybe he didn't talk much at all. Or he smoked a pack of cigarettes a day—which shouldn't sound so good. But it did. He had an accent—something Southern. And despite his apologies he sounded . . . rough.

Something weird was happening to my heartbeat.

"You know mine," he said.

I nearly closed my eyes as that dark tone sent chills across my back like a cool breeze.

"Dylan," I said. "It said your name on the phone."

"Right. Well, I guess you don't have to—"

"Layla." The name came out of nowhere. Layla was my

cousin, a wild girl I'd only met once but a name I'd heard over and over again in Mom's warnings and stories of forbearance. *"You don't want to end up like Layla, do you?"*

Which was hilarious, because last I'd heard Layla was an extremely popular makeup artist in Hollywood and happy.

So, Mom's horror stories had worked, and no, I didn't end up at all like Layla.

But in this new life . . . maybe I'd endeavor to be more like Layla.

Layla had been bold. And confident. Embarrassingly sexy to utterly staid and uptight me. Annie McKay.

"Are you okay?" Dylan asked, pulling me away from thoughts of my cousin.

"What makes you think I'm not?"

"People don't end up in the Flowered Manor Trailer Park and Camp Ground because everything's going great in their lives."

"Tell me about it," I laughed. The relief of sitting still, letting go of some of that fear I lived with, and the . . . weirdness of this call made me giddy. I felt like a stone kicked downhill. Rolling faster and faster toward something.

This run-down trailer park had the market cornered on last-ditch efforts. Everything and everyone from Kevin to the morning glories out front seemed to be holding on with a white-knuckled intensity.

"You know the brochure did promise modern amenities, but I haven't caught sight of the spa," I joked. "And weedy watering holes don't count."

There was silence after my words. And I knew silence as well as I knew sighs. The variations, the cold undertones. The hot overtones.

The razor-edged silence that came before *You got a smart mouth, girl.*

The heavy echoing silence that came before a backhand.

Stupid joke. It was a stupid joke. I am made of stupid jokes.

"You just can't trust advertising anymore, can you?" he asked.

"Especially when it's on a bathroom wall in a truck stop."

We both laughed, and this was officially more fun than I'd had in years.

"Are you safe?" he asked.

The question with its implied concern bit into me, sweeping away my laughter like someone taking his arm over a dinner table, sending plates crashing to the floor. Tears burned in my eyes.

No one had worried about me. Not in a very long time.

"Layla?"

"Yes." My voice was gruff and thick. "I'm safe."

"You sure?"

I got the sense that if I told him no, that I felt threatened or scared, he would *do* something about it. Arrive at that metal door to *help* me.

The temptation to trust him was not insignificant.

But that was not the point of having run so far.

I collapsed onto the seat, taking in my new home in all its glory. The fake wood cupboards of the kitchen, the narrow hallway with its curtain divider between the bedroom and this main area. I saw the edge of the bathroom's accordion door.

Mine, I thought, and something wild and bitter rose in my chest.

"I am." I was safe. Hundreds and hundreds of miles from my old life. "I really am."

"Good," Dylan said as if he knew what I wasn't saying. And hell, maybe he did. Maybe the story of Annie McKay was a familiar one at the Flowered Manor.

"Do you know where Megan went?" I asked. "I'll mail her phone."

"No," he said. "It's not her phone; it's mine. She worked for me."

"Can I mail you the phone?"

His silence seemed loaded, but not dangerous. "Are you always this nice?"

I laughed, because this was nothing compared to the bending over backward to accommodate people I'd done in my past. I'd been able to fold myself up into nothing.

But this man's concern made me grateful.

"It's your phone, isn't it? Only seems right to get it back to you."

"Most people don't go out of their way for a stranger."

"Would it make you feel better if you told me something about yourself?"

I'd said it flippantly, but the silence that followed my words was oddly heavy, as if I'd opened a door he hadn't expected.

"I'll tell you why Megan had the phone."

The sudden lack of laughter in his tone, the new element of seriousness, made me sit up straight.

This is when you hang up, I thought, sensing that we'd slipped past banalities. I was not in the practice of talking on the phone to strange men.

Hoyt would— The sudden thought of him and what he would and wouldn't do about my behavior—like a cancer in this new Febreze-scented world of mine—galvanized me, sent new steel running down my back.

I'm not Annie. I'm Layla. And fuck Hoyt.

"Why?" I asked, noting there was a change in my voice, too. As if there were a sort of intimacy between me and this stranger who asked about my safety in a lifetime of people not caring.

"There's a trailer, two away from you. To the north. You can see it out your window."

I twisted and pushed aside the curtain on the north-facing window.

"Did you look?"

"I did."

I heard him breathe into the phone and something electric pulsed over me. An animal instinct made all the hair on my neck stand up.

"An old man lives in that trailer," he said. "Megan kept an eye on him for me."

"Is he sick?"

"Not that I know of."

"Does he need help of some kind?"

Again that rumbly dark laugh, again that weird reaction of my heart. "No. He doesn't. In fact, I made it real clear to Megan that she shouldn't get to know him at all."

"So, she just spied on him?"

"She did. And I paid her well to do it."

"Did she do anything else for you?" I asked. It hardly seemed a job a person could get paid for.

In his silence I realized what he might be thinking, and I felt blood pound through my body in horrified embarrassment.

"What are you asking me, Layla?"

Oh, his voice was suddenly thick with intimacy and now I could not pretend otherwise. Somehow this had gotten sexual. It was the Layla thing that had started it and it was a stupid thing to start. I did not play this kind of game. Didn't understand it. Was completely embarrassed by it.

Suddenly restless, I stood up. My skin felt far too keenly the rub of my clothes against it.

"Nothing," I said quickly. "Just seems like something a person should do without being paid."

"Are you offering to look in on him for me?"

"Sure." I picked up my bag and walked down the hallway to the tiny bedroom in the back. The double bed was stripped. A stack of clean sheets sat at the end of the faded flowered mattress.

"That easy?"

"That easy."

"When's the last time you said no to someone?" he asked.

"Why does it matter?"

"I have a sense, Layla, that you give away your yeses without thinking."

Oh, he was right. So damn right.

"And you want my noes?"

"I want something you don't give away."

My knees buckled and I leaned back against the wood-paneled wall, feeling light-headed. *How . . . how did we get here? What has happened to me?*

"Tell me no, Layla," he murmured.

No was dangerous in my old life. A red flag in front of a murderous bull.

I wasn't brave enough.

"No." It was barely a whisper. A breath. A rebellion that screamed through me. It was like *Les Misérables* in my chest cavity.

"Do you remember my name?"

Inherently, somehow I knew what he was asking. *Say my name.*

"No, Dylan."

The sound he made—half sigh, half groan—was easily the most erotic sound I'd ever heard, and suddenly there was no more wondering, no more innuendo. He wasn't asking what I was wearing, but the effect was the same. The *intent* was the same.

This is . . . oh my God, this is phone sex. I'm having phone sex with a stranger in a shitty trailer in the middle of nowhere!

I pulled myself away from the wall. My hands in fists.

"Don't call me again." My voice sounded firmer than I'd expected. Firmer than I'd sounded my entire life, and I was proud of myself.

"I won't," he said.

"Promise." Why I expected him to keep that promise I had

no idea, but having acted so stupid I felt the need to at least attempt smart behavior. *God,* that lie about cleaning the trailer was so see-through. He knew where I lived. He could find me in the middle of the night, break through those flimsy locks— "I promise. You're safe. Goodbye, Layla." And he hung up.

I hung up a moment later, staring down at the phone as if I'd never seen its kind before.

It's just a phone, I thought, despite its near pulsing heat in my hand. Its strange aliveness. It echoed in me, a foreign nature that was not entirely my own. Something hot-blooded and impulsive.

Don't be stupid. Or stop being stupid. Or . . . something.

I walked back into the kitchen. Turned off the phone and threw it up in a high cupboard. A phone would be a handy thing to have in case of an emergency, and when he stopped paying for the service, I'd find a way to get my own.

My hands were shaking. My whole body quaked like an aspen leaf. I stepped sideways into the tiny bathroom and turned on the faucets. Cold water blasted out, ricocheted off the sink, and sprayed across my body, soaking through my white cotton blouse.

I sucked in a shocked breath.

"Damn it," I muttered and cranked the water back off.

I pressed cold hands to my eyes and cheeks and then opened my eyes to stare right at the woman in the mirror. My shirt, thanks to the water, was see-through, and I could see the pink of my flesh beneath it. A white bra. My nipples . . . there. Painfully, obviously, *there.*

Slowly I unwound the sheer, floral scarf from around my neck.

The bruises under my chin and at the sides of my neck were turning yellow at the center. Green at the edges.

The one at the corner of my mouth was still dark and ugly and red.

This is my body. Those are my bruises.
The hands shaking on the sink, those are mine, too.
Those words I said to that man.
Dylan.
Those were mine. My words.
This is me.

I took a deep breath, feeling overwhelmed by the empty space around me, usually filled in with so much fear. Without that fear, without the rules—said and unsaid, implicit and explicit—I felt undone. Unmade. As if I'd been pruned, allowing—*God, please, please allow*—new growth.

My hair, the thick, pretty red curls replaced by a lopsided cut I'd given myself and then dyed black in the Tulsa bus station, made me unrecognizable to myself.

"So," I said out loud to the reflection in the mirror. That stranger staring back at me. "Who are you?"

2

DYLAN

Make no mistake, Dylan Daniels was the beast. He was the bad guy in the stories. Some other asshole could be the hero, save the day and get the girl.

Alone and gruesome, he'd stay up on his mountain with his money and his work, as far from people as he could get because that was how he liked it.

It was better. For everyone.

But every once in a while he got to worrying about the monsters that lived off the mountain and he called to check up on Ben.

Carefully, like it was a bomb with a lit fuse, Dylan put the phone down on the workbench in front of him.

Pencils rolled onto the floor, but he barely noticed.

For five years he'd had the old man looked in on. By six different people. Four women, two guys.

The first question any of them asked was what was in it for them.

And that worked for Dylan. The voices on the other end of

the phone belonged to people who were all disinterested and influenced only by the stupid amount of money he paid them. The six people he'd hired didn't get invested. They didn't give a shit about the old man or why Dylan wanted him watched. And Dylan didn't have to worry if they got hurt. Or if they vanished without a word, which was what happened more often than not in that crappy trailer park.

Five years. Six people who were only a disposable set of eyes and ears. Nothing more.

Until now.

Layla.

What the fuck was that?

It wasn't just the country-girl kindness that got him, which was a novel change in the world. The offer to mail him back the phone? *Christ*. The trailer park wouldn't reward that sort of sweetness; he knew that for a fact.

He'd been able to tell the moment she was about to hang up, and the moment she decided to be brave and keep talking. And the moment . . . the hitch in her breath, the sigh, the husky edge to that drawl-tinged voice . . . she'd been turned on.

That small reveal of a colossal internal shift. From indifference to desire.

When was the last time someone had shown him something so personal? So intimate?

Maybe never.

And he'd felt her excitement like a physical touch.

Well, like he remembered a physical touch to be. It had been a while. In fact it had been long enough that he'd actually forgotten what *want* was.

But a ten-minute conversation with a stranger and he was hard as steel. His body primed. Ready.

Craving more.

Dylan had a sixth sense about inevitability. An awareness of things out in the dark he could not avoid. Of events stacking up, paths being forged, the result of which would not be seen for years to come. Usually these inevitable things were bad. For him, anyway.

Layla felt different.

Fuck. Enough, he thought; she was a woman with a nice voice who got turned on thinking about phone sex. *Move on.*

Around him work was piling up. Deadlines were approaching and his team was getting anxious. Not that any of them bothered him here in his home. But he could feel them, just down the road at the warehouse. He could smell their nerves, their growing doubt. Blake, his business partner, was threatening to actually show up one of these days to see what the hold up was.

So, he shook off the conversation and went back to work on the engine schematic spread out over the bench. They were working on an adapted planetary gearbox for a manual transmission. And it was a thing of beauty. Simply put, it consisted of one large gear—the sun, surrounded by smaller gears—the planets. And around that, there was a larger carrier keeping it all in place.

That was how his world worked best, all parts in sync. He was the sun, the people around him the planets, and the rules he lived by kept it all in line. Controlled. If one piece was dirty, or out of alignment, if the steel had the slightest imperfection, his world simply didn't work.

There was no room for distractions. Strange obsessions. Sweet girls on the other end of the phone.

So he shoved those thoughts away.

But four hours later he was still thinking about her.

Layla.

3

ANNIE

In the dream, I was leading a crew of detasselers. Teenagers mostly, only a few years younger than me, but somehow they seemed so much younger. Childish with their summer jobs and packed lunches, the early hours making them grumble. One girl, despite being told to wear long-sleeved shirts and pants because corn rash was a bitch, stood there in cutoffs and a bikini top.

"You are going to get corn rash. And corn rash hurts," I said, lifting my Del Monte cap and setting it back on my head over and over again. A nervous tic.

The girl glanced sideways at a boy who had his paper-bag lunch over the front of his jeans and was pretending so hard, so painfully hard, not to notice Bikini-girl's attention that the corn could practically detassel itself, under the power of his discomfort and lust.

"I'll be fine," the girl said, flashing the boy the coyest of smiles.

"Stop saying that!" I yelled, startling everyone. I didn't yell, as a rule. A rule I'd learned the hard way. I swore like a sailor, but I didn't yell.

I took my clipboard with all the crew lists and the leaders and the fields they'd be going to and I started to smash the clipboard against the hood of my truck.

Stop. Smack. *Fucking.* Smack. *Saying.* Smack. *That.*

You will not be fine.

None of us will be fine!

I woke up, the tension reverberating up my arms, my hands clenched in painful fists. My heart pounded in my throat.

Did I yell? I waited, agonized, for the creak of the bed when Hoyt turned over. But he wasn't there. His side of the bed was empty.

Where is he? Did I oversleep?

Quickly, I put it all together: the surprisingly great mattress, the sunlight through the beige curtains, the smell of Febreze.

The trailer.

Hoyt's not here.

More importantly, I wasn't *there.*

I could have wept.

There was a sudden pounding on the door and it felt like the top of my head might explode. That was the banging from the dream, someone at my door. Carefully, I pulled out the top drawer of the small bedside table between the bed and the wall of the trailer.

The black rubber grip of the .22 felt awful in my hand. Awkward. Cold, and both too big and too small.

"Annie McKay?" a voice asked, a Southern drawl coloring it.

It took me a second, freaking out as I was, but I finally recognized the voice. *We don't truck with no nonsense.* That's what that voice outside had said to me. It was Kevin, the guy in the office, knocking on the trailer door.

Adrenaline and relief made me dizzy.

And the fact that I hadn't been sleeping or eating in days kept me dizzy.

The world was spinning.

"You don't have a phone number for me to call," he said, still talking through the weak metal door with the shitty lock. "And it's half past nine. You said you were going to start work at eight."

"Oh no," I said, scrambling up. I'd slept in my clothes, despite the heat, ready to run if I had to. I wasn't sure if that was still necessary, but I couldn't quite convince myself not to do it. I put the gun back in the drawer and pushed my feet into my shoes. "Just a second!" I yelled.

I brushed my teeth too hard, too rushed, and I split my lip again.

"Shit," I hissed, pressing cheap toilet paper to it.

"You coming, or what?"

"Sorry!" I yelled.

The toilet paper stuck to the cut and I left it there, looking like a guy who'd nicked his face shaving for church. In the mirror, my bruises seemed to be greener than they were yesterday. I put the scarf back on, despite how stupid it looked with my tee shirt and cutoffs, and then I put on my big movie-star sunglasses.

Could I be any more obvious? I wondered, carefully peeling the toilet paper from my lip.

But the thought of *not* wearing the scarf and the glasses made me feel naked.

So obvious won.

KEVIN WAS A BIG MAN. TALL, WIDE, BIG STOMACH, BIG SHOULDERS. His belly peeked out beneath his giant red tee shirt, already sweaty in the August North Carolina heat. He had big feet wedged into Adidas shower flip-flops that looked like they'd been welded on at some point. He wore his gray-black hair in a long ponytail down his back, with ponytail holders at regular intervals, keeping it all in line.

"Morning," he said without much of a smile. He didn't seem like a smiler.

Kevin was a still waters kind of guy. Or maybe he just didn't give a shit.

"I'm so sorry," I said, pushing up the edges of the scarf. "I overslept. I usually don't sleep so late."

Last night it had taken me hours to fall asleep. I'd jumped at every sound, and there were lots in the trailer park. People yelling, doors slamming. Wind and trees. A car alarm.

But finally I'd drifted off after two in the morning. Usually I'd be up at dawn, but sleep since I'd left Oklahoma had been in fits and starts.

And honest to God, who would have thought that mattress would be so comfortable?

"You're the one who said you wanted to start today," he said, his eyes wide under bushy eyebrows. "I thought you was nuts."

"Nope, just broke." When I'd asked about work in the area while doing the paperwork for the RV, he'd told me they were hiring at the park to do some groundskeeping, and I'd jumped at the opportunity.

Physical labor, right where I was living. I wouldn't have to go into town. Meet other people.

My gut, which had been silent for my entire life—seriously, not a peep out of the thing for twenty-four years—had been yelling at me nonstop since I woke up on my kitchen floor two weeks ago. And my gut seemed to think this arrangement, this job, was not to be passed up.

"Did I tell you what you'll be doing?" he asked, walking in front of me down the dirt track between my trailer and the next one.

"No. You just mentioned some lawn work."

Kevin laughed, but I didn't find any comfort in it. I had the distinct impression he was laughing at me. "Well, that was clever of me," he said ominously.

The trailer next door was nearly identical to mine, though it seemed to be a newer model. White, where mine was totally '70s beige, with a darker brown racing stripe down the side. *American Dreamer* written in sort of an old-timey Western print.

Yep, she was a beaut.

But the white RV next door had a wooden deck on the outside with a chair, a table, and an ashtray.

Deluxe.

I had trailer envy.

"Does anyone live there?" I jerked my thumb over my shoulder at the neighbor's trailer.

"Joan," Kevin said. "Keeps to herself. Not too friendly. If you're smart you'll stay away. She's kind of a bitch."

The skin on the back of my neck prickled as I walked by, as if someone was watching me from between two slats on the blinds. But when I glanced back there was nothing.

I'd been paranoid most of my life—it's not like I could just make it stop.

"Ben, on the other hand," he said, pointing past Joan's trailer to the trailer the man . . . *Dylan* . . . had asked me to look in on.

Just the thought of his name electrified part of me, like a filament in a lightbulb starting to glow.

Don't. Don't think about him.

"Nice guy. Quiet, but not rude about it. Grows a hell of a garden." He pointed over at the far end of the property, where I could see fencing and some plants.

Hardly sounds like a guy worth watching, I thought, wondering if Dylan wasn't looking after the wrong person.

"Other side of the park," Kevin said, jutting his chin out at the trailers just visible over a giant rhododendron bush, "that's where the families are. Some are great. Some are screamers and drinkers and scene makers, so I try to keep the people without kids on this side."

"Are you quarantining them? Or us?" I asked.

He gave me an arch look. "Hell if you won't appreciate it by next Friday."

Probably true.

We walked single file across a wooden bridge over a rain ditch that because of a recent storm was gurgling along happily under my feet.

Black-eyed Susans and forget-me-nots and tons and tons of Queen Anne's lace covered the banks of the small stream. Crickets were loud and jumping into my legs. The highway was a bunch of miles in the distance, but I could feel the hum of trucks on asphalt rumbling in the boggy ground beneath my feet.

"It's nice," I said.

"What is?"

"This place." I flung out a hand toward the flowers, the stream. A cricket smacked into the back of my leg and then buzzed away.

Kevin's look made it clear he doubted my sanity. "You must see some real shit holes if this is nice."

Oh Kevin, you don't want to know.

Because the truth was, I hadn't seen anywhere. Shit hole or otherwise.

Mom had been on a campaign practically since the moment of my birth to convince me that the world outside of the farm was a godless, terrible place. Full of selfish people doing selfish things. Men who'd want nothing but to hurt me, and women who'd look away while they did it.

When you are told that shit day in and day out, you start to believe it.

It's probably why I stayed so long with Hoyt. Because the unknown was just so . . . unknown.

But here I was, in the thick of it, and so far, my new life was a million times better than my old life.

So, yes, it was nice.

"And here it is," he said, coming to a stop in front of an overgrown field full of black garbage bags torn open by animals. Cans, dirty diapers, and newspapers spilled out in the weeds growing as tall as my head. He had to shout over the drone of black flies.

And the smell . . .

Oh dear God, I take back all that "nice" stuff.

Behind the wall of weeds was a giant oak with a ratty old rope hanging from one of the branches.

"What's the rope for?" I asked, because surrounded by all this filth it looked like the scene of a terrible crime. The cover of a horror novel.

"Behind the weeds is a real nice watering hole."

"That's a watering hole?" I'd been joking about a weedy watering hole last night on the phone, but this was ridiculous.

"Kids play in it all summer, but it's quiet now that they're back in school."

"So . . . what is this supposed to be?" I looked at the surrounding field. It was huge. An acre at least.

"The Flowered Manor Camp Ground," he said.

"You're joking."

"Absolutely not." Kevin looked only marginally affronted by my slack-jawed surprise.

"People actually camp here?"

"They will when you're done." He nudged my shoulder with his massive one and I was nearly knocked off my feet.

"You really can't believe the things you read in a bathroom stall," I muttered.

Dylan would laugh. The thought made me smile before I could stop myself and my lip split again. I licked away the warm copper tang of blood.

Dylan.

I remembered his laughing groan. Low and explicit. Dirty, really. One of the dirtiest things I've ever heard. Last night, staring up at the plastic dimpled ceiling of the trailer, I'd convinced myself that the conversation had been a product of exhaustion. The fact was, stepping into the trailer for the first time, my fear slipping nervously into tentative relief, I'd been momentarily . . . not myself.

It would seem only logical that after the stress and focus of the last week, I'd go a little nuts.

And that's what that conversation was. Nuts.

That's why I'm not talking to him again.

Because in that wild nuts moment—that moment when I was just not myself—something had changed. Shifted.

And I *wanted* to talk to him.

I still did.

Which was weird, if not terrifying, because that bikini girl in my dream looking over at that boy, saying everything was fine, whose skin was about to be shredded—I'd already been her.

Only I had been wearing a wedding dress.

"Come on, now," Kevin said. "I'll show you our tools."

Good. Right. Tools. Kevin led me over to a shed and opened the padlock on the door. "I'll give you a key," he said. "Once I'm sure you won't steal nothing."

"Steal?" I'd never been accused of stealing in my life.

"No offense," he said. "But we've had some real unsavories looking in on this job."

Inside the shed it looked like I'd have everything I needed for campground cleanup: a tractor mower, a weed whacker. Rakes, shovels. Granted, they were all older than I was, but I could work with it. There were even some gloves and boots by the door.

"You sure you want to do this?" Kevin looked sideways at me and I wondered what he saw. What story my scarf in August in North Carolina, my hair so black it swallowed the light, my increasingly alarming thinness, told him.

Probably nothing good. And frankly, probably a story far too close to the truth.

I am, after all, wearing the official costume of a woman on the run.

"I mean . . . you're a kid, ain't you?"

"No." Childhood had blended right into adulthood for me, and there had been nothing in between. Like a rainbow that went from yellow right to indigo. "And I'm totally sure I want to do this." I was used to physical labor at the farm. I liked it. And after a week on the road, I felt listless. Too in my head.

And my head was a shitty place to be.

"Suit yourself. Watch out for snakes."

"What?" I squeaked.

"And bears."

"You're joking, right?"

He shrugged.

"That's not funny, Kevin."

"I don't know, it kinda is."

Kevin winked—which was weird in and of itself—before he lumbered off, leaving me unsure if he was joking or not.

For my own peace of mind I decided to go with joking. Physical labor—yes.

Snakes? No.

Bears? Hell no.

I traded my tennis shoes for the boots and slipped on the gloves. There was a box of black garbage bags and I tucked five of them in the back of my pants. I grabbed a shovel and rake and headed back over to the weed-and-garbage-filled field.

My feet slipped in the too big boots, but I was grateful for them when I stepped into the weeds and something squished underfoot and a wall of flies buzzed up and away.

The smell made me gag.

I pulled my scarf up over my nose. *This is so gross.*

But it was still better than what I'd left behind.

BACK HOME, IN THE FLATLANDS OF OKLAHOMA, I'D BEEN ABLE to see for miles. And at the beginning of my marriage—not the very beginning, but when I realized that the chicken potpie incident wasn't going to be a onetime thing—the openness seemed like protection.

Like a moat around me.

Hoyt couldn't sneak up on me. I could be anywhere on the property, but I'd see the dust behind his truck rising up into the sky, long before I'd even see the truck. And in all that space, that open air, that blue sky with its towering clouds, my fear was like a radio signal that never bounced back. It just went and went and went—flying out over the prairie, fading away into silence.

And at some point during those days, at the beginning, anyway, I could empty myself of that fear. For just a few minutes. As if the dust and the work and the emptiness sucked it all from me.

It's not like it was a huge transformative event. Like for a few minutes, I took off my clothes and sang Broadway tunes to the corn.

Hardly.

I just got to not be scared for a while.

And it was enough.

But here in Carolina, I was surrounded by a forest and insane amounts of kudzu vine. Which truthfully—as far as plants went—had to be the scariest plant. The way it climbed and grew over anything that stood still, preserving the shape of the thing underneath but killing it dead at the same time. Like a mummy plant.

So damn creepy.

There were strange animals in the forest. Strange bugs buzzing around my ears. Every noise made me jump and every shadow seemed to watch me.

Here, my fear bounced back at me tenfold.

Like I transmitted doubt and it came back as terror.

By the second hour of working, my entire body slick with sweat, I started to doubt if I'd gone far enough to get away from Hoyt. Because I was partially convinced he was watching me from the weeds around the watering hole.

"Hardly seems like a job for a girl," a quiet voice said.

Wild, I turned, shovel over my head like a weapon.

4

"Whoa, there," said an old man, lifting one arm up in the air. His other hand held a plate. "I take it back. It's a perfect job for a girl."

Heart thumping, I lowered the shovel. "Sorry," I said, with the best smile I was capable of. "You startled me."

"I can see that." The man had a silver buzz cut and wore a pristine white tee shirt with a pair of jeans. On his forearm a tattoo snake twined its way around his elbow and an eagle was swooping down from his biceps, talons stretched to grab it.

"Here," he said, holding out a plate toward me. "Watching you work made me hungry, so I figured you had to be starved."

On the plate were two pieces of bread covered in mayonnaise and ragged slices of tomatoes, like they'd been cut with a spoon. The tomatoes were so red, so beautiful, they looked like gems. The juice like blood.

My stomach roared.

The old man's lip twitched. "Go on," he said pushing the plate toward me.

"I'm fine," I said, squeezing my hand around the splintery wooden handle of the shovel. Hunger made me dizzy.

He shot me a puzzled look.

"Really," I said. "Totally fine."

"Well, I'll leave it for you, then," he said, setting down the old plastic plate on top of a boulder.

"You don't need to—"

"I got about seven hundred pounds of tomatoes right now. I can't eat them all myself."

I had this half-clear, half-fuzzy memory of one of the last times Mom and I went to church, when it must have been getting obvious Mom was sick. The various circle groups and outreach ladies had unleashed an unprecedented wave of charity upon us. Tater-tot-covered casseroles, sheet cakes, a dozen kinds of chili, clothes, and blankets knit by hand—it all just rained down on us. So much that we couldn't carry it all. There were hand squeezes and whispered, tearful promises to Mom that I would be looked after when she was gone.

I'd been relieved, delighted even. My fear of what would happen when Mom died was washed away in that flood of care. I had friends, I had community. I wasn't totally alone. I didn't need to lie awake at night scared, listening to Mom shuffle up and down the hallway, restless from the pain, and wonder what would happen to me.

Who would take care of me?

These people would!

Mom smiled at those friends, my potential new families, she nodded, made two trips to the car to get it all home, but once we were home and safe and alone, she went apeshit. Dumping all that free, delicious homemade food in the garbage.

We don't need their pity, she'd said.

I do, I'd wanted to cry. *I need their pity. And their chili!*

We never went back to church after that and Mom died a few months later.

"Honestly, you're doing me a favor," the old man lied, but he did it without blinking, without smirking.

Oh, for God's sake. Take the sandwich, I told myself, staring down at the juicy tomatoes resting on the bed of creamy mayonnaise. *Wanting something doesn't make it bad.*

"Thank you," I said. "I'll eat it in a bit."

I'd take the charity; I just wouldn't eat it in front of him. Seemed reasonable.

He nodded as if accepting my terms. "How old are you, girl? If you don't mind me asking."

"Twenty-four." Twenty-five in two months.

I waited for that "old soul" comment I used to get a lot. *Old soul* was code for a lot of things, and I figured most of them had nothing to do with my soul and more to do with growing up with my mother.

He nodded, saying nothing about my soul or age one way or another. "If I could offer a little advice, about the work?"

"Sure."

"Start earlier. Out of the heat. Quit at noon. Ain't nothing gonna come from working outside in August past noon except heatstroke. And drink more water."

All of it I knew, but I'd been so flustered starting the day by sleeping in. Still, it would be rude to say "I know" when all he was doing was being polite. And frankly, he'd been kinder to me in two minutes than anyone had in a very long time.

So, I said, "Thank you for the advice. And the sandwiches."

In reply, he ducked his head and walked away. Beneath the thin fabric of his white shirt I saw the shadow of a black tattoo in a strange shape, like a big square.

"I'm sorry," I called out, though I was pretty sure I knew the answer to the question I was about to ask. "What's your name?"

"Ben," he said. "Yours?"

"Annie."

"Pleasure to meet you, Annie."

"Likewise, Ben."

He walked back over to his trailer, the one two north from mine.

Ben was the man Dylan had watched.

Why?

Once he was out of sight I dropped the shovel and picked up the plate, nearly shoving one of the open-faced sandwiches in my mouth.

"Oh God," I moaned around the mouthful of food. And then again because really . . . I'd had tomatoes before, and mayo and toasted cheap white bread. But somehow this combination, on this day—it was transcendent.

Flavors exploded in my mouth, sharp and sweet and tangy.

I scarfed both of them down, and used my finger to pick up the crumbs on the old plate.

If there were a dozen more on that plate, I'd eat them too.

The sun blazed overhead and my clothes were soaked and exhaustion made my feet weigh a hundred pounds.

My stomach was full, my hunger satiated.

Suddenly, I wished I could tell my mom that sympathy, pity, or concern—whatever it was that came with those tomatoes, much like the tater-tot casseroles—weren't anything to be afraid of. Or angry over. They were no slight to pride or self-sufficiency.

All they were, really, was delicious.

And when you were hungry, they filled you up.

DYLAN

It was late. So late it was about to be very early. The gearbox design was done, his team was manufacturing the prototype, and Dylan should be collapsed, face-first on his bed, beginning to sleep the first of two days away.

But instead, Dylan stood at the windows, looking out at the black night.

There was a glimmer of a campfire on the mountains on the other side of his valley, just visible through the dark trees.

He used to camp with his brother. Well, not so much camping as sleeping outside when shit got bad with his parents. But Max had made it seem like an adventure.

Max. He pressed his forehead against the glass. *Why am I thinking about Max?*

He'd put these memories, these thoughts away. Because they hurt. Because they made him angry. Sad. Thinking about Max led to missing him. And nothing good ever came of that.

I'm tired, he thought. Exhausted. That's why he was thinking of Max. And Layla. Thoughts of her were a burning coal in the center of his brain. A constant hum while he'd been retooling the design.

Was she still at the trailer park? Was she okay?

He couldn't outrun thoughts that something might have happened to her. He couldn't outrun the fact that he wanted to hear her voice again. Wanted that brief and strange moment of intimacy repeated. Again. And again.

The usual chorus of dissent was too tired to stage an intervention. He knew all the reasons why Layla was a bad idea. He just didn't care anymore.

This is fucking idiotic, he thought and finally grabbed the phone, because he couldn't stand himself anymore. *Just call her.*

He paused with his thumb over her number on the screen.

It was very nearly dawn. Phone calls at this time were only scary.

And I made a promise.

She had to call him. It was the only way it could work.

Resigned, he tucked his phone back into his pocket. Margaret had made him some dinner before she left and it was bubbling away on the stove.

Margaret was his business partner Blake's mother. And somehow the care and feeding of Dylan had slipped under her umbrella. She was his half-cook, half-housekeeper, all pain in the ass. Though he imagined she was exactly what a mother would be like, if one managed to get a good one.

But as good as whatever she'd cooked smelled, he wasn't hungry. Not for food.

Two years since he'd ended things with Jennifer. He was twenty-nine years old and he lived like a monk. Margaret said it was because he had trust issues. He didn't argue. Though Margaret was implying that he didn't trust other people.

Which was true—to a point.

The person he really didn't trust was himself.

What would he do to someone as innocent as Layla? How would the blood and dirt on his hands ruin her?

But Layla didn't know anything about him. The accident. His past. His money.

She knew nothing. And her voice had still broken with interest and desire.

That's what he couldn't shake.

It was obvious she'd lied to him about not living at the trailer park. Probably her name, too. So maybe he wouldn't tell her about himself. Those things he didn't want anyone to know. He wouldn't lie; he just wouldn't tell her.

If she was going to pretend to be someone else, so would he.

As long as she didn't find out his last name, or what he'd done, he could be *anyone*.

Suddenly the ache was back in his flesh. In his blood.

Thinking about her—the potential of her, the potential of who he could be with her—he was hard, again.

He sighed and put his head against his fist where it rested on the window. It was dark out there, the only light the bright spark of that campfire in the distance. And it was dark in his house.

It was dark in him. Always had been.

How easy it would be to lick his hand, slide it into his pants, and take care of this ache. Hard and fast, until at least for a brief bright moment, he could let himself go. Let all of it go.

But he didn't much like easy.

He didn't question how he knew it, but Layla would call him.

And he would wait for her.

But perhaps he would send her something. Just to move things along.

ANNIE

THE NEXT AFTERNOON, THERE WERE SIXTEEN BAGS OF GARBAGE stacked out near the road for trash pickup. Blistering and sunburnt, I stumbled back to my trailer only to find, there on my stoop, three giant tomatoes, each the size of my fist, and a small jar of mayonnaise.

Oh.

I glanced around, looking for Ben. But the park was quiet in the late afternoon hush. His garden was empty. Clutching the tomatoes and the mayo to my chest I brought them back inside, a smiling squirrel with forbidden nuts.

Despite being gross and in need of a shower, I toasted the last of the bagels that I'd bought from—believe it or not—a truck stop and slathered them with mayo and tomatoes. And I ate my lunch standing up.

Truck stops were kind of amazing places.

Once I'd bought the car, I made a study of truck stops from Pennsylvania down to North Carolina. And in most of them I'd been able to take a shower, as well as buy fresh fruit and some milk. And car parts, because the POS Toyota leaked oil like a sieve. Once I even splurged and had a club sandwich delivered to my parking spot. For a few quarters I'd been able to check the internet. Which I did religiously, searching the online versions of Oklahoma newspapers for news of my disappearance.

Everyone slept in their cars at truck stops, so no one came around at dawn to shoo me away.

If I'd wanted to, I could buy a new cell phone. A pet dog. A time-share in Florida. A gun. And jerky made out of camel meat.

But that was nothing compared to what I could have gotten at night.

At night I watched through the window of my car as the young girls came out in short skirts and heels so high they could barely walk. Or boys in tight pants, playing with their nipples through net shirts, talking to truckers who watched them like if they could, they would unhinge their jaws and swallow them whole.

Those girls and boys climbed into the trucks, smiling and licking their lips, only to come out an hour later, smiles vanished, tucking money into their pockets.

And I got it—I understood, they were playing a part. I knew all about that in my own life. But they were so convincing. So illicit and knowing. Forbidden and confident. The parking lots reeked of sex.

I watched them and wondered and thought about what went on in those trucks.

What I knew about sex could fit in a shoe box. A terribly small shoe box. And I knew that the reality of what was happening in those trucks was totally illegal, probably cold at best, and degrading more often than not.

But what if it wasn't always? What if one of those truckers and one of those men or women were kind? Were excited? And careful? What if they were able to take something that could be awful and painful and scary and made it . . . nice? Or more than nice?

It's not like I thought it was *The Notebook* happening in those trucks—I wasn't stupid. I was just . . . hopeful.

And if I had hope for them . . . couldn't I have hope for myself?

I thought about that in my car in those truck stops until I was . . . hungry.

And that was a hunger I had no idea how to feed.

A HALF HOUR LATER, STILL SWEATING, EVEN AFTER THE COLDEST shower in the history of cold showers, I stood in the bedroom of my trailer and considered doing something I'd never done before:

Dropping the towel and lying down naked across my bed so the breeze coming through the screens would blow right across my hot body.

My naked body.

Because I could do that. No one was here to care. Or stop me.

I put my fingers against my neck. It was a sick habit, but I caught myself pressing my thumb against the worst of the bruises—just until it hurt again.

A reminder. An anchor . . . *Don't move too fast, Annie. Remember where you're from.*

Crouching down slightly, I caught sight of the world outside when the breeze came through the window. *What if someone was standing right there? Just when the wind blew and someone saw me . . . naked on the bed?*

The chances were minuscule. The idea ludicrous, surrounded as I was by walls of metal. Thin metal—but still.

The truth was I was more self-conscious alone than I was with other people.

In the end, twenty-four years of conditioning won out. Defeated, slightly ashamed of myself, I got dressed.

Annie McKay, you're just not the kind of person who lies down naked in her bed in the middle of the day.

In the drawer next to my bed was the phone programmed with only one number. Dylan. I felt the world in a new way these days. Since pulling myself up off the floor and leaving my life behind. I was new.

And I wanted to call Dylan.

And I was terrified of that. Terrified of what it meant. About me, about my decision-making. All of it. Everything about Dylan felt risky.

Calling him was an invitation to something dangerous.

Not yet, I heard his voice in my head, that dark purr. *But soon.*

There was a knock on my trailer door and I jumped like a scalded cat, yanked from my utterly impure thoughts.

"Hey, Annie. I think a package arrived for you." It was Kevin outside my door. Just Kevin. I put a hand against my throat and felt my heart pounding hard.

"There's got to be a mistake," I said, opening the door. "There isn't anyone who would send me a package."

"Well," he said, looking down at a small box, wrapped in regular post-office brown paper. "It's addressed to 'Layla-slash-the new cleaning lady.' And you're the closest thing I got to a cleaning lady around these parts."

Layla.

That box was from Dylan.

Kevin held it out toward me but I couldn't get my hands to move. I could barely get my lungs to move. He'd sent me something.

"You want me to pitch it?" he asked, dropping his hand to his side with a shrug.

"No!" I cried. "No, I'll . . . I'll take it."

Of course I would take it.

It was a package from a man I could not stop thinking about. It was a bad idea, I got that, but what was just one more bad idea? I was kind of on a roll these days.

"Here you go." He handed it to me and left, walking back across the dirt path to the other side of the trailer park.

I closed the door and put the box down on the table and slid into the settee. The handwriting on the top was a woman's handwriting. Weird. But whatever.

I grabbed a knife from my drawer and slid it between the edges of the cardboard, cutting open the brown tape that sealed it shut.

Inside was a phone charger. And a note.

For the phone. For emergencies, the note read in very different handwriting than what had been on the box. This was a man's handwriting. Sharp and slashing across the white paper in dark ink.

I hope you are all right.

A phone charger. For emergencies. The breath I'd been holding shuddered hard out of me. I had no idea what I thought was going to be in there, but a phone charger was not it. I grabbed the note and phone from my cupboard and went into my bedroom where I plugged the charger into the wall and hooked it up.

Manners dictated I say thank you. I had to contact him.

You know, because of manners.

A dark thrill, a sort of giddy misgiving, rolled through me.

I pulled up his number on the phone but instead of calling him, I texted.

I got the charger, I wrote. *Thank you. So much.*

I deleted the *so much.* No need to go overboard.

You're welcome, he wrote back.

I pulled my bottom lip between my teeth and waited for him to say more. But the screen stayed the same.

Either write something or put it down, I told myself. *Because this is ridiculous.*

In the end I put the phone back in the drawer and shut it.

But I thought about it—about Dylan—for the rest of the night.

5

"HEY KEVIN," I SAID, WALKING INTO THE OFFICE A WEEK LATER. Kevin sat directly in the path of the rattling air conditioner in the window, playing computer solitaire. "I'm going to need more garbage bags and a new rake."

"There isn't a rake in the shed?"

"There is, but it's broken."

"You can't fix it?"

And I thought *I* was cheap.

"Nope."

"A shovel won't work?"

I sighed. "No. Kevin. I really need a rake. And some hedge trimmers. Heavy-duty ones."

"Why?"

"I'm going after the kudzu."

Kevin nodded, impressed maybe by my antagonistic nature toward the creepy mummy plant.

"I'll get that for you tomorrow," he said. "You done real good out there. Most people don't get past the flies and the garbage."

"Well, I figure the garbage had to be the worst part." And it had been disgusting, but I did it. I shoveled it. Bagged it and cleared it.

"Amen to that," Kevin said. "And here."

He slid the key to the shed across the counter.

"You saying I'm not unsavory?" I asked, smiling.

"That's what I'm saying. And take the day off. Too hot to work anyways."

"But . . ." *We don't talk about money.* That had been one of Hoyt's rules. *About how much we got. Or what we need. We don't say a word about any of it. It's low. Vulgar.*

Those rules wouldn't get me very far in the outside world. I would starve to death trying not to be vulgar.

"I need the money."

Kevin leaned his heft back in his office chair, which squealed against the weight.

"I'm paying you a salary," he said. "Just make it up another day."

I'd worked on the farm my entire life and not once did it earn me a penny. All my money I had to ask for, from Mom and then from Hoyt.

Until I took that three grand from Hoyt's safe.

Back wages, I'd told myself.

"Now, go on." Kevin shooed me out the door. "Take a day off."

"You sure?" I asked. "Because if there's anything else that needs—"

"No. Nothing else needs doing. Now go."

Still, I lingered at the door. It's not that there weren't a thousand things I needed to get done, but all of them meant leaving the trailer park. This small island of safety. Of work.

I totally tore my life up by the roots and now I was too scared to actually live it.

"Were there any other packages delivered for me?" I asked.

Every night I looked at that phone and thought about calling

Dylan. About texting him. Every night I chickened out. Or resisted, like that was a virtue.

"Nope. You gonna stand around here all day?"

"Nope," I said, pushing the door open and making the bell overhead jingle. "I'm leaving."

I would go twenty miles into town to get some groceries, because that's what normal people did when they ran out of gas station food and dish soap. And then I would see if there was a library with an internet connection so I could check on the news from Oklahoma.

Woman Runs Away, I imagined the headlines. Though considering Hoyt, the headline should undoubtedly be more like *Lying Wife Runs Out on Husband, Leaving Him No One to Smack Around on the Fifth Day in a Row Without Rain.*

Heading back to my trailer I saw Ben in his garden, curling the delicate stems of peas up twine runners tied to the top tier of his fence.

"Sugar snaps?" I asked as I approached.

"No," he laughed, not looking up, which frankly was a relief. I wasn't good with eye contact. "Nothing so fancy. I'm trying runner beans for the first time."

"I wanted to thank you for the tomatoes and the mayo."

"You did. I got that note. Both notes. You want to write me a letter, too?"

I smiled at the rusty teasing. Smith used to tease me that way, too. A long time ago.

Oh God, Smith.

In my house we had this front hall closet. Right off the foyer next to the front door no one ever, ever used. That front hall closet was where we put the stuff we didn't know what to do with. Christmas decorations. My grandfather's old coats. My grandmother's formal dress, in a garment bag I liked to open when I was a kid, to see the sequins and the peacock pin at the dress's neck.

And I had one of those closets in my brain. That's where I'd put all my memories of Smith. All my guilt over what had happened. What . . . I'd done to him. And I hadn't thought about him in years, but for some reason, Ben opened that door and the memory rolled out.

"Well, I wanted to thank you in person, then," I said, pulling myself away from those awful memories.

"My pleasure. I've got fifty more tomatoes I can put on your doorstep."

I had a sudden brainstorm of homemade pasta sauce, with ground beef and Ben's tomatoes. I learned how to be a lousy cook from my mom, the lousiest, but one year Mom—before things with Smith got so strange, and the new minister, and Mom getting sick—got it in her head to volunteer to make the meat sauce for the church spaghetti supper. She found this recipe on the back of a can of tomatoes and it was such a huge hit that she ended up making the spaghetti sauce for the church for years.

It was the one thing we could make that didn't involve opening a box and preheating the oven.

And I could give Ben some spaghetti sauce. The quid pro quo of it appealed to me.

"I'll take whatever you care to give me."

His garden had everything. Peppers, cucumbers, beets, even. Along the far edge of the fencing were herbs. I saw basil and oregano, which would be pretty awesome in the pasta sauce.

"You want something you should ask for it, girly."

"I don't . . . that's not—"

"What do you want?" His eyes were nearly black they were so dark, and when they looked into mine I felt pinned to the ground.

Ugh. Eye contact.

"Nothing."

"Go away, girly. I got no time for this."

His dismissal stung. "The basil," I said.

"Yours. Anything else?"

I shook my head, far too uncomfortable to answer.

When I'd needed help, really needed it—life-or-death stuff—I'd been unable to ask. There was no way I was asking for more from this guy's garden.

"I'm running into town," I said. "Is there anything you need?"

"Nope." His thick, gnarled fingers were busy with the delicate work of making sure his beans grew up the twine.

There were tattoos on his knuckles. A word, each letter on a different finger that I couldn't quite make out.

"Okay," I said, "sorry."

"Sorry for what?"

I blinked. *Sorry for not being able to ask for what I want. Sorry I can't get anything for you from town. Sorry for being here . . .* Christ, what was wrong with me? Apologizing was an old habit.

"I don't know, I guess."

"I guess I don't either. So stop."

Right. So stop. That easy. I might be off the farm, but parts of the farm were still very much in me.

Making a grocery list in my head I walked back to my own trailer, my eyes on the dust of the track between the RVs.

"Hello, neighbor," a woman said and I looked up to see Joan, sitting on a lawn chair on a small improvised deck on the side of her RV. She wore a short, green silk robe and a bland expression of disdain.

"Hi," I said, feeling utterly grubby in the face of Joan's inexplicable trailer-park elegance. She was actually kind of regal, sitting there. It was the rhinestones on her toes, maybe. Or her straight posture in the lawn chair, the casual way she held her cigarette.

Because it wasn't her dirty-blond hair piled up on her head, or her pale blue eyes. The scars on her cheeks from long-ago acne.

But her legs, beneath that green robe, went on for miles.

"I'm Annie," I said, into the silence.

"Joan."

The trailer door opened and a man came out, pulling a shirt on over his head. He was thick and muscled, hairy all over, not just his chest. Even his stomach was hairy. When his head popped out of his shirt, he smiled at Joan, his face covered in a thick black five-o'clock shadow. "See you, babe," he said leaning over the small railing as if to kiss her. Joan took a drag from her cigarette, blowing the smoke toward him, and he pulled back, rebuffed. Though he didn't seem to be too upset about it.

"I put a little something extra for you on the counter," he said to Joan before turning away. He gave me a wink and a smile that was so slimy it made me want to take a shower in my clothes.

If my life depended on it I could not look back over at Joan.

A prostitute? Am I living next door to a prostitute?

"A little hot for a scarf, don't you think?" Joan said.

I put my hand up to it, wincing slightly as I touched the bruises. Joan smirked, like she knew what was under the water-lily print. Like she had been there that night in my kitchen. Like in the ten seconds we'd stood in front of each other, Joan knew all about me.

And all of it was sad.

Without another word, I left, my cheeks on fire.

Dylan had it all wrong. Ben was about as threatening as a mouse.

It was Joan I had to watch out for.

THERE WAS NO GUIDEBOOK FOR RUNNING AWAY FROM AN ABU-sive husband. I had to go with my gut nine times out of ten, and my gut hated towns.

CNN was on in most bars all day. Magazines shouted scandalous, salacious headlines: *Wife Missing! Man Grieving!* in every grocery store.

Internet access was everywhere.

The potential of being spotted—found—just seemed so much higher in a city.

But that's where grocery stores were.

In this case, Cherokee, North Carolina. There was an Indian reservation just outside of town and its influence was heavy in all the gift stores, with women and men in full headdress sitting out front, selling the chance to take a picture with them for five bucks.

All the restaurants had the word *Chief* in them.

It was a strange place.

The Appalachian Trail also went through here, or near here somewhere. There were men and women with giant backpacks, and filthy legs beneath their shorts, walking along the side of the road with their thumbs out.

Hitchhiking? Really?

Who the hell got to be so naive? So trusting? They were literally asking for trouble.

But when I caught sight of their faces in my rearview mirror, I realized they were probably my age. Just out of college, maybe. Having a little adventure before finding a job, or going back to grad school.

I stopped looking at them. Angry at all their opportunity. Their youth that looked so different from mine.

An IGA sat on a corner and I pulled in and parked in the shadows closest to the dumpster. In the silence of the car after turning off the engine, I went over my plan.

Get in, get out. Don't make eye contact. Be forgettable.

That had been my credo for my week on the run.

Forgettable, I could do. I'd perfected it, really.

Once inside, I sped through the aisles, picking the same

things I had for years until I stopped, my hands on a box of cereal that Hoyt loved.

I'm not . . . I don't have to get this. I put the Cheerios back on the shelf and then turned to get the generic Froot Loops. My favorite. Glancing down in the cart, I realized I'd gotten all of his favorite things.

Cottage cheese.

I hated cottage cheese.

As I walked back to the dairy section to put the cottage cheese away, I felt someone watching me, and I looked out of the corner of my eyes at a woman with three kids hanging off the cart. All of them staring at me.

I accidentally made eye contact and the woman smiled.

"Do I know you?" she asked. "You look really familiar."

Panic slipped over me like delicate, poisonous lace.

"I don't think so," I said, resisting the urge to put my sunglasses down over my eyes, leave the basket, and run.

"You're working out at the Flowered Manor, aren't you?" she said. "We live there."

She looked like a teenager, covered in babies and toddlers. One of them, a little boy, was pulling down on the hem of her ratty Old Navy tee shirt until I could see the dark edges of a bruise on her shoulder.

The woman yanked her shirt out of the little boy's hands. "Stop it, Danny," she hissed. She smiled over at me, her eyes somewhere on the floor. "We gotta go," she murmured, and then pushed her cart in the other direction.

Fast.

I stood there in front of the yogurt and shook for a moment. *How many times have I done that? Without the kids and the diapers, but how many times have I dashed away, eyes on the floor? Shame a thick, awful taste in my mouth.*

Should I find her? Talk to her?

Hell, no, my gut spoke up. *Get what you need and get gone.*

In and out.

It really was for the best.

My cart was far from full, but somehow impossibly satisfying, full of all the things I liked. I even splurged on a big bag of generic chocolate chips. I'd put them in the freezer and let myself have a few every night.

Mom would hardly approve, but that sort of seemed the point.

The woman with the kids had left the store. Her abandoned cart sat next to the manager's hold desk, the big box of diapers wedged in next to a gallon of milk and a bag of apples.

She'd left it all. Everything she came here to get she just abandoned.

I asked the cashier for directions to the library across town and tried to pretend that cart full of things a family needed wasn't even there.

6

INSIDE THE LIBRARY, IT WAS QUIET AND EMPTY AND SMELLED like old books and air-conditioning.

Without looking too closely at the kind-seeming woman at the desk, I headed right over to the bank of computers on the far wall.

"Excuse me, miss," the woman said, using that quiet librarian voice that somehow managed to travel across the room. I wondered if there was a class for that in college.

"Yes?"

"You need to sign in to use the computers."

"Pardon?" I glanced around the empty library.

"We just need you to sign in, so we can prove that people use the computers here. That they are an asset to the community."

"I'm not part of the community—I'm just passing through."

"I still need you to sign in," she said with a smile.

I'm being ridiculous, I thought, walking back over to the desk and the clipboard there, the red pen attached with a string and masking tape. Panic fluttered in my belly. I wasn't a good liar and I'd been lying about my name all across the country the last week.

What if she asked for ID?

"You forget your name, sweetheart?" the woman asked, eyes twinkling.

I wish.

With a quick breath, like I was about to dive underwater, I picked up the pen and scrawled *Layla McKay* across the form and thought of Dylan.

He lurked in the back of my brain all the time. When I stopped thinking of something else, there he was. Filling my head with thoughts that made me uncomfortable.

"Thank you," the librarian said.

"No problem."

I sat back down at the computer and scanned the headlines for Oklahoma papers. No mention of me in Tulsa. Oklahoma City. Or in the *Bassett Gazette*, the town newspaper closest to the farm. I'd been checking that one religiously since I'd left.

I did a quick search of my name and all that showed up was my marriage announcement, my mother's obituary, and the announcement of the land Hoyt sold to the electric company to put up windmills.

Nothing. *Oh dear God. Nothing.*

It had been twelve days since I'd run. And it didn't seem like he'd even gone to the police.

I sat in the chair a little bit longer because my legs felt like jelly, my arms useless spaghetti noodles. There was no big search underway for me.

I had never made a will, but I imagine if he claimed abandonment or whatever, he could do what he wanted with the land. I had no idea how these things worked. But he was my husband after all. No one would argue with him.

This was the best possible outcome of my leaving. There would be no fuss. No scene of him in front of reporters with flashing cameras, pretending to cry, pretending to care.

But it meant that I'd vanished ... everything I'd been.

Twenty-four years of being alive, of being a daughter and a student and a member of a church. Of working, sweating, crying, laughing as Annie McKay. Gone.

No one missed me. Or worried. Or wondered. I'd vanished and the world just kept on spinning.

That no one seemed to be searching for me was a relief. Yet behind the relief . . . there was something else. Something I couldn't look at yet.

Relieved was enough for now. Relieved was all I could handle.

"I know you said you're not from around here, but we're having a book sale this week," the librarian said. "Paperbacks are a dollar, hardbacks are three."

I got to my feet, bracing myself against the table for a moment when it felt like my knees were wobbling.

The librarian pointed to a little rack of books by the door, full of beat-up old bestsellers and hardback textbooks and literary novels.

I loved books. Loved reading. It not only gave me an escape from my own world, but opened a door into other worlds. It allowed me, at the beginning of my marriage, to suffer with some grace. As long as I had another world to go to, what did I care about how small and strange and terrifying my own life had gotten?

Then Hoyt took away my books. Put them right in the burn pile, and the smell had been worse than anything. Like every dream going up in smoke. I'd tried to get some at the library, telling him it wasn't costing him anything. But he didn't like it.

And then I snuck them when I could, hiding some garage sale books in the barn.

But he'd found them.

And that had not gone well for me.

"I'm fine," I said to the woman, feeling unbelievably outside of my body. Like I was floating somewhere near the ceiling, watching my thin arms and legs all scraped up from the work I'd been doing. The stupid bad dye job.

The scarf.

Stop. Fucking. Saying. That.

Everyone can see you are not fine.

"Actually," I said and stopped at the shelf, "let me see what you have."

In the end I bought ten paperback books. One of them was *Fifty Shades of Grey*, so worn the cover was nearly falling off. Chunks of pages were threatening to fall away from the spine.

"We've had to replace that book three times," the librarian said with a twinkly smile.

"I've never read it." I could not imagine the shit storm that would have fallen on my head had I tried to bring that into my home. But news of it had even managed to make its way to the rock I lived under. It had caused something of a revolution.

And I was ready to be revolutionized.

I clutched the plastic bag of books to my chest and headed back to my car. My hands were shaking so bad I barely got the key in the lock, barely got my body inside the car, the door shut behind me.

It was hot, and it smelled like the peaches I'd bought off the clearance rack at the grocery store.

I rested my head against the steering wheel.

He wasn't looking for me.

I bought chocolate chips.

And a dirty book.

I pressed my hands to my lips, unsure whether I was going to laugh or cry. Until I was doing both. Loudly. Like a crazy person.

A sudden knock on my driver-side window made me jump, spilling my books all around me.

A cop stood out there. I must have shot him the worst look, because he stepped back and lifted his glasses up onto his head. He smiled.

I'm a nice guy, that smile said. *I swear.*

I used the old crank to unroll my window, brushing the tears away from my face with my other hand.

"I didn't mean to spook you," he said. He had a nice face. Round, with a little blond scruff around his chin. An uncommitted beard.

"It's all right," I said, my voice reedy and thin.

"I just . . . I saw you and I wanted to be sure you were all right."

He saw me in the middle of some kind of freak-out. A panic attack. I was caught in that wide chasm between what I'd had and what I could have. What my life had been and what I wanted it to be, and every step, every huge step I'd taken away from what I knew and into the unknown, felt terrifying.

"I'm fine." I gave him my best smile, which apparently wasn't convincing, because he asked, "Are you sure?"

No. I'm not, but I'm trying here. I'm trying harder than I ever have and it's so damn hard.

"Yep," I said. "I'll be fine."

Funny, but I felt like this time it wasn't totally a lie.

In the twilight, hours later, the heat had broken and the breeze coming in through the windows was cool. My little trailer was ripe and delicious and homey with the scent of pasta sauce, bubbling away on one of the burners of my two-burner stove.

But my body was restless. Aching.

I sat up from where I'd been lying on the settee and put the book down on the table.

God.

I mean. God.

Between my legs, I throbbed. Actually throbbed. I felt swollen and wet and . . . throbby.

Honestly, I'd never felt this way before. Like my skin was too tight and aching and I needed something . . . something to split me open. To relieve this pressure.

No wonder that book was so popular.

I clasped my hands to my lips, closed my eyes, and tried to will the feeling away, but the more I thought about it, the worse the ache became, until it was in my bones.

I turned my head, staring back at my room.

The phone was in there.

Dylan.

I call him and . . . what? Have phone sex? Honestly, Annie McKay, is that what you're thinking? You have no idea how that starts. How it even happens.

But I would bet my last seventeen dollars that he did.

Before I could talk myself out of it, I went back and grabbed my phone and took it back into the kitchen.

Away from the bed.

See how crazy you are?

Its face was dark and my intentions uncertain.

I'm twenty-four. Girls my age do this shit all the time, and worse! Why do I have to be different?

Dylan wanted to know about Ben, I thought, searching for a respectable reason to call the man. Something more . . . me. More passive and meek. Ben, a man with a penchant for tattoos and tomatoes. A harmless guy. So what would be the harm in calling Dylan and letting him know that the old man was fine?

Because Ben was not the threat.

Dylan is.

No, not even that was the truth.

I am the threat.

I'd promised myself in that bus station in Tulsa that I wouldn't lie to myself anymore. The self-deception would stop. Because it had made me complicit in my abuse to some extent.

All married couples fight. That was one I told myself quite a bit.

Hoyt's just under a lot of stress—that had been a doozey.

I'll be fine.

That had been the worst of them.

So I wasn't going to lie to myself now.

The phone was in my hand because I wanted to call him. Because my belly was full and my shelves were stocked with food I liked. Because my hands were raw from honest work, because I'd had a week of safety in this world I'd carved out for myself.

Because between my legs I was sore with . . . desire. Lust.

Those were such strange words. Foreign to my life.

Because I wanted to see what would happen if I talked to Dylan again.

What I might do if he asked.

Tell me no.

Because I wanted to be asked to do something I couldn't quite do on my own.

I pressed the power button and the phone slowly blinked to life.

7

HE ANSWERED A BREATH AFTER THE FIRST RING, BUT INSTEAD OF his voice all I heard was the revving of an engine. Or lots of engines. I pulled the phone from my ear.

"Just a second," Dylan yelled into the phone and then I heard his voice, muffled as he yelled to someone else on his end, "I'll be in my office."

A second later the roar of the engines was gone. "Hello," he said.

Oh.

His voice made me ache harder. I sat back down on the settee and crossed my legs, squeezing them together until sparks shot out through my nerves.

"Is this Layla?"

I closed my eyes in a kind of embarrassed relief, because truly his voice sounded like he was smiling. "It is."

"You okay?"

No. I've been reading a dirty book and it's worked on me and I don't know what to do with myself, and I thought if I called you, you might tell me.

"Fine." My voice was shaky. Everything about this was shaky. "Everything is fine."

Lie! Lying liar!

"I'm real glad you called."

"You are?"

"I didn't like thinking I'd scared you."

No more lying. So, instead, I went with total naked honesty. "Truthfully, I kind of scared myself." He made a rumbly curious sound that raised goose bumps across my spine and the silence after my words was loaded, filled with questions I didn't have the answers for yet. "You . . . you're at work?"

"I am always at work."

"You work in a garage or something?"

"Why do you ask?" Something cold laced his words, something slightly defensive. Or accusing. Very distrustful. Like I had no right to wonder about him. Or ask.

"Because when you answered your phone it sounded like engines in the background," I said quickly.

"Right. Yeah, you could say I work in a garage."

Still, the small note of suspicion and distrust in his voice cooled me down some and made me doubt what I was doing all over again. *Jesus, what do I know about this man? He could be worse than Hoyt.*

"Look, I just wanted to tell you that Ben is fine—"

"You talked to him?"

"Sure. Wasn't that the point?"

"No. It's not the point. You're supposed to watch him. Not talk to him."

"What?" I laughed, imagining myself peering through the blinds at him. "Like a spy?"

"You need to keep your distance. He is not a nice guy."

"I really don't think we're talking about the same person," I said. "An older gentleman, with a silver buzz cut—"

"The words *Free* tattooed on the knuckles of his right hand and *Dead* on the knuckles of his left?"

So, that's what those letters were. "Well . . . I couldn't actually make out the words . . . but—"

"It's the same guy. I know he seems innocent, and probably real likable, but that's not real. That's not the real him."

"He gave me a bunch of tomatoes. I made him some pasta sauce."

He was breathing heavily into the phone and his voice was hard. Not the way I'd heard him before. If he'd sounded like this the first time we talked, I wouldn't have called him back. I would have been too scared. Of him. Not myself. "Layla, I know you have no reason to trust me, but please . . . please don't get messed up with him."

"Okay," I said, placating him. I'd promised myself I'd stop with the self-deception; I didn't say anything about lying to some stranger on the phone.

"Do you trust me?" he asked, sounding doubtful. "Because I need you to trust me."

"I don't know you."

His chuckle felt like a hand across that tender skin at the nape of my neck. The skin that had never been touched before. Not in kindness.

And I didn't know if Dylan's voice was kind. Or if he was. All I knew was that my body reacted to him.

"I guess that's true."

"Are you an ax murderer?"

"No. You?"

"Nope. Well, at least we got that out of the way." I laughed. "Though maybe it would be funny if both of us were, you know, ax murderers. Like the worst coincidence. Or maybe a dream come true—I imagine that ax murderers don't get to date—"

"You sound nervous."

My mouth was hot and dry. Worse than the creek bed back home in August. "I . . . ah . . . a little. I guess. Yes."

"Are you trying to be brave?" His voice tipped into that familiar place where we'd been last time. Like, he was letting me know there was something more he wanted to talk about. Underneath the laughter and the banalities, there was a darker place we could go.

"I've never been brave in my life," I said, longing so hard for that darker place. If having a dirty book would have gotten me in trouble, wanting this forbidden thing would have gotten me hurt I don't know how bad.

But not here.

Not with him—this stranger on the phone.

This is why I called, because I don't know how to find these dark, forbidden places on my own.

"You're talking to me, aren't you?"

"Are you telling me I shouldn't?"

"No, but you said you scared yourself last time we talked."

The trailer was small and dark, and it was as if there were only the two of us in the wide world.

"I did," I murmured, feeling almost powerless. But in a good way. Like I was giving up the power instead of having it taken from me. The act of willing surrender made all the difference.

Made it okay.

"Then talking to me is brave."

"I guess so," I said, giving myself some points when I was usually so damn stingy.

"What else do you want to be brave about?"

Everything. My life. My body.

"I bought a dirty book today." I closed my eyes and slapped a hand to my forehead. Honestly, could I be any less cool? I felt like a teenager.

His chuckle was low. Rough. "Did you? Was it good?"

"I'm not done. But yeah . . . it's hot."

"Was that brave?" he asked.

"Very. You tell me one," I said, mortified and on edge.

His sigh was the kind of sigh that came after a long, hard day, when it seemed to be you against the world. I was pretty familiar with that sigh. "Well, I fired a guy today. A friend's brother. I let it go on for too long because I owe my friend a lot. But in the end, I had to let the guy go."

"I'm sorry. That's a hard thing to do."

"You ever fire anyone?" He sounded surprised.

"Once," I said, not wanting to remember. "It was awful."

"Yeah, today sucked. You go."

"A brave thing?"

"Yeah."

I couldn't tell him about the cereal and the chocolate chips. I already sounded like an idiot with the book.

"Yesterday, it was so hot I wanted to lie down on my bed in the middle of the day naked and let the wind blow over me."

I bit my lip and he exhaled slowly through his nose and I sensed that I'd shocked him. Or excited him. I sure as hell shocked and excited myself. But it was happening. I'd said those words and my body was coiled, hot and anxious. Full of restlessness and embarrassment and a kind of yearning that hurt.

For sex. Lust. Orgasms. Oral sex. Red rooms with whips. Blindfolds and handcuffs. Kisses in elevators that changed a person's entire life.

Things other women took for granted that had been denied me, my entire life.

I wanted to feel my body from the inside out, in a way I never had before.

"Did you do it?"

"I chickened out."

"Why?"

"Self-conscious, I guess. Too much sunlight maybe."

"No sunlight now."

I held the phone away from my face for a moment and took a deep breath.

"No," I said. "There isn't."

"Why don't you do that now? Open your windows, take off your clothes and stretch out on your bed, and then you can tell me what else you want to be brave about."

This is why I called. Exactly why I called. I can't chicken out now.

I got up from the settee and walked to my bedroom. My fingers opened the fly of my shorts and when they fell to my ankles, I stepped out of them and kept walking. I took off my tank top. I hadn't bothered with a bra because of the heat, and I didn't have much up top anyway.

The underwear stayed on. I was still Annie McKay after all.

The windows were open, the breeze making the little beige curtains wave.

In my threadbare pink bikini underwear, I lay down on my made bed.

The wind danced across my stomach. Over my nipples, turning them into hard beads. I almost touched one. Almost.

It was like when I cut my hair and felt the wind against my neck for the first time. I felt exposed and raw.

Brand new.

"How's it feel?" he asked, his voice somewhere between a whisper and a murmur.

"It feels good." I was lost for a moment in the cold and heat of it. The strange vulnerable thrill of it.

"Yeah? Tell me."

I swallowed. *Oh God.* I didn't have the guts for this one.

"It's been hot for days, hasn't it?" he asked, as if he knew I'd hit a limit. "And that breeze just cools down all that sweat. Makes you almost cold in places."

"Yes, exactly."

"Good girl."

I shouldn't like those words. I wasn't his good girl. I wasn't anyone's. But my eyes fluttered shut and I lifted my fingers to my nipple. For just a second. It was hot and hard. Burning, nearly. And then I put my hand down on the quilt beside my hip.

But I couldn't quite stop the hitch in my breath.

He made a sound—that sound—again. Something had turned him on.

"What else do you want to be brave about?" he asked.

"I'd like to eat dessert for breakfast one day."

His laughter was dark and rich like brownie batter and I wanted to eat a bowl of it. Of him.

"That's an easy one," he said.

Not if you're me. Not if you were raised by my mom.

"I want to give a man a blow job."

The silence on the other end pounded.

"You haven't done that?" he asked.

"No."

"Jesus, how old are you?"

"Twenty-four. How old are you?" God, I hadn't thought to ask.

"Twenty-nine."

"We could be lying," I said. "Both of us."

"I'm not," he said. "I'll never lie to you."

I couldn't make him the same promises—I had, after all, lied about my name, about staying away from Ben. About being totally naked. I wasn't ready to tell him the truth.

Or willing to.

"I'm not lying about my age," I said.

"Are you a virgin?"

"No." Those memories, cold and uncomfortable, terrifying and sad, were in my brain's front hall closet too. "Just . . . not experienced."

"Has a man ever gone down on you?"

I shook my head, my mouth dry, words gone, but then I realized he couldn't see me.

"No," I said.

"Did that happen in your dirty book?"

"Yes."

"It turned you on."

"Yes."

"That's why you called me?"

Oh my God. "Yes," I breathed, and he groaned.

Sex with Hoyt had been awful on a bunch of levels and the memories spilled, uncontrolled, out from where I'd tried to hide them. At the beginning, before I knew better, I'd asked him once if he'd like that . . . like me to put his penis in my mouth.

He smacked me right off the bed.

Whores talk like that, he'd said.

I closed my eyes, my arms lifting to cover my breasts, an old awful embarrassment filling me right to the top, pushing away all my excitement. Tears burned behind my eyes.

I can't do this. This isn't me. This isn't for me.

I opened my mouth to tell him I'd made a mistake. I never should have tried this, no matter how bad I wanted it.

"You're missing out on one of life's great pleasures, Layla," he said.

My eyes sprang open at the fake name.

My cousin's name.

I'm not me. This isn't me, having this conversation.

I'm Layla. And Layla isn't embarrassed. Layla doesn't give a shit what some asshole like Hoyt thinks about her. Layla's probably had phone sex half a million times.

Recommitted, I cleared my throat. "I've never been skinny-dipping."

"Well, now you're killing me."

"There's a swimming pond here. Maybe I'll try it."

"That sounds like a good idea."

"What about you?" I asked. "What—"

"Hold on now, we're not done with you."

"Oh." I flushed at the attention, the focus this man put on me. It was uncomfortable, but I forced myself to take it. Absorb it. So different from Hoyt's mercurial, violent focus.

"Can I ask you a question?" he asked.

"It would be weird if I said no after all this, wouldn't it?"

"Are you touching yourself?"

"What, like . . . masturbating?" I shrieked. Actually shrieked. *So impossibly not cool, Annie.*

"Not necessarily."

"Then . . . what are you talking about?" I asked.

"Just touching. Just feeling your skin. Your body."

"No. I'm not doing that." I'd never done that.

"Put your hand over your belly, spread out your fingers as wide as you can."

I did what he asked, the tips of my fingers touching the edge of my panties. My thumb and pinky brushed the small indentions next to my hips that were somehow ticklish and directly attached to the ache between my legs. The skin there was so soft. The hair on my stomach white-blond and fine. I'd never noticed that before.

I ran my palm over my skin and then the back of my hand, from hip bone to hip bone.

I couldn't stop my gasp at the electric sensation.

"You doing it?"

"Yes."

"Now take that hand and slide it up your stomach, your chest, to your throat. Trace your collarbone."

"I don't . . ." *My collarbone? Really?*

"This is why you called me, baby. Let me do my job."

I was panting—which I'm sure he could hear, but I didn't care. I did what he asked, tracing the top and bottom edges of the delicate fluted bone.

"Touch your lips. Go real slow with your thumb. How does that feel?"

"Good. All of it . . . feels so good." My lips were chapped, and somehow even that skin was attached to the ache between my legs because I was dying. Restless and achy and hurting.

"Lick the tips of your fingers. Feel your tongue."

It was surreal, these parts of my body that seemed so pedestrian, so bland and normal every other moment of my life, but right now . . . they were electric. The air I breathed, the skin on my body—my entire self—was electric.

"Do it, baby."

"Do what?"

"Slip your fingers between your legs."

"I don't . . ." I closed my eyes and moaned. There was too much happening inside of me—too many things. Desire and embarrassment. A terrible, sharp sense of my own ridiculousness.

"You don't what?"

"I don't . . . I just . . . I've never—" How could I explain my life to this man? The extreme temperatures I'd endured that left nothing . . . nothing for me. There was not a moment of my day spent on anything but appeasing first my mother and then my husband.

"You've never . . . ?" he asked.

Once, I thought, but the memory was a bad one. Sour and awful. Terrible and unfinished; I couldn't even count it.

"Never."

"Oh, fuck, baby, I don't even care if this is some kind of game you're playing. I'm in. Whatever it is, I'm so fucking in."

"It's not a game."

"Okay," he said, and I could tell he still didn't believe me. And God, wasn't that easier? Wasn't it easier if he thought I was worldly and experienced enough to think of this dirty little phone sex game to play with a stranger?

"Are *you*?" I asked.

"What?"

"Touching yourself?"

His low chuckle sizzled from my ear over my body. "No, this one is about you."

About me. Oh God, why did that even turn me on?

Nothing good had been about me. Ever.

"Tell me what to do," I whispered.

His breathing was hard and I heard the shift and squeal of a chair, like he was turning, or leaning back.

"God, you're good, baby."

I didn't give a shit what he thought as long as this feeling was filling my body. "Please," I whispered.

Again, that groan. "Slide your fingers down between your legs."

My fingers slipped under the plain pink cotton of my underwear and I whimpered when the pressure of my hand made the ache worse. Sharper somehow.

"I like that sound you made," he said.

"What next?"

"Cup yourself in your hand, your fingers low . . . you feel yourself there?"

"Yes. I'm . . . I'm wet. Hot."

Dylan swore.

"Good, baby. Now take those fingers down between your lips, just keep following your wetness until your finger slips . . ."

I gasped. "Inside."

"Yes."

"Oh God." I closed my eyes, sliding my finger out slowly and then back in. I lifted my knees up, arched my hips so I could get more of my finger inside, but somehow, as good as that felt, there was something entirely unsatisfying about it. "It's not—"

"Use two fingers."

I did and immediately the pressure inside was fuller . . . better. My fingers slipped and slid, buried between my legs. I felt the muscles of my channel against the skin of my hand in a way I never had before.

"You know where your clit is?" he asked.

"Yes." Entirely in theory.

"Slip your thumb up to the top of your pussy—"

Oh God, that word. That filthy word . . . "Say that again."

"Thumb?"

Impossibly, a wild gust of laughter blew through me. My fingers *inside* my body and I was laughing. He laughed too, and it was a whole new layer of connection.

But then somehow in the same breath, we both sobered.

"Pussy, baby. Slide your thumb to the top of your pussy."

I did what he asked, so hard and so fast that when my thumb brushed my clit, I cried out.

"There you go," he breathed, sounding somehow satisfied. "Work it with your thumb."

"It . . . it hurts, a little."

"Good hurt or bad hurt?"

"There's no good hurt," I told him, my voice harsher than I'd intended. Good hurt. What an oxymoron. My thumb lifted from the kernel between my legs that was so sensitive right now I could barely stand to touch it.

His silence went on for a long time, long enough that I pulled my fingers from my body. The breeze over my body was not cool—it was cold.

I crossed an arm over my chest as if he could see me.

"Dylan?"

"You're not playing, are you? This isn't some hot virgin kink game with you?"

"Sure it is," I said, trying to sound coy or something, not like my lungs were being crushed by failure and embarrassment. "You don't like it?"

"Don't lie." His voice was harder than it had been and I responded instinctively.

"Not . . . really. No."

"You've really never done this?"

Virgin kink. My entire awful, sad, and lonely sexual experience could be summed up as virgin kink?

I sat up, breathless and embarrassed again. My body's humming, its ache and throb—the slick heat between my legs, on the top of my thighs—shameful more than pleasurable.

"Never mind," I stammered. "Forget it. Forget everything."

"Layla, stop. Don't hang up."

I didn't hang up, but I didn't say anything, either.

"Are you there?" he asked.

After a long moment, I said, "Yes."

"Did that feel good, that stuff you were doing?"

"Yes." It came out as a sob. My body felt combustible. My emotions impossibly wild. Totally out of control. I wanted to hit and scream and cry.

"It's gonna go somewhere, baby. I promise. All those feelings, it's going to get better and better. Let me . . . let me tell you what to do."

"Are you . . . going to laugh at me?"

"Laugh? I'm the fucking luckiest man on the planet tonight. The only thing I'm going to do is help you come."

I flopped back down on the bed.

"Put the phone on the pillow beside your ear," he said. "I want you to use two hands."

"This sounds advanced," I whispered.

His chuckle was sexy and warm, and I smiled at the sound of it.

"Brush the palm of your hand over your nipple."

I did it and it felt good, but in a watered-down kind of way, considering what my body had been feeling a few seconds ago.

"That's . . . not enough."

"Are your nipples hard?"

"Very."

"I want you to pinch them."

"Pinch?"

"Good pain, trust me, baby."

I pinched my nipples. Hard and then harder until I felt the strange pleasure-pain of it ricochet in my body. I rolled them slightly between my fingers until the lust and heat and desire roared back through me.

A choked gasp slipped out of me.

"There we go. You want to come?"

"God. Yes."

"Roll over on your stomach."

I did, fumbling slightly with the phone, until I was on my belly and could still hear him.

"Grind your pussy against the mattress. It'll make your clit—"

He didn't have to finish his instructions before I was doing it, so ready to have this happen. To have all of this panicky, edgy sensation tearing through me—do something. Go somewhere.

"Oh God," I muttered, lifting myself up on my palms slightly to get the pressure exactly right between my legs. Back and forth. Up and down. It was all the right pressure without hurting.

"You got it?"

"Yes, God . . . I want . . ."

"More?"

"Please."

"Put your two fingers in your mouth, the ones you had buried in your pussy."

I did what he asked. I could feel my fingers shaking against my lips.

"You can taste yourself, can't you?" he asked. "Salty and earthy. Best fucking taste in the world."

It was different. And strange. Tangy.

"Now put them back between your legs."

"Inside?"

"Inside. But go slow."

I lifted my hips and slipped my fingers under my panties again. I bypassed my clit, traced the edges of my lips, until I found the entrance of my body. Wet. Waiting.

"One finger at a time," he said. "Don't hurt yourself."

I laughed.

"What?"

"I . . . want it so much it seems impossible to hurt myself, you know?"

"Like you could do anything to yourself right now and it would feel good?"

"Something . . . something like that."

"Push that finger inside," he said, his voice low and dark, and I closed my eyes and did what he told me to do.

But then I couldn't get the grinding pressure right against my clit so I used my other hand, to push against my vulva, mashing my clit.

"Ahh!" I cried. "Ahhh, fuck. Oh God."

"Tell me."

I braced my forehead against the mattress. "There's some kind of weird pulsing thing happening on the bottom of my foot," I told him, not even caring how ridiculous I sounded. "And my nipples . . . oh God, they're smashed against my quilt and it's rough. It's so rough. And my fingers . . ."

"Yeah?"

"My fingers feel so good in my body. So good."

"Go, baby, make yourself come."

It took a while, a few minutes anyway, and I thought at one point I might just give up or ask him what was wrong with me, but then I slipped my fingers down to directly touch my clitoris and everything changed. All of it.

Bold, I squeezed it between my fingers and there was an explosion behind my clit, behind my eyes. In my head. Every muscle along my back spasmed and jerked and I had to pull my fingers away because it hurt again, but I kept grinding myself against the mattress and the explosion went on and on.

Until it faded away, leaving me sweating and panting and utterly changed.

I lifted my head from where I'd buried it and looked around for the phone, which I'd knocked from the pillow to the edge of the mattress.

Now what? I thought, trying to catch my breath. I had no idea how long that took. What he might have heard.

A hot wave of mortification practically lifted my skin right off my body. I was light-headed with shock at what I'd done. At how far that had gone.

Despite wanting it, despite manufacturing the moment, despite *actually doing it*—the reality was too much. Like my body had traveled far too fast for the rest of me and now I was yanking it ruthlessly back.

Without checking to hear if he was there, without saying thank you. Without any of that.

Cowardly, ashamed and buzzing, I hung up.

And I quickly turned off the power and threw the phone in the drawer.

This was dangerous on every level. That man—Dylan— undoubtedly knew where I was. He could find me. He could *find* me.

God, I couldn't think of that an hour ago?

Quickly, I flew off the bed and went to check the locks on my door. And then made sure the windows were closed. So that not even fresh air could find me. I turned off all the lights, pulled the blinds until the moonlight was filtered and dim.

Mom caught me when I was ten, rubbing myself on the edge of a chair. She took me right to church. Every day after chores. I didn't go to school for the week. I prayed for forgiveness in the church, in my pastor's office. Under my mom's careful eye and the pastor's terrifying sermons about hell, I prayed those feelings right out.

In a cerebral way I understood that I didn't deserve that. But I had a set of mixed-up scales in my head that told me over and over again that what I deserved was what I got. This awful belief was reinforced every day with Hoyt. Every moment.

And I couldn't shake it. In my lowest moments, when everything was stripped away, that was all I had left.

I got what I deserved.

No, I thought.

I am better than this, I thought, squeezing my eyes shut. I'd run so I wouldn't feel this way.

But somehow I couldn't quite stop it.

The shame was old and familiar.

And unstoppable.

A tide that rolled and rolled and rolled, over me.

DYLAN

Dylan was a rich, distrustful son of a bitch. So rich he owned the mountain where he lived and worked. So distrustful his employees—just to get to work—had to pass through an iron gate.

Clients were dealt with by Blake, who did all the face-to-face stuff. Dylan handled steel and engine schematics. The garage employees.

All of which meant it had been a very long time since Dylan had been surprised.

And tonight he had no fucking idea which surprised him more.

That Layla had called him for phone sex.

That she'd just gone from never having touched herself to having what sounded like a pillow-biting orgasm.

Or that she'd hung up on him.

Despite the raging hard-on nearly boring a hole in the zipper of his jeans, he tipped his head back against his chair and laughed.

What the hell just happened?

Part of him was suspicious, as he'd been taught to be, over and over again by hard experience. No one was that innocent, and that eager at the same goddamn time.

But somehow he knew, down in his gut, that this wasn't an act with her. Or a game. And she was undoubtedly sitting out there embarrassed by what they'd done. Maybe punishing herself.

The thought just brought him to his knees.

Because what he heard in her voice told him everything he needed to know about her. That she was scared, but she was trying; in order to get what she wanted she was pushing past her own bullshit fears and being brave. In her voice, he could hear every dark and forbidden thing she craved. And he wanted to give it to her. Everything she wanted and the things she didn't know to want, yet.

How far would she go?

She wanted dark? He had all the dark. All of it. And he'd show her every midnight corner of it.

The shiny surface of the phone in his hand reflected his face, macabre and twisted, back at him.

He wanted to call her. Well, that was bullshit. What he really wanted was to drive down off his mountain and find her in that shitty trailer park and get a front-row seat for what he'd just heard. He wanted to see her in action.

But that would never happen.

She'd take one look at him and this would be over. She'd run for safety.

There were rules, after all. And those rules were there for a reason. When he broke them, people got hurt.

Someone pounded on his office door.

Tonight, he and his team were working out in the warehouse on the engine build and he was sitting in the smaller office attached to it. It was a windowless box, dark and closed, the way he liked it. The only light was the lamp next to his computer. No one would dream of coming in here without knocking.

He'd been short-tempered and impossible and basically every single kind of a dick he could be. But he paid his guys a small fortune to offset his strangeness, and the glory helped too. His gearheads loved the glory.

"What?" Dylan yelled and Blake opened the door. He and Blake had been together since the beginning. The good years before the fire. The better years since. Blake rarely came to the garage anymore; that was Dylan's kingdom and Blake didn't like to get his manicured hands dirty, but today had been that kind of day.

"We heard you laughing," Blake said. He'd traded in his suit for a red tee shirt with a black smiling skull on it and *989 Engines* beneath it. Their company logo. "Thought the world might be ending."

"Hilarious," he said. "How's it going in there?"

"We got the planetary gearbox working."

"How's it look?"

Blake's bottle green eyes lit up. "We will be gods and people will bow before us."

"Well, that is the plan. Be there in a second," he said.

"I wanted to thank you for giving my brother a chance. Mom appreciated it."

"I'm sorry I fired him without talking to you first."

"The garage is your world. You did what you had to do."

Blake was a good guy, one of the best. And his mom was Margaret and both of them deserved better than that shit-bag Phil. But whatever; if everyone got what they deserved, Dylan would be dead a few times over.

"How did he leave?"

"Like a dick, spewed some hate at me and Mom before he finally got in his car."

"Where'd he go?"

"Back to whatever rock he lives under, I guess. It's not like he keeps us up-to-date on his address changes."

"I don't know why the hell you bothered."

"Some of us can't just leave our family behind, man."

"Yeah, well, that's too bad for you."

"Mom wanted one last try," Blake said, making it clear he wouldn't have done it on his own. Blake had inherited his father's darker skin, green eyes, and business brain. He got Margaret's blond hair but none of her soft heart. "And it's done now. For good. Come check out the gear set," Blake said and without another word he left, closing the door behind him.

Dylan remained in his chair, staring first at the door and then at his phone. Without thinking about the consequences, because after all, he was a god, Dylan grabbed his phone and sent Layla a text message.

Call me.

She might be embarrassed. But she was innocent, and she had no idea how fucking compelling, how addictive, what they'd just shared could be.

Dylan was a patient man and it might take her a while, but she would learn.

And she would call back.

ANNIE

A FEW DAYS LATER, I WALKED THE FIELD FOR THE LAST TIME before mowing. The tall grass touched my legs just under my shorts and my thighs were wet with dew. It rolled down into my socks. I pushed and shoved the big boulders into the brush along the edges, shoving a long stick in the ground next to the ones that were too big to move so I didn't accidentally hit them when I mowed.

I worked until my body hurt and my muscles were twitching. My hands, despite the gloves, were raw.

I worked until what happened with Dylan on the phone seemed to be something I'd read. Maybe in that dirty book. But not something that happened to me.

Stuff like that didn't happen to Annie McKay.

Walking back to the trailer after locking up, I saw Ben in his garden, taking bricks out of a wheelbarrow and struggling under the weight.

"Here, let me help you," I said, rushing to his side. I didn't even think about what Dylan had said. His dire warnings about this old man's danger. Frankly, I just didn't believe him.

"I got it," he breathed, clearly straining.

"Stubborn man," I muttered and ignored him. I grabbed a bunch of bricks, setting them down beside his pile. I got another load before he could straighten his back.

"I'm not helpless."

"I know."

"You don't need to treat me like I am."

"I'm not. I'm just helping you."

He grunted, which made me smile.

"You don't got enough work?"

"What else am I going to do?" I asked, taking out the last of the bricks.

He sighed. "I hear alcoholism is time consuming."

I was worn down and thin with all my worries and that joke just made me howl.

"It's not that funny," he said with a smile, watching me sideways.

"I know," I said, wiping my eyes.

He started clearing the bricks off the cement pad that I'd placed my stacks on. "Thanks for the pasta sauce," he said.

"You're welcome."

"It was better once I put some of my oregano in it."

I sobered again, shackled by the reminder of my own gutlessness. *Can't ask for what I want. Can't enjoy what I've got. Can't even touch my body without being pulled apart by all the shit I'm trying to leave behind.*

That night . . . after the thing with Dylan, I'd taken *Fifty Shades of Grey* and thrown it in the drawer with the gun and the phone and shut it. I'd been enjoying that book, was excited to read the rest of it, but I denied myself that because I'm a gutless dummy.

Because in the end, I get what I deserve.

I started an Agatha Christie novel. Because who doesn't love Agatha Christie? But the whole time I wanted to be reading the book in my bedside table.

"I'm sure it was," I said, crouching down beside him to clear the cement pad. After my shower I was going to finish that damn book. I was. No one was going to stop me. Not even myself. "What are you working on?"

"A little brick oven," he said, brushing leaves away with his hand. "It's too hot to cook in the trailer during the summer."

He pulled a piece of paper out of his back pocket and I saw again under his white shirt the shadow of that big, black tattoo.

It seemed ominous.

"Where did you live before here?" I asked.

"A bunch of places."

"What did you do?"

"A bunch of things. Why are you asking?" His suspicion was uncomfortably threatening.

Because I'm trying to figure out why I'm supposed to be watching you.

"We're neighbors," I said with a shrug.

"Where are you from?"

"Oklahoma." I surprised myself with the truth. "A farm."

He grunted and took the wheelbarrow back over toward his trailer, where a pickup truck was parked. I followed and helped him move a bag of cement and a bucket from the truck bed into the wheelbarrow.

"You want me to help you with that?" It was hard watching him struggle.

Smith, who'd helped Mom and me on the farm, broke his hand once fixing a tractor. He'd had the whole thing in this weird splint, and then in a sling, but he wouldn't stop working. Trying to do everything with one arm. I followed him around relentlessly until he snapped and demanded to know what I was doing.

"Waiting for you to need me," is what I'd said.

I was doing the same thing with Ben. Waiting for him to need me.

Memories of Smith were best not contemplated. They were best kept behind their locked door.

"I don't need your damn help," Ben said, and wheeled it across the rough ground toward the bricks and cement pad.

I ignored him and followed. Once he made it there I helped him unload it, despite his grumbling, and he took the bucket over to the hose he had coiled up and hanging around a fence post, connected to a spigot in the ground.

His bad mood, with its familiar undertones of begrudging tolerance, made me feel better.

Smith again.

"What brought you to this place?" he asked over the gush of water into the bucket.

"I was running," I said.

"Now what are you doing?"

He turned off the hose and brought the bucket back over to where I stood. When he set it down, water sloshed over my feet. I watched puddles form around my beat-up tennis shoes and didn't answer. Didn't have an answer.

Running had been such a wild departure—a giant crack—and I was still running. I didn't know what happened after running.

"Seeing the sights?" he asked when I didn't answer, oddly paralyzed by his question.

What am I doing, now?

"No?" he asked, with a smile. "Finding yourself? No, I know . . . finding God."

I shook my head. "I think . . . I think I'm just . . . waiting."

"For what?"

"I have no idea."

"That's not waiting, girly. That's hiding. And I got a lock on both."

Those words were a punch in the gut and I could barely breathe as I watched Ben, shaking and in stages, get down on his knees.

Silent, shaking as much as he was, I crouched down beside him.

Shoulder to shoulder, I helped Ben start work on his oven. We mixed the cement with an attachment to his drill and we troweled a thin layer over the cement pad and then slowly, carefully, started to build something. "What are you hiding from?" I asked.

"Done a lot of bad things. To a lot of people. Here's as safe as anywhere."

"What are you waiting for?" I asked after we'd been working for a long time.

"Something that's never gonna come. Not for me." I wanted to ask more, but we were three layers up and it was obvious he was getting tired.

"You want a break?" I asked.

"No."

But a few seconds later he was coughing and then he was bent over coughing, holding a handkerchief from his back pocket over his mouth as he hacked away.

"You all right?" I asked.

"Fine," he said. "But let's call it a day."

"Really?" I looked down at the bucket of cement. It was going to harden and be ruined.

He got to his feet, refusing help from my outstretched hand.

"Yeah, too hot." He walked away, looking bent and frail.

I watched him walk to the trailer and then I bent and kept working a little bit longer, spreading the cement on with a trowel. Placing the bricks, scraping away the curl of excess. Repeat, repeat, repeat.

Until the cement was gone and the first few layers of the brick oven were in place.

Ben's trailer was silent, his hiding spot secure.

LATER, I TOOK ANOTHER COLD SHOWER AND THEN, STILL TOO hot and too out of sorts to eat, I crawled into bed.

I'd made that promise to read the book, but I didn't want the book.

I wanted Dylan.

In the bedside table I practically heard the phone taunting me.

Annie McKay—runs away from her old life only to keep living by its rules. It was sad.

And it made me angry.

I opened the drawer, grabbed the phone, and made a deal with myself.

If he'd called or texted, I would call him back. If he hadn't, I'd forget about this whole situation, finish my book, and if and when I felt like it—masturbate on my own like a normal person.

And honestly, why would he call? *I* wouldn't call me. I would quickly forget the whole thing.

My first ever orgasm to the sound of his voice probably didn't even register in his life.

I turned on the phone, my heart pounding in my clumsy fingertips.

Call me.

That was it. One text message.

And say what, I wondered. *I'm a freak. A total mess. I don't know what I want, other than it's not what I have.*

Other than it's more.

I didn't give myself a chance to be scared. Or nervous. I

called him back. I was utterly and totally compelled by that demand.

"Layla." He answered right away. How had his voice gotten so familiar? I felt like I'd been listening to his voice on a loop for a week.

"Yes."

He sighed and that was it. Just a sigh and then silence. And I didn't know how to fill it. All I knew, really, was to keep my head down and work. I'd done one audacious thing in my life, and that was steal three thousand dollars from my husband and run out in the middle of the night.

And that night—with Dylan. That had been pretty audacious. So two, I guess.

"You all right?" he asked.

"Fine." My voice was shrill. Strange. And I closed my eyes, praying for some kind of map in this situation. For that voiceless instinct to rise up and lead me out of these terrible, dark woods. But the instinct must have been taking a nap, because it was silent. "I'm fine."

Memories of that night landed like sparks from a fire against my skin.

The brush of my thumb across my hip bone.

The chapped skin of my lips.

The way the bottom of my foot felt hot.

The quilt against my nipples.

The way I'd felt . . . for a while there . . . like I could do anything to myself and it would feel good.

Good. What a ridiculous understatement.

For a while there I'd craved everything. Anything.

The things in the half-read book, the things those girls did in those trucks at the truck stop. The things his voice alluded to.

I wanted all of it. And with equal force I wanted to not want any of it.

"I didn't think I'd hear from you again."

"I turned off the phone."

"You embarrassed?"

"That's one way of putting it."

"That's bullshit, you know. You shouldn't feel bad about anything that feels that good."

"I think that's easy for you to say."

"It's easy for you too. Just say it."

Laughter humphed out of me.

"You're twenty-four years old. How come you never touched yourself like that before?"

"It's complicated." Understatement of the century.

"What kind of complicated?"

"The kind I'm not going to talk about it," I snapped, and then winced. But I had no intention of telling him who I really was. What my life was really like.

"I'm sorry," I sighed. "I just . . ."

"Don't want to spill your guts to a stranger? I get it. We all have secrets."

Of course, immediately, I wanted to know his.

"Thank you," I whispered. "For the other night. Really. Thank you. That was—"

"Good for me too. Until the end when you hung up."

"Sorry."

"It was pretty intense."

"It's not . . . I'm not . . . virgin kink. Or whatever."

I'm just me.

"No shit," he said. "You might be all the kinks."

There was a delicious amount of respect in his words. And that respect delighted me.

"I appreciate you texting me."

"I want you to call me again," he said.

"To tell you about Ben?"

"Right now I don't give a shit about Ben. I want you to call me so I can listen to you come again."

My breath clogged in my throat. And those random sparks of desire, they coalesced into something big. Bigger even than my body.

"All right."

"But Layla?"

"Yeah?"

"We are going to do this my way."

"What does that mean?" Why did that thrill me somehow? Currents sizzled up my legs.

"It means there's no embarrassment over what we do. None. The second you think about embarrassment or shame, forget it. Because it's pointless."

"But—"

"Tell me you understand that."

"I don't like bossy men," I said, avoiding the question because really he was asking the impossible. I would *try* not to be embarrassed. I would work really hard at that, but he couldn't make the feeling go away just by demanding it.

"No?"

"No," I answered because I did like this. Because I was contrary and full of opposing forces. And he seemed impervious to these swipes I took at him. Seemed in fact to like it.

He chuckled, proving that he appreciated my claws, and it was just too much. I curled over onto my side, tucking my knees up, holding the thrill between my legs.

"You liked me the other night. You called me when you wanted to come, Layla. I think you like me fine."

"I don't want to be . . . controlled."

"You can hang up whenever you want. Say the word and this is over. But if you want to keep going, it's my rules."

I clutched the phone in my hand.

"Yes or no, Layla?"

"Yes."

"Good girl. Now, you won't call me again until you eat dessert for breakfast and go skinny-dipping."

"Are you joking?" Skinny-dipping and dessert for breakfast? What the hell was this?

"Do those things," he said. "And then call me. And Layla?"

"What?" I sounded extra angry with him and I was rewarded with that half-groan of his that reverberated down low into my belly, sending all this desire and itchy, angry lust into hyperdrive.

"Hurry."

And then he hung up.

I PUT THE PHONE BACK IN THE DRAWER AND LIKE I WAS TESTING the waters, waiting for some kind of protest, or someone to tell me to stop, I eased my hand under my tank top and spread out my fingers over my belly, making the heat coil under my skin.

I wanted to wrench everything out of me that was left over from my old life. The voices, the fear, the guilt and shame—I wanted it all gone. Like the garbage I was clearing out of the campground.

Feeling defiant—rebellious, more like Layla than I had the other night—I jumped off the bed and made sure my door was locked and all my curtains and blinds were shut. In the bedroom I kept the windows open for air.

I took off my shirt and then my shorts, but I left on my underwear. The last of my clean ones. They were a little too small. A pair—blue, with little white flowers on them—that I'd had forever, since I was sixteen, maybe? The elastic bit into the skin of my butt and the front dipped real low, to the point that some of the hair between my legs peeked out. Slipping my hand down low, I felt the wide patch of moisture from my body, and as I traced its edges, it got wider. Wetter.

I slipped one finger past the sharp elastic, pulling the other side harder against my skin, which made me gasp and pull it tighter, until the elastic brushed up against my clit.

"Oh my God," I breathed and then, experimenting, I pulled both sides of my underwear down between my lips and I nearly shot off the bed. Carefully, I used the pressure, slow and driving, sharp and fast, to find out what I liked better.

And the truth was—I liked it all. Even the touches that didn't add to the stone-rolling-downhill of orgasm, I liked. The side trip of my fingers against the skin of my leg. The act of pushing my hair—sweaty and damp—off my face. The lift of one arm up and over my head.

It was as if my body—which had seemed my entire life to be stupid and heavy, an entity to be pushed and smacked, a blind and dumb creature made only for work, its only skill a certain kind of stillness, a trick of getting smaller so as not to be seen— had been transformed.

No, not transformed. Not really.

It was as if I'd found buried beneath the skin a secret wisdom. A dark knowledge.

Like it had just been waiting for me to find it.

I came, minutes later on my stomach, my pillow between my teeth. Part of my underwear—a sly little instrument of pleasure— in my fist, the rest of it buried between my legs.

Huffing for breath, I pulled the blue cotton with the white flowers off my body. It was wet. Totally wet. My hand, too.

I laughed, delighted and embarrassed. Horrified and pleased. Exhausted and exhilarated.

As I rolled sideways on the bed, stray sparks shot up from my pussy, from where I'd crossed my legs, giving my clit a sort of thick pressure.

Oh God. Again?

I put my head down, my fingers eased between my legs.

Again.

10

AN HOUR LATER I HAD GATHERED UP ALL OF MY DIRTY CLOTHES, my generic laundry soap, and another one of my books—*Pride and Prejudice*. The cover was new and featured a Hollywood actress. The one that was all chin and cheekbones.

My dog-eared and beloved copy from high school English class had been burned in the burn pile.

The laundry was on the other side of the rhododendron with the families, where the trailers were packed in a little tighter. But most of the trailers were in really good shape and a few families had worked hard to make them look homey with scrappy flower gardens, and a few of the little wooden decks were hung with twinkle lights.

Or maybe those were just Christmas decorations that never came down.

The trailer right next to the laundry was one of the few double-wides. And there were balloons tied to the door. Birthday streamers across the back of the trailer.

A line of kids screamed around the corner of the trailer, five in all; a few of them I recognized from that day at the grocery store. Danny was there. The others were strangers. But they all had face paint on. There were two pirates. A tiger and a Spider-Man.

I sidestepped the kids and flattened myself against the aluminum siding of the laundry.

"Boys!" The mom, the woman from the grocery store, came out of the trailer, carrying a little tray of paint and a paintbrush in her hand. Two little girls clung to the long, colorful dress she wore. One daughter had a rainbow across her forehead. The other, in diapers, had half a sun. "Boys, take it over to the playground. We're going to have cake in a half hour!"

The boys switched direction on a dime and raced over to the swing set and slide that were set up across the dirt road.

The mom turned to go back inside and I wished I could somehow vanish before she saw me, but no such luck.

"Hey," she said, looking as awkward as I felt. "You do live here."

"Over there," I answered, jerking my thumb over toward the rhododendron. "It's your son's birthday?"

The woman reached down a hand and cupped it over Rainbow-face's blond hair. "Yes. Danny. He's five."

"That's great."

"It's loud is what it is," she laughed. "I'm Tiffany, by the way."

"Annie." The second I said my real name, I wished I could suck it back.

"Mommy!" cried the girl with half a sun. "Finish me."

"I'd better go," Tiffany said.

"Have fun," I said.

"Thank you."

I ducked into the laundry as fast as I could. For some reason my heart was pounding hard. That woman stressed me out.

All my clothes together made only one load. Tee shirts, bras. Cutoff shorts. My nightgown. A few of the towels. Underwear.

I shoved the blue ones with the white flowers in first, as if someone might come in and see them. Smell them, even, and guess my secret. Know what I was doing.

I was smiling as I dumped in the half-cup of soap and a few of my precious quarters.

In the far corner of the small room there was a lawn chair with frayed plastic ribbing and I grabbed it, took it outside to the other side of the building, away from the birthday party and Tiffany with the bruises and dark eyes who somehow managed to still give her son a birthday party with pirate face paint.

A gesture so full of love and hope it made my heart hurt.

I settled the chair down in a small copse of dandelions next to a dark trailer that seemed empty. The sun was hot today, but there was a rare breeze blowing, keeping things moving, and in the shade of the trailer it was actually quite nice.

It had been years since I'd been able to sit down in the middle of the day to read. It felt . . . decadent. Sighing with pleasure, I opened up my book and slipped seamlessly into Mr. Darcy and Elizabeth Bennet's world.

It took a while for me to notice the girl standing nearby, but when I finally did, I jumped, startled. The little girl had three suns, one on each cheek and one on her forehead, with a flower on the bridge of her nose.

"Hi," I said with a smile.

"Cake?"

The girl held out a plate with a piece of yellow cake with chocolate frosting and roughly a pound of sprinkles on it.

"For me?" I asked. The girl nodded and walked over to me, nearly tripping on the uneven ground, but I caught her and the cake in the nick of time.

"Thank you so much!" I said.

"You welcome," the girl said, with very nice manners and a sparkly grin revealing a mouth full of little teeth. She had a pink barrette barely hanging onto her curly light brown hair.

She skipped off as quickly as she came. And I looked down at the cake. The sprinkles, the half a Y written in blue frosting.

Birthday cake.

God, how long had it been . . .

Even though I didn't want to, because the memories were bound to disappoint, I tried to remember the last time I'd had one. For myself. Or for Mom. Hoyt. And the only one I could remember was when I was really young. Walking with my mom out to the cabin behind the barn where Smith lived. He'd opened the door to his cabin, wearing his jeans and a white undershirt and nothing else, and Mom had looked away, her eyes on the far fields.

I stared at his tattoos. He'd had lots. Army stuff from the Gulf War.

"Morning," he'd said with that rough, gravelly smoker's growl he had, but Mom had stayed silent. Eyes averted. Cheeks red in the dawn.

"We made you a cake!" I had said, jumping a little because there'd never been a cake-making experience in my life.

"Take it," Mom had said, still not looking at him. She shoved the plate at Smith, who caught it just before it went all over his white shirt. "Come on, Annie, we got work."

And there'd never been a cake-making experience again.

My long sigh came out in shuddery stages, the memory an uncomfortable one. All those adult motivations and feelings still shrouded in shadow and mystery. Mom had been . . . unfathomable, at best.

I stood, my butt numb, and went to push my wet things into the dryer.

In the distance there was the rumble of a car engine that needed a serious tune-up. Which was weird, because almost no one got off the highway on this road, or used it to get to the highway. It was nothing but swamp and forests past the campground.

The engine roar got louder and then nearly deafening as it turned into the drive of the RV park.

Heart in my throat, I glanced out the door of the laundry only to see an old blue Dodge muscle car come to a stop right next to Tiffany's trailer. Blue and red balloons collided and bounced off the side of the trailer.

When the man behind the wheel turned off the motor, the silence was deafening. And my old sixth sense about danger crackled.

This wasn't good.

"Hey, Phil," Tiffany said as she came out of the trailer. No little girls clinging to her. No face paint. Just her and enough tension to make the air too thick to breathe.

There was not anything about Tiffany that I didn't recognize from my worst memories. That false smile spreading only so far over a fear she could not hide. The rounded curve of her shoulders as if she was already figuring out how to protect herself from his fists. The preemptive kiss, dry and full of self-loathing, placed on the rough plane of the man's cheek once he got out of the rusty blue car.

"I didn't think you were going to be home until next week," Tiffany said to a small man wearing a tee shirt and jeans a few sizes too big. He had mean eyes and big hands. A terrible combination.

The hair rose on my neck.

My throat closed with fear.

Quickly as I could, I ducked back inside the concrete walls of the laundry room, but through the open door I could still hear Tiffany and Phil talking.

"No, I fucking quit that bullshit job," he said.

"Wait. What?" Tiffany asked, her voice suddenly shrill.

Careful. Oh God, be careful.

I moved my wet things from the washer one at a time into

the dryer, wishing truly that I were anywhere but that laundry room.

"What happened?" Tiffany asked, obviously strained.

"It was bullshit. The whole thing. Supposed to be such a hotshot, but that dude was just an asshole like the rest of them."

"Phil, we need that money—"

"Jesus Christ, Tiffany, I just got here and already you're ragging on me?"

"I'm not . . . I'm not, I'm just saying, we're already behind on everything—"

"Maybe if you wasn't spending money on shit like this?"

"Don't! Phil!" Tiffany cried, and I jumped at the sound of a balloon popping.

I wiped my hands under my eyes because I was crying. Terrible stress tears.

Desperate, I looked for a back door or something, some way to get out so I wouldn't have to walk by them. Wouldn't have to see them.

"It's Danny's birthday," Tiffany breathed.

"Where is the little shit?"

"Please," Tiffany begged. "Please don't ruin this—"

"Ruin it? The fuck you talking about, Tiff? I'm paying for this shit. Your mom sure ain't giving you enough to pay for jack."

"You're right. Phil. I'm sorry. I'm so sorry. But we're having a nice party. Look, there's cake, honey. Why don't you have some cake?"

This conversation was engraved on my heart, beaten into my brain. I knew exactly how this was going to go.

Tiffany would keep apologizing. Over and over again, swallowing all her anger so that this man wouldn't raise a fist to her. To her children. So he wouldn't demolish the small bubble of normalcy she'd so painstakingly blown for her children with all the air and hope she had in her.

But in the end it wouldn't work.

It never worked.

Because guys like Phil—like Hoyt—they walked into the room knowing what was going to happen. Whether they would smack a person around or not. They had all the power. Her apologies were for naught. Her pain and fear—irrelevant. All that mattered was what that man wanted to do to her and he'd made that decision way back in his lizard brain—miles ago. Maybe years ago.

I have to leave.

It didn't matter that I couldn't sneak out, that I had to walk right past them and their awful domestic drama, the miserable unhappy end of which I knew too fucking well. Gathering up my book and laundry soap I ducked out the door, my head down, hoping not to garner any attention. This was the last situation I wanted to get pulled into or bear witness to.

Holding my breath, I got past the rhododendron bush and ran smack into someone.

"Careful," Joan said, picking up the book I had dropped. Joan wore a pair of short cutoffs and a tee shirt with the neck and sleeves ripped out, the ties of a bright pink bikini visible underneath. She had her eyes over my shoulder, trained on Phil and the blooming catastrophe.

"You shouldn't go over there," I said.

"I shouldn't?"

"No. It's . . . they're fighting."

"And you think we should all just stand around with our thumbs in our asses while he beats her up?"

That was what was going to happen. That was exactly what was going to happen and I was walking away. Head down. Eyes averted. Thumb in ass. "No . . . but—"

"Get out of my way, kid," she said, clearly through with me. Joan brushed past me, stomping past the rhododendron, making the leaves quake as she went by.

"Hey, a birthday!" Joan cried, out of sight. "Sorry I'm late, Tiffany. Hey, Phil—"

"Get the hell out of here!" Phil yelled. "You fucking bitch."

"Honestly, Phil, you should dress up like a clown for birthday parties. You'd be great," Joan said. "Is there assigned seating or can I sit anywhere?"

"You're not wanted here!" Phil said, low and mean, and I could just imagine him saying that through his teeth, right in her face.

"Joan," Tiffany said. "I'm fine. It's fine."

"Bullshit it's fine," Joan said.

"You know something?" Phil yelled. "Fuck this shit. I don't need this. Later, cunts."

A car door slammed and the Dodge revved back up and drove away.

"Now look what you've done!" Tiffany snapped in the silence after the car's deafening departure. I could see, through the leaves, Tiffany yelling at Joan, who stood up slowly from her seat, looking older. Looking pained.

"Saved you from another black eye, so . . . you're welcome!"

"We have no money! Oh my God! What am I going to do?" Tiffany cried as she collapsed onto one of the seats at the picnic table.

"I can float you—"

"I don't want your fucking money!" Tiffany yelled and I knew what she was doing, how Tiffany had all this anger and rage toward herself and her husband and her life and it was only because Joan was standing there that she got it smeared all over her.

"Fine," Joan said without any heat. "If you need help—"

"You've done enough," Tiffany said, low and defeated.

Joan came back around the bush before I could get my legs to move. I stood behind that bush like a gaping coward, and when Joan saw me she didn't even spare me a sneer, she just walked on by, head up, shoulders back, armored in her righteous bravery.

"Come on, kids!" Tiffany yelled, her voice just a little broken. A little worn. The fake amount of cheer she had to put into it nearly hiding the trauma. Nearly. She'd clearly had lots of practice. "Let's open presents!"

The kids came back from the playground, more subdued. Their eyes wary. Their smiles gone.

"Did he leave?" Danny asked.

Tiffany nodded.

"Good," Danny said, his chin up, and Tiffany sagged against the picnic table.

Enough, I thought, feeling sick and wrung out and worse, so desperately glad I'd never had kids with Hoyt that the guilty relief made me nauseous.

I went back to my trailer and hours later, when it was dark and silent, I went back to get my dry clothes.

And there on the counter, the sprinkles glittering silver and blue in the moonlight, was the piece of birthday cake the little girl had brought me. I picked it up to take it back to Tiffany—I didn't want it, and there were three kids in that trailer who'd probably love another piece of cake.

Outside the door, Tiffany's trailer was quiet. The balloons drifted slightly on the breeze, dark bruises against the lighter sky.

"Take it." Tiffany's voice made me jump. I saw one of the shadows by the rhododendron shift and detach and Tiffany walk over toward the door of the laundry room. She had a garbage bag and was dumping a handful of paper plates into it.

"Is everything . . . okay?" I asked, lamely.

"Define *okay.*"

I didn't know how. What did okay look like to her? To any of us?

"He'll come back," Tiffany said. "He always does."

"Would it be better if he didn't?"

Once Smith had taken me out to check a trap he'd set for a coyote that had been harassing the animals, eating chickens and killing the barn cats. And we'd found the coyote, caught in it, crying, its strength nearly gone. Tiffany's laughter sounded like that coyote crying.

"I have three kids under the age of six," Tiffany said. "I can't do it without his money."

I thought of the three thousand dollars I'd taken from Hoyt's safe and knew that was the truth sometimes. Sometimes, a woman's freedom all came down to money.

"Take the cake," Tiffany said. "We've got lots. My kids will be eating it for breakfast."

Dessert for breakfast.

"Thank you."

Tiffany nodded and went back to cleaning up what was left of the party in the dark.

I took the cake and my dry clothes and headed back to my trailer.

Birthday cake for breakfast.

It felt all wrong, and not in a good way.

11

THE NEXT MORNING DAWNED HAZY AND CLOSE. AND THE HEAT made my head ache right above my eyes.

Sweltering, I pulled open my little fridge, steam rolling out of its depths as the cool air hit the hot. On the top shelf, next to my milk and butter and what was left of the pasta sauce, was the yellow cake with chocolate frosting and sprinkles.

For a long moment, the cold air brushing across the exposed skin of my thighs and arms and neck, I stared at the cake.

She said you could have it.

But the cake felt like a means to an end for me, like I was building a palace on top of bones.

"Stop it," I muttered and grabbed the cake, shutting the fridge door.

I took the first bite and it was a bit stale, the cake nearly hard, the frosting thick to swallow.

That's right. I should not enjoy this.

I took a sip of coffee and then another bite and my mouth must have been warm enough, because the thick frosting melted slightly against my tongue.

Oh. That wasn't bad.

But the thought made me feel guilty and awful.

Just eat it.

The second bite was at the center of the cake, where it was moist and untouched by the cold air of the fridge.

The next bite was practically a mouthful of sprinkles.

When the cake was demolished, only crumbs and thick waves of chocolate frosting against the paper plate, I stared down at a blue sprinkle and green colored sugar and felt like vomiting.

And I didn't know if it was from the sugar or from last night.

Buzzing and jittery, I dropped a few ice cubes in my coffee and headed out to the field.

I thought about Phil, and I thought about Hoyt.

And then I thought about Dylan.

I'd never felt so safe with a man. And I didn't know if that was because we were on the phone and not in person, or if it was just because of who Dylan was.

Or maybe it was because of who I was becoming—I didn't know. And it didn't really matter.

I was safe with Dylan and I would do all the things he asked because of it. The realization warmed me from the inside.

For the first two hours I mowed the northernmost part of the field, which was largely in the shade, giving the big rocks I'd marked a wide berth. But by eleven a.m. I was soaked with sweat, and on the far side of the field, that oak tree with its rope swing and the swimming hole were too powerful to resist.

I rode the mower to the side of the watering hole farthest away from the little bridge and the rest of the trailer park.

The weeds and cattails were dense, their tips waving far above my head, and I had to push them aside in order to get to the edge of the pool. Which was surprisingly wide and big. The water was clear, with no scum or algae. It drained off in a stream to my left.

Must be spring-fed, I thought.

The oak tree was on the other side, and on this side, the swimming hole had a muddy little beach and a few big rocks close to the shore.

For a skinny-dipping location, I supposed it didn't get better than this.

"I'm going to do this," I muttered, bouncing on my toes. And then, before I could stop myself, I peeled off my sweaty, awful clothes. Leaving on my underwear, because I was still Annie McKay after all.

And then with a squeal and a smothered yell, I ran into the pond until it got to my thighs and then I dove underwater, touching the grainy bottom with my chest and my hands before rising above the surface again.

"Oh my God!" I cried, panting because the cold water took my breath away. But oh, how good it felt! If dessert for breakfast had mixed results, skinny-dipping was utterly amazing. All checks marked yes.

I kicked up off the sandy rocky bottom and floated on the surface of the water, my breasts bobbing just slightly out of the water, where the sun felt hot on the white skin that had never, ever seen the light of day before.

The water felt lush, like not just a liquid, like something magical, even. It lifted me and wrapped around me like ribbons. Between my legs, across my chest, over my waist. Under my neck. I scissor-kicked in the water and laughed out loud as water slid up and into my body, slipping through my pubic hair.

My short hair was plastered onto my forehead and I pushed it off into the water, still lying on my back. For the first time since I'd cut it off, I wished for my hair back. Because how awesome would that feel to have my waist-length hair floating in the water around my naked shoulders, over my breasts?

I closed my eyes, imagining the feeling.

My face grew hot in the bright sunlight, so I flipped over on my belly and dove down to the bottom of the pond, well aware that my butt and my see-through underwear had just breached the water for anyone to see.

But no one was there to see it.

So I did it again. And again.

When I'd had enough I did long, slow breaststrokes back to the shore where my clothes lay in a heap.

But *damn it*. No towel.

Rookie, skinny-dipping mistake.

I stood on shore and gave myself a big, long shake, trying to get all the water off that I could before putting on my gross clothes.

"Well, well, look who's naked," a sly voice said, and I jumped sideways, surprised to see Joan sitting up kitty-corner from me in a little cleared area in the weeds I hadn't noticed earlier.

"Oh my God, what . . . what are you doing?" I cried, throwing my arms into my shirt and slipping it over my head. I jerked my shorts up my legs and fumbled at the button.

"Calm down, honey, they're just boobs—I'll hardly faint." Joan pulled an earbud from her ear and stood up. She wore that pink string bikini like it had been painted on. Honestly, Joan's body had to be one of the most perfect things I had ever seen.

"What are you doing?" I asked again, trying not to stare at the sleek, round muscles in Joan's legs or the indentations around her belly button. She looked strong and totally womanly.

What is wrong with me? Why am I staring?

"Working on my tan lines," she answered, and while I watched, Joan pulled one of the strings holding her top on and the piece collapsed off her body. "I work down at The Velvet Touch and the better my tan lines, the better my tips. Guys like it when they think they're seeing something forbidden. Even when they're paying to see all of it. Go figure."

The little lines bisecting her back and the small triangles around her breasts were white, like milk white, made all the whiter by the dark skin surrounding them.

Joan stepped into the water and when it was deep enough, dove under.

I shoved my feet into my socks and tried to put on my boots before Joan got back to the surface. I could guess what The Velvet Touch was; I could guess Joan was a stripper.

"Running away again?" Joan asked, and I whirled to face her.

"No."

She smirked. "You sure? Because I think that's what you do."

Oh, fuck you, Joan, like you know a thing about me.

Just to prove the woman wrong, I sat down on one of the big boulders on the beach and crossed my legs.

Two could play this rude game.

"Why'd you get in between Phil and Tiffany?" I asked.

Joan leaned back, her white breasts bobbing up, and I watched them for a moment. And then I looked away, cheeks on fire.

Heatstroke. I have heatstroke. Only reason I'm here. Staring at her like a sixteen-year-old boy.

It was the truck-stop parking lot all over again and everything about Joan was carnal and I couldn't look away.

"Someone should, don't you think?" Joan asked. "He's a son of a bitch and she thinks she needs him."

"She does."

"No one needs an asshole like that."

"The kids—"

Joan stood up, her dirty-blond hair a slick down her back.

"Would be a whole lot better off if they didn't watch their mom get beat up."

"That's true, but without money, what's Tiffany supposed to do?"

"Stop looking for excuses to stay, I guess," Joan said. "You forgot your scarf."

I clapped a hand to my throat. The bruises were fading. Mostly blue and green smudges now, but someone who looked hard could tell they were fingerprints.

"Look, kid," Joan said, walking out of the water like Venus on the waves. "Forget the damn scarf—it's like a fat kid wearing a tee shirt to the swimming pool. All it does is make the kid look fatter."

I dug into the heart of the bruise just under my chin until it throbbed.

"All it does is make you look more beat up."

I swallowed hard.

"That's what you are, right? Beat up?"

No. *That's not what I am. That's not all I am. I have a hundred more things about myself that I'm figuring out. I like skinny-dipping. I don't like cake for breakfast. I like grinding my pussy against my hand until I come.*

But what I said was, "I guess so."

"And you ran?"

"I'm running."

"Good for you."

Joan walked back over to the weeds she'd stomped down to make herself a little cove along the shore.

"But I had money. Not a lot, but some. Tiffany has none."

"I've offered Tiffany plenty. No strings. She knows that. She wanted to go she could go."

"You make it seem like it should be easy for her. Like it's really black and white." I was getting angry on Tiffany's behalf. On my own behalf, too, maybe. Because I'd stayed for years with no reason other than fear. Fear and habit.

With no hope that things would get better. No love I could cling to and pretend about.

Nothing but fear that life without Hoyt would be worse than life with him.

"It's pretty black and white. Guy hits you, you leave." She took a drag from a cigarette. "Better yet, avoid them altogether. You want a joint?" Joan asked, holding it up toward me.

I shook my head and she shrugged, sitting down on the thick blanket she had spread out. She had an iPod and a few magazines and . . . a gun beside her.

"Don't worry," Joan said, taking a drag of the weed. She slipped the gun under one of the magazines. "I just keep an eye out for Phil and some of the other shitheads who live here."

"Are there a lot of shitheads?"

Joan laughed, a plume of smoke sliding out of her mouth. "Enough."

"You don't seem so bad," I said, sort of joking, and Joan laughed again.

"That's because you don't know me. And there are plenty more around here worse than me."

I had no intention of finding out. I was minding my own business. Well, I guess my business and Ben's business.

"What's the story with Ben?" I asked, and Joan jerked back. "Why?"

"He seems nice."

Joan laughed. "The really crazy ones always do. The guy's like Phil—they're thugs. Just thugs. One-dimensional—what you see is what you get."

"You're saying behind Ben's garden he's a sociopath?"

"Where are you from, kid, that you don't understand that guy's tattoos?"

"A farm in Oklahoma."

Again with the truth. A few more weeks of blabbing like this and I wouldn't be hiding at all.

Joan smiled. "That explains it. Trust me. Just give him a wide berth."

"What about his tattoos?"

"That big black square on his back, that's a biker gang tattoo that's been blacked over. He got booted. And you gotta do some bad shit to get booted."

"What did he do?"

"I don't know, and I'm not eager to sit down and have a chat with the guy. You shouldn't be either."

I looked away from Joan, out at the water sparkling in the sunlight, as if diamonds had been scattered over its surface.

"Why are you being nice to me?" I asked.

"This is nice?"

"Nicer."

"Because I'm high. Because I just saw your tits. Because . . . those goddamn bruises around your neck."

Again I reached up and felt them like they were still pounding against my skin.

"You're a stripper?" I asked and she stared at me blankly, and I wondered if I'd offended her. Or if she didn't want people to know. "You mentioned The Velvet Touch. I don't want to make assumptions . . ."

"Yes, Sherlock Holmes, I'm a stripper."

I ran out of courage for what I had intended to ask.

"You got something else you want to ask, you should ask," Joan said.

"That guy . . . in your trailer the first time I met you." What the hell was I doing? My mom would kill me for asking these questions. For prying. She used to yank on the end of my ponytail when I started asking too many questions. "Never mind, this isn't my business."

"Spit it out."

"Are . . . I mean . . . do you?"

"Fuck men for money?"

I blushed so hard my eyes hurt.

"No. I fuck them for pleasure. But some of the girls do at the club. There's one of those old-school comfort rooms in the back."

"Oh." I had no clue what an old-school comfort room was. No clue. And I was suddenly on fire to know. But I wasn't about to ask her. I didn't have quite enough courage to reveal my total ignorance.

We sat in silence for a minute.

"How long have you lived here?"

"Too long," Joan said.

"It seems nice."

Joan's silent laugh made her breasts shimmy. "Depends on context, I guess."

"Oh," I said, "you're from someplace wonderful?"

"No." Joan shook her head and then slid her sunglasses down over her eyes. "I'm not." She stretched out on her back and didn't say another word.

After a minute I got back on my mower and rode through the weeds, avoiding the sticks marking unseen hazards.

12

AFTER LOCKING UP THE MOWER AND THE REST OF THE TOOLS, I followed the scent of something delicious being cooked over to Ben's garden.

Part of me insisted that I heed both Dylan and Joan's warnings. But a larger part of me was tired of taking other people's warnings as rules. I was done having my mind made up for me by someone else.

Joan had an unforgiving view of the world if she could be angry at Tiffany for being a victim. I wasn't about to take her word about Ben. And Dylan . . . I didn't know enough about him to know his worldview, other than that he was both kind and controlling. I'd never known the two qualities to live in sync like that.

Perhaps Joan and Dylan weren't looking past the tattoos. Perhaps they were caught up in some black-and-white idea that I wasn't interested in. Maybe Ben had never given them tomatoes.

I found the old man sitting in front of a fire inside the half-built shell of his brick oven.

"You've made a lot of progress," I said. Through the unfinished top of the oven I could see a cast-iron skillet over a crack-ling fire.

"Just about done, but I got impatient," he said. "Thanks for what you finished the other day."

"No problem. I didn't want that cement to go to waste. What are you making?"

"Here," he said, pulling out the pan. Inside, bubbling in oil, were little yellow plants. "Zucchini flowers." He set the pan down in the grass and pulled off the mitts he'd used to protect his hands.

"My ex used to make 'em," he said. "She was part Mexican. Fucking amazing cook."

With a metal fork he grabbed one of the flowers and put it down on a piece of napkin he had with him, and the white paper immediately went clear with grease.

"Want to try it?"

I nodded and took the napkin, still so hot I shifted the little flower from hand to hand so my fingers didn't burn.

He lifted the other flower out and put it down on his knee.

"Doesn't that hurt?" I asked.

"Nah." He held out his palms and I could see the thick cal-luses on all his fingers. Three fingers on his left hand reminded me of Smith's hand. They looked like they'd been broken and not set properly.

I blew on the flower and then finally bit into it. It was stuffed with a little bit of cheese, and as I pulled the flower away a long string of it came down and scorched my chin. My tongue was singed.

"Ouch. Ow. Wow."

"Tenderfoot," he muttered and tossed his flower into his mouth. He chewed contemplatively. "Not quite."

I finished mine. It was cheesy and fried, which made it pretty damn great. "That was delicious."

"My ex's was better," he muttered.

From a bowl beside his chair he pulled out jalapeño peppers he'd sliced in half, added them to the still-bubbling oil, and put the whole thing back in the fireplace.

"Are you going to just eat those?"

"Fried peppers? No, I'm going to make cornbread. My wife used to put peppers in hers."

"You're a really good cook," I said. He was thinking about his wife and he seemed sad, staring into that half-finished oven. I wished I knew some way to comfort him. Leach away some of this loss he was so clearly feeling.

He shook his head. "Well, I can't drink, I can't smoke. Don't ride no more. Friends are in jail or dead. This is what I got left."

"You don't have any family?"

He pursed his lips, staring into the fire as if trying to remember, and then he shook his head. "Nah. My old lady left years ago. Went west to her sister's."

"I'm so sorry," I said, responding more to the grief he couldn't quite hide under those words.

He shrugged. "It's done business, I suppose."

"You don't have any kids?" I asked. I rubbed at some dirt on my elbow, carefully not watching him. I wanted someone—Dylan or Ben—to tell me that they were related, that Ben was Dylan's father. Otherwise, I didn't know why Dylan wanted Ben watched.

"Why are you being so nosey?" he asked.

"I can't drink, can't smoke. This is all I've got left," I joked. He smiled into the fire.

"No. No family." He reached into the kiln with his fork to poke at the peppers.

That killed my theory that Dylan was his son. I'd been so sure.

"You took off your scarf."

I resisted the impulse to hide the bruises with my hands. "I don't think I was fooling anyone."

"No," he agreed. "Your daddy do that? The bruises."

"Husband."

"No shit. I thought you're too young for that kind of stupidity."

"That kind of stupidity is made for the young."

It felt oddly crowded around this fire. Like we had all our ghosts with us.

"He didn't start off mean," I felt compelled to explain it to him. Maybe to myself. To Joan. I'd never put any of it into words, never looked at how Hoyt had managed to isolate and hurt me so effectively. How I'd let him.

"They never do," he said, staring into the fire.

"I suppose you're right. My . . . mom died, and I was really young and I suddenly found myself alone and in charge of a farm. Mom never taught me about payroll or taxes, or how much credit we had at the grain elevator or who we owed money to. I was in so far over my head, I had no idea what to do. And Hoyt started to help me. Told me he'd take care of things at the grain elevator. Helped me pay bills and talk to people at the bank. He'd been working there a few years already, and he just kind of came up alongside of me so I didn't have to be so alone. And he seemed . . . solid, you know? And interested. In me. Like . . . that." I'd been able to feel him watching me. His eyes under that hat made me blush. Made me . . . aware. That and a few polite howdys and I'd . . . *God,* I'd been so easy.

"Interested in your land, more likely."

And yes, wasn't that just a stunning assessment of my appeal?

"Yes, in the end, I guess, that was true. But I believed he was interested in me. And I was lonely."

"You didn't have no one else telling you he was suspicious?"

"One man," I said. "Smith. Our . . . foreman, I guess." Smith and his relationship to Mom and to me and the land kind of defied description. "He warned me that Hoyt was bad news."

"Smart man."

"You remind me of him. Of Smith."

Ben looked up, startled at that. "Well, that's a mistake. I'm not smart, or I wouldn't be put out to pasture here."

"Still," I said, smiling at Ben. "You two are a lot alike."

"I guess I'm supposed to take that as a compliment?"

"Yep." Smith had been the best man I knew, despite the rumors about him. Despite . . . what I'd done to him.

"Fine." Oh, Ben was so crusty, it made me laugh.

The jalapeños popped in the grease.

"You stay away from that fuckwit Phil," he said. "In the double-wide by the laundry. He's bad business. He'd hurt you and not think twice about it."

"He was here last night, nearly ruined his son's birthday party, but Joan stepped in," I said. "Our neighbor—"

"Oh, I know Joan. And that crazy bitch *would* do something so stupid."

I bristled at the name and Ben's tone. "I thought it was pretty courageous."

Ben's eyes lifted to the bruises around my neck and then quickly away.

"Sometimes I miss Maria more than I can stand," he said. "I wake up at night so lonely it's like someone chopped off my leg. And then I remember how shitty we were together. How we hurt each other over and over. How much I fucked up, and I think it's probably better this way. Better to be alone."

I'd had that same thought just the other day, but somehow it was lonelier when he said it.

He wasn't a dangerous sociopath. He was a lonely old man trying to re-create something from happier days.

"Thanks for the zucchini flower," I said. "And for listening, I guess."

"You're welcome. I'll save you some cornbread."

After my shower I lay down on my bed, the cell phone in my hand. But somehow I couldn't quite turn it on.

I'd had dessert for breakfast. I'd gone skinny-dipping.

I'd expected anticipation and lust and the throb between my legs and the tightness of my skin.

But somehow the world seemed like it was just too heavy a place right now. All the hard edges were out tonight and I felt each one of them.

I turned the phone on and a text message appeared from earlier in the day.

> Dylan: I'm really hoping you found yourself some pie for breakfast . . .

I smiled, and despite the melancholy, something dark ignited low in my body.

> Annie: I did. Well, cake. And I went skinny-dipping this afternoon.

I didn't expect him to write back right away, but within a minute his answer appeared on the screen.

> Dylan: You gonna call me?
>
> Annie: It was kind of a weird day . . . and night.
>
> Dylan: Call me.

There really wasn't any question. We were doing this his way. And my way left me alone in my bed and sad. His way I got to call him and maybe . . . maybe come against my hand.

I called him.

"Layla?" Oh, his voice. His voice just killed me. Part drawl, part growl.

"Hi."

"You all right?"

I took a deep breath, trying to keep the strange comfort of his worry at arm's length. "I'm fine."

"What happened?"

"It's a long story . . ."

"You got something else to do?" he asked.

"No."

"Me neither. Might as well tell me."

I flung an arm out across the bed. Night was falling outside the trailer. I could hear the sounds of the kids on the other side of the rhododendron playing at the swing set. Someone somewhere was grilling hamburgers.

"This . . . is just kind of a sad place, is all. Sad people."

"And you're feeling sad?"

"Not very sexy, is it?" I said with a little laugh. "How about I call you—"

"How about you tell me what happened?"

Something sharp and thorny turned in my chest. "A guy showed up and almost beat up his wife. Nearly ruined his kid's birthday party. I ran away but this other woman just . . . charged right in. Made the guy leave."

"Christ, that was risky."

"I know. But it was really brave, you know? And I ate the kid's birthday cake for breakfast and that's my brave and I just felt . . . stupid. And awful."

"Well, that's not really fair, is it?"

"Fair has nothing to do with anything. Ever." I sounded bitter, far more bitter than I thought I felt. But it was there all along, this bitter and angry sea, dark and awful and full of monsters, just waiting for me to dive in and get eaten.

Dylan laughed. "This is true. My whole life . . . I just wanted to be like my brother. My whole life. He was the toughest. The bravest. The most badass guy around. And I just followed that guy around trying to do the shit that he did."

"What happened?"

"I learned I'm not that badass. And that some people just don't give a fuck what happens to them. And I don't know if that's brave or just crazy."

I thought of Joan beside the pond today and how she seemed

to have a thick armor of I-don't-give-a-shit. And how lonely that was.

And Ben. *God*. So lonely it hurt. So lonely he was like a feral mountain man or something. Cooking food that reminded him of a woman he'd driven away.

"I'd rather care," I said, thinking about the night I ran and the dozen nights before that, when I felt myself slipping, slipping, slipping into not caring. I'd run away so that I could find something to care about.

That was my brave, I realized. Risking everything so I could feel something again. And I suddenly felt proud of myself.

"Me too. Every time. All the years I spent not caring. Or pretending I didn't give a shit—they were bad years. I'm not saying she wasn't brave trying to protect that woman. I'm just saying what she did doesn't make you not brave."

"Thanks," I said, more sigh than anything else.

"No problem. But the dessert . . . what was it?"

"Yellow cake with chocolate frosting."

"And?"

"Can't say I loved it."

"You gotta try tres leches cake."

"I have no idea what that is."

"It's pretty much the best thing going."

"Noted," I said with a smile.

"So dessert for breakfast was a bust," Dylan said. "How about skinny-dipping?"

I smiled and rolled onto my back, eager to think of something else. Eager to not be lonely. This connection with Dylan was strange. But it was real. And the world could be a cold place without connection.

"Skinny-dipping was awesome."

"Yeah?"

"It was so hot today and I'd been working hard and the water was so cold. So . . . perfect."

"Sounds like you did it right."

"There was another woman there."

His chuckle lit me up from the inside. "Do tell."

"We just . . . swam. You know?"

"Tell me *swam* is some kind of code word for making out."

I laughed, but I couldn't lie; I felt hot at the idea. A blush rising up my body making me dizzy. "No . . . but I saw her kind of naked and . . . she has an amazing body. She's a stripper."

"Oh Jesus, baby . . ."

Somehow, somehow I'd gone from uninterested and sad to hot. Hot and wet in no time. A chuckle from this man and I was ready to go, my hand in my underwear, testing the swollen edges of my lips.

"I want you to touch yourself tonight," I said.

"Why?"

"Because . . . I don't want to do this alone. Alone . . . isn't the point when I'm with you."

"With me?"

"You know what I mean."

"Baby, you can't be building any fantasies around me. Around this. I'm not . . ."

He trailed off and I held my breath, waiting for him to reveal something about himself. "You're not what?" I prompted.

"Anything a girl like you should build fantasies around."

"A girl like me?" I asked.

"Innocent, young . . ."

"You're only twenty-nine," I said, because if there was one thing I didn't feel most of the time it was young.

"On the outside," he said. "Inside I'm ancient."

Inside I'm ancient. I totally got that. Maybe that's why this thing we were doing worked. Because we were ancient on the inside.

"But what we're doing . . . this is all this is. All it's ever going to be."

"How do I know you're not building fantasies around me?"

"Oh, I am," he laughed. "I'll be thinking of you and a stripper swimming later on tonight. But a man's got to have rules, and I know nothing comes out of breaking them."

Nothing comes of fantasies.

"I know." *Because I'm lying to you and you might be lying to me, and I'm breaking every rule there is because I'm married.* "But I still want you to touch yourself tonight."

He was silent for a long time, as if he were sizing up the reality from his side. *God,* he might be married too. And he said he wouldn't lie—but he could have been lying. "Okay."

"I want you to do it right now." I bit my lip, incredulous at my boldness.

I heard the clink of a belt, the loud undoing of a zipper.

The connection between us buzzed and I wondered if he was waiting for me to tell him what to do—like he'd done the other night.

Good lord, if he was waiting for that, this would take forever.

"I don't . . . Tell me what you're doing," I whispered.

"Where's your hand, baby?"

"Between my legs."

"Good. Keep it there, but don't come . . ."

"What?"

"Not till I tell you. Not until I let you. You feel yourself about to come, you pull your hand away."

Sweat broke out across my body. Between my legs I was wetter than ever. "Okay."

"Say yes."

"Yes," I swallowed. "Yes, Dylan."

"You been doing this all week?" he asked. "Touching yourself."

"Yes."

"You figured some stuff out? Shit you like?"

"Yes."

"Details, baby. You need to give me details."

"I used my underwear the other day, between my legs. It hurt a little—"

"Good hurt?"

"Yes. Good hurt. I got so wet. So . . . it was all down my legs and my underwear was soaked." His groaning laugh made the hair stand up on my body. "Now, you tell me."

"I've been hard all day thinking about you," he said.

I doubted that was true, but whatever. It was hot.

"And it's quiet here now. Quiet and dark, and I got you in my ear and my cock in my fist."

My breath shuddered in my throat.

"You like that word?" he asked.

"Yes."

"I stroke myself slow, because that's how I like it. Hard and slow. Bottom to tip."

I whimpered, closing my eyes, imagining it as best I could, a dirty movie on the back of my eyelids, gathered from bits and pieces. The book. That one time when I was sixteen with my cousin in town. Dylan's voice.

"I got come leaking out the tip, and I smear it all over my cock . . ."

Again that word. I pulled my fingers away from my body, the tension in my belly, between my legs, about to explode.

"I go faster," he said, his breath sawing in my ear. And I could hear his movements. The click and squeal of the chair maybe. The slap of his skin.

"Tell me," I whispered. The lake of bitterness and anger was gone, replaced by a desire for everything. A hunger for it all. I felt empty and wide open to the world. Waiting for experience to fill me up. To satiate me.

"I gotta slow down," he moaned.

"No," I said, reaching for myself again because I could feel the orgasm coming, touching myself or not.

"Stop, Layla."

I pulled my hands away. "Come on," I moaned.

"No, let's slow down for a second."

I growled at him but he only laughed, panting a little.

"How many men you slept with?"

"Why?"

"Cause we're taking a break . . . slowing shit down."

"One."

"One man?"

"Yes."

"Other than that dirty book of yours, you ever watch any porn?"

"Oh my God," I laughed, trying to imagine how that would even work. How or where I would find it, much less watch it. "No. No porn."

"What's the naughtiest, dirtiest thing you've ever seen in real life?"

I barely had to think; the memory was right there. Plugged in like it had been waiting.

"My cousin . . ." *Shit*, I was already using Layla's name. "Annie. My cousin Annie and my aunt came to visit my mom and me on the farm. And I think . . . maybe because my aunt was there, Mom let me take my cousin into town for ice cream. She never, ever let me go into town by myself."

"How old were you?"

"Sixteen." It was a year before Mom got sick. Hoyt had just been hired but I hadn't really met him yet. Saw him in the barn every once in a while, a big blond guy with his hat pulled down low.

God, it seemed like a lifetime ago.

"What happened?"

"Town was like a half hour away and we drove the old station wagon in, but once we got there my cousin decided we should get beer instead of ice cream."

"Naughty girl. Were you on board with that?"

"I was terrified, but I didn't want my cousin to think . . . or to know, really . . . how weird things were in my life, with Mom and being out so far. I mean she probably knew, but I wanted her to think I was . . . normal."

"Normal?"

"You know . . ."

"No. I got no damn idea what a normal sixteen-year-old does."

"You were sixteen once."

"But I was never what anyone would call normal. So what happened?"

"We went to the liquor store parking lot and sat out on the hood of our car . . . just waiting I guess for someone to come by and offer to buy us beer. It took like five minutes. My cousin was real . . . pretty."

"So you got a six-pack and got loaded?"

"No, the guy . . . the guy asked if we wanted him to buy us beer and my cousin said yes. And he asked what was in it for him? And my cousin told him she'd give him a hand job in the back of the station wagon."

I remembered that night like it was yesterday all of a sudden. The hot summer air, the smell of the fried chicken place up the street and Layla's clove cigarettes that truly did make her seem like the coolest girl in the world. The cowboy had been rail thin, his belt buckle nearly bigger than his waist.

"How old are you girls?" he asked, his eyes making me feel dirty. And scared. And . . . excited.

"How old do you want us to be?" Layla said, twirling the end of her ponytail with her finger.

"What happened, baby?" Dylan asked.

"He said yes," I said, "but he wanted me to watch. My cousin shrugged like it was no big deal, like she gave hand jobs to strangers with me watching all the time, and she just hopped off the front of the car and then climbed in the backseat. The guy jumped in after her and I . . . I went to sit in the front seat."

"I want you to watch, sugar," the guy said. "Back here with us so you get a good view."

"She can see just fine," Layla said in the backseat. "Just tilt the mirror, Annie."

"I tipped the mirror," I told Dylan. "So I could see what was happening in the back."

"And did you see?"

"It was dark, too dark really. I could see her hand . . . moving. But mostly I just heard it."

"What did it sound like?"

"Wet, sort of. And the guy talked a lot." I squeezed my legs together remembering what the guy said, the filthy things that came out of his mouth about what a good girl Layla was, and how he wanted to fuck her.

"Were you turned on?"

"I guess . . . I mean, I think I'm more turned on now, thinking about it, than I was then. Mostly, then I was scared." But I wasn't now. The ache was back. That empty throb.

"Did he buy you beer?"

"Yep. I drove around while my cousin drank a six-pack and talked to me about how to give a hand job."

"Yeah, what was her advice?"

"Spit. She said you need to spit on your hand."

At the time I'd never heard anything so disgusting, but right now I wasn't so sure.

"I've never told anyone that story."

"No?"

"Not a single person in my life would appreciate it."

"I appreciate the fuck out of it, baby."

I laughed. "How about you? How many—"

"How many men have I slept with? None."

"Hilarious. How many women?"

"Lots. But I used to be wild."

"Wild?"

"Following around my badass brother. It wasn't pretty and I'm not proud of it, but it was wild."

"What's the wildest thing you've done?"

"Baby, it's not—"

"Tell me."

"A couple women at once, I guess."

Lightning struck my body. "How—?"

He groaned as if my curiosity turned him on, or maybe he was remembering those women. "Truthfully, I was so messed up I barely remember. Mostly, they did each other and I watched. By the time I got around to actually fucking one of them it was over pretty quick. I was wild, but I was young."

"Well, there's the difference between us. I've never been wild."

"You want to be, don't you? That's why you're calling me?"

"Yeah, I guess . . . maybe . . ."

"Yes or no. There's no one else here to hear you and I ain't judging."

"Yes. Yes, I'd like to be wild."

I had my doubts that I'd ever really get there. I was after all still in my underwear. But just today I'd gone skinny-dipping. There was no telling what could happen. A girl had to have goals.

"All right, you listening? We're going to get back to it in a few seconds and we're gonna come and then I gotta go, but before you call me again, I want you to go out to that strip club your friend works at and watch the girls dance."

"What?" I cried. How did I graduate from cake for breakfast to going to a strip club?

"You heard me, and before you start acting like you're not interested, remember it's just you and me here right now. And I do not judge you."

I do not judge you.

The problem was not him. Not at all. It was these ghosts in my head. My mother and Hoyt and a lifetime of trying to appease the unappeasable by suppressing everything about myself.

That's Annie, I thought. *Annie is the one with ghosts.*

Layla is the one giving hand jobs in the backseats of cars for a six-pack of beer.

"Okay," I whispered.

"Okay, what?"

"Okay, I'll go out to the strip club," I said.

"You want that?"

I thought of Joan's perfect body and how hard I'd tried not to stare at it.

"Yeah . . . I do."

Again that laugh of his did something to my blood because my whole body got hot.

"Fuck, that'd be something to see, baby. That would be something to see. Now, where's your hand?"

"In my pussy," I whispered, feeling brave and bold and flush, and the word came out of my mouth on a gust of air, so easy. "Where's yours?"

"Around my cock," he moaned.

We were silent for a moment, just the sound of our breath between us. Harsh and raw.

"Dylan," I groaned.

"Right here. Right fucking here."

It was fast and hard and quick and over in seconds, and I listened to him gasp and groan and wished, more than I could say, that I could see him right now.

"Layla?" he asked after a moment.

"Yeah?"

"You okay?"

I laughed, boneless and weak on the bed. "Yeah. I'm good. You?"

"I'm good, baby. Real good."

"Can I ask you something . . . that's not dirty?"

"As a rule I only answer dirty questions."

"Dylan," I laughed. "I'm serious."

"Shoot."

"Have you ever done this before?"

"Phone sex? Sure." Part of me was crushed at his words, though it was ridiculous. I had no reason to care. "But this other stuff?" he continued. "Talking to a total stranger like this? Totally new."

Ah, not so crushed anymore.

"Me too."

"You grew up on a farm?" he asked.

"Yeah."

"Where?"

"Worlds away from here. Where did you grow up?"

"You changing the subject?"

"I am. My past . . . is . . ."

"Complicated?"

"Very. So where'd you grow up?"

"Outside of Jacksonville."

"Now where do you live?"

"Does it matter?"

Because we're never going to meet. That's what he wasn't saying. We were never going to meet, so this . . . small talk didn't really matter.

"I guess not."

The silence between us hummed for a second, nothing bad. Just quiet. Just space between two people. It was kind of comforting.

"Why are you going to all this effort to watch Ben?"

"You're full of questions, aren't you?"

"I guess so. You have any answers for me?"

"And sassy. I like this."

I did too. I really did.

"Tell me about Ben."

"Are you talking to him?"

"No. Not really. Today I did a little bit. He said he has no family."

Dylan didn't say anything, and I guess I'd been hoping that he'd tell me Ben was lying.

"Why are you having him watched?" I asked.

"He's fucked up my life more than once. I feel better knowing where he is and what he's doing."

"How did he fuck up your life?"

"I'm not talking about this."

"But—"

"Layla, we've got to have some rules about this thing between us. And one of them is I'm not talking about Ben."

There was something so naked in his voice. So raw, and I was suddenly sorry to have put it there.

"Okay," I breathed.

"What are you going to do before you call me again?"

"Go look at naked ladies."

He laughed, sounding satisfied, and though I had no basis to even consider it—or know—he sounded happy, too. "That's right, baby. Do that and call me when you're there."

"Call you?"

"Yeah."

"Like while I'm watching?"

"Yes."

Heat bloomed again in my stomach, between my legs. The idea was unbearably exciting. Unbearably hot.

"What are you going to be doing until then?" I asked.

"Waiting for you."

13

THE NEXT DAY I STEPPED INTO THE ARCTIC CHILL THAT WAS THE
Flowered Manor office.

"Hey, Kevin, the lawn mower died again."

"What?" he cried, looking up from the game of solitaire he
was playing on his computer. In the three weeks I'd been working here, it was really just about all I ever saw him do. "You're
kidding. This is like the third time this week."

"Fourth." And I'd been in here telling him about it every
time, too. Kevin didn't seem to have a whole lot of concern that
I wasn't going to be able to do the work he was paying me for.
But I did. I had oceans of concern. "And I've done everything I
know how to do to keep it running. Can you get someone to
take a look at it? It's in the field."

"Can you ask Ben to have a look-see?" he asked, unable to
make eye contact for very long. As though the solitaire had mag-
netic powers over his eyeballs.

"Sure," I sighed and opened the door back, the hot air rushing into the small office.

"Oh, hey, I think there's a package for you."

"For me?"

"Well, it's addressed to Layla. I figure that was you last time. Must be you again."

The wild thump of my heart was ridiculous.

"Where is it?"

"There." Kevin waved his hand behind him toward the far end of the counter, where a white box sat tied with a red ribbon.

For some reason just looking at that package made me blush. It looked like a secret. A delicious, dirty secret.

"I'm . . . it's . . . Layla is my middle name."

"Whatever," he said, clicking on a Jack of Hearts. "Ask Ben to look at the mower."

"I will." Clutching the box to my chest and acting as nonchalant as I could, I raced back to my trailer to open it in private.

I set it down on the table and pulled one end of the red ribbon, until the bow came undone and the box opened a little. Like it took a deep breath. There was the name of a bakery in Asheville embossed in gold on the front. Looked fancy. My fancy scale was skewed to the low side, and so this was the fanciest thing I'd ever seen.

There was a note folded on top.

Call me.

That was all it said.

I lifted the lid to find a large piece of yellow cake with white icing covered in coconut. It was oozing sugary, creamy liquid.

Smiling, I went to grab my phone.

As I had become accustomed, he answered on the first ring.

"You got it?" he asked.

"It's beautiful. What is it?"

"Tres leches cake."

"Your favorite thing for breakfast," I sighed, touched so much that he'd gone to this effort.

"I couldn't let you settle for that shitty experience. Try it."

"I will. I just wanted to thank you—"

"Try it while you're talking to me, Layla."

I swallowed and blinked. This . . . this seemed oddly intimate.

A chill raced over my skin, and my nipples were hard. My mouth was salivating. It was a full-body response to this gift. To its implications. I was . . . utterly charmed.

Delighted.

Turned on.

By cake.

By Dylan.

I smiled and pulled one of my three forks out of the drawer. The first bite made me moan. "Oh my God," I sighed. "That's . . . that's amazing."

"Tell me."

"It's so moist. And sweet. Really sweet. It's kind of carmelly somehow and coconutty."

"That's how my mom made it. With the coconut."

I took another bite, the sweetness gathering in the back of my throat. "Oh, God . . . Dylan. It's so good."

He was breathing hard. I was breathing hard.

I felt the emptiness inside of me. The place in my body where he would go if he were here. I wondered, suddenly, what else he would do if he were here.

"The frosting is whipped cream." I put some on my finger and sucked it off.

"Do that again," he said. "That sound."

"I'm sucking the whipped cream off my finger."

He groaned a little, in the back of his throat.

"It's perfect," I whispered. "It's so perfect."

"Take another bite," he said.

I did. Moaning, because I knew somehow that was really what he wanted to hear.

"No more," I said.

"What?"

"I want to save it. Stretch it out."

"You're the kind of kid who had her Halloween candy until Easter, aren't you?"

"I didn't get to trick-or-treat much," I said, putting the box of cake in the fridge. My body was humming, from the sweetness of the cake.

The sweetness of him.

"But usually, I'm . . . greedy. I like all my treats at once." The door closed with a small snick. "You don't have to do these things, you know."

"What things?"

"These . . . nice things."

"I like to do these nice things."

"I don't know how to thank you," I said, smiling a little. Enjoying playing coy. Because I knew how to thank him. I knew what he wanted. I wanted it too.

"Take off your clothes, Layla," he breathed. "I'll tell you how you can thank me."

I went back into my bedroom and did every single thing he told me to do. I didn't think, not for even a second, of saying no to him.

"You can do it, baby," he breathed, when I was sobbing that I couldn't take any more. I had three fingers in my pussy and my clit was on fire. He wouldn't let me touch it. "I want you to do it."

He wanted it, so I did too. I wanted it for myself, because it felt so sharp and real. Painful and so good at the same time. And I wanted it for him.

I wanted to please him.

So, inside my tight, aching body I slipped a fourth finger. I was stuffed, so full. Too full. My hand hurt, my arm ached. My body was shaking.

"Dylan," I whimpered. "Please . . ."

"Now, you can touch your clit."

I did. And the world exploded. My world exploded. It was dark and bright at the same time. And I didn't recognize myself in it. I didn't recognize my body, as if it had been fundamentally changed by this pleasure.

Changed by Dylan.

DYLAN

DYLAN WALKED FROM HIS HOUSE TO THE WAREHOUSE, WHERE the rest of the team was still working on the engine. They weren't gods yet, but they were getting close.

Yet instead of contemplating improvements on the bit slopes, he was thinking about vibrators.

Specifically, sending one to Layla.

And maybe some lingerie. Expensive, classy stuff. He had a thing for black lace, but he could send her something in every color. But he didn't know what size she was, so that made it tricky.

He'd go with the vibrator.

It wasn't hard to imagine her shocked; she'd be shocked. But then she'd be interested. Very interested.

The thought made him smile. And hard. An entirely new and weird sensation. But one he was getting used to when he thought about Layla.

"Dylan!"

Margaret was waving him down from the door of his house. She was actually waving a kitchen towel at him. As if he were a plane, or a soldier leaving for war.

"What?"

He'd spent too much time arranging to send cake and talking to Layla. His team—Blake, actually—was getting pissed, and he really needed to get to the warehouse or he'd have a mutiny on his hands.

"There's a call for you on the landline," she said.

"Take a message." He turned, folding and putting away thoughts of Layla and vibrators, and tried to get his head to focus on the work.

"It's from the hospital down in Cherokee."

That made him pause and Margaret took advantage, coming at him with the cordless phone. "I think you should take it," she said.

Dylan stared down at the phone she was holding out to him. Layla wouldn't use this number, so it couldn't be her.

"Everyone on staff is here, right?"

She nodded.

Which meant it was someone in his family.

"What do they want?" He didn't touch the phone.

Margaret's sympathy vibe was turned way up and he realized whatever was waiting for him on the phone, it was bad.

When he was a boy and Mom was using again, he and his brother would hide all their nice shit. Anything that might be worth some money that she could sell. Bikes got buried beneath the weeds behind the apartment. Swiss Army knives and video games, shoved beneath a floorboard in Max's room. When Dylan started racing, bringing home hundreds of dollars, Max got him a cash box and they buried it in the side yard. He'd been sixteen years old and making more than Dad as some petty soldier in the Skulls. Sometimes they didn't see it coming until it was too late, and shit was gone before they had a chance to hide it, but they got better. Faster. Started hiding everything they got the second they got it.

Just in case.

In his head, in his gut, he was doing the same thing. Hiding everything that made him happy. Everything that made him soft. Anything that might hurt when it got ruined or driven away by whatever was waiting for him on the other end of the phone.

I've been an idiot, he realized. He'd let down all his guards.

"Give me that," he said, grabbing the phone from her hand, too rough. Too mean. Margaret didn't deserve it, but he was sharpened to an edge and anyone that got close got hurt.

"What?" he said into the phone, braced for impact.

"Dylan Daniels?" a woman asked. A nice-sounding woman, which only made him colder. Sharper.

"Speaking."

"Are you next of kin to one Ben Daniels?"

He shifted his foot in the dirt. Widening his stance. Bracing himself for impact. "Is he dead?"

"No," the woman rushed to say. "Gosh, no. I'm sorry I led you to think that. He's not dead—"

"Is he dying?"

"No," she laughed. "The man is tough as nails. I'm calling because—"

"He's not dead and he's not dying?"

She paused. "No, he's not."

"Then don't call me until he is."

He pressed the end button and handed it back over to Margaret.

"I need to get to work," he said and headed back toward his garage. Toward his work. It had saved him from his family once before and he could count on it to do so again.

Pop used to do this thing when he was drunk, when Dylan and Max were young. He'd take those big fists, with the tattoos across the knuckles, and pound them against their shoulders, as if Dylan and Max were stakes and he wanted to drive them into the ground.

Remember who you come from, he'd say with every punch. *Remember who you little bitches come from.*

Dylan used to wobble under the force, fall to the side. His knees buckling.

Max never did. Not once.

All of Pop's friends . . . *his brothers,* would laugh and get Max a drink. A shot. A joint. A girl. Whatever reward for toughness was available. Dylan never learned that toughness from his dad. He wanted his pop to be like other dads, his mom to be like other moms. He wanted them all to be a family, like the ones on TV. The ones that did nice things for one another.

Sweet things.

It wasn't until he got sent away that he learned how to be tough. The toughest, actually.

He was forged steel.

And he was forgetting. Layla was making him forget.

He came from a long line of villains. And that shit couldn't be forgotten. Couldn't be erased with cake.

You need to remember who you are, he thought. *Because you told her not to go building any fantasy around you, and now look at you.*

Cake. What the fuck was he thinking?

He'd send another package. More honest this time.

Dylan Daniels was still the beast. The bad guy in the stories. Layla just didn't know it yet. And he was forgetting. He was letting himself forget. Because he'd somehow gotten addicted to the sound of her voice. The way her voice made him feel.

Sometimes it was nice pretending to be the hero.

But it was time to stop.

ANNIE

ANOTHER PACKAGE ARRIVED FROM DYLAN THE NEXT DAY.

"What are you doing, girl?" Kevin asked, handing me the package. He'd brought it out to me as I was locking up the shed after work. It was a perfect, hot day. Bright sun. Cool breeze. I'd jumped back in the swimming hole today and felt cool and sleek all the way through.

"Nothing, why?" I had no experience playing it cool and I failed miserably at it.

"Seems to me like you got yourself a long-distance admirer."

"And so what if I do?" I asked, laughing. Because I did! I had myself a long-distance admirer! Blood rushed to all of my skin, a full-body blush as I thought of yesterday. How I couldn't say no to him. Wouldn't say no. Why would I?

"You . . . sure that's smart?" he asked. I blinked, surprised he would ask. "It's just . . . you know when you showed up here, you looked like you'd—"

I stiffened and turned away, horrified by the memory. That he would bring it up. "I'm fine."

"Yeah, I hear that a lot from people and they're lying to me," he said.

"I'm not lying."

He looked like he was about to say something else. Something about the box. Maybe about the guy who gave it to me and I was touched, I really was. But I didn't need his concern.

"Thank you, Kevin," I told him. "But you don't need to worry about me."

I walked away from him, back to my trailer. But I felt his eyes on me the whole way.

Once inside my trailer, I tore open the box. On top was a folded-up piece of paper, two twenty-dollar bills, and a sticky note.

If you still decide to go, buy yourself some drinks at that strip club, the note said.

Still decide, I thought with what could only be called a giggle. He'd told me to go; he'd set down the rules. I was going.

I was well aware that building some kind of infatuation around this guy was dumb . . . but it was also fun. And fun was a rare enough bird in my life that I was going to let it stick around if it wanted to.

Good God. Forty dollars' worth of drinks? Was he nuts? I'd buy myself one. Maybe. And then a box of hair dye, because my roots were coming in and I looked like a weird off-color skunk.

But beneath the drink thing, it said, *This is why I watch him. This is why I want you to stay away.*

The folded-up piece of paper was a photocopied news story from ten years ago.

GANG MEMBERS ARRESTED AFTER TRIPLE HOMICIDE

Beneath the headline was a picture of a younger Ben and two other men in handcuffs being led into a police station.

Quickly, I closed the article, pressing my thumb along the crease as if I could seal it shut. Forever.

Triple homicide?

Gang member?

Joan had said that, remember? She'd said, that day at the lake, that he'd been a part of a gang. He'd been kicked out for doing something awful.

Was this it? Was this the awful?

It seemed ludicrous. Like a joke. He fried zucchini flowers and told me to stay out of the sun. He gave me tomatoes from his garden. The other morning I woke up to find a loaf of cornbread on my stoop. Still warm.

He was a man whose regrets and remorse sat on his shoulders, nearly visible.

This . . . article didn't make any sense.

With shaking hands, I opened the paper back up.

Three members of the Skulls Motorcycle Club have been arrested in relation to the October house fire that killed two men and a young girl that took place in the Tallyrand area of Jacksonville.

According to local law authorities, the two men who died in the fire were tied up and alive at the time the fire was set. The girl was apparently asleep in an upstairs bedroom. The house, area residents claim, was used to make and distribute methamphetamines.

"Between DNA testing and eyewitness testimony, we're confident we've got a case," says county prosecutor Edward Hayes. "All evidence points to the three suspects tying up those two men, setting the house on fire and leaving them to die. Those two deaths I have no doubt were premeditated. Whether or not they knew the girl was upstairs is a matter we will have to determine in court."

I closed the article again and fumbled for the phone. I texted Dylan.

Is this article real? Did he kill those people in the fire?

A little girl?

Was I living next to a murderer?

The phone rang and I answered it before the first ring was over. "Is this a joke?" I asked.

"No," Dylan said. "It's not."

"What happened, did he go to jail?"

"Not for this. The whole case was thrown out because the prosecutor fucked with some evidence. He was a little too keen to get those guys behind bars, and so they all walked."

I paced the very small distance the charger cord let me.

"Is that . . . did he?"

"Set the fire so those guys would burn to death? Yeah. I think he did. He was some kind of enforcer for the MC."

"MC?"

"Motorcycle Club."

"Oh Jesus, oh God." I sat down on the edge of my bed. That little girl . . .

"You are safe."

I didn't even think about that. If Ben wanted to hurt me he'd had a month to do it.

"Why did you send that?"

"So you know who he is. And who he's not." His voice was loaded and hard. Mean sounding. Like he was angry.

That article and what I knew of Ben did not connect in any way. "I have no idea who he is," I cried. "Not after this."

"He's someone you can't trust. He's someone you do not want to get close to. Not for any reason. I don't want you to be scared; I want you to be informed. To be smart. I shouldn't have asked you to look in on Ben and not tell you the whole story."

"Did he go to jail for something else?" I asked.

"Yeah. He was in and out of jail until the club kicked him out a few years ago."

"Why did they kick him out?"

"I don't know, Layla. Just . . . keep away from him."

I sat up straight and blew out a slow breath.

"You okay?" he asked.

"No. And why do you sound mad at me?"

"I'm not mad at you—"

"Then don't talk to me like that." I was stunned those words came out of my mouth. Stunned. But I was too angry myself, too freaked out, to process any of it.

"Baby," he sighed. "I'm sorry. I just needed you to know."

"Well, now I'm pissed at you." I was pissed at him for his tactics. I felt bullied. I shifted on the bed and the money slipped down over my hand. Bullied and cared for. What the hell?

"But . . . thank you for the money. Forty bucks is too much, though—"

"Forty bucks is nothing. Look, I gotta go. I have this party thing . . ."

"Yeah, sure," I said. "Me too. Well, not a party thing. But I need to go." It was Thursday night and I had my weekly date with the laundry building. He had a party thing. Awesome.

What the hell are you doing, Annie?

"Will I talk to you later?"

"We'll see."

"No. Layla. No 'we'll see.' If you're done, be done. If you're not, I'll talk to you later."

"Where in that choice is there room for me to be pissed at you?" The words choked me as they came out of my mouth. Was that me, saying that?

His laughter was unexpected, a husky curl that would usually make me close my eyes and shiver a little. "Both choices have that room. Depends on how pissed you are. You can still be mad, baby, and keep doing the things we do."

I didn't really know how. How to hold both my anger at him and my desire for him in the same hand. But I knew I didn't want this to be the end.

"Okay," I breathed. "I'll talk to you later."

"Good," he said, the relief in his voice obvious. He'd been worried I would end it.

I hung up and then walked over to my stove, where the foil-wrapped loaf of cornbread sat in between the burners.

How could the Ben I know be the Ben that was in that newspaper?

How can you be the woman lying on a kitchen floor begging your husband not to kill you and the woman having phone sex with a man you don't know? How did those two realities live side by side inside of me?

That was the truth, wasn't it? We could all be so many things. Victims and criminals. Sinners and saints. Devious and virtuous.

That was what my mother was really scared of, why she kept us so alone out on that farm. Why she tended that garden of radical fear and suspicion. Because we were editors of our own selves, revealing only what we wanted to show. Being only what served us best.

Trust was an enormous act of faith.

And faith . . . *God,* faith was hard.

Who was Ben? Really. Who was I?

And who the fuck was Dylan?

14

THAT NIGHT REALLY WAS LAUNDRY NIGHT, SO I LOADED UP MY stuff, including the last book I'd bought at the library, a historical romance that was the second in a series, so I was a little lost, but hooked all the same.

To my surprise, Tiffany was sitting out at her picnic table, the twinkle lights on making the dusty little yard actually seem quite lovely. And she was sitting with a woman who looked just like her but without the bruises and the dark circles under her eyes.

But the real kicker was that Tiffany was laughing. Head thrown back, hand pounding the table—laughing.

"I'm not kidding, Tiff," the other woman was saying. "He said, 'I'm the pitcher, he's the catcher, and there's nothing gay about that.' On a blind date! Who says that?"

"Oh, Bebe," Tiffany sighed, wiping her eyes. "That stuff only happens to you."

"Well, I'm super lucky then, aren't I?" Bebe took a swig of some unnaturally green concoction in a plastic Spider-Man cup.

I was actively and positively envious. Of the whole thing.

The laughter. The green drink. The fact that Tiffany looked . . . relaxed. I wanted to look relaxed.

Had I ever looked that way?

Shit. I needed a friend who was not a potential murderer or a stripper with a chip on her shoulder or a man I have phone sex with but know nothing about.

And frankly, not a one of them could I really consider a friend. A friendly acquaintance, a begrudging neighbor, and a man who turned me on like a blowtorch, but to whom I only lied.

Tiffany looked up and caught me staring. I smiled and tried not to look like some kind of weird friendship stalker.

"Hey, Annie," she said, still relaxed. Still smiling.

"Hey, Tiffany."

"This is my sister Beatrice."

Bebe rolled her eyes and kind of half stood up, reaching out her hand. I stepped farther into the backyard to shake it. "Please, call me Bebe."

"Nice to meet you, Bebe."

"Come over and have a drink," Bebe said. "I brought over like ten Buckets-o-Margarita—"

"Buckets-o-Margarita?" Tiffany asked.

"It says that on the label, Tiffany. I'm not making it up. Anyway, I took them from work. So it's free and there's lots of it."

"I . . . I don't want to impose . . ." I stammered, when I really did. I really wanted to impose.

"You're not," Tiffany said. "Honestly, we've got to drink all this green booze before my kids come home and think they're slushies."

"Well . . ." I smiled. "As long as I'm doing you a favor."

"Oh," Bebe said, nodding, her face all serious, "you are."

"Let me just put my laundry in and I'll come back."

I practically threw my laundry into the machine with the

soap and the coins and then walked back out to the picnic table. Tiffany was coming out of her trailer with one Spider-Man and two Barbie cups filled to the brim with icy green booze. She was licking the top of one like an ice-cream cone.

"You're right," she said. "It says Bucket-o-Margarita."

"I told you," Bebe said. "Who'd make that shit up?"

Tiffany handed out the cups and we all took a half-sip, half-bite from our drinks. It was shockingly sweet and really boozy and very cold.

Perfect.

"Where are your kids?" I asked.

"My dad's away on business for the week, so my mom took them for two whole nights," Tiffany said. She put her hands up in the air and did a little swaying dance move. "I'm gonna get drunk. And sleep in late. And then I'm going to mop the floors and go to the grocery store without anyone—"

"No," Bebe cut in. "We're going to get drunk, yes. Sleep in, yes. And then we're going to flop out on that couch and watch bad TV all day."

"I vote with Bebe," I said and took another swig/bite of my drink. It was melting fast in the heat. "Bad TV, no mopping."

Tiffany smiled affectionately at her sister. "Bebe does have all the good ideas." She clapped her hands like she'd had a suddenly great idea. "Hey, I have chips." She stood up, wobbled slightly, and then made a beeline for her trailer.

"Bring out a bucket!" Bebe yelled.

Without Tiffany, we both took another drink and the silence was thick. I'd never been good with small talk, especially with other women. "You don't live here, do you?" I asked when the silence went on way too long. "I haven't seen you around."

"No." She shook her head. "I live with my folks in Asheville."

"Wow," I said. Tiffany had a sister, a mom, and a dad who goes on business meetings, who all live in Asheville—an hour and a bit up the road—and she's stuck out here in a trailer park with three kids and a fuckwit like Phil? Hardly seemed right. But then I was no great judge of family dynamics.

"When she got pregnant with Danny and married Phil, Dad disowned her," Bebe said, like she knew what I was thinking. "Mom and I do what we can behind his back—"

"Like take the kids when he's on business?"

She nodded. "I send her some money when I can. Stuff for the kids."

"You know Phil hits her?"

Bebe jerked back, her face turned aside.

"I'm sorry," I muttered, putting down the drink. "I should—"

"She says he stopped."

I shook my head.

"Goddamnit," she whispered.

Tiffany arrived in the doorway of the trailer, holding a bucket aloft. She looked years younger. Radiant, even. And drunk as a skunk. "This one is Bucket-o-Daiquiri."

"Bring it on," Bebe said, waving her forward.

"Forgot the chips," Tiffany said and darted back in.

Bebe grabbed my hand. "Stay," she said. "Let's have fun. A lot of fun. For Tiffany. She needs this."

"Sure," I said, because I needed it too. The proverbial rug had been yanked out from beneath me and I didn't know how to process it. Processing Dylan while drunk seemed like a great idea. I had never in my life gotten drunk with girlfriends. I'd never really had girlfriends. This night seemed paramount to me. A matter, quite frankly, of survival.

The slush was now mostly liquid and I took another big swig. Alcohol burned down my throat.

Tiffany came back out with the bucket and the chips and an ice-cream scoop. "Hey, Annie," she said, sitting down and pointing the ice-cream scoop in my face. "I've been meaning to ask you something."

"Yeah?" I asked, leaning out of the way. Bebe cracked open the daiquiri bucket and took the ice-cream scoop out of Tiffany's hand, using it to dish out giant balls of yellow booze.

"What the fuck happened to your hair?"

AND THAT IS HOW I FOUND MYSELF IN THE KITCHEN OF HER trailer (really, those double-wides were so spacious!), a towel around my neck and Tiffany putting peroxide in my hair. She'd already trimmed up my ragged edges and bangs. I felt like I'd had short hair before, but now it seemed . . . really short. Boy short.

I couldn't quite work up the sobriety to care.

"It'll just take some of the black out," Tiffany said. "So you don't look so fucking scary."

"I look scary?" I asked, and tipped my head back so I could get the last bit of Bucket-o-Daiquiri out of the bottom of my Barbie cup.

"Don't listen to her!" Bebe warned from the couch. "When I was five she said she was only going to give me bangs and I ended up with a weird sideways Mohawk."

"Shush," Tiffany said, in her best stern mom voice. "You're gonna scare her."

"I'm not scared," I said. And I wasn't. This was all too much fun to be scary.

Tiffany applied the peroxide, which stunk, and Bebe refilled my cup, and all was really quite right with the world.

Until Tiffany touched one of the bruises on my neck. I jerked, thinking it was an accident. But then she touched another one. I opened my eyes only to find her looking down at me. All her pain, every time a fist had touched her skin, bruised her, broke her. It was all right there on her young/old face.

I know you, I thought. *I know everything about you.*

I reached up and grabbed her hand. "I got away," I breathed.

"I left him. He can't hurt me anymore." I don't know why I said any of that, other than it seemed like the answer to the question she was too scared, maybe, to ask.

Her smile was lopsided. "Good."

"Anyone want to try Bucket-o-Colada?" Bebe asked.

"Me!" Tiffany and I both said.

Bucket-o-Colada was the best one yet, and Bebe started telling the story of her five-year high school reunion, which apparently included the Prom Queen starting a fight, and we all lost track of time.

"Holy shit, your head!" Tiffany shouted, who the hell knows how much later. She jumped out of her seat and bent me backward over the sink. "Isn't it burning?"

"I can't feel anything," I told her. Which wasn't true. I was feeling those drinks. I was feeling them hard. The world was actually kind of swimming around me.

I closed my eyes and Tiffany's fingers worked through my hair. After it was all rinsed out, she towel-dried my hair and then ripped the towel away, yelling, "Ta-da!"

"God love a duck," Bebe gasped. "You look fucking fantastic."

"Not too shabby," Tiffany said, finger-combing it. "Go check it out in the bathroom."

I stumbled down the hallway to the bathroom, which was full of little-kid toothbrushes in the shape of whales and bath toys in a bucket by the sink, a little kid's potty seat on top of the toilet.

God, I thought, touching a ribbon tied to a towel rack with a ton of little barrettes on it. How did she do this? How did she do all this with Phil like an evil shadow over her shoulder?

I glanced up in the mirror and then did a quick double take.

My hair was blond. Like *white* blond. My eyebrows looked darker, my tan, tanner. And my eyes. Wow. Were those mine? They were huge. And so blue.

What I looked like was totally not myself, and that was all that really mattered.

But I did have to admit it was better than the black. Way better.

I thought of Dylan and my body ached in response. A sharp lightning bolt of feeling—of lust—zapped me, and I wondered what he would think of my hair.

If he would like it.

I tried to shake off the thought, because I knew I wasn't supposed to be thinking that way about him.

But the thought stayed.

Dylan.

Always Dylan.

"Like Miley fucking Cyrus," Bebe said when I came back into the main room. Tiffany was passed out on the couch, her hands tucked under her face.

"How old is she?" I asked.

"Twenty-three," Bebe answered, picking up everyone's glasses and putting them in the sink. The buckets were stacked up in a pile by the door. There were a lot of buckets.

She was a year younger than me. With three kids.

"I gotta go," I said. I needed Dylan. I needed his voice. I needed those things he asked me to do. I needed all of it—suddenly worse than ever before. "That was fun."

"That," Bebe said with a smile, "was epic. Good luck tomorrow."

"Ha!" I said and stumbled home.

Inside the trailer it was cool and dark, and I locked the door behind me and slipped right into bed without brushing my teeth.

It took me a few tries to get the bedside table open, but soon I had the fully charged phone in my hand. I texted Dylan.

DYLAN

IF DYLAN WAS GOING TO BE A GOD, HE WAS GOING TO BE A GOD among these men. NASCAR officials, team owners, sponsors, drivers, and crew chiefs. Wearing tuxes and drinking scotch, making million-dollar deals over cigars.

None of them looked him in the eye. Not one. Or looked at his face. When these people talked to him, they talked to his nose. Or the black tie around his neck.

The drivers couldn't even look at him, as if he were bad luck.

There but for the grace of God and all that shit . . .

There is no grace of God, he wanted to tell those drivers. *Put your faith in the machine and the crew and the feeling in your gut when you're on that track.*

Dylan knew he made them nervous and he could enjoy throwing around that kind of vibe.

But now this shit was just getting old. Which was why Blake usually did these things by himself. But Blake had insisted Dylan come this time, and that was a rare enough request that Dylan felt obligated to play along. *They're scars, people. Just scars.*

"How is that transmission of yours coming?" Jimmy Morrow asked, his hair so white and thick it was like a cat had taken a nap on his head. Jimmy Morrow wanted Dylan's transmission. Every man here wanted it. Jimmy was willing to pay him a lot of money but Dylan wasn't sure he could work with a man who had hair like that. For a second, just a flash, he thought of what his brother would have said about that man's hair and nearly smiled.

"It's coming along," he said.

"I heard you're getting more horsepower than any other engine builder."

"It's a game-changer, gentlemen. I won't lie."

Dylan could feel their excitement; they were like circling sharks.

"My offer still stands," Jimmy said. "I told that partner of yours and I'll tell you the same thing. I'll buy 989 Engines. I'll give you enough money that you can buy yourself another couple of mountains. You can still run the whole operation, build the engines you want, how you want. Think about it, son. Offers like this don't come around every day," Jimmy Morrow said to Dylan's chin, smiling at the other men as though he had Dylan eating out of the palm of his hand.

But Dylan wasn't anyone's pet.

"That's where you're wrong, Jimmy," Dylan said. "I get an offer like that once a week. From men who can look me in the eye when they do it. My company is not for sale. Never will be. You can stand in line like the rest of the owners when the time comes. Gentlemen," he said and took his leave from the silent, gape-faced assholes.

Dylan caught sight of Blake in the corner, surrounded by rich white guys. Blake caught his eye and Dylan tilted his head toward the exit. Blake nodded and Dylan left the stuffy, crowded room that stank of perfume and cigars and stepped out onto the big wraparound porch of the mansion nestled up into the northwest corner of Charlotte.

The humidity was thick away from his mountain and there were way too many people here, but duty demanded he come down occasionally and meet with the men who paid him so much goddamned money. And in the case of Jimmy Morrow, would pay him so much more.

"Hello, stranger."

A woman stepped out of the shadows wearing a classic black dress over a body that made a man look twice. She flipped long brown hair over her shoulder and shot him a sly smile.

"Jennifer." Something warm rolled over in his chest. They'd had some good times not too long ago. She was one of the few people from his life before who didn't treat him any differently now. Though he was rich now, and Jennifer did enjoy money. "I didn't realize you were here."

"Just got here," she said. "I'm surprised to see you here. Someone yank your chain? Force you down off that mountain?"

"Blake insisted I come down and make nice."

"Hmmm," she laughed.

"What about you?" he asked.

"Daddy's looking for a new driver. He's here to grease some palms."

"This is the place for it," he said. The NASCAR corporate gala brought everyone out of hiding. Including him.

"You know," she said, stepping even closer. He could smell her in the darkness, something bright and sharp. "He was asking if I thought you'd be interested in scouting—"

"No."

"But—"

"No, Jennifer."

Her slow prowl across the porch paused for a moment, but she got her stride back. That was the thing about Jennifer: she never got knocked off her stride for long. He actually admired that about her. She pouted at him, making the most of those lips she'd been born with. "You know, you used to be a lot nicer."

"I used to be a kid," he said. And a fool. So damn grateful and eager for what those men at the party could give him. So damn happy to be out of his cage he would have done anything for the people paying his way. He'd enjoyed being one of their golden boys for a few short years. An up-and-coming driver with a bright future. It had been a relief putting the darkest of his sins as far behind him as he could. Pretending his hands were clean.

But then karma, his old friend, came back around. She always did.

Luckily he was a far better engine builder than he'd ever been a driver.

"You leaving?" She'd gotten close enough that she could touch him. She didn't. She wasn't that brave. Or stupid. She'd been the last woman who'd touched him, years ago. And he'd liked it for a long time, until quite suddenly, he couldn't stand it.

"Soon," Dylan said.

"Want some company?" To his surprise, she lifted her hand toward his face, as if she were going to run her fingers over the scars there.

He turned his face aside and stepped back away from her touch. Jennifer had a habit of wanting more. Always more. Too much. And his world didn't work like that. He didn't work like that. Whatever he'd had to give a person had been taken from him years ago.

"You know that's not going to happen," he said.

She dropped her arm and the sly smile vanished. "You've changed, you know that? Ever since—"

"Go back to the party," he said quietly. "Before you say something we both regret."

She turned on her heel and headed inside.

Everyone in there thought the accident had ruined him. But he'd been ruined long before.

His phone buzzed in his pocket. A text message.

Layla.

All the bullshit inside that house and inside his head—it vanished.

And he smiled as he stepped off the porch and into the darkness of the tree line surrounding the mansion, having known somehow in his gut who it would be, texting him at this hour.

Sending her that article had been a risky but necessary move. He couldn't have her thinking Ben was tame. He couldn't have her getting hurt because he'd put her in that situation. And reading that article had brought so much shit to the surface, reminded him of what a scumbag Ben was, how capable he was of hurting the people around him.

After mailing that article to Layla, he'd sent one of his guys to a hotel in Cherokee because he wanted someone close to her if things went south.

Because that was the thing about Ben. Shit always went south.

Her first text was sent an hour ago; he must have missed it in his arrival at the party.

> Layla: Hey.

And then her second one was just a few minutes ago.

> Layla: helllllloooooooooooo

Dylan smiled before texting her back: Hey yourself.

> Layla: You're there!!
> Dylan: I'm here.
> Layla: I'm drynk
> Dylan: Drunk?
> Layla: Very. But I'm still mad about the article
> Dylan: That's why you're texting? To tell me ur mad?

He knew she wasn't texting because she was angry. She was texting because she was as addicted to this shit they had between them as he was.

> Layla: Not at this moment

His blood thickened and he would give anything to not be at this party. Half of him was ready to step farther into those shadows and tell her to do all the things that got her off. But that couldn't happen here. He was very careful about how his worlds touched, like a kid who couldn't let his carrots touch his potatoes.

There was no cross-contamination in his world.

> Dylan: Cause you're drunk
> Layla: very. call me
> Dylan: Why?
> Layla: I want to hear ur voice.
> Dylan: You like my voice?
> Layla: Makes me very hot. Wt
> Layla: Wet. Drunk texting is hard

Dylan smiled before looking up at the glittering windows of the three-story house full of people who kissed his ring but didn't make eye contact. Jennifer was in there. That smile on her face that told him everything he needed to know about how good his chances were that she'd be willing to lift that skirt of hers in an upstairs bedroom.

Everyone in that party thought he was a hermit and he wondered if the fact that he preferred this faceless woman, a woman he'd never met, over Jennifer only proved their assumptions.

Good thing he didn't give a shit what the people at that party thought of him. And he would give anything to be alone in his house, sitting in the dark, listening to Layla's voice, that sweet voice with the country twang and the nervous laugh. What he wouldn't give to have his hand around his cock, pushing her to try more. To do more. To test the edges of that pleasure and pain.

But he had to put in another hour or Blake would kill him.

Dylan: you're going to have to do it alone tonight.

Layla: but it's better with you

Groaning, Dylan texted back: But I'm still at this party.

Layla: I was at a party 2! There were buckets of booze. And I dyed my hair.

He wondered briefly what color her hair was. What she looked like. But as the reality didn't matter, he pushed those thoughts aside as useless and irrelevant.

Dylan: Sounds like a much better party than this one.

Layla: What kind of party is it?

DON'T. The word was loud and clear in Dylan's brain. *Do not do this thing.*

But in the end, because he was bored, because of the way the people at that party made him feel like an animal and not a man—and because somehow she'd cracked a hole in his life that he kept trying to stuff more work into, more deals, more money—his warnings were to no avail. He turned the phone around and snapped a picture of himself. From the chin down.

And sent it to her.

Her response came back fast and in all caps.

Layla: IS THAT YOU?

Such a fucking mistake. *What happened to cross-contamination? What happened to the rules?* His life worked because everything was controlled. He knew this, but it didn't seem to matter.

Dylan: Me and my monkey suit.

Layla: send me another

Dylan: Can't. Have to go. Call me tomorrow night.

Layla: boooooooo

Dylan: tomorrow night.

Dylan put his phone back in his pocket. The rules he was breaking were piling up around his feet like metal shavings, razor sharp and about to cut the both of them.

Inevitably, someone was going to get hurt.

AN HOUR LATER HE MANAGED TO MAKE HIS GOODBYES AND leave the party. He ignored the valet and went to get his own car. His F-150, the same truck they used to tow the 989 trailer, looked like a giant beast among all the sleek European cars and the refurbished American muscle cars that surrounded it.

This parking area was a gearhead's wet dream.

He climbed into his bare-bones pickup and pulled off his tie. The engine, one he'd rebuilt himself, roared like it couldn't wait to get off this damn property too.

The back roads leading from the house to the highway were dark and still. He was alone on the road, except for the sound of the engine on a distant motorcycle.

A Harley Fat Boy, if he heard it right.

A Harley Fat Boy that needed a tune-up.

It was the sound of his youth, one that used to wake him up in his bed at night. It was the sound of his father and his brother, coming home or leaving.

Outside the dark trees blurred and he kept his speed, enjoying the night and the open road. He unrolled the window, and the smell of the road and the forest filled the cab. He'd be home soon and then . . . Layla.

The motorcycle showed up in his rearview and Dylan put his hand out the window, indicating the guy could pass if he wanted.

The biker flashed his lights.

And then again.

The fuck?

They were entering the suburbs, and Dylan slowed down for a stop sign at an intersection and the motorcycle pulled up alongside him.

Out in this neighborhood he wasn't much worried about being mugged. Probably a guy looking for the highway.

"You need something?" Dylan asked. The murky light from a distant street lamp picked up the flash of a dirty white badge on black leather.

A cut.

The rider was in an MC.

"I guess you could say that." The guy rolled forward until his face was in the light.

It took Dylan a second to place the man, who seemed vaguely familiar. And then the guy grinned, revealing the two, rotting front teeth that bent inward, tilting toward each other.

"Rabbit?"

"Hey there, son."

"Holy . . ." He couldn't deny the fact that for a heartbeat he was happy to see the man. Rabbit had gotten Dylan started in racing, supported him, found him races. Illegal backwoods races, but it was a start. He'd also fed Dylan to the dogs when the time came.

The heartbeat of happiness stopped. Immediately.

"I tell you what," Rabbit said with that crooked grin and his dark eyes. "You don't come down off that mountain of yours very often, do you?"

"You've been looking for me?"

"Fuck. No one needs to look for Dylan Daniels, we just need to wait for him to show his face—" Rabbit blanched a little in the strange light. The guy always had been a little squeamish.

And his face was exactly why Dylan didn't come down off his mountain.

"What do you want, Rabbit?"

"I need you to talk to your brother."

Dylan laughed and began to roll up his window.

"Hear me out," Rabbit said, putting his hand over the escalating glass. Dylan could ignore the guy's hand. Close the window on it and drag the guy behind him for as long as it took for Rabbit to pull himself free.

And once upon a time that was exactly what he would have done.

He lifted his finger from the window button.

"I haven't talked to my brother in years." Nine to be exact. He remembered the day in absolute clarity. "If the club is having trouble with how Max is leading it—"

"He's gonna get us all killed."

Dylan shook his head.

"You don't believe me?" Rabbit asked, those dark eyes getting sly. Mean.

"No," he said. "I believe you. There's just nothing I can do to help you. Max has been trying to get himself killed since the day he was born."

Dylan rolled up the window and roared away, leaving Rabbit and the past in his rearview mirror.

15

ANNIE

WHEN I WAS LITTLE, SMITH HAD A DOG. A PRETTY SHEPHERD with one blue eye and one dark one. And that dog loved dead things. If there was a rabbit or a squirrel or a bird that died somewhere on the property, Queenie would find that thing and roll around in it. She'd roll around in it in ecstasy. Like her dog life was made. And then she'd eat it.

She'd eat the dead thing.

And then she'd throw it up and then, if Smith wasn't around to shout her name in the serious threatening way he had, she'd roll around in that.

On Friday morning I couldn't tell if I was Queenie, or the dead thing she'd rolled around in, eaten, and thrown up.

That's how bad I felt.

I made my way, hours past dawn, in the bright, sticky heat of the day toward the field, unsure if I was going to be able to work. Or if I would even really survive the day.

Stepping across the bridge, I caught sight of the tractor in the far corner where it had broken down yesterday.

Shit. I'd forgotten.

I was supposed to ask Ben if he could fix it.

Ben.

Forget it. Forget all of it. I turned around, ready to head back to my trailer, where I could pull the blankets up over my head and die in peace.

But there, like he'd been summoned. Standing on the bridge, in a gray tee shirt and a pair of khaki pants, toolbox in hand. Like a regular guy. Just a regular guy who'd never planned to kill two men and accidentally killed a little girl, was Ben.

He looked old. And frail. His skin was nearly gray. White around his mouth.

He was a sick old man who'd been kind to me. Very kind.

And I was scared of him.

I couldn't stop myself from stepping back. Reeling back, actually, I was so startled. So off balance.

And all I could think of was this guy tying two men to a chair, leaving them helpless, and then starting a fire for them to die in.

Did you know about the girl? The question surged, angry and righteous, to my lips—but I swallowed it back, where it smoldered in my belly.

Was Dylan somehow related to the little girl? Was that how this man fucked up his life?

"Hey, girly," Ben said. He was smiling. Actually smiling. And it somehow made him even more menacing. "You all right?"

"Hung over," I said, grateful for the rock-star sunglasses so he couldn't really see my eyes.

"I like your hair."

I'd forgotten. I lifted my hand to my hair, which felt unbelievably dry and stiff. Like a head full of hay. "Tiffany thought it would be a good idea."

"It's better than the black."

I was silent. Lost and shaky in the hangover and what I knew about him. What I thought about him now and what I'd thought about him yesterday morning.

"This is where you say thank you," he said.

"Thank you."

He walked past me toward the tractor. "Come on, now show me what's wrong with the engine."

I shouldn't, I thought, standing still, unable to move. Dylan . . . that article . . . even Joan had said stay away. My gut was screaming *stay away, now.*

And I had to listen to my gut.

"Annie?" he asked. "You coming?"

"No," I said. "I'm taking the day off. I can't . . ."

"Yeah," he laughed. "I can see that. I'll see what I can do about getting your tractor fixed."

And then he was gone and I . . . *Christ,* I was in ruins.

There was no chance of my going to the strip club that night. All I could do was lie in bed, eat chocolate chips by the handful, and look at that picture of Dylan in a tux. I could just see a slice of his chin, pink skin with a shadow of darker scruff. But the chest beneath that white shirt with the small black buttons looked wide. Solid.

The fact that Dylan went to parties in tuxes was mind-blowing in about a million different ways.

He goes to parties in tuxes and I go to parties in double-wides.

But he sent me that picture and that seemed . . . like something. Like . . . trust. I didn't know. I didn't have any kind of context for this fucked-up relationship. All I had were a million questions.

Starting with who the hell was Dylan?

When the phone rang, I was dozing but I woke up in a heartbeat, reaching for the phone.

"Layla?" Oh that voice, that eager jump in my heart, in my body at the sound of it.

"Hey."

"You okay?"

I smiled at his familiar opener. "Why do you always ask that?"

"Because that's the only thing that matters. Did I wake you up?"

"Not really. What about you?"

"I'm fine."

"I didn't get to the strip club."

"I guessed. Too hung over?"

"I feel like part of my soul is dying."

He laughed. "You'll get over it. Was that your first hangover?"

"No, actually." I shifted on the bed, pushing the chocolate chips away. Who needed chocolate when I had him on the other line? "I got very drunk at a wedding when I was a kid. While everyone was dancing I drank all the half-full glasses on the table. Amaretto stone sours were big."

"You barf?"

"Big time. What about you?"

"I don't drink much anymore," he said. "I used to."

"When you were wild?"

"When I was the wildest. Too many mornings with my head in a toilet."

"Now you're a man who goes to parties in tuxes."

He was silent for a minute. "I guess so."

The silence was thick. Telling. He did not want to talk about this. But I didn't really care.

"What do you do? Like for a job?"

"Something kind of stupid that people pay me a lot of money for."

"What—"

"Look, Layla, I told you I'd never lie to you. And I won't, but I can't tell you this."

"Are you a spy?" I tried to joke. "Is that it? You'd tell me but then you'd have to kill me?"

"I'd tell you and . . . shit would change."

"Because you're rich?"

"Because a lot of things, Layla. A lot of weird, shitty things that I really don't want to talk about."

It's not like I didn't understand; there were things that if I were to tell him would blow everything apart.

"Okay," I said.

"Did you see Ben today?"

"He's fixing something for me."

"Jesus Christ, Layla! What do I have to do to convince you?"

"Nothing. Nothing. I'm convinced. I didn't help him. I walked away."

"Good."

I put my head in my hands.

"But . . . he made me cornbread, Dylan." How does a guy kill two men and make cornbread?

He sighed. "Just because someone can be cruel doesn't mean they are incapable of kindness."

"Yes, it does," I said. The words were out before I could stop them. I didn't want to talk about Hoyt. I didn't want to even think about him. His cruelty had left no room for kindness. And the basic decency he'd shown, combined with his calculation, had, in my lowest moments, convinced me he'd been kind. And it had been so easy for him, so easy, because I'd been so starved, so impossibly void of kindness.

I'd been a fool. An easy mark.

Dylan was silent for a long time. "Who hurt you, Layla?"

I stared up at the pocked ceiling of this trailer I'd claimed as my own and the words, the real words—*my husband, my husband hurt me*—didn't come. But it's not like Hoyt was the only one who'd hurt me. My mom had unknowingly spent years tenderizing me for Hoyt. Teaching me to be small and to be scared.

"My mom was . . . not well. Mentally. Not really."

"Like what?"

"You don't want to talk about this—"

"Let me be the judge of that. What was wrong with your mom?"

"I'm not sure. It's not like she went to the doctor. Or like we ever really talked about it. She was real paranoid and she'd go through these weeks when she'd be . . . just furious. The world wasn't right. And everyone was coming after her. And then it would go away and she'd be . . . sad. Hard to get out of bed some days."

"Jesus."

"It was what it was, you know? I learned how to stay out of her way when she was mad, and how to try and cheer her up when she was sad, and I learned how to work . . . like so fucking hard all the time in the hopes that she wouldn't be either. It never worked, but I kept trying."

"Where was your dad?"

"Not around and not talked about. Not ever." I closed my eyes, the past, its mistakes, so close I could touch them. I could hold them in my hand where they burned and hurt. I deserved this . . . the pain over this was one I shouldn't have been shoving away.

"There . . . there was one man, Smith."

And suddenly, I felt tears burning behind my eyes.

Oh, I wasn't sure I could talk about this. I'd never talked about Smith and what I'd done to him. I'd actually managed to stop thinking about him; in the constant triage of my life, I'd been able to push this awful thing out of my mind, but now it was here.

From the moment I'd met Ben, Smith had started to haunt me.
"Layla?"

My hands were shaking and my stomach hurt and the regrets on my shoulders were so big and so awful I couldn't pretend anymore. What I did to him, I could no longer hide from.

"He worked on the ranch most of my life and he was kind of a father to me. Taught me how to change tires and shoot a gun. We used to play chess at night on the porch in the summer and he'd never let me win. Not ever. So when I finally beat him, it was like . . ." I smiled, remembering how I'd done this victory lap around the porch and Mom and Smith had laughed. "A big deal."

"Sounds like a good guy."

"He was the best. The best guy. And I think my mother loved him. As much as she was capable of that stuff."

That was my best guess. My best understanding through the filter of my strange childhood. Mom loved him, this virile cowboy, a former marine.

There were rumors in town that he used to drink, or that he'd had some dark past, and every once in a while some woman at church would get brave and ask Mom if she thought it was such a good idea to have a man like Smith out at the farm where we were so isolated. So alone.

Mom ignored those women.

I, of course, had no idea what those women were talking about. Smith was . . . Smith. With the rusty teasing and the broken-up hand and the up-at-dawn work ethic.

He was silent and steady.

He would never have hurt me. Hurt us.

And I crushed him. Kicked him out of that house, out of the only home he'd ever known.

"Did he love her?"

"I don't know. He must have felt something for her to stick around . . ."

"Maybe he loved you. Thought of you like a daughter."

My breath was broken and sharp and hurt inside my body.

"I think . . . I think you're right."

Smith had stood behind me at Mom's funeral, his hand on my shoulder. Holding me up when I wanted to fall down.

Don't marry that boy, he'd said when Hoyt and I announced our engagement.

It's fine, I'd said. *We're in love,* I'd said. *Hoyt's a good man,* I'd said.

"He's the man I fired," I told Dylan. "After Mom died, there was another . . . person who started helping me with the farm and I . . . I was convinced I had to fire Smith."

Oh, it was awful to remember. A sickening day.

Hoyt convinced me—I don't remember what words he used, what argument he could offer that would turn me against the one person in my entire life I could count on. My only friend. All I remembered was his hands around my wrist, holding me so hard I thought the bones would break. Like he'd just grind them to dust.

"Annie," Smith said. *"I can't leave you here alone. I can't."*

"I'm not alone, Smith. I'm married, and my husband and I are making some changes."

"You regret it?" Dylan asked.

Regret, God. What a tame word. What a silly cage for all the awfulness I felt about Smith.

"When I think about it, I want to throw up," I said.

Who knows how different my life would have been if I hadn't fired Smith? I would have had help. Support. Hoyt would never have been able to sell that land. To hurt me.

And that's why Hoyt convinced me that Smith had to leave. Because he knew.

"Do you know where he is?" Dylan asked.

"He had a sister in Wyoming. That's all I knew. I . . . I made a point of not knowing." Because I was a coward.

He made a low, rumbling sound of dissent. Like he had some problem with that, of my making a point of not knowing.

"What?" I asked.

"Nothing, baby. It's late, and hangovers have a way of bringing out all the garbage. Go to sleep. Things will be better in the morning."

I had my doubts that anything would be better in the morning.

16

THE NEXT MORNING THE TRACTOR WAS FIXED AND PARKED JUST outside the shed. Ben had changed the oil, too. And at the end of the day, Kevin shuffled out to the field to pay me for my third week of work.

"I didn't see you yesterday," he said, giving me the envelope with the small amount of cash tucked inside. The rest paid the rent on my trailer.

"I wasn't feeling very well."

"Yeah, I heard about your little party. Next time—"

"Keep it down. We will." If there was a next time. The one-two punch of Bebe and the kids being gone seemed like a pretty rare event. And frankly, I wasn't entirely sure I could survive another night like that.

The hangover had nearly swallowed me whole.

"No. Invite me. I love a good girls' night."

Once again I had no idea if he was joking or not.

"You seen Ben around today?" he asked.

"No, why?"

"Nothing. Just haven't seen him. He usually comes up to the office to get a paper. Didn't get one yesterday, either."

"Maybe he's sick," I said, thinking about that cough he had. How he hadn't looked all that good yesterday on the bridge.

"Yeah. You're right," Kevin said, and lumbered off in his Adidas shower sandals toward the ice-cave office.

Christ, I thought, *is that it?* Really? Kevin was just going to turn around and not check on Ben? Who might be sick?

We keep to our own, he'd said when I first met him. And he wasn't joking.

I put my cash in my pocket and headed back over to the laundry building to grab my things from the dryer. I'd had to rewash everything because it spent that night I'd been so drunk in the washing machine, getting stinky.

Tiffany was out in front of her trailer, emptying a bucket of water in the bushes.

"Hey," I said with a happy leap in my chest at the sight of her.

She turned and gave me a wan smile.

"Still feeling rough?" I asked.

"So rough. Oh my God, Bucket-o-Colada was a bad idea. But your hair looks fucking awesome."

"It's really dry," I said, feeling the brittle edges.

"Yeah. You gotta condition the shit out of it."

"I'll have to get some next time I go to town."

"Wait." Tiffany went back inside her trailer and came out with a few foil sample packs. "Take these—"

"I can't," I said, thinking about Phil and her kids and how she'd said they were late on all their payments.

"Take them," she said. "Please. It's . . . it's nice to give someone something for a change, you know?"

I nodded and took the packets, shoving them in my pocket with the money.

I was so rich all of a sudden.

"Your kids must be coming home soon."

Her pale face lightened at the mention of her kids. "Yeah. Mom's gonna drop them off in an hour."

"How was the bad television marathon?" I asked.

She smiled. "I slept through it. And Bebe had to leave at two, so it was kind of anticlimactic."

"Your sister was pretty awesome."

"She is. She's going to college at night and works full time, so she doesn't get a whole lot of time to take off like that. Bebe is the best. I wouldn't—" She stopped and shook her head, and I remembered her finger against my neck, that grief in her eyes. And I knew that place so well. Not that I ever had friends, or encouragement or help, but I remembered feeling like an open wound to the world.

"Would she help you get away from Phil?" I asked, taking a leap off the bridge right into her problems.

Her eyes narrowed at me. "It's none of your goddamn business, but I don't need to get away from Phil. I need him to hold down a job."

I blinked at her tone, surprised. That night at the sink, she'd looked so broken. "I'm sorry," I said. "I didn't mean to—"

"Put your nose in? God, what is it with you and Joan? We're married, we're working shit out, and I don't need you guys."

"I'm sorry."

"Whatever," she said, and went back inside with her mop and bucket.

After a moment I turned away and got my clothes, ratty and holey. But clean.

I put my things away and caught sight through my bedroom window of Ben's trailer. Dark. Quiet. I went into the kitchen and looked out the window at his garden. Dark. Quiet.

Shit.

What if he was really sick in there? Or worse? What if he was dying—right now—and Kevin couldn't be bothered to check up on him?

And I was too chicken.

Gah.

I slammed my way out of my trailer and stomped past Joan's. Inside I could hear the bass line of some heavy rock song. The closer I got to Ben's, though, the quieter it seemed. The darker.

As I knocked on the door, I could feel my heartbeat in the palms of my hands.

I really didn't want to have to break in there and find him sick in bed or dead on the floor or anything, really, in between.

"Ben?" I said when initially there wasn't an answer.

I knocked again and from inside the trailer I heard a thump.

"What!" he said, wrenching open the screen door. He looked awful. Up to this moment, I'd only ever seen him in neatly pressed tee shirts, his hair tidy, his pants clean. But now, he wore dirty sweatpant cutoffs and a white tee shirt stained with dark red and black spots down the front.

"Ben!" I cried. "Are you all right?"

"Peachy. Fucking peachy. What do you—" He coughed hard into his hand, where he held a red bandana. He coughed for like a minute and then when he was done, he spit into the bandana, wadded it up in a ball, and tossed it into the sink. "What do you want, Annie?" he sighed, sounding utterly worn.

"I just . . . I wanted to check on you. Kevin said he hadn't seen you today."

"I'm under the weather."

"I can see that . . . Do you need anything?"

Ben's eyes were dark. Very dark, nearly black it seemed, and utterly unreadable. Whether he was grieving or angry or sad or scared, I couldn't tell. They were blacked-out windows, through which I could see nothing.

"I'm fine," he sighed. "Thank you for asking. It's just . . . just a cold—" Then, right in front of my eyes, he blanched and his eyes rolled back. I jerked open the door and grabbed his shoulder with one hand and his arm with the other, and held him up as best I could.

"Ben!" Was he fainting?

"Christ, girl, I'm right here," he whispered, pulling away from me.

"Come on." I wouldn't let him pull away. I put my arm around his shoulders and half-led, half-shoved him toward his settee. Once he was sitting, I started opening up cupboards, looking for water glasses.

"Where are your cups?"

"In the sink," he said. "I've got one in the sink."

I filled the cup with water and set it down in front of him. With both hands shaking, he picked it up and managed to dribble half of it down his chest. "Fuck," he breathed, setting it down. "I feel like shit."

"It's just a cold?"

"Flu maybe? Who the hell knows?"

"You got anything to eat?"

He pointed over to the stove, where he'd been pouring chicken noodle soup from a Tupperware container into a saucepan.

"You want this?"

"Yeah." I put the rest of it in the pan and then turned on a burner.

"You made homemade chicken noodle soup?"

"No. I got a lady-friend that made it."

From outside, a woman shouted, "Hey, you old fart, I got you some meds!"

You could have knocked me over with a pin when Joan walked into the trailer like she owned it.

I turned and lifted an eyebrow at Ben. Was Joan his lady-friend?

"Don't be ridiculous," he muttered.

"Well, well, you guys are cozy. Is his hacking all night keeping you up too?" Joan asked, stepping over to the table. She tipped a plastic bag out, dumping all kinds of cold medicine onto the table. Daytime formulas, nighttime formulas, sinus stuff, pain reliever. There was about a hundred dollars' worth of over-the-counter medicine on that table.

"Something here should fix you," Joan said, and then she turned to me and crossed her arms over her chest. "What are you doing here?" she asked.

"Making sure he's not dead." I stirred the soup when it started to bubble on the stove.

"Yeah, we can't have Ben die, can we?"

"I'm alive," he muttered. "Now both of you go away."

"Later!" Joan said, lifting her hands up. "And you're welcome. For the medicine."

"Fuck your medicine."

"Lovely," Joan said. "You coming?" she asked me.

"Yeah, just . . ." I tested the temperature of the soup and then poured it into a bowl, turned off the stove, and put the bowl down in front of Ben. "Are you sure you're okay?" I asked him. He really looked sick, and what was the deal with the weird dried blood on his shirt?

Not my business was what it was.

"Fine," he said with a wan smile. "And thank you."

"Right," Joan muttered, "her he thanks. Let's go, Florence Nightingale," she said, nearly dragging me away.

Once we were outside and on the other side of her trailer, she turned.

"What the hell did I say to you?" she asked. "Stay away from the old man, Annie!"

"What were you doing bringing him a hundred dollars in cold medicine?" I asked.

"A hundred and fifty—that sinus stuff is expensive. He wakes up at six in the morning hacking away like he's going to cough up a lung. I get home at three, I can't fucking take it."

"Right. Kevin asked me to look in on him," I lied.

Joan heaved a big sigh. "Fine . . . just, honestly, Annie. Don't get friendly."

I wondered if Joan knew about the fire. The girl asleep upstairs. Probably, I decided. Joan seemed to know plenty.

"I gotta get to work," Joan said, checking her watch. "I'll see you later."

Oh God, she would. She would see me later at The Velvet Touch. Or rather, maybe I would see her.

A lot of her.

WHAT DOES ONE WEAR TO A STRIP CLUB?

It wasn't like I had a whole lot of choices. In the end I picked my nicest shorts—which meant they didn't have any holes. They were black and shorter than my other ones, which I thought made them sort of sexy. And I wore my maroon tank-top camisole, which I usually slept in.

I used two of the conditioner packets on my hair and it was actually soft and lying at least a little bit flat against my head, instead of sticking up like a haystack.

With my tan and a little lip gloss and mascara . . . it wasn't half bad, I thought.

I spent the evening re-reading my favorite parts of *Fifty Shades of Grey* and I didn't touch myself once, so I would be too worked up to chicken out. And truthfully, it would have been nice to have a bucket-o-something to get my courage up.

But at eleven o'clock I put down the book, grabbed my keys, and crossed the point of no return.

The Velvet Touch was three exits back on the highway. It was a dark, cement-bunker-type building sitting in a vast sea of parking, with a billboard so big and so pink it could probably be seen in space.

The parking lot was half full of pickup trucks and big rigs, and there were a half dozen motorcycles lined up near the entrance. The chrome reflected the lights and the black silhouettes of naked women on the billboard.

My courage was flagging, so I pulled out my phone and called Dylan.

"Hey, baby," he said. "You okay?"

"I'm sitting in the parking lot of the strip club."

The sound he made low in his throat was sexy. "Having second thoughts?"

"No. I mean . . . I'm nervous."

"Nervous is okay. Nervous is exciting. This is naughty, baby. And you like naughty."

"Yeah, but . . . what do I do?"

"You're going to walk in those doors, order a drink, find a dark corner, and you and me, we're going to talk about what you're seeing. How it makes you feel."

"What if it doesn't make me feel anything?"

"Slip your fingers down your pants, baby."

"Dylan . . ."

"Do it."

Rolling my eyes despite the fact he couldn't see, I sucked in my belly and shoved my fingers down my pants past the thin elastic of my underwear.

I gasped when my fingers brushed my clit and then again when I felt how wet I was. In my nerves I hadn't noticed.

"What did you find?" he asked, like he knew. But of course he knew. Somehow he knew everything about this.

"I'm wet," I whispered.

"Tell me."

"I'm so slippery," I moaned low in my throat, giving in to the feeling.

"Don't come," he said, his voice sharp, like he knew what I was doing.

"I'm so close," I protested.

"Go inside. Call me when you get there."

He hung up, and reluctantly I pulled my hand out of my pants.

I didn't give myself a second to doubt what I was doing. It was just like getting out of my car in front of the grocery store.

Here goes nothing, I thought and started to pull open the big outer door, but just as I pulled, someone pushed and I nearly fell back on my ass.

"Whoa there," a man said, reaching out to grab me before I fell. He was big, with a round belly and a long beard.

"Knocking women over again?" asked another guy coming out behind him. They both wore black leather vests over their shirts. A third man came out, younger than the other two, and taller. Bigger seeming, though he was actually kind of thin. He had dark hair and his eyes, when they ran over me, made me wish I had on a bunch more clothes. Like a snowsuit.

Bad news. That's what my gut said. That man was the worst kind of news.

"Let's go," he said, dismissing me the moment after he saw me.

"You all right?" the bearded guy asked and I nodded, and the men got on three of the bikes and roared away.

Shit, I thought. This was ridiculous. I would tell Dylan that he had to come up with something else. Something less . . . extreme. I could go skinny-dipping again. Or watch some porn— I'm not sure where, the library? Could I do that at the library?

Anything would be easier than this.

But you want this, I thought. And you like that it's hard.

"You coming in?" a giant black man standing on the other side of the open door asked me. "It's Ladies' Night."

"Ladies' Night?" I stammered.

"You get in free and drinks are half off."

"Are there . . . other women in there?"

The man's face broke into a smile. "Yeah. You ain't alone, you little perv."

He said it with such easygoing affection that I laughed.

Oh Lord, I thought, stepping into the club. *If my mother could see me now.*

THE MUSIC WAS LOUD.

So loud that it actually kind of emptied my head of some of the noise I was producing. Some of the fear. The rug under my feet was threadbare and shabby and the lights were low. Some of them fluorescent.

Nice big chairs were gathered around small round tables and most of them were full. The stage was lined with men watching the act and girls walked in and around the tables, flirting and smiling, selling drinks. Selling sex.

I don't know what I expected. Something shabby, and yes, it was shabby. Lewd, too.

I totally expected something degrading. I expected women with soul-dead eyes to be pawed at by men with cigars clamped between their teeth and a kind of awful shaming lust in their eyes.

And maybe the women dancing and walking around in G-strings and sitting on men's laps and leading them into dark and shadowy corners, maybe they felt degraded, but they were hiding it really well. Lying about it.

And the whole place was in on the lie.

I was in on the lie. I needed to believe these women were all right. So . . . I just did.

One thing was for sure: they had amazing bodies. Like truly . . . lush and feminine, but strong, too. The woman onstage did some kind of crazy maneuver where she grabbed the pole and somehow turned herself upside down and then, from the top of the pole, using only her legs, slid down in slow circles.

Her breasts—they had to be fake—didn't even twitch.

And I wondered what I would do if I had a body like that. If I could do that. Would I choose to shovel disgusting torn-up dirty diapers out of a bed of garbage and weeds, gagging the whole time, making far less than minimum wage? Or would I do something like this?

A man in the front row, a young man in a backwards cap sitting with some of his friends, held out a twenty-dollar bill, and the girl crawled over on her hands and knees and took it from him with her teeth.

Her eyes and her smile were inviting and flirty. Sexy.

Layla would have done something like this. For sure.

The thought of Layla, the persona of her, slipped over me, and the screaming of my raw nerves and terrible misgivings became muted. There, but in the background. Something I would worry about tomorrow, maybe.

I stepped to the left of the entryway and took it all in.

The women were putting on a show. And again, I bought it. I don't know what that said about me. But I bought it and the carnality of it all, the sheer sexual suggestiveness of it, seeped into my skin and turned me on.

Like *holy hell* it turned me on.

"You want a drink?" A woman came up to my elbow, wearing a sheer black tank top that had been torn in half, the ragged hem of it just barely covering the bottoms of her nipples. She wore neon-yellow underwear and thigh-high fishnets that had been ripped in places. She looked like the sexy survivor of an apocalypse. "Hon'?"

"A piña colada?" I wish I could say that that was the first thing I could think of, but the truth was, if my reaction to Bucket-o-Colada was any indication, I loved piña coladas.

"Sure thing."

She walked away, stopping at tables as she went. I expected guys to grab her ass or something, yank on her. But no one did. They looked. And they leered. But it seemed pretty hands-off.

There were giant guys without necks standing in the shadows, keeping an eye on all things.

"What the fuck are you doing here?" Suddenly Joan was in front of me in a red push-up bra and black ruffled panties. She was more covered up than any other woman working in the bar, but somehow the sexiest.

And she was furious.

"Hey, Joan," I said lamely.

"I repeat, what the fuck are you doing here?"

17

SHE PULLED ME OUT OF THE SPOT I'D CLAIMED AND PAST A FEW groups of men who watched us as we went.

"Who's your friend, Joan?" one of the guys asked. His calculating eyes followed us and his joking had a heavy dose of mean to it. "You gonna give her a lap dance?"

"Fuck off, Steve," she said.

"Can we watch?"

She ignored him, still pulling me into the shadows past the chairs around the stage.

Once we were in a corner dark and quiet enough, Joan stopped and turned on me, her hands on her hips. Behind her there was a girl on a man's lap. His hands grabbing her ass, grinding her into him.

My entire body went hot and then cold. Between my legs, I got so wet. I swallowed a groan, watching that man's fingers bite into her ass, the skin turning white and pink beneath his touch.

What does that feel like? I wondered, breathless and riveted.

The stripper had her hand up, braced against the wall behind the man's head, her dark hair thrown back. The guy reached up and grabbed a handful of it and pulled.

I could hear the woman groan from five feet away.

And here's the thing—I'd been on the bad end of all of that. I'd been hurt—but I could see the difference here. I could feel it in my body. In the air that we were all breathing in and out.

"Hey!" Joan snapped in front of my face, tearing my attention away from the couple in the corner. "Why are you here?"

"I . . . I'm . . ." *playing this weird game with a man I've never met, and he told me if I want to have phone sex with him again, I have to go to a strip club.*

No way could I say that.

"Is this some kind of weird stalker thing?" she asked. "Because the last thing I need right now is to have a weird stalker living beside me and following me to work!"

"What? No!" I cried. "No. I'm not . . . I'm not stalking you."

"Are you gay? Because I've seen the way you look at me."

I shook my head, so embarrassed I was pretty sure my cheeks were glowing. That day at the swimming hole. She'd noticed. Of course she'd noticed; I was about as subtle as a sledgehammer. "No. I'm not gay—"

"Bi?"

"Bi-what?"

"Sexual, you idiot! Do you like men and women?"

"I don't . . ." I hadn't really processed that. This weird attraction I had to Joan's body. It was beautiful as a thing. Sexy as a concept. But I didn't want to touch her.

I wanted to touch Dylan.

I wanted Dylan to touch me.

It was strange that I'd never really thought that before. Or looked past the parameters of this thing we were doing. Yes, the phone sex was . . . amazing and exciting, and his voice alone was enough to make me crazy. But what I really wanted was to be the couple in the corner.

I wanted him to grab me like that, to pull me and push me. I wanted him to make me groan.

I didn't have the slightest clue what Dylan really looked like. He could be fat and hairy and all kinds of ugly—but it didn't matter.

Because that was who I wanted. That man on the phone who'd never been a normal sixteen-year-old. Who called me back because he was worried that I was scared. Who texted me pictures of himself in a tux, like he knew he looked good.

"No," I said. "I'm not bisexual or gay or stalking you. I've got this thing with a guy . . ."

"Same guy who gave you the bruises?"

"No." *Oh, God no.* "Different guy. We do this thing on the phone—"

"Say no more," Joan said, lifting up her hand, her face changing from confused and angry to begrudgingly respectful. "I don't need details. And I have to say, I wouldn't have pegged you for the type."

"Here you are!" The waitress who took my order came up the small steps with a big, fancy glass with fruit sticking out of it on her tray. "I couldn't find you."

"Thank you," I said, digging into my pocket for one of the twenties Dylan gave me.

"I got it," Joan said. "Thanks, Denise."

"No problem," Denise said and she walked away.

"So?" Joan asked. "What are you going to do here?"

"Watch women dance, I guess."

She gave me a long look. "How daring do you want to be?"

"It was pretty damn daring just walking in the door, trust me."

"Yeah, but you're here now. What are you going to do?"

"I'm supposed to call him . . ." I trailed off and glanced over her shoulder, back at that dark corner. The girl was now facing me, still on the guy's lap, plastered really all along his chest and legs, like she'd been poured on him. Her eyes were closed and her face . . . well, if she was acting, if she was pretending to be turned on—she was totally convincing.

As I watched, the man's hand slipped down across her tummy to cover her entire pussy, which was bare except for a small heart-shaped patch of hair. She twitched against him, her hand covering his, and as I watched, I wondered if she was going to lift that hand away. If that was against the rules or something.

But instead she held it there, grinding it against her, while she was grinding against him.

This. This moment. This was the hottest thing I'd ever seen.

"That's Destiny," Joan said. "Her real name is Renee, and when the song switches over she's going to stand up, take that guy by the hand, and lead him over there." She pointed to a dark alcove covered in one of those cheesy beaded curtains. "There's a door there that leads back to the VIP room."

"What's she going to do there?" I whispered.

"Fuck him, maybe. Blow him for sure."

Blow him. My entire body clenched tight.

"You want to call your guy and share something with him tonight, go in there now. Sit way back in the corner and watch them."

"What?"

"Happens all the time. Husbands sit back there and watch their wives fuck another woman."

"But . . . won't they care?"

I was considering it. I was. Even before I consciously realized it I was halfway in that room.

"No. I'll let her know you're there. I'll tell her about the phone. As long as you don't take pictures it's cool. She digs that shit. Probably put on a really good show for you."

I was breathing hard. And my hand around the drink was numb from the cold.

"Music's gonna change. Yes or no."

"Why are you doing this?"

"What is it with you and the whys?" Joan asked, rolling her eyes.

I didn't know. I really didn't.

"Your guy is going to dig it," she said, prodding me on.

Yes. He was.

"Okay," I said. "But, Renee, is she . . . ?" God, I didn't know how to say it. "Does she have kids? Or like some kind of terrible drug habit? Or a dad who used to sneak into her room at night—"

"Is she a victim?"

"Yeah."

"Does it matter?"

I gave Joan a long look. "Yeah."

"Oh good God, Annie. I don't ask her about her life. She's tough. She's smart and she doesn't take shit from anyone."

"Really?"

"Really. And she's freaky as shit."

I took one giant long draw of my drink and then set it down on the table, nearly running toward the curtained doorway. I slipped between the beads and there was a small hallway with two doorways, and at the end, a red illuminated exit sign.

Shit. Which door?

I opened the first. Inside it was thick with cigarette smoke, and there was a table with five men sitting around it. All of them turned to stare at me when I walked in.

"Wrong door, sister," one of them said. A thin man with the bluest eyes I'd ever seen. Kind eyes. I have no idea why I got that impression in the three seconds I was face-to-face with him, but I did. And he was wearing a linen suit. At a strip club. That's all I could see through the haze of smoke.

"Sorry," I said, getting out of there as fast as I could. I spun around and opened the second door.

Inside was a small room with two big leather couches. In

the shadows in the far corner there was the gleam of another leather chair, and I made a beeline for it before all my courage deserted me.

I tucked my legs up under me and tried to be as small as I possibly could and called Dylan.

"Are you still in the parking lot?" he asked, his voice teasing.

"No," I whispered. "I'm in a VIP room. I'm going to watch . . ."

The door opened again and in walked Renee, who was like seven feet tall in her outrageous sequined heels. The guy she was with came in behind her, his hand wide across her belly, keeping them together.

God, my breathing sounded so loud. And I shifted in the chair and the leather creaked. I closed my eyes, my hands across my mouth.

It hadn't even started and I was ruining this.

"Hit the button, baby," Renee said. And the man, who'd clearly been here before, reached over and tapped a button on a black box on the wall and music filled the room.

I turned my phone so no one could see the glow. Or at least I hoped they couldn't.

Renee turned them a little better so they were almost facing me head on, though there was twenty feet between us. The lighting was super dim but I saw her face.

She winked at me.

"Layla," Dylan murmured. "Are there people in there with you?"

"Yes," I breathed as quietly as I could, watching Renee and the guy to see if they heard me. They were locked on each other, the music blocking out any sound of my voice for them.

"What do you want?" Renee asked and for a second I thought she was asking me, but the man spoke up.

"Your mouth on my cock," he said, and Renee laughed and

then gasped when the man's hands came up and cupped her breasts. Palmed them.

"Can you hear that?" I whispered to Dylan.

"Yeah, baby, I heard. You're watching a blow job." His voice, *oh, God,* his voice was so thick. So heavy. I could feel how turned on he was.

"What do you want?" the guy on the couch asked Renee.

"My mouth on your cock," Renee said.

His dark laughter rumbled through the room. "This is why we work."

This is why we work. I could say the same thing to Dylan right now.

Renee stepped away from the guy and gave him a shove over to the couch. He fell back willingly, and she grabbed a pillow from beside him and tossed it on the floor at his feet.

"Tell me," Dylan ground out in my ear.

"She's kneeling in front of him."

Quickly, Renee undid the guy's pants, her eyes flicking occasionally up to his. He was biting his lips, his hands up on his head, like he was trying hard not to touch her. Like he didn't want to ruin the show.

And then she reached into the shadows of his open pants and pulled out his dick.

"Fuck, baby, go," he breathed.

Renee closed her fist around him and pumped him slowly, from bottom to top.

Like Dylan.

"She's touching him the way you like it," I whispered. "Hard."

Dylan groaned. The guy on the couch groaned.

"You want more?" Renee asked. And she could have been asking all of us; she had us all in the palm of her hand right now.

"Yeah," the guy said.

"Yes," I breathed.

Oh God. Forget about being quiet. Forget about not being noticed—I was going to go up in flames in this corner. Literally spontaneously combust.

"Touch yourself," the guy said, and again, my mouth fell open. Was he talking to me?

But he was talking to Renee, who slipped a hand down between her legs.

"Show me how wet you are," the guy said.

"Yeah?" In the shadows it was too dark to really see what she was doing, but I got the idea when she lifted her hand and held it up to the man's face.

"Taste how wet I am."

The man opened his mouth and Renee slipped her fingers in. The guy groaned. Renee groaned. I nearly died in my chair.

"She touched herself and put her fingers in his mouth," I told Dylan.

"How do you think she tastes?" Dylan asked.

"Good," I breathed.

"Do it. Touch yourself and taste your fingers for me. Right now."

I wanted to put my fingers in Dylan's mouth. I wanted him to taste me. I wanted him to look at me the way this guy was looking at Renee. The way I was looking at Renee.

But he was on the phone and not here, so I did what he said. Traced the edges of my lips with my fingers, gathered up the slickness there, and then put the fingers in my mouth. I moaned.

"Sweet?" he asked.

"Yes," I whispered.

Renee bent and licked the guy's dick, top to bottom, doing some kind of swirl thing over the head that seemed to make the guy go nuts.

"Suck, just suck, baby," he groaned. "I want to come in your mouth."

"She put his dick in her mouth," I whispered.

"Where are his hands?" Dylan asked.

"On his head. He's . . . watching."

"Does it look good?"

"Yes."

"You want to come?" Dylan asked.

"So bad."

Soon, the guy dropped his hands, tangling his fingers into her hair, and he was holding her head, lifting his hips to ease in and out of her mouth.

"Do it, baby," Dylan whispered. "Make yourself come."

His permission made my heart pound, my fingers clumsy, and my nails scratched my skin as I slipped my hand down between my legs and through my shorts, I pressed up hard against my clit. I flinched I was so turned on.

"Oh, yeah," the guy groaned, and Renee's hand was a blur and I bit my lips against the sounds climbing up my throat. I stuck my hand down my shorts until it was buried in the liquid fire between my legs. It took nothing. One touch, another against the pulsing knot of my clit, and I was coming.

Coming so hard I saw stars.

"Oh fuck, yeah. Fuck—"

It was the guy. Not me. I was biting my tongue until it bled, trying not to make any sound.

And then he groaned and Renee slowly pumped her fist against him, holding the head of his dick in her mouth while he jerked. I tried to get my breath back slowly. Quietly. But I thought I might hyperventilate.

"So good, baby," the guy breathed, reaching for Renee. "Let's do you."

"I need to get back. Zo is going to get pissed."

"Fuck Zo."

She shot him a wry look. "Say that to his face."

The guy stood and zipped up his pants while Renee fluffed

her hair and dug a piece of gum out of the guy's pocket. He gave her a big, wet smacking kiss on the cheek and then opened the door and stepped out into the hallway.

Renee stood in the open doorway and glanced back in the shadows toward me with a smile.

"Hope you enjoyed that," she said, and then she was gone.

And I . . . sweaty and wet and shocked and still a little turned on . . . couldn't be sure what exactly I was. But it was different than I was before I walked into this place, that was for sure.

"Layla?" Dylan asked.

"They're gone," I breathed. Replete and keyed up at the same time.

"You liked that?"

"Yes. Did you?"

"Yes."

"Did you come?" I asked. I'd been so enthralled by what I'd been watching and what was happening in my own body that I wasn't sure if I'd heard him or not.

"No."

"Do it now. Do it for me." Words tumbled out of my mouth, describing what I'd seen, but putting the two of us in the scene. "Imagine I'm on my knees in front of you and I've got your cock in my hand. I'm licking you slow. All the way around, and I put the head in my mouth."

"I've got my hands in your hair," he said. "I'm pushing you down, seeing how much you can take. I want my whole cock buried inside of you."

My hand slipped down my pants again, my fingers squeezing my clit.

"I want that too," I whisper. "I want all of you inside of me."

"I'm gonna come," he breathed.

"Please," I whispered. "Come inside me. Let me taste you."

He groaned and cried out and I did the same.

The only sound in the room was the two of us breathing hard and the forgotten radio playing some dance music.

"You okay?" he asked as I lay there, boneless and sweating. Between my legs I ached.

This isn't enough anymore. The thought came out of nowhere. And for a second I wanted to deny it. This was the hottest, most exciting thing I'd ever done in my life. There was no way it couldn't be enough.

But somehow it wasn't. I felt empty. I ached for more than my fingers and the sound of his voice in my ear.

I wanted Dylan. The reality of him.

"Layla?" he asked when I was silent.

"I'm good," I said. "You?"

"So good."

"I'm going to go home," I said.

"Call me when you get there."

I LEFT THE ROOM AND HEADED OUT THE SMALL EXIT DOOR TO the right instead of going out through the bar, trying to push aside my vague disappointment as some kind of weird reaction to the increasingly bold and daring stuff I was doing.

Instead I concentrated on how freaking crazy it was to have done that.

Me. Annie McKay.

I cannot believe I did that, I thought driving home. I kept laughing. And then cringing. Sighing with anguished excitement.

I cannot believe I did that, I thought in the shower, my hands running over my body. The soap and the water turning everything to silk.

I did not have a stripper's figure. Not by a long shot. But I was strong and my skin was soft and I was living in my body. All the corners. All the edges. There was not a part of me that I did not feel right now and it was so perfect.

For years I'd been rattling around inside my skin, trying to get smaller and smaller so when the smacks and the pinches and the shoves came, Hoyt might hurt my body, but he wouldn't hurt me. I never really thought he could tell, that he'd even really noticed me beyond those moments when he was angry.

I'd been wrong. Really, really wrong.

I dried off my skin and in the darkness I walked from the bathroom to my bedroom where the full moon was filtered out a bit by the curtains, which were blowing a little in the breeze.

I went to a strip club tonight. I made myself come while watching a woman give a guy a blow job.

"Who am I?" I laughed, dropped my towel, and lay down, naked on the bed.

But then, a few seconds later, I sat up and grabbed clean underwear from the drawer. I couldn't explain it. It just felt better to have on underwear. But at least now it was a choice and not a fear.

Point for me.

Excitement and anticipation were battling it out inside me and I felt like Charlie in the Willy Wonka movie when he and his grandfather were laughing and floating up to the ceiling.

I was so damn happy. And proud of myself. I get it—a stupid thing to be proud of, going to a strip club. It wasn't like I was curing cancer. But still . . . I was proud.

For the first time in my life, I was proud of myself.

And I booted up the phone and called Dylan, like a sheep to the slaughter. It rang three times and then his voice mail kicked in.

But it was a woman's voice on the recording.

This is Dylan Daniels. Please leave a message and someone will get back to you within one business day.

18

WHAT WAS THAT?

One business day? A woman's voice—like a secretary?

And Dylan's last name was Daniels. How crazy that I didn't know that. That it was so incredibly shocking to learn that now.

Dylan Daniels.

I hung up before I left a message and stared at the phone like it was a snake.

Quickly, a text message appeared on my screen.

Dylan: Hey. Give me ten minutes. In the middle of something.

It was one o'clock in the morning. Who was in the middle of something at one o'clock in the morning?

After what we'd done at the club?

For the first time it occurred to me to scroll through the phone's features. I checked to see if by some miracle the Flowered Manor had free Wi-Fi and the phone was hooked up to it.

Would you believe no free Wi-Fi?

I would have to go back to town tomorrow, to the library, if I wanted to find out anything about him. Stalk him on the internet like other girls my age.

My phone buzzed in my hands with an incoming call. I felt somehow as if I'd slipped into water way over my head. Why did everything feel so different now?

"Hey," I said. So much of my excitement and anticipation had taken a turn and I was anxious. Uncomfortable.

"Hey, you okay?"

"Fine. What are you in the middle of at one o'clock in the morning?" *Who the hell are you?*

"Just a meeting, a fucking boring nightmare meeting. We just finished. Are you—Jesus Christ," he muttered. "Baby, I gotta call you back in a second. I swear to God, I'm going to kill some idiots around here tonight. You gonna be awake?"

"Yeah."

"Good. Don't fall asleep."

I hung up and wondered if I should head back out on the highway toward one of the truck stops with the free Wi-Fi. But then, in some weird moment of clarity, I decided it didn't matter. It didn't matter who he was. All he was to me was the guy on the other end of this phone. The guy that pushed me farther and faster out of my terrified little box than I ever would have gone on my own. Maybe he would tell me in time.

Maybe not.

But I had no intention of telling him who I was. Who I really was, and why I was in this last-ditch trailer park, looking for any crack in my self-made, Annie McKay prison through which I could escape.

I couldn't be hypocritical.

If he was a mobster, a spy, a male model, a politician—none of it mattered.

So he was Dylan. Just Dylan.

And I was Layla.

And I didn't need to know anything more about him, but I still wanted to see him. Touch him.

Have him.

I scrolled through the phone features and found the camera.

I held it up slightly and kind of squished my upper arms against my breasts so they weren't sliding into my armpits and I put my hand down the front of my pink panties. One leg bent at the knee. I took a picture and checked it.

Ugh. Too much knee, no boob.

I tried again and then again.

Finally in the fourth picture my freckles didn't look like a rash against my pale skin, and my boobs were actually in the picture and my hand down my underwear looked sexy . . . really sexy instead of kind of strange. (I'd had to change my underwear, because the pink looked too little girl and that was the last thing I wanted.)

So, in the end I had a pretty hot picture of myself, but not my face.

I sent it to him.

Me. Annie McKay. Sent a picture of my naked body to a man.

One minute later my phone rang. I answered, but before I could say hello he asked, "Is that you?"

"No, it's the stripper I brought home."

"Is that a joke?"

I smiled. "Yes."

"So that is you?"

"That is me."

"You . . ." He exhaled hard. "God, baby you're so pretty. Your skin, it's like . . . it's so fucking beautiful."

I've never been called pretty. Much less fucking beautiful. The only nice thing Mom ever said was that I had nice hair, implying everything else was ugly, and Hoyt said I was a hard worker and a fine woman . . . I know, such a charmer.

But this from Dylan; I was flushed with pleasure. Ecstatic at the idea that someone would think I was pretty.

Because I was. A little.

Not like Joan, but I was me. And I was pretty.

"Tonight . . ." I sighed.

His dark laugh was delicious.

"That was the fucking hottest thing I've ever heard," he said.

"I doubt that. You were wild, remember? I bet you've heard a whole lot worse than that."

"You're wild now, too. And brave. What else do you want to be?"

"I want to be with you."

The words slipped out before I could stop them and I heard him suck in a sharp breath.

The brittle silence told me I'd done something I couldn't ever undo. I'd changed everything.

I knew it with the terrible sixth sense that I'd developed over the years, that specific and terrible skill of knowing when something was falling to pieces around me. "I know that's not going to happen," I said in a rush, desperate to try and put back together this thing that I had shattered. "I do. I get that. I have my own reasons for why that's a really terrible idea. But I watched this girl dance on this guy's lap. She was facing him and he was . . . he was grabbing her ass. So hard with both hands that the skin around where he was grabbing her was white. And it was like he couldn't hold her close enough, or hard enough against him, and I've . . . I've never been held like that. Not once. Not ever. And I wondered what that would feel like. What would it be like to have someone want me that much that he . . . just grabbed me and held on as hard as he could."

"Layla—"

But I didn't stop. I was on a roll. "What would that be like with you? And what would it be like to hold your cock in my hand and to put it in my mouth? Or to slip my fingers into yours, my fingers covered in my—"

"Layla," he said, his voice sharp. Almost a crack. "Stop it. You have to . . . We can't."

"I know. But I want it. Don't you . . . want that?" *Just tell me you want that.*

"Listen to me." His voice was different. Totally different. "This is over now."

"What?"

"It's over now. I told you not to . . . build anything around me and I meant it."

"I don't know anything about you!" I cried.

He was silent for a long moment. "That's not true and we both know it."

"I know you wear a tux to parties," I said. "You work on cars."

"You heard my voice mail message, didn't you?"

Dylan Daniels.

"Yes."

That's when I realized why he always answered the phone so fast. It wasn't eagerness for my calls. It was so I wouldn't find out who he was.

"Is this because I'm poor?" Because I wasn't. I was actually far from poor. My name was on the deed to a thousand-acre farm in Oklahoma, one of the biggest corn providers in the state. I was actually pretty fucking rich in my own right.

Not that I had ever, not once, thought about it that way.

And now, actually, I was pissed. "If it is, fuck you. Fuck you—I don't give a shit about your money."

"It's not money. It's not . . . it's just not anything that should have started. I've had someone look in on Ben for five years and I've never, ever started anything like this. I've barely given a shit about them before, Layla, and then you come around with your bad jokes and wanting to be brave and I'm . . ." He stopped and I waited, breath held for him to keep going.

"And you're what?"

"Breaking my own goddamn rules." I didn't know what to say to that. To the grief and the frustration that filled his words.

Who gave a shit about his rules? He was rejecting me. I'd gone to a strip club for this guy. Laid myself bare for him. Opened myself up to the worst kind of ridicule and he was worried about breaking his own stupid rules? Bullshit! "The phone is yours. I'll keep the plan going."

"I don't want your fucking pity," I spat at him.

He did that groan. That weird, sexy, half-laugh, half-groan thing that I had believed all along meant that he liked what I was saying, that whatever it was that I was saying was exciting to him. And now I didn't know what it meant.

I didn't know what any of it meant.

"It's not pity. I want . . . God, Layla, I want you to call me if you need anything."

"Not fucking likely." I could not believe how angry I was. I was furious with him. And I couldn't stop.

"I'm not kidding. If there's an emergency—"

"I'm not kidding, either. I won't call you again. I won't even think about you." That was a lie and we both knew it.

"That's too bad," he said, sounding sad and tired. "Because I'll be thinking about you. You really are just so beautiful, Lay—"

I hung up. Or disconnected or whatever. I ended the goddamn call and I wished I could call him back so I could end it again.

Fuck you, you fucking fuck, I thought, and threw the phone back into the drawer and slammed it shut. But the stupid thing was so cheap—the whole goddamn RV was a piece of shit ready to fall apart in the next high wind—that the drawer slid back open.

So I slammed it again. And again.

And then it broke.

And so did I. I collapsed back down on the bed, in pieces.

19

WHEN MOM GOT ANGRY, THE WHOLE RANCH COWERED. I scurried away, trying so hard to anticipate and make right whatever
might be the next thing to set her off. It was a useless effort, of
course. On those days, the earth didn't spin right. The wind was
all wrong.

Even the cows looked away when she walked by.

Smith stopped coming to the house for chess games.

My mom was tiny. Like five foot nothing. Yet when she was
angry like that, she was a giant. Blocking out the sun.

The next day, after Dylan broke up with me . . . or whatever,
whatever that was . . . I was that way. The ground shook under
my feet as I stomped out of my trailer.

"Whoa-ho!" Joan said as I walked past her trailer. "What
the fuck is wrong with you? Boyfriend didn't like your little
game last night?"

She was sitting back on her deck in that silky green robe, the
ashtray next to her elbow full of cigarettes. Her beauty was different in the early sunlight.

"What's wrong?" I snapped, in probably the worst effort
ever to get a person to open up.

"With me?" Joan asked.

"Yeah, you look like shit."

"What got you in a snit?" she asked with a smile that indicated my bad mood was entertaining.

"Life, Joan. Life got me in a snit. Now why do you look like—"

The front door of her trailer opened and out walked the guy from weeks ago. The hairy guy with the skeevy wink and smile. This time, though, he wasn't winking or smiling.

"We're good," he said to Joan as if answering a question I didn't hear her ask.

"Fine," Joan said. "See you."

The guy left with barely a backward glance toward me and Joan took a long drag on her cigarette like nothing was the matter.

Fine. We all had to pretend something, didn't we? Out here in this shitty trailer park. We all had to pretend something so we didn't look too hard at what a mess our lives were. We were all excellent editors of our own selves.

"I'm going to town," I told her. "You need anything?"

"You're not working?"

"It's fucking Saturday, Joan. I'm taking a day."

Joan held up her hands like I had a gun but she was still grinning at me. "I'm fine," she said. "I don't need a thing."

I barely nodded at her and I walked over to Ben's trailer and pounded on the shitty screen door.

It took a few minutes but Ben showed up. He looked better than he did yesterday, largely because he'd changed his shirt. He wore one of his unwrinkled tee shirts today and he'd showered.

"You look better."

"I feel better."

I remembered all the reasons why I was supposed to stay away from him. The warnings. But I didn't care. I didn't care about anything. My entire life I'd spent caring . . . soaking up every mood, decoding every silence. So attuned to everyone else around me that I'd practically evaporated.

And I was done with that.

"You need anything?"

He shook his head and I nodded, swallowing back my need to be sure he was all right, to take on his illness like it was my own despite all the shit I thought I knew about him.

"Okay, see you." I lifted my hand in a wave and jumped down off the small step, but then I turned back around.

"Ben," I said. "Have you seen a doctor?"

The screen was a shadow over his face. "Yeah. Lots of them," he said and closed the solid door.

Right, I thought. Not my business.

I got in my car and drove off to town with the windows down, my hair blown back by the wind.

I drove past The Velvet Touch and considered that I didn't need Dylan. I didn't need him at all. I had done all that stuff myself. I'd walked into that place on my own. Ordered that piña colada, watched Renee and that guy. Me. All by myself.

Those were my own hands on my body. Every goddamn time.

But you would never have done that if he didn't ask you, a little voice whispered. *Never have considered it if you'd never answered that phone call. You would have stayed locked up in that trailer, waiting for something that was never going to come.*

"Shut up," I muttered to the little voice and turned the radio up louder.

In the grocery store I bought stuff I usually never bought, Pop-Tarts and a bag of chips.

I still had Dylan's money burning a hole in my pocket. Forty bucks could buy a whole bunch of stuff.

Oranges. The expensive ones.

A can of olives. I loved olives. I was going to eat olives for dinner.

I stopped in the wine aisle, looking for a bucket-o-something, but couldn't find any. So I grabbed the largest amount of white wine for the cheapest price. It came in a box.

It was box-o-wine night at my trailer.

At the library I checked the Oklahoma papers. Nothing about me.

Though there was a front-page story about more windmills going up in the western part of the state. That's where we were. Hoyt must love that.

And then I sat there and tried to be better than my instincts. Tried not to fall into some trap of girlish, woman-scorned curiosity. It was over. And I'd come to a good place in my head about this last night. Finding out about Dylan wouldn't change anything.

Other girls do this—not you.

And somehow that was the argument that put me over the edge. And he wasn't just Dylan anymore. He was Dylan Daniels and he'd dumped me.

I opened the search page and typed in his full name.

There were a lot of Dylan Danielses in the world. A Realtor in Las Vegas. A teacher in Maine. A ten-year-old spelling bee champion in Florida.

There was also a Dylan Daniels who had something to do with stock car racing.

I scanned through the links:

CAR EXPLODES IN NASCAR NATIONWIDE SERIES QUALIFIER.
DRIVER SUFFERS THIRD-DEGREE BURNS, IN CRITICAL CONDITION.
VIGIL CONTINUES FOR NASCAR DRIVER DYLAN DANIELS.

After that—nothing. No news. No mention after August 16, 2011. Not a word after the crash.

I scrolled back up and clicked on the first link.

Beneath the headline about the crash was a picture of a man.

Close-cut hair, intense dark eyes. A square chin. But his lips . . . they made my breath catch in my throat.

Those lips were like . . . I didn't even know. They were beautiful lips. On such a harshly masculine face those lips were like a wink from God or something.

The caption under the picture said: *Dylan Daniels before the accident.*

That was Dylan? My Dylan.

I leaned in closer to the screen, as if I could see him better. If I could reach through that screen, I would.

He was beautiful. Intense. Those eyes . . . those lips. The combination was nearly painful. Divine and wicked all at once.

I skipped ahead to the article.

The world of stock car racing was totally foreign to me and my brain was buzzing, but I understood that in a second-tier series NASCAR race four years ago, Dylan lost control of his car and crashed. He'd been burned in the fire. Badly.

I sat back and gasped for air. I'd been holding my breath. There was a photo of a car in the green area at the center of the track engulfed in flames. A crew in the corner, rushing toward the fire.

"Oh my God," I breathed.

I clicked through and there were dozens more of those photos, the fire from every angle. Crews spraying down the fire, a body being removed from the window.

Dylan. That's Dylan's body.

There were tons of pictures of Dylan before the fire, of that man with the lips and the intense dark eyes and that chin that looked as if it had been carved out of granite. A thick, powerful body. He was often with a tall and willowy brunette, with a giant rack, their arms around each other.

I stared at those pictures, burning them into my brain because I was if nothing else a glutton for punishment.

What did you think was going to happen? I wondered. *That by pretending to be someone else you would actually be some-one else? You're still you.*

And what I had always been was unwanted.

"Excuse me, miss?"

Pulled from this strange horror show, I looked up to see the librarian behind the desk looking at me.

"Your time is up."

"I'm sorry?"

"You signed up for a half hour. It's up. If you'd like more time you need to sign up again."

The library was nearly empty. There was no one standing behind me, itching to use the computer.

"Seriously?" I asked.

"We need to prove that the—"

"Computers are an asset. I know." Truthfully, I needed to get going. I had a backseat full of groceries. And I'd found out what I'd come to find out. Dylan Daniels had been a handsome, play-boy race-car driver.

But after the fire? Nothing.

Not a single image. Not a single word.

It was as if he vanished.

"I'm going."

On my way out, I bought three more books from the book sale.

"Hey!" a voice said as I was leaving, and I turned around and saw a smiling blond guy walking in the door as I was walk-ing out.

"Hi," I said, stepping back.

I had, over the years living in the same place surrounded by people who were not stupid—who probably, if they didn't know specifically, had a very good idea of what my life was like with my mom, and probably with Hoyt—learned how to keep this small sea of distance around me. By keeping my face calm, my eyes distant, by giving no one any reason to think that I cared about their concern, I could usually keep the questions at bay.

Years of practicing this face—and this guy didn't seem to notice.

"We met here at the library a few weeks ago," he said. "I was . . . I'm a cop. I was wearing my uniform. My name is Grant."

I glanced down at his red shirt. The black shorts. Under his arm was a stack of books.

"Right," I said. He'd knocked on the window and asked if I was all right while I'd been having my freak-out. "Good to see you again, Grant. I'm . . . ah, I'm Annie."

"Good to see you too, Annie," he said. God, he was like a golden retriever. All bright eyes and wagging tail. "You have something good?"

"Pardon?"

"Books." He pointed at the stack of books cradled against my chest. "I come in every week. I'm like a library frequent flyer." He flipped his books around to show me. The one on top was the next one in the series of the thriller I'd just bought on sale.

"Hey, look at that," he said, noticing the same thing. Really, he was very . . . smiley. "It's really good. You're gonna love it."

"Thanks. I read one of his earlier ones a long time ago."

"Which one?"

"The one with the aliens and the hotel."

"Oh, God, I loved that one. With the kid . . ."

"And the drawings. Yeah." The smile came before I could stop it and he grabbed hold of it with both hands.

"You know, if you're not busy, it's my day off and I can drop these off and we could go get lunch."

"It's ten a.m."

"Breakfast, then. Coffee?"

A date. He was asking me out on a date.

I'd never been on a date.

Not in high school. Not when Hoyt was . . . *God,* I have no idea what you'd call those six months before he proposed, but you couldn't call it courting. Softening me up, maybe, for the horrors to come?

The closest thing I'd had to a date were the phone calls with Dylan. And those weren't real. They weren't anything.

This man and his offer of coffee might as well have been asking me out to see the dragons. Or raft the Nile. They were on the same spectrum of impossibility.

Why impossible? that voice in my head asked. *This thing you've had with Dylan . . . that wasn't impossible.*

I could lie to this smiley, book-loving cop with the red shirt, the arms of which were pulled taut over pretty impressive muscles, just as easily as I could lie to Dylan. But I wasn't even tempted. Not a little.

Dylan operated in a separate place, far removed from my reality.

Christ, I was just beginning to realize how fucked up I was.

"I'm sorry," I said. "I can't."

"Sure," he said, waving his hand, even taking the rejection with a smile. "No problem. Maybe another time."

"Sure," I lied, scared of giving him false hope, but finding it impossible to do anything else.

I headed home, thinking of Dylan. Trying to put what I'd learned about him on top of what I knew about him, and all the answers that I had to the questions in my head only gave me more questions.

How did he get into stock car racing?

How did he survive the fire?

What happened afterward?

Fire . . . I couldn't even imagine.

And then I forced myself to try and stop imagining.

Because I could cyber-stalk him all I wanted to, but I would never—ever—get the answers I really wanted.

And asking the questions would only get me hurt.

AT HOME I UNLOADED MY GROCERIES AND ON MY SECOND TRIP to my car for the box of wine, Joan was walking back from the laundry building with a basket in her hands.

"Only the good stuff?" she asked, eyeing my box of wine.

"Be nice and I'll let you have some."

She lifted her eyebrows in surprise, and truthfully, I was pretty surprised too.

"You want to bring it over to my porch?" she asked, shifting the laundry basket to her hip.

"You have any food?" I was starving, and olives for dinner was a stupid idea.

She smiled. "I can dig something up."

And just like that I had a date with a stripper.

BEFORE HEADING OVER TO JOAN'S, I WALKED PAST THE RHODO-dendron to Tiffany's trailer. Outside at the picnic table all three kids were coloring. Markers and crayons were in a shoe box in the middle of the table.

"Hi, guys," I said.

Briefly they all looked up, blond hair falling over blue eyes, and then the girls bent back to their work. But Danny kept looking at me. "Hey," he said. The spokesman of the group.

"Your mom around?" I asked, stepping toward the trailer and the closed door.

"Dad's here," Danny said and I stopped. It was silent inside and there was no telling if it was a dangerous or a happy silence. It was just silence.

I spun around looking for the car, only to find it parked in a different spot on the other side of the trailer, like it was hiding. I just caught a glimpse of its bumper.

The car seemed ominous. *Good lord. Paranoid, much?*

"Are you . . . okay?" I asked.

"Fine."

"We're going to McDonald's," one of the girls said. Her paper was a vast rainbow, stretching from side to side. "Dad said."

"That's awesome."

I backtracked slowly, but before I passed the rhododendron I stopped. I might be imagining some of the devils, but at least one of them was very real. "Danny?"

"Yeah?" He was working hard on a Spider-Man coloring book, the red wax of his crayon thick on the page. Shiny.

"Do you know which trailer is mine?"

He stopped coloring and looked up. "First one past the bush."

"Right. If you need anything . . . anything at all. If you're scared or something. Come knock on my door."

He stared at me for a long time, those eyes of his so grown up, and then shrugged. "Sure."

I walked back to my trailer and grabbed the box of wine, thinking about all those people who'd tried to help me that I'd shoved away with both hands. With all my strength I'd shoved them until they never came back again.

20

Joan had heated up frozen taquitos, which were among my top five favorite meals from a box. And she mixed sour cream and salsa together to dip them in—a brilliant combination I'd never once considered. And she had real wineglasses set up on her little table, the ashtray put away.

"Well," I said, stepping up onto the wooden porch. I'd be lying if I said I wasn't nervous. It was Joan after all. I felt like I was trying to make friends with a shark. "Aren't we fancy?"

"We are. Open up that box."

Box wine has a spigot, which cut the fancy down considerably.

"So?" she asked, sitting back with a lukewarm glass of wine and a taquito. She was wearing thin yoga pants and a tank top, and even that somehow looked amazing on her. "This guy you've got . . ."

"I don't have him anymore," I said, dipping a taquito into the sauce. "It's over."

"That's too bad."

"It's probably . . . all right." Though it wasn't. Though I

missed the idea of calling him far too much for it to be normal. "We weren't ever going to be a thing, you know. It wasn't real."

Joan snorted. "What's real?" she asked. "I figure if you're living it, it's real enough."

I shook my head, unwilling to talk about Dylan. Unsure of what even to say. That photo and the article were still swimming around my head. He'd been hurt. Badly. And he was more handsome than I could even believe.

"What about you?" I asked, wrenching the conversation into a new direction.

"Me and men?" she laughed.

"Yeah, the guy that I've seen coming out of your trailer—"

She shook her head. "He's no one."

"No one? Two times coming out of your trailer?"

"A guy I work with. That's all. And—" She pointed her taquito at me. "I am not talking about him with you."

"Okay, okay, I get it. Smiling shirtless guy coming out of your trailer is off limits."

"Fine, you want to be nosey?" She sprawled back in her chair.

"No. I don't."

"Too late. What are you going to do now?"

I blinked. "What do you mean?"

She shrugged. "You got away from the guy who hurt you . . . what are you going to do next? I mean, you can't kill yourself in that field forever."

"I'm thinking of becoming a stripper."

Joan laughed. "Honey, you need a few thousand dollars in plastic surgery on those boobs before you'll make a living."

I put a hand to my chest as if I were stung.

"Seriously." Joan poured herself more wine and the sun sunk down below Ben's garden. I stretched out my legs, which were knobby and scratched. Looking at them made me think of

Dylan's lips, for some reason. Like the worst part of my body was connected somehow to the most beautiful part of his. Opposites—that why I thought of his mouth. We were a combination of opposites, the far edges of the beauty spectrum. "What are you going to do?"

"I don't know. I barely graduated high school; all I've ever done is farm. I don't think there is much I can do."

"That's some grade-A bullshit, right there."

"Joan, you know nothing about me. You have no—"

"I know you're pretty fucking tough. I know you're pretty fucking brave. I know you're a little bit stupid, but all of us can be. The way I see it, you can do anything."

You know those puzzles, the moveable squares inside a frame, that when all lined up correctly make a picture of a cow or something? But they come scrambled and you have to move squares around to try and make the picture.

They're impossible, those stupid puzzles.

But Joan moved a lot of squares for me when she said that.

A WEEK PASSED QUIETLY. NOTHING BUT ME AND KUDZU DURING the day. But at night . . .

At night I thought about Dylan's voice and slipped my hands over my body, finding new things I liked. The edges of good pain. The depths of real pleasure.

I made up for some serious lost time on my bed, the curtains open, breeze fluttering over my body, cooling the sweat I'd made all by myself. Despite my imagination—which was also making up for lost time—I could not imagine anyone else's hands on my body. It was just me. Over and over again.

Another week and it was the middle of September. The nights were cooler. Just a little. We had a few days of storms that everyone seemed to think were out of the ordinary. Ben seemed to get better. Not that I saw him much. His oven sat out in the pouring rain, half finished. His garden growing, untended, into a jungle.

Joan was not around either.

I felt like we were all hunkered down, backs to the wind, preparing for something. I had no idea what.

But my gut said it was going to be bad.

IT STARTED WITH AN ENGINE WAKING ME UP. NOT PHIL'S SHITTY muscle car, a different engine. Smaller. The engine came into the park and roared past my trailer before coming to a stop.

Fuzzy-headed and bleary, I glanced over at the clock by my bed. Two thirty in the morning. On a Wednesday. If it were Friday, I wouldn't think twice. Things got rowdy at the park on Friday. But it was Wednesday.

I jumped when there was a sudden pounding against the outside of a trailer. Not mine.

Joan's?

Oh God, had some freak followed her home from The Velvet Touch? She said that happened sometimes; girls got stalked. Renee had to call the cops and stay with her mother for like a month. Joan said they usually told the owner, some guy named Zo, and he had that shit taken care of, but that first night, the first time the guy followed a girl home—there was no Zo to protect them.

I leaned over my bed and lifted my curtain, just a little to see outside.

Joan's trailer was quiet. Dark. Still.

But there was a motorcycle outside of Ben's trailer.

"Open up, old man!" a man shouted and kept banging on the trailer.

A dog on the far side of the park started barking. A kid was screaming.

This was bad.

Worse than bad.

My gut didn't have to tell me that.

I slid from my bed and crept to the window over my settee. I could see things more clearly from there. I pulled back the curtain just in time to see the light outside Ben's trailer turn on. Moths immediately flew in from places unknown to buzz around it. Ben's door opened and the man standing outside it, big and tall, wearing a black leather vest with some kind of design on the back, shoved his way inside and I saw Ben fall to the side as the man pushed past him.

And then the door closed behind them.

I stood up, my shaking fingers to my shaking mouth. What should I do? Call the cops?

And then the yelling started.

There was no way to understand what the guy was saying, but it was loud and it was aggressive. Ben was an old man. Frail and sick. That guy . . . that giant man could kill him. Easily.

Back in my bedroom I grabbed the phone. The .22 was sitting there, in a small splash of moonlight. Terrified, freaking out, I grabbed it too and then ran out my door.

The plan was—as much as I was able to make a plan—to listen to what the guy was yelling, and if it seemed dangerous, I'd call the cops.

I ran out my door and circled my trailer only to find Joan standing in the dirt track between our two trailers. She wore her green robe and no shoes.

"What the fuck are you doing?" she whispered.

"Making sure Ben's okay."

"Is that a gun?" She was still whispering, but her voice had all the power of a shriek. "Are you nuts? What the hell are you doing with that?"

I could see on the edge of her deck, in easy reach, her own gun.

"The same thing you are," I said, trying to sound bold. It might have worked if the gun felt natural or right in my hand. But it felt awkward and dangerous, and I probably projected that all over the place.

"Look," Joan whispered and stepped closer to me. "Go back inside and call Dylan."

I blinked, blood falling down to my feet, leaving me dizzy. Did she say *Dylan*?

"How . . ." I couldn't even finish the sentence, I was so shocked. I'd never said his name to her. Not once.

Inside Ben's trailer something crashed to the floor and I could hear Ben yelling, and I jumped, a small scream squeaking from my throat.

"Go inside," Joan said, her voice calm and firm. Her eyes locked on mine. "And call Dylan. Tell him Max is here."

"Max?"

"Go!" she said, and for emphasis pushed me back toward my trailer. I stepped inside the dark and relative silence of my trailer and felt as if the walls I recognized were being pulled down around me, revealing darker shadows I didn't even realize existed.

I pressed call on the phone and lifted it with a shaking hand to my ear. It was three in the morning; there was no way—

"Layla?" he said after the second ring. His sleep-roughened voice stroked over me and I could do nothing to stop my reaction. Not one thing. I shivered at the sound of his voice. Goose bumps rising on my arms. "Are you okay?"

"I'm fine. But Ben . . . there's a guy here. Some guy on a motorcycle—"

"Oh fuck."

"Joan . . . knew your name. She knew we were talking and she said I needed to tell you that Max is here—"

"Listen, Layla, listen carefully: I need you to stay in the trailer. Don't go over there. Don't . . . don't even leave your trailer. Get down on the floor by your bed, the side farthest from Ben's trailer."

"Why? What the hell are you talking about?"

I could hear his breath shake as he exhaled and was suddenly a dozen times more scared. "Bullets go through trailers like cheese, Layla. I'm sending a car for you—"

"*What?*"

"I'm sending a car for you. He'll be there in ten minutes. Tops. Don't leave until you see a black sedan in front of your trailer."

"I'm not going anywhere! I'm going to call the cops—"

"You call the cops and I guarantee someone is going to die."

"This . . . you're being ridiculous."

"I wish I were. Stay inside. Stay safe. Someone is coming to get you."

He disconnected and I stared down at the phone. In shock. Truly. If I called the cops someone would die? How did that happen?

The fight continued over in Ben's trailer, but the intensity seemed to have dropped. Ben was yelling too, and now it was just a loud conversation.

In no time a black sedan purred to a stop in front of my window, in the shadows between my trailer and Joan's. And I thought about that day in the laundry room when I'd scurried away while Tiffany and Phil fought. I'd been so scared—for myself.

Ben was my friend. He was. And I couldn't leave him here to be bullied or scared or hurt.

I had to have changed that much. I *had* to have. I couldn't have run this far to still be so damned scared.

I ran around my trailer to tell the driver he wasn't needed. He was standing beside the car, a handsome guy older than me.

"You Layla?" he asked and popped open the back door of the sedan.

"Yeah."

"Get in."

"No. No, I'm not leaving."

"Dylan told me to throw you in the backseat if I had to." He stepped toward me and I stepped back, not about to be manhandled.

"Touch her and I'll put a bullet in your hand," Joan said from the shadows of her little deck. Her green robe caught the light and glimmered.

"Joan!" I yelled. "I'm not going to leave Ben—"

Suddenly from the front pocket of her robe she pulled out a badge. Some kind of government thing.

"What . . . what is that?" I asked. This whole thing was spinning so fast out of any kind of control.

"I'm undercover DEA," she whispered. "Get in the car and get gone."

"But—"

"Go!" she yelled. Truly yelled, as in no longer whisper-yelling, and I jerked into motion, stumbling toward the sedan. The driver yanked open the door, but before I got in I looked over at Joan.

"Come with me," I said. "If it's really dangerous—"

"If it's really dangerous I do my job. Go."

And then I was in the backseat of the car and it peeled out of the Flowered Manor Trailer Park and Camp Ground.

PART TWO

21

ANNIE

THE CAR ROLLED THROUGH AN ENDLESS NIGHT, PARTING THE sea of shadowy kudzu and dotted by islands of neon rest stops. We got off the highway, onto increasingly smaller roads that switchbacked up hills and down again into gullies, until we were up in the mountains.

Panic and a thousand questions sat in that car with me. How could I have been so content not pushing Dylan about Ben? Who does that? What kind of idiot allows herself not to worry about a possible murderer next door because she's too busy having some kind of late-blooming sexual awakening complete with phone sex and strippers?

That guy, the motorcycle guy—I thought for sure I'd seen him at The Velvet Touch.

Was that why Joan—an undercover DEA agent—was there?

What was Ben involved in?

With shaking hands, I fumbled for the button to unroll my window.

"You okay?" the driver asked.

"The window—" The word wasn't even out of my mouth before the window had opened a crack.

The air through the window smelled evergreen.

It was exotic compared to the dust and clay of Oklahoma.

"Where are we going?" I asked the driver. Considering one of the last things Dylan said to me was that he didn't want to see me again, I figured there might be a 50/50 chance this guy's orders were to leave me at a hotel. Or a gas station.

Our eyes met in the rearview mirror. "Someplace safe."

Why did I doubt that? Why did I think that wherever we were headed was infinitely more dangerous than where I'd been?

"Who are you?" I asked.

"An employee of Dylan's."

Dylan has employees that drive to trailer parks in the middle of the night to pick up women and whisk them away to safety.

Of course he does.

The headlights illuminated impenetrable curtains of trees and kudzu, and then the car slowed down and stopped in front of the thick black beams of an iron gate stretched across the road in front of it.

Through the window he opened, the driver punched in a code on a metal box, and the gate slid open and the car eased up the drive.

My heart was pounding behind my eyes. In the tips of my fingers.

I couldn't see the house in the thick shadows of a granite-topped, forested hill. But as the car pulled up, a light flickered on in the murk and I could see a wooden door, the house behind it dark and hulking against all that stone.

Not safe, my gut said. *Not safe at all.*

"This is it?" I asked.

"Yep."

Reluctantly, I got out of the car, freezing in the pre-dawn mountain air. I wrapped my arms around myself as best I could. There was running water somewhere, a brook or a river.

It didn't look like much, this house. There was a back door and a garage attached. A big garage, like a warehouse. It was dark. And had lots of little roofs. Eaves and awnings.

It was a strange little house on a lonely mountain.

Weird and vaguely ominous.

It looked like the evil house in a movie. The one where bad shit happened.

"Dylan's housekeeper, Margaret, will take care of you. Don't be fooled by the Mrs. Santa Claus act—she'll cut you if she thinks you're going to hurt Dylan."

"Wait . . . what?" I turned to ask the driver more about this housekeeper, because frankly, I'd kind of hit my limit on drama tonight, but the driver only waved at me through the driver-side window before taking off, leaving me alone in the parking area. Moths the size of airplanes buzzed over my head toward the light over the door.

Right.

A deep breath.

I stepped across the gravel driveway, wincing as the rocks bit into the bare skin of my feet. I lifted my hand to knock on that dark little door, now totally inundated with moths, but it opened before my fist connected and I nearly knocked on a woman's forehead.

"Sorry—"

"Are you Layla?" She was short and round, with a Hilton Head sweatshirt zipped up to her neck. She had gray-blond hair pulled back into a bun, stray hairs frizzed out around her head making her look like she had a halo.

No. I was not Layla. I was never Layla.

But I said yes, because this was the bed I had made.

"Well, come on, girl, before these bugs make off with you."
She did not look nice. She was trying to look nice, but it wasn't
working. She wore a big smile that should have put me at ease,
but didn't come close. She was worried about me being here, or
tense. Or something. Whatever her reasons, she didn't want me
here. And it was coming off of her like a radio signal.

Jesus, did I need to worry about her having a knife?

Without much choice, I stepped into the house. The door
clicked shut behind me.

"Look at you, poor thing," she said. "You don't even have
any shoes."

"Or a purse," I said. Or money. Or a bra. Such is the nature
of trailer park kidnappings.

"Are you hungry?"

"No, please don't go to any trouble for me."

"It's no trouble," she said, waving me off like waking up at
three in the morning to care for a surprise guest with no shoes
was totally par for the course in her life.

Lord, maybe it was. Maybe Dylan Daniels brought women
up here all the time. Women with no options or boob support.

I followed her through the cave-like foyer. I was beginning to
think Dylan might be a Hobbit. A mole, maybe.

Whew, dodged a bullet there, I thought, giddy with panic;
for a while I was imagining having sex with Bilbo Baggins.

"Well, you must be exhausted. Follow me and I'll show
you—"

"Where's Dylan?" I asked.

"Let me show you to your room," she said, with the kind of
smile that indicated I would get no farther with her. That smile
placed her firmly on Dylan's side.

Dylan had a lot of people on his side. The driver. Joan. Margaret.

I had no one.

The woman led me out of the foyer and the house opened up

into a wide, tall, beautiful room with a wall of windows facing a dark valley. Leather couches with big pillows faced that window. There was a kitchen in the back corner with stainless-steel appliances and a large dining room table, surrounded by chairs. The floors were hardwood, worn but shining. Rugs were scattered on those floors, under the table, in front of the sink, and before the big wall of windows—beautiful ones. Rich person ones.

Everything gleamed and glowed in the low light coming in those big windows.

The whole room looked like a movie set. A beautiful movie set—not for Hobbits.

For a very wealthy man.

Hoyt spent five years making me feel small. Unwanted. Unwantable. He made me feel like a nuisance and a failure. At the beginning I'd been hurt, wounded. But I slowly grew to not want anything. If I never wanted anything more than what I had, I could never be hurt.

So I was totally unprepared for how hurt I was looking at Dylan's house. And I realized how much I'd wanted with him. How far I'd reached.

And I felt toyed with, shamed even. As if I were nothing, a speck, a stupid girl, a puppet, and he was the man with money and drivers and housekeepers and beautiful houses, pulling my strings.

My chest hurt.

Did he sit there? I wondered. Did he sit on that couch, with his feet up on that ottoman and study the mountains while he talked to me? Did he touch himself there? Did he ask me to eat dessert for breakfast and to taste my own come on my fingers? Right? There?

Did he hang up and laugh at me? At my eagerness? My total lack of experience or sophistication?

Was this fun for him, playing with me?

I couldn't breathe; shock and anger had their fists down my throat.

"Are you coming?" Margaret asked, having walked across the room to stand at the entrance to another dark hallway.

"I need to see Dylan."

She shook her head. "He's not here."

Wasn't that perfect? He wasn't even here and I was still being controlled by him. Why did this hurt? I wondered, limping on my sore feet after Margaret down that hallway. There were no pictures. No mirrors. Nothing. Just dark walls and doors that I kept walking past on my way to some room that had been set aside for me.

God, the house was really huge.

Margaret opened a door. "Here's your room. There's a bathroom through there," she said. "I've got a toothbrush and some other things you might need. There are some clothes in the drawers—"

"For me?"

Margaret smiled. "Of course."

"How did you know what size?"

"Dylan said small." She shrugged.

How did . . . ? The picture. He'd seen my body in that picture. "Thank you," I breathed. Horrified and on fire in the same breath. Thinking about the cake. The charger, all the little lures that pulled me into Dylan's life.

"It's no problem—I've got a granddaughter about your size. They were things I'd bought for her."

"I can't take them—they're gifts for your granddaughter!"

"She'll never know. Now, get some sleep, honey," she said. "You look done in."

She closed the door behind her when she left, leaving me alone in a simple room with a big bed covered in a blue bedspread. The far wall was curtained, and I walked over and opened it up. I could hear running water through the sliding glass door.

I opened the door and stepped out onto a small balcony. The sky was pink, the rising sun still behind the mountains. To the left and right there were other little balconies, four of them. Little extra nooks and crannies on a house that just kept going. There was a brook beneath me, falling off the edge of the cliff the house was built onto. This house was built into a cliff. With a waterfall falling under it.

It was like magic, this house.

My back pocket buzzed and I jumped, startled. My phone. I'd forgotten. No bra or shoes, but I had this damn phone shoved in the back pocket of my shorts.

Suddenly all that shit I felt, the grubby bit and the meaningless part—it was all gone. I was still hurt, still impossibly wounded, but I was furious, too.

And if I'd learned nothing else in the last two months of my life, it was that fury felt better than pain. Every damn time. So I grabbed onto my anger with both hands.

"Dylan?" I asked after I answered.

"You okay?"

"I'm in your goddamn house."

"Good."

"Where the hell are you?"

"I'm . . . in my garage."

I lifted my head, as though I could smell him on the breeze. "Here?"

"Here. But—"

"How do I get there?"

"Layla—"

"Tell me how to get there or I'm going to start tearing this place apart!"

His chuckle was unexpected and it did nothing to cool me

down. "I'm not kidding, Dylan. I'm seeing you right now or I'm walking out that door."

"We're in the middle of nowhere."

"And if you think that will stop me you're crazy."

He was silent for a long time; I could hear him breathing. "Go through the big room. I'll leave the door open."

I ran back down the hallway through the big room. Margaret had vanished, thank heavens. And down in the far left corner of the room near the floor-to-ceiling window was a cracked door, a slice of yellow light cutting into the shadows.

With my hands shaking, I pushed open that door.

The garage was big. Like a cathedral. In the center of it was one whole car with its hood open, surrounded by pieces of cars. It smelled of oil and concrete. On a metal table there was a dismantled engine and on the far wall there was a long wooden bench.

Sitting in a pool of light, on a stool at the bench, his back to me, was Dylan.

22

FOR A SECOND THOSE WIDE EDGES OF MY LIFE DIDN'T CONNECT; anger slipped out of my hands. And I didn't know what I was doing here. Or how in the world I'd gotten here. To this house. To this man.

"Layla?"

At the sound of his voice—so familiar, so achingly familiar—all the pieces of my life slammed back together.

Helpless, I closed my eyes and let that voice work its way through my body.

"You okay?" Even that familiar question was somehow bittersweet.

He'd spun around, shifting back out of the pool of light so his face and half his chest were in shadow. The shadows were dense and maybe that was easier . . . maybe that was better. I couldn't see his eyes, but I knew they were watching me. His hands were in fists at his knees.

"Is this where you bring all the women you kidnap?" I asked, coming out swinging, for once in my life.

"No," he said. "I don't bring anyone here."

"Well, aren't I a special snowflake," I said through lungs that felt as if they were collapsing in on each other.

"Layla," he sighed.

Suddenly, I wished very much that I had not sent him that picture.

I felt painfully bared to him, wholly exposed. I'd sent him a naked picture of myself. My pale, thin, boyish body. All my flaws, all my imperfections, my feminine failures—he'd seen them.

And he sat there in the shadows, unwilling to show me anything of himself.

The distance between us throbbed. With anger. With lust. Questions and huge fucking secrets.

Beneath my ribs, I ached. Between my legs I ached. My fucking blood ached at the sight of him. I took a deep breath and clenched my hands together in front of me, as if I needed something to hold onto. And maybe I did. I was so adrift.

"I'd like to go home."

"You can when I know it's safe."

"You are not the boss of me." Really, could I be any more idiotic?

"When you're in danger," he said, "I'm going to do everything I can to keep you safe."

"Why?" I asked, baffled by this protectiveness. By his attention. From the first phone call to now, I didn't understand. *Why me?*

I didn't want his concern to mean anything. I didn't want to be warmed by that in some way. But anger was a blanket that could not cover all of me and my exposed parts soaked it up. I was helpless against that kind of care, I had no . . . defenses against someone's worry. For me.

He was silent, there in the shadows. Like he had no intention of explaining himself.

"I don't need you to do that."

"Not your choice," he said, with a shrug. As if my desires were irrelevant in the equation.

"Well, it's hardly yours. I am not your business, Dylan."

"It's a little late for that, don't you think?"

A few phone calls, some drunk texts, and two ill-advised pictures—that's all we had between us. A handful of paltry, inconsequential things. How in the world did they add up to something so damn heavy?

"You didn't want to see me, remember?" I whispered, revealing some of my hurt. "You ended it."

His silence was agreement. *Yes,* he was saying. *Yes, I ended it. Yes, I didn't want to see you.*

"I didn't ask to be brought here," I said, sounding shrill. His silence was making me crazy. *Shut up,* I told myself. *Shut up and forget about him.*

"You can go home tomorrow."

We were at an impasse. Forty feet between us, and every inch was lined with barbed wire and land mines. And it would be easy to turn around and leave. Wait out the hours until that driver came back to take me home.

But I couldn't do it. I couldn't just walk away and not . . . ever have seen him.

"Come out of the shadows," I said.

He rolled toward the bench, his back to me. "Go on to bed, Layla. It's been a long—"

"Stop!" I cried. The anger and fear and hurt exploded out of me. "Just stop. I've been bossed around, thrown into cars, driven to some kind of mountaintop fortress to . . . you. You, Dylan. You ended it and I still wound up here. To you!" I kept spitting out that word, like it somehow meant something. Like on the stupid weird map of my life he had been some kind of spectacular surprise destination. "I'm exhausted, I'm scared. I'm angry. I'm . . ." I cut myself off. I was not going to admit that I was turned on. Though, undoubtedly he had to know. He always seemed to know. He knew over a phone and now I was standing here, panting, my body shaking . . . *God. Damn it.* He had all the cards and I was standing here barefoot in my pajamas. If there was ever a moment I longed for a bra, this was it. My nipples hurt, they were so hard. I knew he could see them.

"Inevitable," he said.

"What?"

"Nothing."

"I'm not in the mood for games!" I yelled.

I couldn't see him, but I could tell he was smiling at me. I knew what his voice sounded like when he was smiling. "Games are what you like. Dirty little games. That's all we've got, Layla."

I fought back the surge of memories of all of our "games," because I was not going to be distracted. And he was trying to marginalize it, and what we did—what happened between us— couldn't fit within any margins I'd ever known.

"I know about the accident. The fire. I went to the library and looked you up."

"It's not about the fire." He lifted his hand to the back of his neck like he was rubbing sore muscles there. And I got the sense that he was lying. "The fire is nothing. There are a lot of things I haven't told you. Things you'd just be better off not knowing."

"Well, Jesus Christ, Dylan," I yelled. "Let's start with something! Let's start with you telling me one true thing."

He looked down at his hands, shadows playing over his beautiful body. "You are . . . beautiful. You look exactly like I thought you would."

I gasped, the words so unexpected they slid right through my ribs. Right into the meat and blood and bone of me.

"I never imagined you," I said.

"Probably smart," he laughed.

"You just . . . were you. Just Dylan." *Just everything.*

He lifted his head, watching me, and I stood there with nothing. In the face of all that he had, the slimness of my existence, its utter weightlessness, was shocking. But I was out to even the scales. Just a little. Just enough that I could look at myself in the mirror tomorrow. Just enough so I'd know that I'd fought for something. My own worth in this game we'd played. I wasn't a pawn. I was a person.

"And I'm pretty much done with other people telling me what's best. So, either stand up, or I'm leaving."

"Layla—"

I turned for the door.

"There are bears out there!"

"I'm not scared of bears," I snapped over my shoulder, stepping into the living room. Maybe I'd find some shoes in the closet. If I could find the closet.

"Stop," he yelled from the garage. "Stop, girl. You're gonna . . . fine. Fine, Layla! Come back."

I stepped back into the garage, the door closed tight behind me, my arms over my chest. My feet were so cold they were numb at this point.

Slowly, he stood up from the shadows. He sort of unfurled from the chair. He wasn't tall. But he was big. He wore a plain white tee shirt over wide shoulders and a big chest that tapered down to a lean waist. His faded blue jeans were low on his hips, held up by a thick leather belt.

I sucked in a breath, light-headed. His head was still in the shadows and he reached over across the bench, his biceps a beautiful gilded curve, and then he tilted the lamp up so it hit his face.

And he turned, facing me full-on.

The scars were pink and shiny up the side of his neck to his ear. The scar tissue spread across the left side of his face like kudzu, touching the corner of his mouth.

But the rest of his face was the same as those pictures in the articles. Striking. Masculine. Those lips . . . *oh God,* those lips. The shiny taut edge only made them more compelling. More beautiful.

"Happy?" he said, tilting his head so I could see the extent of the scars. He was uncomfortable, standing there like that in the light. On display.

"No," I whispered. "I'm not happy."

I'd thought, somehow, that it would be so much worse. Because the news coverage just stopped. Because he was shrouded in mystery.

But they were just scars. I'm sorry, I wanted to say. I'm sorry for the pain you must have felt. And the fear you must have lived through. I'm sorry that happened to you. But those scars did nothing to change my feelings for him—conflicted as they were.

"Is that why you stopped talking to me?"

He shook his head, the shadows shifting over his face.

"You're not going to tell me anything, are you?" I asked, knowing the answer before he said a word.

I'd told him things I'd never told anyone before. Things I hadn't even conceptualized. But he'd shared nothing of himself, because that made sense. I was the one who'd reached for more. Who'd felt so alone that he'd seemed like a friend.

I had no reason to feel betrayed, but I did.

I looked down at my hands, the calluses on the tips of my fingers. Part of my thumbnail was turning black. I'd smashed it the other day trying to get the damn engine on the mower to work. But this . . . this thing/not-thing between us. It hurt worse.

"Is Ben okay?" I whispered. "Will you at least tell me that much?"

"Probably; he usually is."

"Who is Max?"

"A dangerous guy. A . . . very dangerous guy."

"You know a lot of dangerous guys."

Something hard slipped over his face. Something . . . scary. And I stiffened. An old instinct braced me.

"You should go back to your room, Layla," he said, sitting back down on the stool, rolling belly up to the bench. I was being dismissed and frankly, he was probably right. But I was pretty done with being bossed tonight.

"I'm not going to do that, Dylan. You don't have to tell me anything about yourself, but I deserve to know what is happening at the trailer park." My home.

He spun back out and his eyes, full of hot knowledge, touched me. My shoulders, my stomach. My bruised knees. My breasts.

For a second I thought he was trying to scare me away. With sex. Like he was threatening me. If I stayed, he'd what? Fuck the hell out of me?

Stupid man.

That was not going to scare me away.

Interest, sexual and sharp, flooded me. Warmed me, from the inside out.

"Max is a part of the same motorcycle club Ben used to be a part of," he said.

"The Skulls."

He nodded.

"Did you . . . are you in the club?"

"No, I have nothing to do with the club." He picked up a little screwdriver and fiddled with it like he was bored or needed distraction, and I wanted to stomp across that floor and shake him. "Most of the time Ben and Max have nothing to do with each other either. I don't know why he was there."

"Joan, my neighbor? Do you know her?"

"The stripper?" he asked with that crooked smile. "I only know what you've told me."

"She's actually a DEA agent. Undercover. Did you know that?"

The screwdriver clattered against the bench when he dropped it and I wanted to smile at him. At his surprise. It was nice to know something he didn't. "No. I had no idea."

"Do you know why she'd be undercover?"

"Had to be something about the club," he said with a shrug and then winced, reaching up to pinch the muscles at the base of his neck. I fought the urge to ask if he was all right. I fought the urge to care.

"She said I should call you. She knew about you."

"You didn't tell her—"

"That we were having phone sex?" I spat the words because I was pissed. I was pissed because he wasn't mad. Because he was acting like this was no big deal. "No. I didn't. But somehow when this Max guy showed up she knew I should call you. Why?"

The tension in his silence was razor sharp, and whatever he was going to say, I had the sense I should brace for it. Duck and cover, like when I was a kid and we practiced tornado drills at school.

"I own the trailer park," he said.

I swayed backwards, putting a hand against the wall to catch myself before I fell over.

He jumped to his feet, like he was about catch me, and I shook my head—I couldn't have him touch me. Not at all. And so he froze. Just froze.

"Layla?"

I flinched and turned my face away. Mortification swallowed me whole.

"Then you . . . you know. All about me." *That I'm lying about my name. That I showed up with bruises around my neck covered in a stupid, silly scarf. That half my trailer is paid for with manual labor in the damn field.*

"I own the trailer park because of Ben. The rest of it . . . doesn't matter to me."

"You don't know—"

"What?" he asked, stepping out of that freeze toward me.

"Nothing. Forget it."

"Now who is lying?"

I laughed, throwing my hands up in the air. "Does it matter?"

We stared at each other, long and hard.

"I guess you're right," he said and turned away from me. "Go on back to your room, Layla."

I was being sent to my room like a child. And it would have been the right thing—I should have done what he said, like a good girl, and gone silently back to that bed and stared at the ceiling until he decided to let me go.

But somehow I couldn't.

"My name is not Layla," I said. "I lied. All along. I lied."

He turned back toward me.

"I know."

"What?"

"Well, I figured you told me some lies to protect yourself. You wanted to be called Layla." He shrugged. "It didn't seem to be any of my business."

None of his business. Of course. That, too, shouldn't hurt. But it did.

It was like running into a wall at top speed. "And they worked so well, didn't they?"

"You don't have to protect yourself from me, Layla."

My laugh was ripped from my stomach, nearly a sob. "You don't know anything about what I have done to protect myself."

"Then tell me." He was the sharpened edge of a blade, bright and awful. Violence waiting to happen. Not to me, but on my behalf. I could set him against the world.

For a moment I could barely hold onto my secret.

I turned on shaking legs and went up the steps to the door, desperate to get out of there.

23

DYLAN

IT SHOULDN'T MATTER. ON THE GIGANTIC PILE OF LIES THE TWO of them had told each other, that she'd lied about her name should not matter at all. And it hadn't up until this moment.

This moment, watching her shaking and walking away from him, it mattered.

He'd understood all along that she was doing it to keep herself safe. Because he was a stranger; because the things they were doing were so outrageous to her.

He understood better than most the desire for anonymity.

But it wasn't just Dylan and what they did together that scared her.

Something else had her deep down scared.

He knew the look of terror, the smell of it. The way it could make your body shake like a fever.

Don't, he told himself again. The plan had been to get her out of that park, bring her here where she was safe, but never let her see him. Never let himself see her. But he'd blown that, and the image of her was seared now into his brain. Small and thin but long-legged, white-blond hair, and eyes the color of powder-blue paint.

The smart move was to let her go.

But he couldn't.

Keeping her here was a mistake. For her, potentially a dangerous one.

She'd lied to him. She was scared. Very scared.

And that changed everything.

ANNIE

I OPENED THE DOOR FROM THE GARAGE TO THE MAIN PART OF the house, surprised to see that morning was being ushered in on the billowing clouds of a storm.

Thunder boomed and the air smelled like electricity. No rain, though. Mother Nature was only setting the loud and violent stage.

Margaret was in the kitchen, preparing food, and at the sound of the door to the garage opening, she turned with a tight smile that quickly vanished when she saw me.

"What are you doing in the garage?" she asked, as if I'd been snooping around the place.

"Talking to Dylan. Turns out he was here after all."

Her face was unreadable, but everything about her gave the impression of being shocked.

"Is he in there?" she asked.

"Yeah."

For a second a smile burst through that wall of impassivity. And then it was gone. I didn't know what that smile meant. I didn't know what anything meant anymore.

Margaret set down a pot of coffee on a table full of food. There was homemade bread set out with butter and jam beside it. Cut-up melon and strawberries filled the bottom of a pretty pottery bowl. There were cinnamon rolls. Fresh ones. Still steaming.

If my stomach weren't in knots, I'd be all over that.

"I'm sorry I don't have much for you." Margaret looked down at the food like it had failed her.

"It's a feast." I picked up a strawberry like I had an interest in eating it, but my stomach rolled over at the idea. So, I just held it, picking off the green leaves, one by one.

"Would you like some coffee?"

"Yes, please."

Margaret, in a pale yellow shirt and a pair of black leggings, poured me a mug. "Milk? Sugar?"

"Black." I drank it black because it was cheaper. And faster. Because it didn't bother anyone. "Actually, can I have some sugar? Both, actually."

Margaret fixed up the coffee and handed a dark blue heavy pottery mug to me. "I don't understand people who drink coffee black. It's like they don't want to enjoy themselves."

Huh. Score one for Margaret.

I took a sip of the coffee and nearly grimaced. It was too sweet. And not hot enough with the milk. Come to find out, I liked it the way I'd always had it. Go figure.

"Margaret," a soft voice said, and suddenly Dylan was behind me. I could feel him there in the nerve endings along my back. The hair on my neck stood up.

Him. That's what every part of my body said. *Him.*

And *mine.*

I put the mug on the table before it fell from my fingers.

"Go shopping," he said.

"For what?" Margaret asked, putting her hands on her hips and giving the impression of a woman at her wit's end. A mother, actually—she gave the impression of being a mother. Frazzled but affectionate.

"I don't care. You're always telling me my house needs stuff; go get some."

"You have a guest. Who has had a rough night, and you want me to—"

"I want you to get out of the house," he said, and my skin shrank. It squeezed me tight and I couldn't breathe.

"Dylan," she said, her façade cracking. Her worry visible, but not for me. No, her worry was entirely reserved for Dylan.

"It's fine," he told her. "I'm fine."

Right, I nearly laughed, like I was going to hurt him? Chip that steel edge of his? Impossible.

"All righty!" Margaret said, and she opened up a small closet and grabbed her purse, stomping around a little to make her point. "But I'm using your money and filling up your fridge."

"Go gambling, I don't care. Just be gone."

Dylan walked past me to shut the door behind Margaret.

The door closed with a heavy, loud click and he turned to face me.

Dylan.

Those lips like pillows. The taut, shiny flesh at his thick neck. The scars looked worse here, in this light. But I had no reaction to them, besides concern. They were not repellant or scary. They just were.

His dark, heavy-lidded eyes were unreadable and they walked all over me. My hair, my eyes, the neckline of my cami-sole, my legs beneath my shorts.

I felt naked under that gaze, my clothes stripped away.

"Tell me your name. Your real name."

"No."

His face split into a grin, and I remembered he liked my op-position. My sharp edges. This was how things between us started and I did not have the strength to go down this road.

"It's Annie," I said. "Annie McKay."

He blinked. Again. Smiled a little.

"That suits you."

I didn't have anything to say to that, so I kept my mouth shut. Obstinate even when I didn't want to be.

"I need to know why," he said. "Why you lied."

"Does it matter? You knew all along apparently. It was the most useless lie ever told."

"It matters!" he yelled. "Because, you're here, Annie. It's like you said: despite everything both of us did to make sure that never happened, you're here. It's inevitable, and so, I would like to know why you lied. Even when you knew it was safe. What are you scared of?"

For years, years and years and years of my life, if someone shouted at me I would shrink inside my bones. I would hide deep inside of myself and nod my head. I would nod and say yes. Yes, you're right.

I'd say I was sorry a thousand times. A million. Whatever it took for the yelling to stop.

I fired Smith. I sold my land for windmills. I ducked my head and took it. The yelling, the fists, the disdain and marginalization. I took it all to make the yelling stop.

I laughed, but it sounded nervous, not cavalier. Old habits were weighing me down. "You've lied to me—"

"I've never lied," he interrupted, his anger white hot and barely controlled. I swallowed and took a step back, my hip hitting a chair. He watched the movement and saw all the things I couldn't hide.

"Are you scared?" he asked, and I wished I had enough bravado to tell him no, to shake my hair out of my eyes and yell right back at him.

"You're yelling at me and I'm . . . here. Alone. It would be stupid of me not to be afraid." I wished I weren't, but I was.

My fear seemed to put a pin in his anger and he took a deep

breath. Another. The electric tension in the air dissipating enough that my fear lifted.

"I won't hurt you," he said.

"I've . . . I've had a few people say that to me and then go right on ahead and hurt me."

"Your mother? Who else?"

I shook my head. I wasn't going to talk about it. He could put a barricade around his secrets.

"I won't hurt you," he said, calmly. All that fire in him banked for the moment. Not gone; it would be foolish of me to think that that anger was gone. It was just . . . hidden. "And I won't lie to you. I told you the first night that I would never lie to you. And I just . . . I want to know why you lied."

I swallowed, my hands wrapped tight around the back of the chair beside me. "I lied because I was scared. I lied because I didn't know you. And you were asking me to do things—"

"Things you wanted," his silky voice reminded me. I felt acutely the security blanket of the phone, of distance and anonymity, being ripped away.

"Wanting it made it even scarier! Those things we did, those aren't things I do. I barely knew about them, so it was easier to be someone else. Someone braver and bolder."

"Layla."

"Yes," I sighed, wondering if he could even fathom this kind of choice. The desire to be the opposite of who he was. Maybe when he was a kid, chasing his brother around, trying to be tough.

"That makes sense," he said and I smiled, bitterly, angry to have some of my secrets ripped away.

"Glad you approve."

The air around us seethed, no matter how much both of us would pretend otherwise. "Why Layla? Why'd you pick that name?"

"Layla was my cousin."

He lifted his eyebrow. "Layla with the hand job?"

I nodded, my throat aching. A blush raced up my body from my feet to the top of my head. That night, the night I told him, the sound of his heavy breathing, the sound of his zipper lowering, was like a living, breathing thing between us.

Hard and slow, just the way I like it.

It was impossible to look at him. He filled up the entire room and I felt squeezed by his presence. There was a table between us but it was like I felt him right up against me.

"And you're Annie. The cousin who watched."

I was so off balance with this man, wanting more. Constantly wanting more. More than I should, more than I was really comfortable with. More than he wanted.

I nodded. The cousin who watched—that sort of summed up my entire life before running away. The woman who watched life go by. Who watched her freedom get ripped from her. Who watched herself get smaller and smaller every minute.

"How did you end up at the trailer park?" he asked, as if he could see inside my mind. The pictures there I couldn't get rid of. "What are you so scared of?"

I shook my head. The answer to everything he was asking me was no. No, I would not tell him. No, the things we'd done did not give him the right to all my secrets. No, he could not bully it from me.

"Please," I said. "Don't push."

He seemed stunned that I'd asked. And he rocked back, a little. Our entrenchment not as deep as I'd thought.

"Okay."

I felt a threatening softness toward him at his capitulation. It wasn't his nature and it didn't come easily.

He poured himself a cup of coffee, ate the leafless strawberry I'd been playing with. His fingers were wide and blunt, the nails cropped close. White calluses covered the tips.

I still wanted those hands on me. I still wanted to know what it would be like to be touched by him.

"I'd like to go home," I said.

"Do you? Do you really want to go home?" That voice, that soft, dark, rough voice that led me places I'd never imagined I'd go.

His eyes were hot on my body. He'd been thinking the same thing I had. He still wanted more of me. Despite everything.

"You're the one who didn't want to see me," I said because I could feel all of this turning. I was getting swept up again by him and heading toward water that was inevitably going to be over my head. "You ended it because I said I wanted to see you. I didn't even mean it, I just wanted it, and you said we couldn't talk to each other anymore. And now you want me to stay?"

"I do." I opened my mouth to argue but he held up his hand. "And no more lies, Annie—you want to stay too."

I did, but hadn't I been reckless enough? Wasn't it time to go back to being Annie McKay?

"No. I need to find out if Ben is okay. If Joan—"

"Call."

"What?"

"Use the phone . . . Call . . . what's his name at the desk?"

"Kevin. He's your employee, isn't he?" My words were wasps, stingers out. I wanted to touch him and wound him. Every breath I pulled into my lungs sizzled. Burned.

Anger was no stranger to me. I lived with anger. A low-level seethe every minute. An anger I'd had to swallow over and over again. Because while I might be angry, I couldn't show that anger. Showing anything but a bland and smiling face would get me hurt.

Never, not with my mom and certainly never with Hoyt, had I been allowed to behave this way.

Childish and petulant. Pissy.

It was fucking revelatory. A delight. It felt like I'd unbuttoned a pair of too tight pants. Pants that had been suffocating me.

"It's a means to an end, Annie. Easier to keep an eye on Ben."

"Why do you need to keep an eye on Ben? Were you related to that girl in the fire?"

"Why are you twenty-four years old and never touched yourself before?"

He was not going to pull a single punch. If I stayed, it was open season on my secrets.

From his back pocket he pulled out a phone and looked up a number before handing it to me. "Call him. Make sure your friends are okay."

I pressed call on the screen and walked back toward my room.

"Flowered Manor RV Park." It was Kevin.

"Kevin," I said. "It's Annie. I'm calling to make sure everything is okay."

"Well, we got some power lines down because of the storm, but other than that everything is okay."

"Last night . . . Ben?"

"He's fine. Came in this morning before the rain to get a newspaper. Grumpy as a cuss. But that's usual."

"And Joan?"

"Haven't seen her."

"The guy on the motorcycle?"

"I heard about that. No sign of him this morning. Where are you?"

"I'm . . ." *Christ. Where am I?* "At a friend's."

"You have friends?"

"Very funny. But that guy last night . . . he didn't do anything?"

"He was loud, apparently. Caused some trouble and then he left."

"Okay," I said.

"You stay dry," he said. "And indoors. Not fit for man or beast out there."

"Thank you, Kevin."

I hung up and cowardly felt like hiding in the room.

Because Dylan wanted me to stay and I . . . I wanted to stay. Well, that wasn't the total truth. My body wanted to stay. And my body ached for him. I felt like those phone calls between us were a promise, like the storm rolling in over the valley. And I was flush with the potential to make good on that promise.

My head was trying to make a case for getting the hell out of here.

You are alone in an isolated cabin with a man you don't really know.

I knew enough though, didn't I? Enough to know that if I stayed, something amazing would happen. He would touch me. Kiss me. Make me come. And not by myself. Not alone in a shitty trailer on the edge of a swamp.

The need for connection—for what we had on the phone to be made real. Physical. It was all that mattered.

I was Annie McKay, and I could go back to my strange, hollow, friendless existence later. I could go back to hiding and waiting later.

I did not think about Hoyt. My husband.

Marriage, I decided, was not the word for what I had.

Another time I would figure out what word fit. Another day. But right now . . . Dylan.

In the end it wasn't a decision. Dylan was an instinct. An urge, like a tide in my blood.

I would do this. I would have this.

And then I'd forget it.

I went back into the kitchen to find him standing in front of the windows, watching the storm. The rain and the clouds. The flash and crackle of lightning, spanning the distance between heaven and earth. A link—electric and momentary—between the two.

"Everyone okay?" he asked without turning around.

"Yes. They're fine. Apparently, Max left without doing anything."

He made a low assenting noise in his throat.

I set the phone down on the table and clutched my shaking fingers together. "Now what?"

Lead me, I thought. *Lead me like you've always led me.*

He turned, his face, that nose, those lips, the edges of the scar there on his neck.

Dylan.

"Now, take off your clothes."

24

DYLAN

Truthfully, Dylan expected her to comply. Dylan expected her to do everything he asked. She was twenty-four and she was so innocent. The kind of innocent that never went away. She could watch a dozen strippers give blow jobs and she'd still be innocent.

Pure, that's what Annie was. She was pure.

Pure, but curious . . . it was a killer combination.

That purity, it was a part of her. It was in her eyes as she watched him from across the room. It was in her voice. *Fuck,* it was in the ramrod straightness of her spine, like she knew she shouldn't be here. Like she knew she was better than this place, and what was going to happen here.

Dylan wondered again where she was from, what kind of life she'd had that kept her insulated from the world. What she was so damn scared of. But then he shoved the thought aside, because she'd made it clear it wasn't his business.

He'd never been innocent. He'd been ruined since the moment of his birth.

And he was going to smear her with all the filth on his hands. He was going to get it all over her.

The devil in Dylan Daniels was in charge now. And the devil couldn't wait.

ANNIE

Take off your clothes.

The words ignited inside of me, burning away what was left of my reservations.

"No," I said, the courage coming from I had no idea where.

He lifted his eyebrow, flares of color showing up on his cheeks, because he wasn't expecting me to say that. And he liked it.

Dylan always liked it when I said no.

More fire. More courage. I did not recognize myself in this moment.

"No?"

Instead of answering, I sat down on the leather chair facing him. It was big, that chair, and it practically swallowed me whole. His eyes burned into me and I leaned back, spreading my legs. Slowly, making sure he saw everything. That his eye tracked every twitch of my fingers. I lifted my hand from beside my hip to touch my stomach and then the top edge of my shorts.

I could feel the heat of my pussy on the tips of my fingers.

With one hand Dylan swept all the stuff off the ottoman, magazines and a book. The television remote. It all clattered to the floor, but I didn't jump. His eyes held me pinned to the chair. He sat down on the ottoman, facing me, so close our knees touched. So close I could smell him.

"Show me what you've been doing," he said. "Show me what you've been doing all alone in your trailer."

My fingers slipped down over the fabric between my legs.

My fingers curled and I scraped my short, blunt nails against myself. My eyelids flinched with the pleasure/pain.

"Good pain?" he asked.

"You were right," I whispered. "It does exist."

He clenched his hands around his kneecaps. And I imagined he wanted to grab me and was stopping himself, and that restraint . . . *God,* it was so sexy. And I wanted more than anything in the world at this moment to break that restraint. To test it, over and over again, until he snapped.

"What else do you like?" he whispered.

I pushed the palm of my hand harder against my pussy and arched into it, rolling my hips against the pressure.

"I like that," I said, biting my lip.

"Take off your shorts," he said.

I shook my head, smiling at him.

"You," I told him.

He reached for me with big, thick hands, calloused and nicked. Scarred not by the fire, but by the usual things. Life things.

I held my breath, waiting for their touch. It seemed in that moment I'd been waiting for his touch forever. My whole life. He grabbed hold of the bottom edges of my shorts, his hands brushing over the tops of my thighs in the process, and I gasped. His eyes lifted to mine and he stroked his thumb against my leg again.

I felt that touch inside my skin.

Dylan was touching me. And I read some kind of surprise in his face.

After all this time, we were touching.

After another second he yanked the shorts down my legs, revealing my old bikini underwear. The blue ones with the white flowers.

God. It had to be this underwear.

The elastic bit into my skin and red hair curled over the edges.

"You're a redhead," he whispered, touching those curls, and then he touched the underwear, right over my core. Right where I ached. "You're wet."

"I'm . . ." *on fire, dying. Hurting.*

Unable to wait, unable to do this at his pace, I slipped my fingers beneath the tight blue crotch of my underwear, and we both looked down to see the rolling edges of my knuckles as I made my way down to my clit.

"Spread your legs wider," he whispered and I complied. I lifted my knees, bracing my feet against the edge of the cushion.

"You are so fucking gorgeous," he said, his eyes moving over my body. My shoulders. My breasts. My hand between my legs.

Dylan watching was hotter than I'd expected, hotter, almost, than I could take, and I squeezed my clit between my fingers.

"Does that feel good?" he asked.

I nodded, squeezing it harder and then letting it go. In time with my heartbeat.

Slowly, he reached forward and touched the top trembling edge of my breast, just where it rose above my camisole. Just his finger there across that small curve.

I jumped. Startled, shocked even. His eyes were locked on mine and I couldn't look away. My fingers under my panties slipped farther, lower, until I was inside of myself, reaching deep and high and as hard as I could.

That had always felt good. Always been enough. But somehow with his eyes on me, with his hand on my breast, it wasn't enough. Not nearly enough.

"Dylan . . ." I breathed, hoping he'd understand and he'd just do it. Just push my hands out of the way and take over. That's what I needed him to do, because the things I did alone in my trailer, they weren't enough. Not nearly enough.

"You can do it," he said, cupping my whole breast in his hand, his thumb right over the hard edge of my nipple.

"But I want you."

His face was flushed. Blotchy, almost. His jaw as hard as granite.

"I want you to fill me up," I whispered.

But all he did was press my nipple between his thumb and finger and pinch it, slowly building up the pressure until I groaned. Until I felt like I was being pulled into pieces.

"More," I begged. "More . . ."

"Keep going," he told me, and I lifted my hips up off the chair.

"Dylan—"

"This is what you get," he breathed. "All you get right now."

Oh God. Fuck him. My face twisted and I lifted my other hand, using both between my legs, keeping up that heartbeat on my clit, and slipping two other fingers inside of myself.

Between the look on his face and my hands between my legs I was lost in the pleasure, swept up in some kind of endless tide, and then he squeezed my nipple as hard as I could take it, as if he knew the very specific calibrations of pain and pleasure in my body, and I screamed. I screamed and arched up off that chair.

The orgasm went on and on. Until finally I collapsed back against the leather. Boneless and strange. Different.

I opened my eyes and found him watching me and tenderness unspooled in my chest. Something living and vibrant, a wild . . . affection for him.

It was startling and awful. The wrong thing at the wrong time. And I felt myself flinch away from his eyes. Away from his touch.

"Annie?"

I took a breath, another, trying to rein myself in. Find my footing.

"Are you okay?" he asked.

"Best one yet," I said with a wide, ecstatic smile, hoping he wouldn't look past it at the strange panic I was feeling.

It's just the sex, I told myself. *You're all twisted up because it feels so good and he helped you get it. That's all it was.*

I really, really wanted to believe that. But somehow, nearly naked in front of him, the air between us smelling like sex, I couldn't . . . couldn't commit to it.

He was staring at me, as if he could see what I was thinking, read my thoughts like a book. I put my feet back on the floor, shifting so my underwear wasn't cutting up into me.

"Maybe," I whispered, my voice still shaking. Sweat still dripping down from my hairline. "I should—"

He fell down onto his knees between my legs and reached an arm around my hips and pulled me hard against him.

I squeaked, startled. That soft wet place between my legs, still pulsing with blood, twitching still with pleasure, was tight up against the hard length of his erection in his jeans. He dropped his hand down to my ass and pushed me harder against him.

"Feel that?" he asked.

My mouth dry, my brain dumb, I nodded.

"Every time I talk to you, that's how I get," he said.

He ground us together and I flinched and gasped at the same time.

"Sore?" he asked me, and pushed back slightly like he was ready to give me a second. But his eyes said only a second.

He brushed his thumb over the damp crotch of my underwear and I flinched again, but not as hard.

"Just . . . sensitive," I said.

"I thought listening to you come was hot," he told me, his thumb tracing circles and circles around that damp spot, making it grow.

"That's the only time anyone's ever touched me . . . while I did that." The second the words were out of my mouth I realized how much I'd revealed. It's as if I couldn't help it with him; even as I tried to keep all my own secrets, I managed to let too many spill.

He cocked his head. "You've never come with anyone else?"

"No," I breathed.

He pushed against me again, so hard I was amazed his jeans didn't tear. "Then this is going to get much better. Put your arms around my neck."

Carefully, as if he were a live bomb, I wrapped my arms around his shoulders. Shocks zipped between us as the storm outside electrified the air.

"I'm gonna kiss you," he said. I felt my skin flush. I liked when he talked that way, the announcement before the act. I guess I had a thing for dirty talk, maybe from the phone calls. Or maybe that's just what I liked and never knew it. Like black coffee.

"Yes," I sighed and, slowly, carefully, he put his mouth— those beautiful lips—against mine.

He exhaled and I inhaled, breathing him in. I exhaled, he inhaled. He moaned against my mouth and I breathed that in, too.

As beautiful as those lips looked, they felt better. Infinitely better. The scar tissue at the edge of his mouth was harder skin than the rest of it. Just one of Dylan's textures.

I had no experience with which to measure this kiss. It wasn't as if Hoyt had never kissed me. He had. Perfunctory pecks that meant nothing, that felt like . . . nothing. That were as special as shoving my feet into shoes.

But this, this long, slow pressure. This sweet tasting. The careful breathing—it felt special. Like one kiss in a thousand. A million, maybe.

I reached up and touched his hair. It was silky between my fingers and he sighed against my lips, which I took to mean he liked it, so I ran my fingers through that hair. Up the back, past his scars toward his ears. Rough, then soft. And he pushed against me like a pet looking for more affection.

I smiled against his lips and gave him a good rub.

He grabbed the back of my neck, holding me still, and opened his mouth. His tongue touched my lips. I couldn't quite swallow my gasp. Surprise and pleasure. His tongue slipped into my mouth. Intimate and invading. And for a moment I could just sit there, passive, and experience it. The slick slide against my own tongue. My teeth.

But then, very suddenly, it wasn't enough. And I was struck with the very real fear that nothing was going to be enough with him. Not ever.

I could do every single sexual thing I've ever thought of and it wouldn't be enough.

Starving for him, for what he could give me, I wrapped my arms hard around his neck and tilted my head, opening my mouth to accept him. To let him in. As far as he wanted to go.

Take it, I thought. *Take me.*

There was nothing careful anymore, nothing tentative. It was as if we'd both realized we were starving for the other. Like we wanted to devour each other. My lips ate at his, my tongue was in his mouth, and he pulled me even closer, until my arms and my legs were wrapped hard around him. He jerked me against him, even tighter. Even closer.

It was going to take an act of God to get me out of his arms.

His hands slipped down my back to my ass and he started to pull off that thin, little-girl underwear.

"Grab me," I breathed against his mouth.

"What?"

"Grab me. Grab my ass."

It was the thing with the stripper and I didn't know if he'd remember. Or care.

But then he palmed my ass in his hands, gripping me hard. I

pushed against him and he squeezed, lifting me, the tight elastic of my underwear cutting across his hands and my skin.

"Why do I like that?" I groaned. "Why—"

The tips of his fingers teased the crease between my cheeks and I shook in his arms. The pressure to come again was nearly painful and I put my teeth against his neck, hurting him, just so I hurt less.

He jerked against me, tipping his head, giving me more room to play.

"Harder," he said. "Bite me harder."

So I did.

"Fuck," he groaned.

"I want—" I stopped, laughing, because I really didn't know how to put all of this into words. How to make sense of it. There was a storm raging inside my skin.

"Tell me."

"More. I want more. Your hands—"

"Where?"

I pushed my hips at him, hoping he'd get the message.

"Don't tell me you're shy?"

"Please . . . just . . . touch me."

He kept one hand on my ass and shoved the other through the curls between my legs until he finally got his fingers inside my slit. His middle finger slid past my clit and I jumped in his arms, arching toward him, hoping to lure him back to my clit, but he wasn't interested.

"I'm going to fuck you, baby," he breathed against my neck. "With my hands. My tongue and then my cock."

God, I was so wet. So wet. I bathed his fingers right there at the entrance of my body. But very suddenly this felt far too lopsided. It was the phone calls all over again. Him with all the cards, me panting for more. And he could do all those things to me, with his mouth and his tongue and his fingers and body.

And I would let him. I wanted him so bad I could barely understand it. But there were things I wanted to do to him.

There was an equality in this that I needed. So much of this was wrong. So much.

But a little equality would make so much right.

I remembered what Tiffany said the other day outside her trailer—sometimes it felt good to be the one giving something.

"Stop," I breathed.

"What?"

I pulled away, shoved myself back so I could get my hands between us. The flesh of his stomach was hot against my fingers as I shoved his shirt up and started to open the fly of his jeans.

"I want . . ." I shook my head, the short blond hair falling over my eyes.

"What?"

"I want to suck you. I want to put you in my mouth."

From the book. The fucking stripper.

"So bad, Dylan. I want that so bad." I nudged at him when he didn't seem eager to move. He was watching me with those unreadable eyes, but I was burning too hot to wonder what he was thinking. "Get up," I said. And he braced himself against the arms of the chair and pushed himself up. He grimaced as if it hurt.

"Are you okay?" I asked, reaching for his neck, which he held so stiffly.

"I'm good," he said, standing up straight. Because of his height and how I was sitting, that rod in his pants was at eye level.

My fingers, thick and clumsy, fumbled, but I got the zipper open and then my hand was around his cock, pulling him free of his pants and the cotton of his boxers. He was huge in my hand. Wide and long, the head purple, nearly, and damp. I blew out a long breath, which feathered across his skin. He hissed and put a hand to my neck, cupping it in his palm, his thumb pressed against my pulse, as if he were feeling my heartbeat.

Anticipation stretched so thin between us, it could shatter like glass with the wrong move. And I was suddenly paralyzed with indecision. I didn't know the right move from the wrong move and all that was pushing me along was instinct.

But maybe my instincts were as fucked up as I was.

"Go ahead, baby," he said, tucking a piece of hair behind my ear. "Do whatever you want."

Whatever I want? That was some big territory.

I LEANED FORWARD AND LICKED HIM. HE WAS SALTY AND WARM and soft. I licked him again, tracing the edges of the head. Finding the veins along the shaft. Again and again until I felt like I'd mapped him. Dylan kept twitching against me and sighing and it was all so intimate. So personal.

I'd never experienced anything like this before. The vulnerability and power that each of us had in this exact moment. All his strength, restrained. All my courage, unleashed. It was a moment that spun and spun and spun between us.

He was silent, letting me find my way, letting me look at him, and kiss him. Taste and touch. Soft and slow. Until finally I ducked my head and licked him from root to tip. I stopped and looked up, only to find him watching me with hot, deep eyes.

Approval and affection and respect poured off of him. It rained down on me and I knew . . . without a shadow of a doubt that I was in real trouble.

Real. Trouble.

I would leave this house in a few hours and go back to the trailer to sort out my life, to get back on my feet. I was going to go back to being Annie McKay. But I would be leaving a part of myself here—a part of myself I liked, and I didn't know if I would ever get that back. Or find it again.

My pleasure was now tinged with a kind of grief that made it sharper. Sweeter. It twisted harder inside of me.

Good pain. It was all a kind of good pain. It was happiness pushed as far as it would go.

Feeling his eyes on me, I ducked my head and slipped him past my lips. The head of his cock slid across the top of my mouth and then touched the softer muscles at the back of my throat.

"Oh God, Annie . . ."

I slipped him out of my mouth. "Is that . . . is this okay?"

"So good, baby. You're killing me."

I smiled up at him, at the bright color in his cheeks, the heat in those dark eyes, and then took him again, into my mouth.

He took my hand and wrapped it around the base of his cock. He squeezed my fingers until I was holding him hard in my hand. Sucking him hard in my mouth. My lips stretched tight around him.

His hand left mine and then touched my ear and then the back of my head and he pushed me, just a little, into him. Pushing me just a little past what was comfortable.

I hummed in my throat, hoping he got that I liked that. That I wanted that.

I looked up at him, just to be sure he understood, and he put both hands in my hair, the strands tangling on calluses, caught between fingers. The small licks of pain adding to the fire building inside of me.

He stopped me, pushed me back, which I resisted, because I wasn't done. Because there was a whole world of experience I was aching to have. Right now. With him.

"I want to fuck you," he said and the words, *God,* his words, made me crazy and he slipped out of my mouth with a pop. A string of saliva between my mouth and him.

"Yes," I breathed. "Yes." Yes to all of it. Yes to everything.

He tore out of his clothes. The white shirt thrown over his

head, revealing a tattoo on his chest. The other half was pink with scar tissue.

His chest, stomach, and arms were thick with muscles.

If he wanted, he could hold me in one hand. That was the sense I got, anyway. He could hold me or tear me apart—with one hand.

"Take off your clothes," he said, and then jumped over the couch, heading for the other hallway.

I was astounded to see that I still had my top on. I ripped it over my head and lay down on the couch, which felt like butter, soft against my skin.

How odd to be lying down in this strange room in front of a wall full of windows when I couldn't do it in my own trailer, the curtains shut.

Suddenly shy, I sat up, looking for my underwear.

He came back into the room and stepped around the couch to stand beside me. He had a silver strip of condoms in his teeth. Watching me, he pushed down his pants and stepped out of them. His boots had been kicked off in his bedroom. He tore one condom off the strip and tossed the others down on the ottoman.

I reached for him, touching the bottom of the soft sac behind his penis, and he twitched and then reached for me, skipping my thigh, skipping everything but the heart of me.

His fingers spread my folds and then slid right inside of me.

I gasped. Arched. My breasts shimmied with the motion.

He added another finger and I groaned.

"It's good?" he asked.

"Yes."

"It's going to be better when it's my cock. I'm going to fill you all the way up, Annie."

"Hurry," I breathed. He ripped the condom open with his teeth and pushed it on and then sat down at my feet on the couch.

"Come here," he murmured. And I must have moved too slowly because he pulled me up into his lap. He pulled me so hard I practically flew against him. He kissed me, deep and hard. And I kissed him back just as hard. Just as frantic.

And then he grabbed my ass. Grabbed all my ass he could. Grabbed my ass like he wanted to rob it.

"Oh God, oh my God. Please, do something. I need you to do something," I whispered into his neck. "Or I'm going to do it myself." I reached my hand down my body like I was going to make myself come, but he grabbed my hand and held it behind my back.

I leaned away from his neck, looked him in the eye.

"Lift yourself up," he said.

And I did, wobbling a little against his chest.

With his free hand he reached behind me and then slowly began pushing me down onto him and I felt him . . . there at my pussy. Too hard. Too big.

I cried out. Moaned. Suddenly scared. Suddenly worried. I tried to climb off of him.

"Does it hurt?"

"Too . . . it's too much."

"Go slow. Take me slow."

I shook my head.

"Annie, baby, look at me," he said. And when our eyes met the fear was gone. The worry evaporated. It was just us. And he cared.

"Do you want to stop?"

I shook my head, words beyond me.

The hand on my shoulder did not hold me or force me. It was just . . . there. Letting me set the pace. Which was slow, my body accepting his inch by inch. And what had seemed foreign was just . . . right.

"It's never felt like this before," I whispered.

Sweat poured off of me. Pooled between us. We were slick

and we were heaving. And his patience and my trust made this something totally new.

Finally, I was seated hard against him. Our hips so tight it nearly hurt, and I was gasping with every breath.

"Now what?"

He smiled. "Hold on," he whispered. My head was too heavy to hold up, my body too cumbersome to control, so I put my head down on his neck and let him do it. Let him move me. He grabbed onto my hips, pushing and pulling me against him in a slow, hard grind.

I could feel him inside of me, brushing up against nerve endings I didn't know existed, creating a kind of burn I'd never dreamed of. But when he pulled me toward him, he pushed up against my clit, creating the pressure I loved, and the combination of the two things with the heat of him, the strength of him all around me . . . very soon, it wasn't enough anymore.

I shifted harder against him and I could feel his breath catch, felt it in my chest cavity. And suddenly it was game over.

He tilted us sideways and laid me out on that couch, my legs spread wide around his hips, my hands on his shoulders.

"You okay?" he breathed through clenched teeth.

"Good. So good."

He pulled out, almost all the way, and then pushed back into me. Again. Harder.

"Still good?" he asked.

All I could do was nod and clutch at his back, his body, try to hold on as the seas rose around us.

He growled, swearing under his breath, and then grabbed onto the arm of the couch, using it for leverage as he began to pound into me.

"Touch yourself," he told me.

"No," I said, because what was happening was new. What was happening was different. "I'm going to come. Just like this. Keep. Just. . . ."

I didn't have to tell him twice. He pounded into me three more times, each time so deep, impossibly deep, and then I was coming, unraveling beneath him. My nails digging into his back.

"Oh . . . fuck. Annie," he cried, and then he buried himself inside of me and came.

I held onto him, stroking his hair, his back, the scars on his neck, and wondered what happened after something like this?

How was I supposed to still be Annie McKay after this?

25

I WOKE UP SLOWLY, ROLLING SLIGHTLY, ONLY TO FIND MY BACK
stuck to whatever I was lying against. My skin peeled as I sat up.
Leather. I'd fallen asleep on the leather couch.

There was a soft blue blanket over my very naked body.

My very naked, very . . . sore body. I felt stretched wide between my legs. The muscles in my back, in my thighs—they felt
like they were made out of water.

I felt like I was made out of water.

I pressed my fingers against my lips as if I could hold back
the giggle. I wanted to giggle. A giggle was going to happen.

I laid my head back against the cushions and like the
seventeen-year-old girl I'd never been—I giggled.

Ho. Ly. Shit. That . . . had been amazing. Dylan had been
amazing.

What I'd had with Hoyt followed—to the letter—what my
very uncomfortable high school health teacher had told us about
sex. Or procreation. There had been the hardening and the in-
sertion and the ejaculation.

It had been cold and clinical and painful.

What had happened with Dylan? I didn't even have words

for it. But if I'd had a wish list for what sex could be like, Dylan just crossed everything off the list.

I fell sideways back onto the couch, my hands between my legs, where I was warm and sore. Who knew . . . honest to God . . . who knew my body was designed to feel so much?

What a fucking miracle that was.

When I turned sixteen, our church got a new pastor. The first time he spoke from the pulpit, Mom and I went to church in the best of our Sunday best. We sat in our pew, right side, third from the back, and waited with bated breath to hear the new guy.

I remember exactly his sermon. Exactly. Tolerance. That faith was not just faith in God, or faith in people who looked like you or were attracted to the opposite sex. Faith was faith in humanity. God loved all of us. And we should do the same.

It had been a revelation to me.

Not so much for Mom. We didn't go back until that pastor left.

It was weird, my body sore from sex, my mind blown from the power of what I could feel, but at that moment, more than any in the past few years . . . I missed church.

The power of those two things—the spiritual and the carnal—were connected, like the arc of electricity between heaven and earth.

From behind the cracked-open door that led to Dylan's garage, there was a thump and a muffled curse. Dylan was up.

I pressed a hand to my heart where it pounded, barely contained by my ribs and my skin. Part of me wanted to vanish. Just . . . not be here. Not look at him. Not try to make conversation after what had happened between us. I didn't know how to do that. Not with any grace.

But another part of me, alive and hungry and curious, wanted to do all of that again.

I grabbed my clothes from the floor but they smelled like sex and sweat, so I wrapped the blanket around my body and walked back to the room that was mine.

In the drawers I found a clean set of pajamas. Size small, the tags still on the soft fuchsia tee shirt. And the dark navy flannel pants with the stars and moons and bright yellow suns scattered over them.

They fit. They fit perfectly and they were pretty.

Dylan didn't pick them out, I got that. Margaret had. For her granddaughter. But they were pretty pajamas with little suns on them and I loved them.

The storm had not stopped. Rain fell in sheets on the windows. Outside it was just a swirl of gray. I looked down out the window and wondered if there was a chance this house might slip right off this mountain.

I wondered if I'd slipped off a mountain.

I'm married.

I watched the rain fall into a dense cloud of mist, where it just vanished.

I'm a married woman.

It was one thing to lie about my name . . . but I'd just made Dylan a participant in adultery. I swallowed and rested my head against the window. And tried, really, really hard, to convince myself that it didn't matter. What Dylan didn't know couldn't hurt him.

But it mattered.

And I knew it.

I put on a pair of thick socks I'd found in the top drawer and made my way back across the house and then slipped through the cracked door into his dark garage.

The light was on over his bench, and he sat there in a pair of jeans and boots and nothing else.

He was beautiful, his skin dusted with gold under that light. His muscles flexed and shifted under that skin.

"Dylan?" I said, standing on the cement stoop, three steps up from the floor of his garage.

"You're awake," he said. He didn't turn, the muscles of his arms twitching faster as he finished what he was working on. "Just . . . one more second."

In that minute, I honestly didn't breathe.

But then he turned around, and I blew out my breath as coolly as I could before I got light-headed.

"I was tired." *Awesome. Awesome response.* "It was a long night."

"Sure."

He was still looking at me. Not quite smiling. Not quite not smiling, either. It made me nervous, that look. Like I was something he was slowly taking apart and putting back together, over and over.

"So . . . what is all this stuff?" I looked around his garage because I didn't know what else to do.

"All this stuff is cars," he said. "Those are tires. Anything else you're unfamiliar with?"

Oh . . . I couldn't. I was too raw for teasing now. "I'm . . . I'm not . . . I haven't done this."

"Fucked a guy and then talked about cars?"

The laugh barked out of me.

He crossed the room and climbed the three steps, his eyes on mine, burning away the embarrassment and insecurity until all that was left was my heartbeat in my chest and the heat in his eyes.

"Hey," he said and kissed me lightly on the mouth. Just enough. Just enough that I could taste him. The salt and spice. He'd brushed his teeth and had coffee. I could taste all of him on his lips.

"Hey," I whispered and kissed him back. Wishing I'd had coffee and brushed my teeth.

He stepped back. "Nice pajamas. I like the suns." He reached out and touched one of them on the front of my thigh and just like that, I was ready. I was hot and damp and . . . ready.

"So," I said, stepping back for just a little distance. "What's going on here?"

"I fix cars." He took his own distance, taking the steps down to the floor.

He was being evasive—I knew, because that's how we were with each other. So, I slowly gathered all those things I knew about him, the crumbs he'd left, and I followed him down the steps to the floor.

"You fix cars and go to parties in tuxedos. You live on a cliff in a beautiful house—"

"Don't come down here," he said. "You don't have shoes."

He was wearing steel-toed boots. Boots and no shirt.

I glanced down at my feet in the thick wool socks I'd found. My toes were curled over the edge of that cement step, like I was about ready to jump.

"You told me people pay you a lot of money for something stupid."

"I fix cars."

"You're telling me you're the best-paid mechanic in the world?"

He laughed and glanced over his shoulder at me. "Yeah. Sorta."

"Dylan . . ." *Please,* I wanted to say. *Throw the girl whose mind you just scrambled with what will undoubtedly be the best sex of her life a bone.* "We just had sex." What a stupid, inadequate word for what had passed between us. "And I know nothing about you!"

"That's not true. We . . ." His throat bobbed and this cavern, this great cathedral of space, shrank to nothing. To zero, and I could hear his heartbeat. The sound of his swallow. "We know plenty about each other."

Heat exploded between us. His beautiful, scarred lips, my

scarred knees. Every car and machine between us—it just incinerated.

What I knew about him I could hold in my palm and when he looked at me like that, it didn't matter.

"I fix race cars," he finally said. "Build engines. I . . . invented a fuel injection valve that . . . sort of made some money."

I nodded, fighting a smile. "Sort of."

"Trust me," he said. "No one is more surprised than me."

He walked back over to his bench and I sat down on my step. I was pretty sure that he was going to shoot me down if I tried to talk about the accident, but it was worth a shot. And maybe his mind was a little scrambled too. "After the accident you started fixing cars."

"Before the accident I started fixing cars. That's how most drivers start. Souping up the engines on their dads' old Fords to see how fast they can go before things fall apart."

I watched him putting tools away in big metal cases, like filing cabinets on wheels. He grabbed greasy rags and threw them into a cloth bin in the corner.

"So," I said, stepping lightly into this conversation. "When you were a kid, messing around with your dad's Ford, he didn't mind?" I watched him out of the corner of my eye because I knew what I was doing, the sleeping dog I was poking at.

Dylan stilled, his back to me. "My dad taught me. I keep forgetting that."

I pulled the sun on my knee into a fold. Obliterating it.

"Ben said he didn't have any kids," I whispered, my voice carrying through the cavern right to him, and he flinched. Just once. But then he started moving again. Pushing himself back into motion.

"Put that together, did you?"

"I thought for a long time you were related to the girl in the fire."

"Nope. I'm related to the murderer."

"Dylan? Why would he say he doesn't have kids?"

"Because he stopped being my pop a long, long time ago."

"But you didn't stop being his son?"

Dylan turned. Amazing how inscrutable he was. He could close a door so fast, so hard, there was no chance to get in, no chance to see anything but what he wanted to show.

I nodded like I understood, and the silence between us started to get chilly. "So that makes Max—"

"My brother."

"The badass you wanted to be like."

Dylan watched me a long time. "Yeah," he said.

Looking at Dylan, strong and fierce in this beautiful house, with Margaret and the money implied in all of it, I could not connect the dots between him and Ben. They were so many miles apart.

"Is your mom Maria?" I asked. He could not control his shock. His drop-jawed astonishment.

"How did you know about Mom?"

"Your dad—"

"Ben," Dylan said with a mean laugh. "That man is no dad."

"Fine . . . Ben told me about her."

Dylan blinked as if he really couldn't believe what I was saying. "What exactly did he tell you?"

"That he missed her, but they were bad together."

"Bad together," he laughed, humorlessly. "That's one way to put it."

"Did he hit her?" I asked, wondering how Ben could look me in the eyes when I was telling him about Hoyt. How could he look me in the eyes and have done the exact same thing to another woman?

"No. Good Saint Ben never lifted a finger against her, like that was what made all the other shit he did all right. There is more than one way to hurt a woman, and Ben found them all."

I did not need to be sermonized on the many ways men could

hurt women. I glanced away from the intensity of his eyes. They saw too much, those eyes of his. He started throwing tools back into the toolboxes. Each one landing with a clatter and a bang that made me jump.

"Is it really dangerous at the trailer park?" I asked.

He leaned back against one of the cars and crossed his arms over his bare chest, looking like every single sexual fantasy I never allowed myself to have.

"Ben is an old fucking man. Harmless. But if Max is coming around, then, yes."

"There are other people there. Families. Young kids."

"Yep."

"That's all you have to say?"

"The world is rough all over, Annie. My brother is an outlaw. My father was an outlaw. They are both involved in shit that's not safe."

I put my head in my hand. I ran away from Oklahoma to try and get safe. To get away from violence and abuse. I thought I'd done it, in my Febreze-scented escape.

"Annie, listen . . ." He came over to stand in front of me.

How odd, I thought, to know that skin so well. The taste of it. The feel of it. And to know the man inside of it not even a little. At that moment I let the fact that I didn't tell him about Hoyt be okay. Cowardly, yes. Awful, sure. But I let it. "I have a house in Charleston. You can stay—"

"No!"

"Why no?"

"Because I don't know you! I'm not going to live with—"

"Slow down there, killer. I'm not asking you to live with me. I have a house where you can stay. If you're going to be uptight about it you can pay me rent."

"I don't like cities." My gut made me say that.

"What's wrong with cities?"

"People."

He laughed. "That I can understand. You don't have to tell me right now; you can think about it. But I gotta say, it seems like a pretty easy call to me. Shitty trailer or a beach house in Charleston."

"It's a beach house?"

"Oh, that changes your mind?" He laughed.

"I've never been to the beach."

"Not ever?"

"Not ever."

"Jesus Christ, honey. Did you live in a box before you answered that phone?"

The smile died on my face and I ducked my head, rubbing my cheek against my shoulder. I did. I lived in that box. And I smashed it right open.

"Anything else you want to get off your chest?"

"What day is it?" I asked.

"Thursday. The twenty-fourth."

"It's my birthday."

For a minute he gaped at me.

"Everyone has a birthday," I said when it seemed his shock went on a bit too long.

"You're twenty-five? Today?"

I nodded, back to nervously obliterating the sun on my pants, but then he smiled. Not one of his half smiles, or mocking grins. It was a smile that revealed a very real amount of happiness. Of joy, even.

It did not make him more handsome, he was already far too good-looking, but it made him very human. And again, that dangerous affection for this stranger curled through me.

He pushed off the car and . . . well, he prowled over toward me. Loose-hipped and gleaming, he came to me. To me. Annie McKay. And he bent down, one hand braced on the wall, the other on the railing.

His smile . . . I swear to God, it was beautiful. Beautiful because it was rare, because of those scarred lips, because it was all for me.

I couldn't stop myself. I tipped my face up, like a plant toward the sun, and smiled right back.

Softly, sweetly, he kissed me. Again. And again. And again, again. A thousand small breaths across my face. His mouth was delicious and I was starving.

"What do you want for your birthday, baby?" he asked, so low, so quiet, I felt the words more than heard them.

"One more day." The words came without thought. Without a plan. I wanted one more day in this magical house on the edge of the cliff. "One more day with you," I said.

I reached up and touched the edge of a scar, a thick, white wrinkle on his neck. He had the Virgin Mary tattooed over his heart. I felt my own buckle in my chest.

And then it's over. It has to be.

He nodded like he heard me.

"One more day," he agreed, and those arms swept me up.

For a second I was awkward in his hold. All legs and arms caught up between our bodies. I jerked away and he gave me a quick jostle.

"You want me to drop you?"

"No . . . I'm just . . . This is awkward."

"Relax." Another kiss. Another jostle and my arms were out and around his neck and my legs were around his waist and suddenly, it was the most natural thing.

I could feel the skin of his waist against my legs, his neck on the inside of my elbows.

This electricity between us found new routes. The tops of my ears burned, the tips of my fingers. The back of my throat.

He carried me through his house, past my room, through the last door at the end of the hallway. It was his room and I barely noticed. I was too busy feeling his lower ribs vibrate as he breathed.

There was fine hair at the nape of his neck. Soft when I

stroked it one way, like the bristle of a brush when I touched it the other way.

I could do that all day.

My twenty-four-hour birthday wish.

Something cold touched the back of my thighs, and he flipped on a light and I blinked into the reflected brightness in the mirrors. We were in his bathroom. A bathroom so big my trailer could fit in it.

His kiss lingered. His hands slid from my ass to my waist and my shoulders and I twitched. I did the same to him. I took all the touches I didn't take earlier. I ran my hands all over his body. All that silky bare skin, the thick muscles beneath it. My fingers brushed over the scars on his ribs and he twitched.

"Does . . . does that hurt?"

"It's not comfortable," he said and kissed me again. I kept my hands away from his scars.

When he pulled back, his lips were swollen and damp. Pink.

I reached up and touched them with my fingers. "You have a pretty mouth," I said.

He sucked my finger into his mouth and then slid back, until it fell from his lips. "I have a girl's mouth," he said. "A cocksucker mouth."

"What?" I cried.

"Pop's words," he said.

"What a stupid thing to say," I muttered and pulled him back toward me. I touched his mouth, all the edges, the soft curves, the hard edge of the scar tissue, and he twitched and tried to pull back but I put my legs around him, keeping him still. "You've got a beautiful mouth." I had no idea if my opinion mattered, but I wanted to say it. I gave him one hard, quick kiss and let him go.

Smiling, he reached into a glass-lined shower and turned on the faucet. Water thundered down from a big, round showerhead and the glass near the floor immediately got foggy.

There was a bathtub next to the shower, one of those big Jacuzzi ones. And a toilet beside that. Outside the window over it, there was only sky.

"Are we taking a shower?" I asked, excited by the idea.

"You are. And you're going to take your time."

"Are you telling me I stink?"

"No. I'm telling you I need twenty minutes to get things organized."

"For what?"

"Your birthday."

He grabbed the hem of my shirt and lifted it up over my head. This was another strange minute when I kind of missed my long hair. It would feel good falling down over my bare shoulders. It would probably look good, reflected back in all these mirrors. And I sort of . . . I sort of wanted him to see it. To see part of the old me and find it desirable. The parts of me that no one found desirable. I wondered what he would think—of my red hair. My Del Monte cap. My cowboy boots.

The steam was filling the room now, and when he reached around me to pull at my pants, I braced my arms behind me and lifted my hips.

He smiled down at the red hair between my legs, his thumb stroked through it, and I looked down to the see the red curls there around his thumb.

Other women shaved. I didn't. I'd never been waxed. I trimmed the hair because it was hot and I felt cleaner when I did it.

"Why'd you dye your hair?" he asked.

Because I'm running from my husband who tried to kill me.

Reality was intrusive. A bully pounding on the door, and I ignored it as best I could.

Twenty-four hours and then I'd go back to reality.

"I just wanted a change," I lied.

His thumb slid deeper and I spread my legs wider, lifting my hips higher, jerking when he hit my clit and then lingered there, rolling it against his thumb.

"Dylan . . ." I breathed, leaning back against the mirror behind me.

He growled but then he stepped back, took a deep breath. "Get in the shower," he said.

"Now?" I blinked.

"Preparations," he said. He pressed a quick, hard kiss to my shoulder and then was gone.

26

THE DIFFERENCE BETWEEN EVERY OTHER SHOWER I'VE EVER had and Dylan's shower was the difference between what happened between Dylan and me on the couch and what happened alone on my bed.

The shower was huge, the hot water endless. And it came out of that showerhead like a spring rain.

I was considering moving into that shower. Maybe I could sublet it.

There was a razor in the shower and masculine-smelling soap and shampoo. I used it all, until I smelled like Dylan. I shaved my armpits and my legs and then, staring down at my pubic hair, I decided why not.

Using plenty of shaving cream and sitting on the bench on the far end of the shower where the water didn't hit me, I shaved my pubic hair. Not all of it.

Still Annie McKay after all.

But some. The edges. The top and then down between my legs. I rinsed off the shaving cream and felt . . . bare. Deliciously bare. Like a harem girl in the historical romance I'd read.

The hot water turned tepid and I cranked it off, opening the glass door to a room full of steam. When it cleared, I found a towel and a black robe on the marble counter where I'd been sitting.

He'd snuck in while I'd been shaving. I wondered what he'd seen. I wondered if he'd watched. Between my legs I felt puffy. Totally different.

The robe was silk and way too big and even though I rolled up the sleeves and looped the belt around my waist twice, I was still swimming in it.

But it was silky and perfect against my skin and Dylan had laid it out for me, so why would I change? The bedroom when I came out of the bathroom was dark. A king-size bed covered in a dark duvet monopolized the room. There was a dresser on a far wall. A closet in the corner, with the door left partially open. Inside I could see suits. Three or four suits. A tuxedo. I stepped forward and reached into the closet, touching the black sleeve of the tuxedo jacket. There was no label inside, which I gathered to mean he'd had it made custom. And the fabric was the softest, finest thing I'd ever touched.

One day, I thought, looking at that jacket, pushing aside the anxiety it gave me. I have one day in this magical house. Try not to ruin it. The door to the rest of the house was open and I could hear music from the kitchen. And I could smell food. Good food.

My stomach got excited. It had been many hours since the cornbread I'd eaten with peanut butter (a terrible combination) for dinner.

I got even more excited when I stepped into that kitchen and found Dylan drinking beer and putting food out on that barn table. He was listening to music I didn't recognize. But I never recognized music.

"Wow, these are some serious preparations," I said, trying to be light to hide all my misgivings. My nerves. The nonstop pounding of reality.

"Hey!" He looked up, his eyes taking in the dark robe and my damp hair. "That looks real good on you." I did a little preen, pretending to poof up my hair or something. "Can I get you something to drink?" he asked.

"You have anything in a bucket?" He shot me a quizzical look and I waved it off. "I'll have whatever is easy." My pat answer.

"Well . . ." He turned and opened up the silver fridge. "Margaret took this shit pretty seriously, so I have a fully stocked fridge right now. But I think we'll start with . . ." He pulled out a big bottle. "This."

"Champagne?"

"Only the best."

I almost told him I'd never had champagne before, but I thought maybe there'd been enough revealing how little I knew of the world.

I sat down at the table while he opened the champagne.

"What is all this?" I asked, looking at the food he'd set out.

"That," he pointed with the champagne bottle toward a plate, "is some kind of cheese that you are supposed to eat with those kinds of crackers. I don't really know, to tell you the truth. Margaret did this."

There was a bowl of olives on the table and I ate one. There was a pit in it. The pit must make it fancy. As discreetly as I could I took it out of my mouth and placed it in a little bowl that must be there for just that reason.

"Margaret came back while I was in the shower?"

"No, I imagine she came back hours ago. She lives in another house on the property. I called her when you were in the shower."

"This is quite a compound you've got here," I said, eating the cheese with the appropriate cracker. It tasted expensive. I was used to Velveeta and stale Ritz.

The champagne cork popped and he handed me a flute. And

I sat in a mountain home in a silk robe, drinking champagne, and truthfully, I didn't know how I got there.

Do not, I thought again, ruin this.

Dylan had put on a shirt while I was in the shower. A dark plaid button-up shirt, with most of the buttons undone. The sleeves were rolled up revealing his forearms, and somehow that was even sexier than his bare chest.

I put the cracker and cheese down on a plate and took a sip of my champagne. The champagne was amazing. Like sweet-and-sour sunlight. I took another sip.

"You don't like it?" he asked, glancing down at the cheese.

"It's good," I lied.

He half-smiled, half-frowned at me. "You can say you don't like it," he said. "You can actually say, 'Dylan, this cheese sucks.'"

I would never. Not ever.

"It's good," I said with a laugh. "Strong."

He tipped his head toward me. "You can change your mind, you know."

"About what?"

"About staying."

"Why . . . why would you say that? I don't want to change my mind." I knocked back half the champagne in one long gulp. Did he want me to change my mind? The thought made me feel incredibly naked under the robe and I pulled the fabric up into my lap.

"You seem wound up."

Wound up. Right. For some reason the voice in my head, the voice that kept wanting to remind me that I was married, would not shut up.

"Do you want me to leave?" I asked, and he shook his head.

"I don't turn out birthday girls on their birthdays."

I thought of the brunette I saw in those pictures, that beautiful girl who clung to his side, the two of them looking like they were in the pages of a catalog. A catalog where you could buy a richer, more exciting life.

I handed him my now empty champagne flute.

"More?"

"Please."

He filled my glass back up and handed it over to me, and then pulled a tray out of the oven. He tipped the tray onto a plate, and little pastries rolled off onto the plate. Two landed on the floor and he grabbed them with his bare hand, shoving one in his mouth.

"Jesus," he muttered. "That's hot."

He put the plate down by my hip and ate the other pastry. Watching him do all these small domestic things on my behalf, seeing the trouble and expense he'd gone to for me and my birthday, made me feel worse.

"Is this where you talked to me?" I asked, twirling the champagne glass in my hands. "At this house?"

"Yeah. I mean, usually. I have another building here. A bigger garage with an office. I talked to you a few times there."

"This house, another garage, and Margaret's house? All here?"

"I own the mountain, Annie."

I glanced away, my breath skittering around my lungs. *He owns the damn mountain.*

"Truthfully," he said, "I rarely leave this mountain."

"You go to parties in tuxedos."

"Yeah, I think that will be the last one I'm invited to. I pissed off one too many people."

"Were you always like this?" I asked.

"A hermit?" He laughed.

"No."

"Rich? No. Not at all," he said.

"Alone." He seemed intrinsically alone. Self-contained and solitary. Even surrounded by people, he would seem alone.

"I'm hardly alone," he said. "I've got a crew of guys here every day. My business partner. Margaret's here constantly."

I wondered if he believed the lie, but I did not. I knew alone. I'd been painfully alone and I only realized it now, after a month at the Flowered Manor. It only took a few friendships of exceedingly shallow depths to show me how alone I'd been. And not by choice.

"Why me?" I asked. The question surprised us both.

"Why you, what?"

"Why'd you do all this with me?" His face was blank, like he didn't understand what I was asking. "Was it a power thing? Was it like a . . . I don't know . . . a test? A joke—"

"What the fuck are you talking about, Annie? A joke?" He sounded offended.

"I mean look at you, Dylan. Look at all that you have. You could get down off this mountain and have any woman you wanted and instead . . . you were having phone sex with some stranger who could barely make rent on her shitty trailer in a shitty trailer park. And my guess is you knew that. You knew I was living in that trailer from the very beginning, didn't you?"

"Yeah, I knew, but—"

"So was it some kind of game to play around with the poor girl?" What did he call it that night, virgin kink? Was this poverty kink?

"You think any of that matters to me? What I have and what you don't?"

"I have no idea what matters to you," I said, and he blinked.

"Well, that shit doesn't."

"So . . . why me?"

He finished what was left in his champagne glass and then filled it up. He gestured to me to finish my glass.

"A little liquid courage for the birthday girl," he said, sounding . . . dark. Angry. As if my questions had wounded him. I drained my champagne and held my glass out for more. "That first phone call, I knew you were lying about living in that trailer. You are a shitty liar."

Oh, I thought, *you are so wrong. So impossibly wrong. You have no idea the lies I'm telling.*

"You kept doing this thing, every time we talked. You'd get scared and be about to hang up, but then . . . it was like you forced yourself not to be scared anymore. To keep talking to me. And every conversation I'd push a little harder, ask you to do more, and you'd . . . keep coming back for more. Over and over again and . . . Fuck, Annie. Watching that, being a part of that kind of bravery. It was exciting. Addictive."

"You didn't laugh?" I asked. "You didn't hang up and laugh at me."

"Never." It was a solemn vow from him and my nipples got hard. My body wet. "Every time you called me I felt so damn lucky."

He finished his glass of champagne and stepped over toward me. His hands on his hips. "Now, why me?"

I stared at him blankly. "Are you serious?"

"Yeah, I'm serious. Why'd you do that with me?"

I took a sip of champagne and it fizzed through me, so I took another. And then one more. "I like your voice. And . . ." I held out my glass. "I like your champagne."

Silent, he poured more champagne into my glass.

"Tell me, Annie. The truth."

Oh, the truth. Wouldn't that be something? What would happen if I just opened my mouth and told him the truth?

"You asked me if I was okay. Every time," I said, watching the bubbles explode in my glass instead of watching him. "And you apologized. And you seemed to . . . care about me and I was a total stranger to you. I felt safe," I said.

"You are safe."

I gave him an arch look. That was not the song he was singing earlier, urging me to leave the trailer park.

"With me," he clarified. "You are safe. I won't hurt you, Annie."

I think I'm already hurt, I thought. *I think I'm bleeding and I don't even know it.*

This was, without a doubt, the nicest thing any man had ever done for me. Ever. The champagne, the disgusting cheese. It was all so kind. It was the most trouble. The most care.

And I didn't deserve it.

I was lying.

I was married.

I knew I should just leave. Hadn't I gotten what I wanted? That something amazing I knew he'd be able to give me—I'd gotten it. He'd touched me. Kissed me the way that a woman should be kissed. With passion and care. Some of the ugliness of my life before was wiped away by the last few hours.

But to accept more . . . it was too greedy.

Wanting more only got me punished. Wanting more got me hurt. I had to carefully calibrate what I wanted to what I deserved.

A penny more, an inch more, and it would rain something awful down on my head.

I'd let myself have this terrible, terrible thing. And I should end it. Now. Before it got worse. Before I wanted even more. Before . . . before I ruined everything and told him.

"I have a question for you," he said. He came over to my chair, and with one hand, he picked me up and set me down on the table and then he pushed in between my legs, bracing his hands on the table beside me.

He was crowding me and I wanted to push him away and pull him closer. All at the same time. I pulled in a deep breath and my breasts touched his chest. The robe had split over my legs and I could feel the denim of his jeans on the insides of my thighs.

He tilted my face up so my eyes met his.

"What are you scared of?" he asked.

27

DYLAN

Dylan knew fear. He knew how it smelled. What it tasted like—the bitter, coppery taste of blood and adrenaline in the back of the throat. And he knew what it looked like when someone was trying not to be scared.

After he turned sixteen he'd had four long years learning every inch, every side of fear.

"I'm not scared," Annie whispered.

"And now you're lying."

She shook her head and he eased his grip up under her chin.

"Are you scared of me?"

She shook her head, that white-blond hair falling over her eyes. Dylan reached up and brushed it away, taking in all her softness. Her skin. Her hair. All of it. Her entire body communicated her fear. The white-knuckled grip on the champagne glass, the way her eyes wouldn't stay locked on his. Her shoulders were up at her ears.

"Then who are you scared of?"

"No one," she breathed. "I'm fine. Just . . . maybe nervous."

Why the fuck was she lying? He'd kicked women out of his life for far less than lying to his face. If Dylan was thinking at all, he'd pack this girl up and send her on her way.

But he wasn't thinking. And that always meant trouble.

"No one's ever gone to all this trouble for me," she said, putting her hand out toward that gross cheese Margaret insisted was the best and the olives.

"It's not that much trouble," Dylan muttered. Truthfully, he would break every rule he had, every promise he'd ever made, and go to all the trouble in the world for this girl and she had no idea. None.

He'd made a joke earlier about her living in a box before. And he knew he wasn't wrong. She'd talked about her mom, and Dylan had the sense that she wasn't the only one that had kept Annie small and pushed down.

"I don't need champagne," she said, setting down her glass. She was doing it again, that thing that made him nuts. Pushing past her fear to be brave, to reach out, however scared, for what she wanted. "I don't need fancy cheese and all this . . . stuff."

"It's a seduction, Annie. It's about want. Not need."

"You've already seduced me," she whispered. "All I want is you."

She reached up and pulled the lapels of the robe off her shoulders, revealing herself to him. That creamy skin. The small, round, tight breasts with the pink nipples. She pulled open the belt and the rest of the robe fell away and she sat there surrounded in black satin, like a present just for Dylan.

And *Jesus* . . . she'd shaved.

That tender sweet spot between her legs was nearly bare.

"Oh baby, look at you . . ."

"Finish this," she said. There were two terrible, trembling inches between them. She couldn't hide how much she wanted him. But she also couldn't hide how much she didn't want to want him. "Just . . . let's finish this."

"You think if we fuck each other hard enough it will go away?" he asked her. He was already hard as steel behind his zipper. "We'll get it out of our systems?"

"That has to work," she said. "It has to."

Dylan pushed back her hair, holding her face in his hard hands. He was worlds too rough. Worlds too wrong. But he was going to take what she was offering. "You really are innocent, aren't you?"

She shook her head and he could feel her shaking in her skin. Her eyes were frantic on his.

"If we do this right, it's only going to get worse."

Dylan didn't give her a chance to argue. He picked her up again, his hands under her armpits, and she wasn't awkward this time. She put her arms around his neck and her legs around his waist and he carried her down the hallway again, this time straight to his bedroom. Where it was dark and still.

No one had ever been here with him. Not ever. And when she left, he knew her ghost was going to haunt this bedroom. This whole damn house. And it pissed him off. It pissed him off that he wasn't strong enough to stop it. That he had no shred of control left with this girl. She stripped it all away with her wide eyes and her clenched fists and all her secrets and lies.

"Lie back," he growled into her ear, and when he let go, she fell back onto the bed, naked and beautiful against the dark, silky duvet.

Dylan stood over her, fully clothed, his dick so hard it hurt.

Who the fuck was this girl to do this to him?

No one, he wanted to say, wanting her to be nothing. Wanting her to not matter. She was just a lying bit of trash from a trailer park who happened to pick up a phone call.

But it wasn't true.

She was fucking killing him.

"You got something you want to tell me, don't you?" he asked.

She blinked up at Dylan and then tried to scoot away to the other side of the bed, but he grabbed her leg. Not hard. Just enough to hold her.

"No," she said. "I'm not going to tell you. And you've got no right to be mad. You're not telling me things either."

Wasn't that the truth? In a heartbeat he saw what a dead end this was and how fast they were rushing toward it. And because it was his nature to destroy, he put his foot on the gas and made sure when they hit that dead end they were really over. That there would be no pieces for them to pick up.

"Past this," he said, his eyes locked on hers. "You can stay in my place in Charleston. I want you to. I want you to be safe. And you can call if you need help. Margaret will take care of you. Or one of my guys. But it won't be me. We are never going to talk or see each other again. Ever again. Do you understand that?"

She nodded, her cheeks bright. Her eyes brighter.

"Do you still want me?" he asked.

"Yes," she said on a sobbing gust of air, sounding nearly hopeless against this thing between them. "I do."

Dylan knew the feeling. But there was no point fighting it anymore. The new rules were set. Today and then over.

He tore off his shirt, the buttons flying from the fabric to ping against the wall. He felt her eyes on his chest, the Virgin Mother and his own mother's name. He felt her picking apart his secrets, gathering up sharp broken pieces of him and trying to put them back together. Just like he was doing with her, trying to pick apart her lies and her secrets to find the truth of her.

And they would keep on doing that if he didn't stop it.

"Spread your legs," he said. And she did without hesitation. Without fear. "Wider."

She braced her heels on the bed and spread her legs as wide

as she could. *God*. She'd totally shaved. She was bare and sweet between her legs.

"You shaved your pussy. For me." He couldn't help himself anymore—he reached out and touched her, ran his finger down the seam of her fat, soft lips. It came away wet. She wanted this just as much as he did. The reality of it was kerosene on a fire.

She jerked and groaned at his touch, gathering the bedspread in her fists. "I thought you'd like it."

"I do like it. But you are going to love it," he breathed, and then he got down on his knees beside the bed and pulled her by her hips to the edge. "Keep your legs apart," he growled, and she snapped the leg back that had curled over his shoulder.

He licked her with the flat of his tongue, all along her lips, and she closed her eyes, her breath a ragged gasp. It was better if she didn't watch. If he didn't feel her eyes on him. He used his thumbs to part her, to stretch her wide, and she flinched, so he eased up. Until she moaned with pleasure again.

"Look at you," he breathed, staring down at all that pink flesh. With the tip of his tongue he touched her clit, licked it, and rolled it. And then sucked it into his mouth. Hard. She shot up off the bed, her legs jerking, clasping his head between them.

"Don't make me tell you again," he said, breathing all over her pussy. "Spread. Your. Legs."

"I don't like bossy men," she groaned but did what he asked, and he felt like he had her all staked out for his pleasure. The only places they touched were his mouth, his fingers, and her pussy. And yet he felt that connection all through his body. Like they were skin to skin with not even air between them.

He teased her with that long, slow lick over and over again and he could feel her arching up toward him, searching for something solid to grind against.

"Touch me," she whispered.

"I am."

"More."

He curled his tongue over her clit, barely touching it.

"Why . . . why are you being so far away?" she asked.

"Because you're lying to me about something and I don't mind getting used as long as I get to use you right back."

She flinched at his words. The ugliness of them.

But then he slipped a finger down to her pussy, entering her just enough so she could feel it, and then he pulled back and slid his finger down from her pussy to her asshole, burning a trail against the slick flesh there.

"Dylan," she sobbed, pushing against him. Wanting more. The fucking truth of her was that she would take everything he had. They could burn down his whole mountain with this fire between them.

And the knowledge sucked.

"This is what it's like between two liars, baby," he said, his finger rimming her pussy. "This is what you get."

"I want more, please."

"There is no more."

"Don't," she breathed. "Don't be like this." She sat up, reaching for him, tears in her eyes, and he couldn't fucking take it. He stepped back away from her, trying to get his breath. His bearings. The ragged, burning edges of his control kept slipping through his slick fingers.

He could smell her on him. On his fingers. His face. She would be all over his sheets when they were done.

He undid his pants, pushed his underwear down until his cock sprang free.

She reached for him, her eyes hotter than the fire that scarred him.

"No," he said, an act of self-preservation if ever there'd been one. Her eyes flew to his. "Don't touch me," he said, and she dropped her hands.

He didn't know if he was hurting her. Scaring her. If she'd tried to leave at this point, he would have let her. Part of him wanted to scare her enough that she would leave. Part of him wanted her to stand up and call him an asshole. Smack him. Because he deserved that. And she deserved to be pissed.

But this fucking hunger they had for each other kept them here, locked together in this tragedy.

She sat there, her hands in her lap.

Trusting him.

"Don't," he said, the word bursting out of him before he could stop it.

"Don't what?" she whispered, her eyes wide.

He didn't have just one answer, he had a thousand.

Silent, he took a condom off the bedside table and slid it on. He could barely touch himself he was so turned on. Whatever was going to happen between them right now was going to be fast and hard.

He felt angry and awful. Which, he figured, was how he should feel. Guilty and miserable.

"Roll over," he told her.

"What?"

She was too slow, he was too wild, and he lifted her hips and rolled her himself, pulling her up onto her knees. He climbed onto the bed behind her and then held his cock, notching himself against her, slipping through her hot, wet pussy to get inside.

With a hiss, she pulled forward away from him and he stopped, lifting his hands away from her. But his cock was just inside of her. Waiting.

Carefully, she pushed back against him and then stopped.

Christ, he didn't want to hurt her. He began to pull out but she reached around and grabbed his thigh, holding him still. "Don't . . ." she whispered. "Don't leave."

"Jesus Christ, Annie, if it hurts, say it. If you don't want this, say it." Their secrets were making a mess of them; all their sharp, jagged edges were out, waiting to hurt each other.

"It . . . doesn't hurt."

"You want this?" he asked, because he wasn't sure. She was wet and she was hot, but he wasn't about to take something she didn't want to give.

"Yes."

"Say it, Annie. Just fucking say what you want."

"I want you inside me."

Her words lit him up but he didn't push into her.

"Take me," he said, and then watched as bit by bit she eased back on him.

Slowly he pushed forward until she had every inch of him.

"You ready?" he breathed, and she nodded. Her arms braced against the bed were shaking. His legs were. The bed was trembling under all their restraint.

Slowly he eased back and then forward. And she eased forward and then back and they found a terrible rhythm. Deep and then deeper each time, turning them inside out. He tried not to touch her, but his hands slid over her hips, holding onto her waist. The pressure built in him. A beautiful pressure. Pleasure and pain. Light and dark. Guilt and ecstasy. Grief and happiness.

He was close. Too close and unable to stop. He reached around her, slipping over her bare skin toward her clit, and she grabbed his hand in a grip that was surprisingly strong. Fierce. The rough and raw edges of her calluses and blisters brushed over his. She laced their fingers together.

And somehow that was more intimate than anything else.

Last time, he thought, letting himself absorb the intimacy. Like drinking all the water he could before heading out into the desert.

Last time. Last time.

"Come on," he growled and shook off her hand, unable to take it. "Fuck. Come, baby."

And she did. She exploded under him, crying out and falling down on the mattress. She pulled him down with her and he blanketed her. Covered her. And filled her.

Perfect.

The orgasm rocked him.

Crushed him.

And he lay there, heaving against her. Feeling her shake and tremble beneath him.

God, she was so small. He could feel the knobs of her spine against his stomach. The fragile bones of her rib cage against his arms. He could carry her in his pocket.

He *wanted* to carry her in his pocket.

He'd learned the hard way to keep his wants and desires on a short list. Wanting too much, either one thing or a million, only meant he wouldn't get it. He was clumsy with fragile things—always trying to hold onto them so hard they broke.

The thought was enough to make him pull out, holding onto the edge of the condom.

He went into the bathroom, dumped the condom, and peed.

Twenty-nine years old, and some of those years had been wild, and he'd never experienced anything like Annie. Not once.

The physical reality of the connection they had on the phone blew his mind. Destroyed it. And he didn't know how he was going to let her walk away from him.

How did anyone walk away from what they'd just shared? They couldn't. He couldn't.

One more day, at least, he thought. *Fuck the secrets.* He just wanted to test this thing between them as far as it would go. Find the red line and hold it there until they both fell apart.

When he stepped back out into the bedroom she had curled up on the bed, her knees to her chest, and when she heard him she pulled the blanket up over her body like she didn't want him to see her.

"Annie?" he asked, worried suddenly that he really had hurt her. He'd been rough. And angry. Raw. Maybe—

"I'm married."

He blinked. "What?"

"I'm married, Dylan. That's what I haven't told you."

28

ANNIE

My words echoed. In my head. In the room. Probably all over this damn mountain.

Get up, Annie. Get up. Get dressed and get gone.

What had happened between us on the bed had been the most amazing experience of my life. It was like we'd used our anger to make it all somehow better and worse at the same time. Beautiful and awful. That's what we were.

And guilt was shredding me to pieces.

With shaking arms I pushed myself up off the bed. I could see him out of the corner of my eye, standing there in the doorway to the bathroom. His hand on the door frame like he couldn't stand up on his own.

"I'm sorry," I said, tears clogging my throat. "I'm so sorry . . ." A sob slipped out and I shook my head, gathering the duvet around me as best I could before slipping off the bed and heading for the door.

I had to get my clothes. Maybe . . . maybe he'd let me take the socks. It was cold. I'd leave everything else. The pajamas and the soft shirt. The robe. I'd leave it all. And I wouldn't ask for one more thing. Except the socks and . . . *Shit.* I had no way home.

"I don't . . . can I get a ride to a bus station or something? And I'll need to borrow some money. I'll pay you back—"

"Stop," he breathed, as if he'd just woken up. "You're married? Like right now, you're married?"

I took a deep breath and forced myself to look at him.

He was naked and still braced in the doorway, as if his feet wouldn't work. Sweat still gleamed on his chest, across those tattoos. His cock, so pink, lay against his leg.

"Yes," I said. "Right now, I am married."

He glanced away and wiped a hand over his face and head, making all the dark hair stand up.

"I didn't have anything with me when you brought me here," I said. I wished more than I could say that I could throw on some clothes, grab my keys, and drive out of there, but I was totally at his mercy. "I need help getting home."

He let out a long breath and when he turned to look at me, his eyes were wide. "Home?"

"Back to the trailer park."

"Get dressed, Annie," he said. "You're not going anywhere just yet."

He went back into the bathroom and came out with my clothes, which he tossed at me. I caught them with one hand; the other still had a death grip on the quilt. "Go get dressed. We're going to talk."

In my bedroom I put on the sun-and-moon pants and the pink shirt. A pair of socks. I found a hoodie sweatshirt, too, and slipped that on, burying my ice-cold hands in the front pockets. Slowly the shaking stopped. The shock of telling the truth wore away, leaving me somehow stripped. I felt weightless somehow . . . impossibly sorry and deeply guilty, but a boulder had been rolled off my back.

I found Dylan in the kitchen, leaning back in the corner of the counter space. He was drinking a beer. He wore jeans and his inscrutable expression; otherwise he was naked.

When I came in he took a long drink and then set the beer down, very carefully, as if everything hinged on his getting that beer down on the right bit of countertop.

Back on the farm, I used to have a rib that kept popping out of place. And it made it hard to sleep, to breathe. Impossible to work. I'd walk around trying to manage the pain, only half-living. My whole life lived in halves because I couldn't do anything. And then Smith would notice, give me hell for not saying anything, and he'd give me one of those big bear hugs and it would pop right back into place.

Telling the secret was like that.

For the first time since I answered that phone call, I could take a deep breath. A real one. I had no idea what was going to happen next. But at least I could breathe.

"I'm sorry I got you involved in this," I said, feeling oddly calm. "I . . . I didn't think it would get this far."

"Adultery?"

I nodded.

"Well." His words had the sharp edge of sarcasm all over them. "It's a first for me."

"When . . . when we were just on the phone it didn't seem so . . . wrong."

"Where's your husband?" he asked, and I couldn't quite stop my flinch. *Husband*. That word always sounded like a threat. And he spit it out like he wanted to wound me with it.

"Still on the farm, I think."

"Are you separated? In the process of getting a divorce?"

I shook my head, my hands in knots in my pockets. I couldn't even give him that kind of comfort.

"Jesus, Annie, tell me what the hell is going on."

"I ran." I swallowed, hard, my throat impossibly dry. I

grabbed what was left of my champagne on the table and finished it, my throat raw and painful. Had I screamed when I came in his bedroom? Or was it just the pain of telling what I'd never told anyone?

"Two months ago, I packed up a bag and I took all the money I could get my hands on and I waited until three o'clock in the morning, until he was sleeping, and I ran."

He straightened up from the corner and took a step closer to me but stopped when I stiffened. I could not be touched right now.

"Why?" he breathed.

The tears it felt like I'd been holding back forever spilled over my cheeks. A hot waterfall trickling down over my chin onto my throat. "Because he was going to kill me."

"*What?*"

"If I stayed my husband would kill me somehow. It was only a matter of time."

"Oh, Jesus, oh . . . Annie." He stepped toward me and I stepped back, my hand up to stop him. He ignored it. For the first time he ignored it and I realized for all his anger the last day, he'd been mine to control. If I said stop, he stopped.

Not now, though. Now, he pulled out a chair and helped me sit down in it as if I were an old lady. As if I were as old on the outside as I felt on the inside.

"Tell me," he said, crouching down in front of me.

The urge to touch him, brush back his hair, trail my fingers over that scar tissue, was real and difficult to manage. But he was not mine to touch. Not anymore. Not ever, really. He was something I never should have reached for.

"My mom died when I was eighteen, and Hoyt was already working at the farm. I didn't know how to run the farm, the bookkeeping and the paperwork. Mom did all of it. And when she died I was just so lost. So totally lost. Smith wasn't good at that stuff, though he tried. We both did. But then Hoyt kind of stepped in. And he offered to do more and then still more. All the stuff I didn't know how to do or was scared of—he just took over. And then I don't . . . I don't really know how it started, but it seemed like . . . we were dating. Like I was his, already. And that's what I was used to, you know. I was like an appendage—first my mom's and then Hoyt's. I didn't know how to be my own self. And I was really alone and really scared and when he asked me to marry him, it seemed like the right thing to do."

"You were eighteen." I nodded. "Did you love him?"

I smiled and tried to stop my tears. "I don't know anything about love, Dylan. All I know is survival. And I didn't think I was capable of surviving on my own. But I did like him at the beginning. I . . . I wanted to be in love. And my mom, over the years, had sort of convinced me that being alone was the worst thing that could happen. Being alone meant no one loved me and I was terrified of that."

"Then what happened?" He tucked a piece of hair back behind my ear and I flinched away from him.

"Annie?"

I closed my eyes. "Please . . . I'll answer all your questions, but please don't touch me."

I felt him move back, pull up a chair so he was close, but no longer close enough to touch. I dragged in a ragged breath.

"Then we got married. A little civil ceremony at the courthouse and for . . . I don't know, a few months, everything seemed fine. Happy, even. Or maybe I was just forcing myself to believe that. To want that to be true. It's not like I had any scale with which to measure that, you know?" I thought of those evenings on the porch, learning chess with Smith. Or when he taught me to drive. Those were my happy times at the farm. So few and far between, like flowers growing out of asphalt. Since running, though? That evening in Tiffany's trailer with the buckets and the hangover the next day. Cleaning up that field. Skinny-dipping. All those conversations with Dylan on the phone. How sad that those were really my happiest times.

"Annie?" Dylan said, pulling me from my thoughts.

I cleared my throat. "After a while Hoyt stopped me from going to church. Or into town if I had to. What few friends I had, he didn't like and I . . . stopped seeing them. Stopped seeing anyone. And then he had me fire Smith. We were already isolated out on the farm, but he turned it into a prison. And I didn't even realize." I turned my face away.

"Do you need a drink?" he asked.

I shook my head. I felt like I was going to throw up. "The first time he hit me," I said, "it wasn't even strange. It was like he'd been conditioning me to expect it. Like he spent months making sure that when he smacked me and told me it was my fault I would believe it. That I wouldn't even think it was all that shocking. It had been over a chicken potpie that was still frozen in the middle or something. And he hit me and I . . . I just picked up the pieces of that potpie he'd thrown. The whole time my cheek was on fire and I'd bitten my tongue so bad I was swallowing blood."

"Jesus," he breathed, and I tried very hard to tell myself that this was not my shame; it was Hoyt's. I did not have to be embarrassed that I'd been hit. That I'd been systematically hurt. That I couldn't see a way out of it.

And maybe someday I'd believe that with my whole heart. But today was not that day. I was embarrassed. Embarrassed that I'd trusted a man like that. Married him. Held myself accountable to him. Let him do that. Over and over again. And I'd convinced myself it was okay.

"How long did this go on?"

"Four years. Until . . . he wanted to sell the majority of the land to an energy company to put up windmills. And I agreed only so far—"

"Is it your land?"

I nodded.

"Annie, it's your farm?"

"Yes." I snapped, hearing everything he wasn't saying. About how I'd been a coward to leave all my land behind. That I should have been stronger and gotten Hoyt to leave somehow. I knew all of this in my gut, but running with no plan and nothing but fear and three thousand dollars had, at the time, seemed smarter. Easier. I'd left my legacy behind, my livelihood and the only home I'd ever known. The truth of it sat like a ball of fire in my stomach. "It's been in my mom's family for three generations and I didn't want to sell any more of it. And I wouldn't change my mind."

"What did he do?"

I put my hand to my throat as if I could still find the bruises he put there. I wanted to dig my thumb into one of those black wounds and remind myself of the pain. "He strangled me until I passed out on the kitchen floor. And he left me there. Went to bed. Just . . . like I was nothing. Like he could do anything to me and it didn't matter. And I sat on that floor and had to convince myself that it wasn't true. That I did matter."

It took hours. Days to build up that courage. To believe I mattered. That's how far he had pushed me down.

Dylan stood up and paced away from me, hands locked on his head. I watched his agitation as if from a long ways away. I felt increasingly numb to the whole thing. To all of it.

"I waited a few days and then ran."

He turned, his jaw clenched so hard I worried he was making gravel out of his teeth.

"What about divorce?" he asked.

I shook my head.

"It's your land, Annie!"

"What's the good of it if I'm dead?" I cried.

"I have lawyers, Annie. Good ones. Ones that can keep you

safe and get you free and make sure he crawls away with nothing. Goes to jail and never comes out."

"I don't have money for that, Dylan."

He stared at me, his eyes so sad. "Do you think I wouldn't give you that money? Do you think I could let you just walk away after you've told me this?"

I blinked. "Yes," I said.

"What kind of man do you think I am?"

I shook my head and turned in the chair, toward the bedroom as if to go grab more of my things. But I didn't have anything. Nothing. Not even three thousand dollars of stolen money and a box of hair dye.

"I think you should take me home."

"Listen to me, Annie," he said, stepping close, but not too close as if the boundaries between us had been rearranged. "Do you really want to go back to that shitty trailer park and hide for the rest of your life?"

I wished I could say I wasn't going to do that. But I had no other plan. I was . . . hell, I was just like Ben, hiding and waiting for something better to come along.

"Let me help you," he said.

"How?"

"We can talk to the lawyers today, Annie. And . . . I want you to stay in my house in Charleston. It's safer, Annie. It's so much safer."

"No." I shook my head, denying him, denying myself, because I should have done that a long time ago. The first time I picked up the phone. Every single time afterward. At the very least when Margaret had put me in the blue room, I should have stayed there. So much would be different if I hadn't been so curious and selfish. If I'd left Layla out of it and just stayed Annie McKay.

"Baby, listen. You got this far, on your own and with nothing. There's no shame in taking help now."

"I don't want you to get any more mixed up in this. I feel so bad for lying to you."

"Don't, Annie. Don't feel bad. Just take my help."

He kept talking, something about restraining orders, and to my great shame, my horrified disbelief, I wanted to nod and say thank you and *yes, please, help me. Take care of these things for me, because I don't understand them and I'm scared. And I feel so damn small in the face of all I need to do.*

It was exactly, exactly how I felt when Mom died and Hoyt walked into the office, looked at the computer, and told me he knew how to do payroll. And he could help.

I stood up from the chair so fast it screeched over the hardwood floor. I wished I could say no to all of his help. That I had the resources to do this on my own, but I didn't. But just because I needed help didn't mean that I needed to pull him in any deeper. I had to have a fence around his help. For my sake.

For his. I could not rely on him for any more than those things that I could not do without.

"I wish I could say I don't need your help . . . but I do. Clearly, I don't even know where to start. And your lawyers would be a big help. I'll pay you back."

"Don't worry about it."

"No, Dylan," I snapped. "I'm not without means. I have money. I'm not as rich as you, but I can pay you back."

He watched me, solemn and serious, and nodded. "All right. Why don't you go lie down for a while," he said. "And I'll set up a conference call."

Oh, what an incredible comfort that would be! To go lie down on that bed, curl up in those sheets that smelled like Dylan and let him make a few phone calls.

But it was comfort I did not deserve, and could not take. Not if I had any intention of being able to look myself in the mirror with any kind of pride.

I had to go home.

I took a deep breath and began the painful process of removing all but what was necessary of Dylan Daniels from my life. "I'm sorry," I said again. "For lying."

"I understand why you did."

"You . . . seem so calm." I thought that if I'd found out that everything I believed about a person was a lie and that I'd been sucked into something as filthy as adultery, I wouldn't be quite so forgiving.

"Baby, I'm fucking furious. I'm . . . crazy pissed, and if I ever have the pleasure of getting my hands on this Hoyt asshole, I will end him. But I'm not mad at you. You were protecting yourself. And that I understand."

"Thank you," I said. "For . . . all of this. For . . ." *calling me. For letting me call you. For keeping me safe. For the pleasure you showed me how to give to myself and the even greater pleasure you gave to me. For making me tell you this secret. For . . . for helping me now, when I feel so alone.* "For everything."

I sobbed again and pressed my hands to my face. It was over. This was goodbye and I couldn't believe how sad I was. How grief had carved a hole in my stomach. I wanted to walk away from him with my head held high and perhaps a lying smile on my face, but I couldn't even manage that.

"Shhhh," he said, pulling me into his chest. I soaked him in as best I could. His scent. His touch. Everything. I memorized as much as I could for the Dylan Daniels–free days ahead of me. All of them. "Shhhh. Why don't you go lie down for a while," he said. "You got about twenty more hours on that birthday wish."

No. I didn't. I had about twenty more minutes.

I wrapped my hand around his shirt, feeling his heart pound under my fingers.

"I can't stay."

"Come on, now," he said against my temple. He put his arms around my shoulders. "You haven't slept much in two days. Take some time."

I'd taken all the time I could. I'd been greedy. A liar. So much so I didn't recognize myself. Now that the secret was out, I couldn't look back at the things I'd done and see any of it that wasn't desperate and selfish.

I'd played at being Layla and I allowed myself to use this man in a pretty unconscionable way.

"I'll take your lawyer's phone number, but I won't be going to Charleston—"

"You're going to Charleston."

"Dylan, please, don't make me more indebted to you than I already am."

"It's not a debt, Annie. It's help."

"I used you, Dylan. To make myself feel better. To allow myself to forget that I was married."

He shook his head, and those sleepy hooded eyes were so sad. So serious. "I used you too, Annie. I have things I'd like to forget too, and for a while, being with you let me."

"It's not the same."

"It is exactly the same."

"Then . . . I need to go home for both of our sakes."

He watched me for a long time and then, maybe, he agreed with me. Or maybe he just saw that despite my tears and my grief I was more than serious. "I'll get the car."

I shook my head. "You're not going to take me. Margaret can take me. Or the man who brought me here. Not you."

"What the fuck are you talking about?"

"A clean break. For both of us. Nothing has changed, Dylan. We still need to end this. And I think it's better to end it now. Like we'd planned before I told you about Hoyt."

"Everything is different now, Annie. Everything."

"No. Nothing is different. Not one thing. You just know who I really am. This is how we end, Dylan. The only way for us to end." He looked like he was going to argue. "Are you forgetting that Ben is down there?"

"I don't give a shit about Ben," he snapped.

I lifted my eyes to his and told him what I didn't fully understand yet, that despite Ben's crimes, the ones I knew about and the ones I didn't, I still cared. "I do."

And I care about you, too much to drag you off this beautiful mountain into my swamp. Even for a minute.

He stepped back, rubbing his hands through his hair. "This is what you want?"

"This is what I want."

"Fine," he said, stepping back again. "I'll get Margaret. But you're keeping that damn phone. And when I call you're going to answer. It's nonnegotiable."

"Thank you," I said.

For one long moment the attraction between us, the connection, the desire and all that lust, tied us together in a bond so strong I had no idea how we were going to break it. Maybe it couldn't be broken. Perhaps for the rest of my life I would feel this way for this man I could not have.

Or maybe, in time, things could be different between us. I could stand up on my own two feet. Divorce Hoyt, see him punished for what he'd done, and then come back here to this mountain. To Dylan. I could pay him back the money I owed him.

I smiled through my tears, pierced by a bittersweet ache.

"There are things you still don't know," he said, as if he could read my thoughts. "About me. I'm still not a man to be building fantasies around."

I shook my head, because there was nothing I could find out about him that would change how I felt. "It wouldn't matter."

"You can't know that."

"I know you," I breathed, putting my hand out to touch him, but he shrugged away. Flinched. My heart squeezed at his rejection. My eyes burned.

"No, baby. No. If I touch you," he said in a voice like a gravel road, "you won't leave, not for a while. So I'm not going to hug you. Or kiss you. But I want to. Leave here knowing that. I want you."

I'd never been wanted. Maybe somewhere deep in the recesses of my mother's heart she'd wanted me, but Hoyt certainly never had. But I believed Dylan when he said that and I held onto his want as hard as I could.

"I want you too," I said. He nodded once, giving a heavy jerk, and then he headed for the front door. "I'll get Margaret."

I knew when he walked out that door he wasn't going to be back. And that was good. Better. Easier.

My stomach churned. Feeling like I might throw up, I ran into the bathroom. But there was nothing in my body but nerves and regret and half a bottle of champagne. I splashed water on my face and washed my hands. My body smelled like sex and Dylan and I wasn't ready to wash that away, so I resisted the siren song of the shower.

When I came back out of the bathroom, Margaret was there. Putting all the food in big Ziploc bags. And then putting the Ziploc bags in another bag.

"You all right?" she asked, watching me with narrowed, knowing eyes.

I nodded; words were really beyond me.

"Ready?"

"Yes," I breathed. She stuck two of the bottles of wine from the fridge into the bag and some other things. Strawberries. Melon. More cheese. "Here you go," she said, holding the bag out to me. "You got some cookies and cinnamon rolls. Some of the wine. The good prosciutto. I gave you all the fruit—you're going to want to eat that soon, before it goes bad. Some of that cheese and a bunch of crackers."

"I don't . . . That's . . ."

"Oh, it will only go to waste here, honey. You just take it."

"Margaret—"

"Please. He's going to lock himself up in his garage and tell people he's fine, when we can all see he's not. He's always been that way, hiding himself away when he's hurt. It's how we all ended up on this mountain."

"Because of the accident?"

"He was hurt long before that. And he won't let anyone take care of him. So, let me take care of you. Just a little. Just . . . so I can feel like I'm doing something."

I was extraordinarily glad that Dylan had Margaret up here on this mountain with him. Someone who cared. I took the bag of food because I wasn't sure if anyone down at that trailer park was going to care at all about me and I would take whatever care, comfort, and cinnamon rolls came my way.

I wanted to believe that Joan, Ben, and even to some extent Tiffany would care. But I had my doubts. Life was pretty threadbare down there and we all had our hands full.

So, I took the food.

And when I got in the car my phone buzzed and I read Dylan's text message with the contact info attached.

> This is the lawyer. His name is Terrance, he's a good guy and he's expecting your call. I am expecting you to call me if you need me. But I am also expecting that you are tough and strong enough to do this on your own. And you are.

And I took the comfort of that. I clung to it, holding it against my chest so it would give me strength for the days ahead.

Margaret insisted I sit in the back of the black Mercedes sedan.

"So you can stretch out," she said. "We got a drive ahead of us."

I couldn't remember from the frantic middle-of-the-night drive up to this mountain how long it took, but I settled into the plush backseat, exhausted yet wide awake.

The first of the leaves were turning up here, and in the dense green of the forest, there would be one bright blaze of color. Red or orange. The sign that change was coming.

We drove down a gravel road and I saw the other buildings. A charming house set back in the forest that must have been Margaret's. And a little farther, what looked like an airplane hangar. There were trucks parked in front.

That must be his garage, I thought, turning as we drove by until I was looking out the back window.

He was there, standing in the shadows, and as we drove by he stepped out into the road, watching us as we made our way off his mountain. He wore a black fleece with his jeans, and the late afternoon sunlight slashed across his face.

I pressed my hand against the glass as if I could touch him. Desperately I wanted to believe this wasn't goodbye.

But I wasn't lying to myself anymore.

29

THE FLOWERED MANOR WAS ENTIRELY THE SAME, BUT SOME-how completely different. What had appealed to me before when I'd been scared and looking for a place to hide now seemed utterly astonishing. Repellant in a way.

It was so small. A tiny island of RVs and double-wide trailers in a wide sea of forest and kudzu. The rain and the darkening sky made everything seem sad. Fragile somehow. As if the metal and plastic walls people lived behind were a laughable attempt to keep everyone safe.

A solid wind would blow all of this away.

"I'm leaving you here?" Margaret asked, clearly horrified.

I smiled, weary. I nearly said it was my home, but my home was a thousand miles away from here. A two-story white farm-house surrounded by soy and cornfields and wide, white-blue sky as far as the eye could see.

I had not missed it and I couldn't say that I missed it now, but I felt very keenly that it was mine.

"You can stop here," I said, just as we drove up to the office. Looking at it now I realized it was a modified garden shed, not unlike the one where all the tools I'd been using were kept.

"Are you sure, honey?" she asked.

"I'm sure. And thank you . . . for the food and the ride." For taking such good care of Dylan.

"My pleasure and," she sighed, "I love that boy to death. Like he was my own. But he's not easy. And he carries a burden so heavy he's getting crushed under it and doesn't even realize."

I knew that; perhaps that was part of what we'd been attracted to at the beginning. Both of us knowing, somehow, that we were carrying impossible loads.

"And sometimes," Margaret continued, "I wish he would meet a girl. Someone like you. Someone who doesn't care about his money and his scars. Or what he's done in the past. Who cares about him. Who makes him smile and pulls him out of that garage where he'd spend every living moment of his life, and then I think . . . no. If he met a girl who loved him, she would get crushed under that burden too." She turned to face me. "Don't come back, Annie."

I blinked, stunned.

"It hurts me to say, but you're a good girl. Find yourself an easier man and don't come back."

I stumbled out of the car, my goodie bag of gourmet leftovers banging against my legs. She lifted a hand in a wave and the car pulled away, flinging mud up everywhere. My eyes burned. My throat hurt and my body was sore from Dylan's hands.

Instead of going to my trailer, where I would do nothing but lie there and think of Dylan, I walked toward the office. Toward distraction.

The bell rang over the door as I stepped into the office. Kevin was playing solitaire in front of the blasting air conditioner.

Exactly the same. Like I'd never left.

I appreciated Dylan's offer of the house, but if I was going to divorce Hoyt, I had to stand on my own two feet. And that meant staying here. Working here. Living here. The luxury of my hours with Dylan was a dream. A beautiful dream. But it was time to wake up.

"Hey there," Kevin said, glancing up from his game.

"Just checking in on the storm damage," I said. "You need me to do any work?"

"We got a shit ton of fallen trees in the back lots. One of the trailers nearly got crushed. We're going to need a chain saw."

"We don't have one in the tool shed," I said, jumping with great relief onto the idea of work. Physical hard work would clear out my head. Get me right. If nothing else, it would fill up the empty hours.

"Yeah, I'll need you to go into Cherokee and rent one. Come back in the morning and I'll get you some cash."

"Thanks, Kevin," I said and walked back out the door, the bell tinkling all the same. Coming, going, it didn't matter. I found the consistency comforting. I paused in the doorway and thought for a second that I should ask him about Dylan. What he knew about us. But in the end it didn't matter.

There was no more us.

I walked back through the trailers with the families, where a few people were clearing branches out of their driveways or away from their cars. Tiffany was in the playground with her kids picking up branches, or at least *she* was picking up branches. The kids were in a stick sword fight.

"Stop it now, kids," she said. "Someone is going to get hurt."

"Hey," I said as I walked by.

"Hey," she said, pushing her long hair off her face. She seemed startled to see me. Like she hadn't expected me to come back. "You're here!" She wore men's work gloves that made her wrists and arms seem so fragile. More fragile than the sticks she was carrying. "You weathered the storm someplace else?"

"Yeah, a friend's. It was bad here?"

"Scary. A little," she said. "Kids were freaked out, but Phil was here and he kept us all in the bathroom. Made it seem safe."

I absolutely tried not to react, but my eyebrows hit my hairline anyway.

"No one is all bad, Annie," she said, her eyes blazing, her lips pinched. She looked sour and mean and old. Older than she should. A million years older.

"Some people are bad enough," I said. I thought of how I'd used Dylan, lied to him and pulled him into my misery. That was something bad enough that the good—the pleasure and the kindness—was invalidated. "Bad enough that the good shit doesn't matter. We both know that."

I would never have had the courage to say those words to her before. To stand there, holding her eye contact until she flinched away.

"I'll be here," I said. "When it's bad again."

Her cheeks were bright red and the kids were watching us, the ends of their stick swords dragging in the dirt.

"Mom?" the boy asked, stepping forward like he would use that stick to stop me.

"Hey, baby?" Those familiar words in a man's voice made me start. Made longing open up in my stomach like a giant pit. But it wasn't Dylan. Dylan wasn't going to be calling me "baby." Not for a long time. If ever.

It was Phil, coming across the road to the playground. "You ready?" he asked. He smirked at me, his eyes taking in my pajamas and hoodie. The slippers Margaret had given me. He made me feel naked, despite all my clothes. That's what guys like Phil specialized in, making a woman feel vulnerable.

I straightened my spine and stared right back at him.

"Yeah," Tiffany said with a bright smile. "Let's go, kids. Daddy's taking us out for dinner."

The kids dropped their sticks and ran back to the trailer. Tiffany tossed her own sticks in the big pile she'd made on the far side of the slide.

"I'll see you later," I said, watching this strange scene of family happiness. The rot underneath it. Yes, it was safety and dinners now, but Tiffany knew it was going to turn again and this man would raise a hand to her. Or to her kids.

Inevitable.

Dylan was right. Some things were just waiting for us out there in the dark.

I turned away, heading toward my own trailer.

"Annie," she said, stopping me. Panic laced her voice. Her eyes skittered over my shoulder to the rhododendron. "I'm sorry."

"For what?"

"Tiffany!" Phil yelled and Tiffany ducked her head and headed back to her own trailer. The blue muscle car waiting beside it.

Past the rhododendron my trailer sat closed up and dark. Beyond that Ben was in his garden, cleaning up from the storm.

I took my bag of treats over toward him. "Hey," I said when I got close.

His head shot up. He had his color back and looked infinitely better than the last time I'd seen him—old and frail and gray, pushed aside by . . . Max. *His son.* Big pieces of the Ben puzzle slowly fell into place. One of those people he regretted hurting was Dylan.

"You all right?" I asked, looking him over for signs of harm. For signs that Max had hurt him.

"Fine. Just fine."

"Last night—"

"An argument. That's all. Where you been?" he asked, retying the strings for his runner beans despite the fact that they were ruined. He'd clearly tried to replant some things that had been uprooted in the storm. But the beans looked smashed beyond repair.

"With Dylan," I told him, point-blank.

The string fell from his fingers, which were suddenly shaking.

"Did you know he lived nearby?" I asked, and he nodded, his throat working as if he were swallowing something big. Something hard.

"Did you know he owned the trailer park?"

"Yeah," he breathed. "I know. It's not a secret. Half the people living here know Dylan Daniels owns the park. Phil, the asshole, just got fired from his shop a month ago."

I nearly reeled under the information. Phil was the guy Dylan fired?

"Did you know I was watching you? That'd he'd asked me to keep an eye on you?"

"I figured," he said. "He's had a spy on me for a while. None of them like you, though."

"What does that mean?"

He smiled at me. "None of them made me pasta sauce."

"He told me to stay away from you."

"Well, you didn't listen to that, did you?"

"He said you were dangerous."

Ben sucked on his cheek. "Makes sense he would say that—it's all he's ever known from me. You two a thing now?"

I shook my head.

"That's for the best, I imagine."

"Why?"

He looked at me for a long time and then shook his head.

"Because he's my son," he said. "And some apples don't fall far from the tree."

"Dylan's not dangerous."

"If you honestly think that, then you don't know the whole story."

"I know Dylan."

He looked at me for a long time like he was trying to talk

himself out of something. Or into something. "You can't go walking around thinking he's something he's not. You can't keep thinking he's . . . tame."

"If you're going to tell me something, Ben, just do it. I've kind of had a long few days."

Ben took a deep breath and let it out slowly. "He was arrested when he was a kid. Sixteen. He and his brother got into trouble for stealing cars. Illegal racing. Dylan went to jail. Juvie. It was supposed to be a short sentence; he . . . he was a good kid. Never in trouble. But in jail he changed. He was fighting. A lot of it. More and more violent. Until he stabbed a kid—"

"You're lying." I held up my hand as if I could get him to shut up. As if I could shove those words back down his throat.

"I'm not. I'm not lying. And he didn't tell you, did he?"

"Shut up, Ben! Shut up, you're just . . . this is a game you're playing. Some awful way to punish Dylan. To get me not to care. Something—"

"I don't give a shit if you care for him. I'm telling you not to trust him. Not to trust . . . yourself with him."

I wanted to yell and scream that Ben was lying. That I knew Dylan, I knew what mattered, knew the soul-deep goodness of him. Dylan and Ben might both be closed up, locked down, hiding a kindness they didn't entirely trust within themselves.

"He's not like you. He wouldn't do what you have done."

Ben was watching me, with those eyes that I recognized in Dylan's face. Deep-set, heavy-lidded. Eyes that saw everything.

"Ask me," he said. "I know you've wanted to for a while."

"Did you know about the little girl? In the house?"

He slowly shook his head. "I didn't." A long, ragged breath sawed out of his chest. "I wish I had more than anything else in my life—I wish I had known that girl was there."

I understood that I had a will to believe the things that made my life easier. That fit the way I needed to live in my world, and yes, it was easier to believe that Ben—a man I liked, Dylan's

father—did not kill an innocent girl in cold blood. And I should
have, perhaps, doubted my belief. My faith.

But I didn't. I believed Ben was telling the truth.

Did that also mean I had to believe Ben about Dylan?

I was torn in half. My head pounded. My heart ached.

"Dylan said he didn't think you knew the girl was there," I
said, wondering if the words would bring him any peace. Or me.

What would bring me peace?

"You look so tired you're about to collapse," he said. "Go
lie down."

"But—"

"Go. We can talk later."

Right. Okay. It was too much. The last few days were too
full and I was officially overwhelmed. I turned slowly, the bag of
food banging into my leg. "Oh," I said. "I brought you some
stuff. Would you like—"

I pulled out half a cantaloupe covered in Saran Wrap. A
small piece of Dylan's world in this unlikely place. I offered it to
Ben.

"No, girly. You take that stuff. I got all I need." Those were
nearly the exact words Smith would have said, and I nodded, my
throat swollen. Why, I wondered, thinking of Smith and Dylan
and Ben, were the men in my life so good at self-denial? So good
at holding at arm's length the things they wanted?

Even Hoyt, to some degree. There was something really
awful in him and he just tried to keep it covered. Deny it. Until
it came leaping out.

"I'll talk to you later," I said and walked back over to my
trailer. I stopped at Joan's and knocked on the storm door. But
no one answered. Maybe she was working tonight. I wasn't even
entirely sure what day it was. Sunday? Monday?

It hardly mattered.

It hardly mattered.

Perhaps it was my exhaustion. Perhaps it was finally telling my secrets to Dylan. Perhaps it was finally hearing the truth from Ben.

Or maybe under the shock I realized . . . I knew . . . what I had always known about myself, about Dylan, about life.

When we were pushed to the edge we were capable of anything. Surviving was the only thing that mattered.

I didn't know exactly what had happened to Dylan. But he survived.

I stumbled to a stop in the middle of that dirt track between my trailer and Joan's and pulled the phone out of my back pocket. Its weight and heft had grown so familiar. I liked the way it felt in my hand, how it centered me, in a way. Connected me, to a version of myself I wanted to be. To Dylan.

To the future.

Quickly, I texted:

I know about jail. I know what happened. It doesn't change anything for me. It doesn't change who you are. When this is done, when I am done . . . I'm going to come back to you. To hear the story from your lips. To finish what we started.

I bit my lip. Somehow, after all that had happened between us, now I felt the most brave. The most vulnerable. In this moment.

If you'll have me.

30

DYLAN

"DYLAN? JESUS. EARTH TO DYLAN!"

Dylan jerked when Blake punched him in the shoulder.

"What? What the fuck?" Dylan snapped. There was a precision wrench in his hand, and he didn't know what he was doing with it. The transmission in front of him was in pieces, but he could not for the life of him remember what he was doing. Was he putting it together or taking it apart?

Stop. Just stop. I've been bossed around, thrown into cars, driven to some kind of mountaintop fortress to . . . you. You, Dylan. You ended it and I still wound up here. To you!

Annie's voice ran in a loop in his head.

She'd been inevitable, all along. From the moment she picked up that phone, every road led them to each other.

And now . . . now the roads were empty. And the work that had satisfied him, that had pulled him out of the shit of his past, away from the ghosts and the demons that haunted him, was stretched out in front of him and he did not care.

He was going to miss her for the rest of his life. Every minute she was gone, he was going to be eaten up by a kind of loneliness he'd never thought he'd feel again.

Not since Max. His parents. Those long, awful nights behind bars.

The kind of loneliness that came from the absence of one specific person.

But the jagged hole made by Annie's leaving was sharper somehow, because for so long he'd mastered feeling as little as possible.

And he didn't know if she was going to come back.

The rest of his life was going to feel this way.

He felt like he had after the accident. The fire. High on pain-killers, staring down at his body like it was meat. Like he was somewhere buried inside of it, or floating above but not at all a part of it.

Not a part of anything.

"Get out of here," Blake said. "You're a fucking mess."

He was. He was a fucking mess. He threw the wrench down and left the warehouse. His guys . . . Blake, they could do it all at this point. No one needed him.

I need you. Please, I need you.

He'd go down off this mountain to her. To make sure she was safe. That he hadn't made a mistake letting her go down there alone with just her phone and the number of his lawyer.

But she'd insisted on going alone and he respected that.

Fuck.

His phone in his back pocket buzzed and he fished it out. His heart stopped when he saw it was a text from Annie.

I know about jail. I know what happened. It doesn't change anything for me. It doesn't change who you are. When this is done, when I am done . . . I'm going to come back to you. To hear the story from your lips. To finish what we started.

And then:

If you'll have me.

Something like hope burned through him, igniting in his gut and blasting out through his fingers, the tips of his hair. And he landed squarely in his body again. Squarely inside himself.

And that hope-like thing crystallized into a happiness-like thing.

Part of him screamed out a warning, but he ignored it. He'd been living alone in his regrets for too long. He would not let Annie be another regret.

I do owe you a few more hours on your birthday wish, he texted back, but then erased it, because he didn't need to try and make it seem like he wasn't invested. Like he didn't care.

Instead he wrote: Yes. I will always have you.

ANNIE

Yes. I will always have you.

I tucked my happiness, my glee, behind all my serious thick walls of worry. About my life. My future.

But that hope kept me lit up, and I felt like I glowed, like a lantern. The future was not entirely scary. Not entirely unsure. When the bad stuff was over, there was something good waiting for me.

Something amazing.

Dylan.

The door to my trailer was unlocked. I hadn't had time last night to find my keys, much less lock up after myself.

Had it only been last night? Really?

How much time did it take for everything to change? I'd moved like a snail through my life before. So slow to know what I wanted. So slow to change. That was over now. I was changing with every breath I took.

I took the metal steps up into my trailer, set down my bag in front of the stove, and turned to shut the door. I slammed it hard the first time so it didn't bounce.

"Hello, Annie."

The voice stilled my blood. My lungs. The world swam around me. Instinctively I glanced back toward those captain chairs I never sat in, just to be sure that my exhausted, overwhelmed mind wasn't playing tricks on me.

But there he was in his faded Wranglers and the dark short-sleeved shirt with the pearl snaps. His hat, sweat-stained and dusty, sat on the chair next to him.

Hoyt.

In my trailer.

The half second it took me to process what was happening was a half second too long, and by the time I was fumbling with the door trying to get it open, trying to get out, away, he was on me.

My arm was locked in his hand, his fingers pushing the nerves on its underside hard into the bone. Immediately my hand went numb. His other hand was so big that when it covered my mouth it partially covered my nose, too, and I couldn't breathe. I couldn't . . . breathe.

"Annie," he whispered. That little smile on his face revealing the crooked eyetooth, the chipped incisor from his days in the rodeo. "Please don't make this worse. I need . . . You need to be good," he said. "And not scream. Can you do that for me? Be good for me?"

His breath smelled like coffee and Halls. He used to eat cough drops like candy, and the scent, familiar and nauseating, sent terror through me. My eyes rolled in my head and I strained away from him. I sank my teeth into the meat of his hand.

"That's a no," he said, his face turning hard and awful, and I knew what was coming.

Perhaps it had always been coming. Despite running. Despite that zigzagging escape. Despite this sudden belief that I'd committed to just hours ago to stand up to him, to demand he get off my land and pay for what he'd done.

This moment had been what was in store for me all along.

Some things we just can't outrun.

He hit me so hard my head bounced against the edge of the stove.

And the world went dark.

Annie and Dylan's darkly emotional, wildly intense
romance continues in the breathtaking sequel

THE TRUTH ABOUT HIM

Coming soon from Bantam Books

Continue reading for a sneak peek

1

ANNIE

Annie McKay came to slowly. Aware in pieces of her surroundings.

The pebbled linoleum of the trailer floor dug into her cheek. Her ankle was twisted, wedged against something hard.

The hot copper smell of blood made her stomach roil and she gagged.

"Annie, I'm sorry."

That voice . . . *oh God.*

It was Hoyt. Her husband. Standing over her.

For heartbeats, lots of them, she wasn't sure he was real. Perhaps she'd tripped and fallen, hit her head coming back into her trailer. She was hallucinating. Pulling Hoyt out of old nightmares. That made much more sense.

Because there was no way he could have found her here.

I was careful. I was so careful.

Two months ago, she'd run from him. Taking only the bruises around her neck and three thousand dollars from his safe. Desperate and scared, she left in the middle of the night and made her way in circles to this place. A patch of swamp called the Flowered Manor Trailer Park and Camp Ground in North Carolina.

Miles from Hoyt. From Oklahoma. From the farm where she'd lived her entire life.

And she'd been happy. The happiest she'd ever been. Not even two hours ago, she'd left Dylan and his magical house. Her body had been flush and alive and *pleasured*. And her mind had been clear.

She'd had plans, real plans, for her *life*, not just panicked and terrified reactions.

Everything had been about to get better.

"Annie?"

This is not a hallucination.

Be smart, Annie. Think!

"You hear what I said to you?"

She lay there silent. Hoyt hated her silence. Apologies were to be met with immediate acquiescence. His guilt immediately assuaged.

But she said nothing. Because fuck him.

"Get up."

She kept her eyes closed, because she wasn't ready to actually *see* him. Not here. Not in this trailer. Her home.

Hoping to feel her phone still in her back pocket, she rolled onto her back.

Please, please, she prayed, *please be there.*

But there was nothing under her butt. The phone was gone.

"There you go. It ain't so bad, is it? Get yourself up off the floor." He said it like she'd fallen, like she'd landed on the floor through her own clumsy, stupid means.

Despite her best efforts, hot tears seeped under her lashes.

"Come on now." His hands touched her hip and her armpit to help her up and she flinched away; her body screamed in pain.

Unsteady, she got herself to her feet. She opened her eyes and the world swam. She grabbed the edge of the table, landing half on, half off the cushion of the settee.

"You're getting blood all over the place." His familiar hands, with their small scars and close-clipped nails, held a pink washcloth toward her. It was the washcloth from her bathroom. He'd probably gone through everything, touching all of her things. Everything was contaminated now.

There was no way she could take the washcloth. Not from his hand.

"Fine," he muttered, tossing the washcloth on the table. "Do it yourself."

Pissy, he stomped off to sit in one of the captain's chairs at the front of the trailer.

The reality of Hoyt being in this previously Hoytless place was shocking.

She forced herself to look at him. Really look at him.

He was a big man. Over six feet tall, and he used to rodeo when he was younger so his legs and arms and chest were thick with muscle. He had white blond hair that made his eyebrows and eyelashes nearly invisible, which gave his face a terrible expressionlessness. A vacancy. She'd never ever been able to tell what he was thinking.

Sincerity looked like deceit. Anger looked like forgiveness.

She used to think he was calm. Other people did too; at the very beginning of their marriage that's what everyone said about him.

He's so steady, they'd said. And she'd clung to that. With both hands and all her fear after Mom died. She'd clung to the version of him she wanted to believe in.

But it was a lie. Everything about him was a lie.

And Annie had been a fool.

That he was so totally the same, wearing what he always

wore—jeans, his brown cowboy boots and the dark blue western shirt with the pearl snaps, his bone-handled knife in the
sheath on his belt—made it even more surreal.

New place. Same nightmare.

Her missing phone was balanced on his knee. He'd taken it
from her, gone through her pockets, while she lay unconscious
on the floor.

Because he was an animal.

"I'm sorry," he said with utter and terrifying sincerity. "I
know at home, you were scared. What I did . . . that night in the
kitchen?" He said it like she might have forgotten. "It was too
much. I understand that."

An incredulous laugh she could not let out stung her throat.
Do you? Do you understand that?

"It won't happen again. I swear it won't."

"How did you find me?" She tried to clear her vision, get her
brain to focus.

"Do you believe me?" he asked. "That things will be different?"

No. Not in a million years.

"I believe you," she lied, putting her heavy, throbbing head
in her hand. "Just tell me how you found me."

"It was actually pretty cool." He smiled, with what she
guessed was modesty, like she was about to be real proud of
him. "*The Bassett Gazette* has this widget thing—that's what
they call them—on their website and it shows a map of the
United States and on that map are little pins that track the places
where people are logging on to the website. The gal I talked to
at the office was real excited about it, said it showed that there
were people all over the state reading their newspaper online.
And there was this one dot . . . this one little dot that I started to
follow. You know where that dot went?"

Sick to her stomach, she nodded. She thought she'd been so
clever.

"It went around in circles for a while. And then it went north to Pennsylvania and then back south. And then it just stayed in Cherokee, North Carolina. Over and over again. Every few days it'd show up. Cherokee, North Carolina. Every week. Once a week. Tuesdays. That's the day you liked to go shopping." He said it like he was offering her proof of his affection. A nosegay. A dead bird dropped at her feet from his bloody jaws. "You thought I didn't notice. But I did. You liked to shop on Tuesdays. So, I drove out here. I saw where you signed in for computer time at the library—Layla McKay. That's your cousin, right?"

In one of the historical novels she'd read, there was a character who had a falcon. And Annie had loved the descriptions of how the guy flew his falcon and cared for it, the bells and the gloves and the little pieces of meat in a bag attached to his belt. And she'd thought, reading it, how great it would be to control something so barely domesticated. Something so very nearly wild.

But at this moment she realized how the falcon must have felt. So free one minute, wings spread, the world a retreating landscape below. The next, hooded and chained. Captured. Freedom a memory.

"I stayed there for a week, hanging out at the library. The grocery store. Driving by all the motels and . . . nothing. I heard about this trailer park out here and came out to investigate and I ran into this man, Phil, at a gas station. He told me all about the park. And when I described you, he told me he thought you might be here. You're like his wife's friend? I'm afraid Phil doesn't like you much."

God, brought down by Phil. How pathetically fitting.

"What do you want?" she asked, unable to pretend any longer.

He looked at her like he was surprised, his mouth gaping open, his translucent eyebrows halfway up his forehead. "I want you to come home," he said. "I want you to be my wife again."

"What does that even mean to you, Hoyt? Your wife? You don't love me—"

He stood up from that chair and she shrank back in her seat.

"I apologized for what happened before you left. I can't do any more than that. It's time for you to come home now. You've had your fun. People are asking about you and I'm getting tired of the sideways glances. Everyone thinks I've done something to you. The police came out to the house two weeks ago. The police, Annie. It's too much."

He touched her hand before she could jerk it back. It was worse when he pretended to care. Or maybe he did actually care and he just didn't know how to do it right.

"We can go back to church."

Annie blinked up at him, unsure if he'd actually said that, or if she was hearing things.

"Annie? Would you like to go back to church?"

"Yes . . . of course," she breathed. Three years ago she would have wept in gratitude. But she was not fooled now. He would let her go to church, once, maybe twice, and he'd find a way to take it away from her all over again.

"And then we've got to talk about selling that land to Encro."

And there it was. That was really why he wanted her home. The land sale to Encro for more windmills. He couldn't do it without Annie's approval. That's why this little scene was happening. "It's time, don't you think, that we thought of our future?"

My future is as far away from you as I can get.

"I forgive you for stealing from me, Annie. The money, the gun. It's forgiven."

Oh my God.

The gun.

The gun in her bedside table.

Did he have it? Was it still there?

She tried to show him nothing. Not one thing.

"I . . . I need to change my shirt." Her spattered and torn sweatshirt was ruined with blood; it would never come clean. She'd had a few shirts like that at home. Clothes that made their way into the rag bag, or the garbage because the truth of her life was sprayed all over it.

Annie got up on shaky feet, her hand braced on the wall as she walked down the short hallway to the bedroom.

Please. Please be there. Please be there. That gun was her only chance.

She closed the door behind her and then, dizziness and headache aside, she nearly leaped over the bed to the small beside table and yanked open the drawer.

It was empty. Sobbing, she searched it, pulling it all the way out, but everything was gone. The books. The gun. The article about Ben. Everything.

She collapsed against the wall and fell to the floor.

The bedroom door creaked opened and Hoyt stood in the doorway. A blond devil. Her gun, like a toy in his great big palm.

In his other hand were her books. The sticky notes from Dylan. The artifacts of her rebellion. Of her entire life here.

Silent, he tossed the books onto the bed. The article. The notes.

She wanted to gather them up, out of his reach. Out of his sight. But it was too late. Everything she owned he'd ruined with his touch. She tipped her head so she couldn't see them. Like a child, she thought if she couldn't see them, they weren't real.

They never happened.

All she had left was getting out of this.

"Who is Dylan Daniels to you?" he asked.

"No one. I don't know who he is." Annie got to her feet without any idea why she was lying when she was doing it so badly. All she knew was that she could not put Dylan in the middle of this nightmare.

"Stop." He held up the phone, the screen showing all of their text messages. The picture she had sent of her nearly naked body. Her breasts and her tummy, the pale white blur of her thighs.

Annie had been unfaithful to a man who smacked her around over chicken pot pies. Strangled her over windmills. She could not imagine what he would do over adultery.

"I know about it all. So you need to stop lying. For your sake."

He was going to kill her. A gasping sob cleared her throat.

"Don't look at me like that," he whispered. His face creased with agony. "I'm not going to hurt you."

Annie nearly laughed. But terror had squeezed her body.

"I don't like it, Annie, but I . . . I guess I understand." He tilted his head like the old yellow lab they used to have. "What I did to you made you . . . act out like that. I know that's not you. That picture, those notes. That's not the Annie I know."

The Annie he knew was a rag doll. A scarecrow. An animated reflection of him. The Annie he knew was gone.

But Hoyt was still talking. "We can go back home and just forget it. Forget this Dylan Daniels. Start over."

That was impossible. There was no forgetting Dylan Daniels. He was burned under her skin. Into her bones.

Move, she told herself, *keep moving, don't just sit here and let him ruin you again.* As long as she kept moving she was alive, and as long as she was alive, there was a chance.

Annie pulled a clean shirt out of the dresser. "You mind?" she asked, when he just kept standing there. That gun held so casually in his hand as if to mock her fear.

A muscle twitched in his jaw and he glanced down at the books on the bed and the phone in his hand, silently asking if she really thought she was deserving of modesty now. But then he bowed his head and walked out of her room as if granting

Annie some privacy was a favor. A silly stupid wish by a silly stupid woman.

Once he was gone, she pulled off her dirty shirt and slipped on her clean one. The windows in here were all too small to climb through, but she pushed open her curtains hoping Ben was still in his garden, hoping she could catch his eye. But his garden was empty. Joan's trailer was still dark.

As lightly as she could, she stepped to the door, listening for sounds from the rest of the trailer so she could try to tell where he was. But it was silent. Eerie and silent and awful.

Shaking, she cracked open the door to see Hoyt back in the captain's chair. He was eating a cinnamon roll from the bag she'd brought down from Dylan's. If Annie was careful and if she was quick, she might get to the door before he did.

Acting as if she was still dizzy, she made her way into the small kitchen with her hand along the wall. Four feet. Three. Two. The door was right there. She paused for a second, holding her head as if she could barely stand. She needed him to think she was weak.

"You want to pack up?" He asked. "I'd like to get home. We've been gone too long." Like they'd been on a trip. A fun excursion.

"Can we have some food, first? I need something to eat. It will make me less dizzy, maybe."

She turned herself around a little, getting her body between him and the door, and then made like she was reaching for the paper bag but instead of the bag she reached for the door, pushing it open, cold air rushing toward her as she threw her body down the steps, but Hoyt grabbed the back of her shirt and then a handful of her hair and yanked her back into the trailer.

And then slammed the door shut.

Annie screamed so loud and so hard her throat ached and he backhanded her, tossed her onto the floor of the trailer and got down on top of her, squeezing the air from her body. His hand closed over her mouth. His knife had slipped forward and the leather tip of the sheath touched the bare skin of her hip, where her shirt had ridden up.

She tried to flinch away from it, but he was too heavy.

With every breath she took that knife rubbed her. Scratched her.

"Look at me, Annie," he said in that calm voice. "I found you and we're together again. There's nowhere for you to go. And you need to realize that."

She shook her head, trying to buck him off with her hips.

"This Dylan man, he's not for you. And you know what? I forgive you for having an affair with this man." His voice said otherwise. His voice and his narrowed eye and the vicious disgusted curl to his lip, they told her she would be paying for these sins. "Some kind of dirty affair. Sending a man who is not your husband a picture of your naked body. You—"

He shifted over her and she felt, to her utter horror, that he was hard under his zipper. This man who had so rarely had sex with her was aroused. She closed her eyes against this new awful terror.

The sheathed knife and his erection dug into her.

"This man you were screwing, did he knew you were married?"

Annie did not respond. Would not. He was playing some sick game. He touched her hair just above her ear, and she could have screamed.

"You smell dirty. Like sweat and sex." He sniffed her. Over and over again, his nose in her hair. Her neck. "I want you to spread your legs, Annie."

Whimpering, she clenched them tighter together.

I am going to die this way.

There was a sudden knocking on the door and both of them stilled. She opened her eyes in time to see a momentary flash of panic on Hoyt's face. But as soon as it was there it was gone, replaced by that terrifying vacancy.

"Annie!" It was Ben. Old frail Ben. "You all right? I heard screaming."

"Who is that?" Hoyt asked.

"My neighbor." Ben Daniels. Dylan's father. And . . . quite possibly, her only friend.

"You don't want that man to get hurt." The menthol smell of Hoyt's breath flowed over her face. He ate Halls cough drops like candy. "And if you say one word to him, give him one reason to think you aren't okay, he'll get hurt. We'll still be going home together, Annie. You cannot change that. No matter what you do."

This whole situation was made worse by the fact that Ben was a former motorcycle gang member and convicted felon. Cops would take one look at her face, and Ben's record, and they'd believe whatever Hoyt said.

Hoyt was very believable.

Bit by bit Hoyt got off Annie, watching her every second to see what she would do. Annie had become unpredictable, and she took some strength from that, from no longer being underestimated.

Shaking, she slowly got to her feet, grabbed the pink washcloth from the table and held it to her head. Hoping Ben would believe the lies she was about to tell him.

Hoyt got out of sight and Annie pushed open the door to her trailer.

"You all right?" Ben asked, looking worried. He wore the familiar clean white shirt, pristinely ironed. He'd been sick recently, and he'd lost weight. No matter how tough he'd been years ago, now he was frail and he was old.

And he could not help her.

"Fine," she lied with a smile. "There was a snake and I screamed and jumped and smacked my head on the cupboard."

"I get those king snakes all the time," he said. "You want me . . ."

She got in his way as he leaned to the side as if to see into the trailer, or, worse, try to come in. "I'm fine."

That lie didn't sound at all convincing, and he pointed up to his own eye. "You smack your eye, too? Your lip?"

"Please," she breathed, unable to pretend anymore. "Please, Ben, just go."

"Annie—"

"For fuck's sake, old man. I'm fine. I'm exhausted and I just want to get to sleep. Leave me alone."

His dark eyes missed nothing and she had no idea what he was thinking, but in the end he surrendered, holding up his hands and going back to his trailer. Taking all hope of rescue with him.

Annie was going to have to do this herself.

About the Author

M. O'KEEFE can remember the exact moment her love of romance began; in seventh grade, when Mrs. Nelson handed her a worn paperback copy of *The Thorn Birds*. It wasn't long before she was filling up notebooks with her own story ideas, featuring girls with glasses and talking cats. Writing as Molly O'Keefe, she has won two RITA awards and three *RT* Reviewers Choice Awards. She lives in Toronto, Canada, with her husband, two kids, and the largest heap of dirty laundry in North America. When she's not writing, she's imagining what she would say if she ever got stuck in an elevator with Bruce Springsteen.

molly-okeefe.com
Facebook.com/MollyOkeefeBooks
@MollyOKwrites

About the Type

This book was set in Sabon, a typeface designed by the well-known German typographer Jan Tschichold (1902–74). Sabon's design is based upon the original letter forms of sixteenth-century French type designer Claude Garamond and was created specifically to be used for three sources: foundry type for hand composition, Linotype, and Monotype. Tschichold named his typeface for the famous Frankfurt typefounder Jacques Sabon (c. 1520–80).